# THE NATIVE AIR

Bonneyville Mennonite Church

# THE
# NATIVE AIR

## Sarah Woodhouse

**ARROW BOOKS**

Arrow Books Limited
20 Vauxhall Bridge Road, London SW1V 2SA

An imprint of the Random Century Group

London Melbourne Sydney Auckland Johannesburg
and agencies throughout the world

First published in Great Britain by Century 1990
Arrow edition 1991

Printed and bound in Great Britain by
Cox & Wyman Ltd, Reading

ISBN 0 09 987640 X

*To P. McC*

# 1

The sound of church bells clamoured down the soft wind of mid June and disturbed the sleeper in the high old bed. There were a great many churches in Norwich, perhaps more than any city had the sense to own, so there were naturally a great many bells: Sunday was unbearable for the bells. The man behind the worn bedcurtains stirred only to stuff the sheets in his ears. If he had forgotten, drowsing on the borders of sleep, that yesterday he had returned to his adopted city, he remembered now. Sonorous medieval sound wafted through the half-open casement. There was the welcome smell of breakfast too, if only he had raised his head.

Even an hour later, shaved, dressed, ready to depart, he still scowled at the intermittent peals, the occasional solitary ding ding, now from some distant quarter, now closer. How often had he heard Norwich's Sunday voices in the past, from this room, from the quiet streets, even from the Hospital though it stood outside the city walls. How he hated bells! He picked up his hat and went to shut the window. It was a beautiful day, a day of bright sun and clear sky. There were martins still busy patching up their old nests under the eaves of the inn, the dear old crumbling Grey Cock crouched humbly in its narrow lane off the Haymarket. He poked out his head, ignoring the bells in his sudden desire to watch the industrious birds, said under his breath: 'I too have returned, like them, after voluntary exile,' swayed a little, saw that with a determined effort he might touch the wall of the house opposite, and withdrew hurriedly. He went down to pay his bill, agreed with Mrs Badcock it was fine weather, uncommonly fine weather, agreed

1

the bed had been as comfortable as he had ever known it these last twenty years, put on his hat and walked out to the small slovenly yard for his pony.

'Doctor, Doctor, your portmanteau!' and he looked back to find a broad, bosomy girl struggling through the door with it, puffing and smiling, her cap knocked on one side.

'I knew I would forget something,' he said sadly, tightening his hold on his case of medical instruments at the same time. He had never forgotten them, thank God.

The pony had short legs, small ears and a perfectly understandable grudge against mankind. It would not lead easily and dragged along behind with a sour expression, the portmanteau bumping on its flank. Its owner paused by St Andrew's – mercifully silent – and wondered whether to mount now or walk on a little. How quiet the city was but for those damnable clanging bells . . . And how well he knew it, this green city laid out in the loop of its river with its unremitting pride in past glories, its slightly foreign air: a Dutch town given style and a sense of humour. It was a place for independent men, stout argumentative men. He had heard it referred to recently as 'that nest of Jacobins', home to revolutionaries. He himself was all for reform – though he would not go so far as annual parliaments, half life would be taken up with elections – but reform after considered discussion; precipitate action brought little good in the long term, look at France. Norwich had seethed and heaved with radical thought for years, the long years of the last war when every village had its revolutionary society, years of bloody confusion in France, years of fervent support for the government and bitter opposition to it, of high taxes, high prices, military tomfoolery, naval miracles, severe winters, bad harvests and riot.

'Come up,' to the pony who was dragging back on the reins. Up past the Assembly Rooms, the theatre, the bowling green, slowly, slowly, man and beast at odds.

2

Another fifty yards and there was the house of a friend and former colleague, Robert Menzies, an assistant surgeon at the Hospital. Dr French sent in his compliments but the servant remained at the door, miserably apologetic. He was a strange misshapen wizened man who had done duty in this post many years and knew Dr French well. Dr Menzies was at the Hospital, he said, called away before breakfast to another accident, it had been a rare week for accidents. The Doctor was welcome to step in if he cared to, but there was no knowing when the master would be home.

'No, no,' said the Doctor. 'Thank you, Creevy, but I shall not wait. Perhaps I might call at the Hospital. Good morning to you.'

But at the Hospital he only drew rein and stared, seeing himself as a young man running in to any number of accidents: men savaged by horses, by dogs, by irate wives, run over by drays, carts, galloping post-chaises. That young man had been a more ardent, less cynical being than the one seated now on the old grey pony, the sun beating down on his shoulders. I was less experienced, he thought, but perhaps more compassionate. He did not like to think so. He did not like to think he had led a pointless, misdirected life but sometimes, as now, he was aware of the gulf between that young man's ideals and this much older man's accomplishments. But then, he had grown introspective of late and supercritical. It seemed only a day or so ago he had travelled this road in search of a new home, fresh from Edinburgh and years of dedicated study to be a surgeon at the Norfolk and Norwich. And of the twenty years he had been a doctor in this place ten had been spent elsewhere as an army surgeon: India, the West Indies, Corsica, Ireland. Now he was returning from a year in Suffolk, a year he had hoped might cure him of a hopeless attachment to Ann Gerard whose home he would pass in about an hour's time if he could persuade the pony to an active trot.

3

His persuasion was crude and not outstandingly effective. The day was growing hot, the hedges laden with dust, and yet there was a heavy, threatening look about the sky over the far hills, a distant and very faint roll of thunder. The pony's steps grew slower, his head nodded. Once away from the post road he revived a little in the shade of the trees and at the ford the Doctor let him drink, standing midstream in the clear shallow beck. Then on, climbing now, leaving woods and fertile fields and entering on a far wilder country, a remnant of the past: great oaks, thick copses, vast stretches of gorse-encrusted space between. At the summit a crossroads where the gibbet had once stood: they had taken it down the year he first arrived here, yet still a horse would shy at that spot some winter dusk or on a fine moonlit evening. The Doctor looked neither right nor left: right to Thorn where the woman he loved was eating an inexcusably late breakfast, or left to Blackow Hall where her late husband had galloped about in an excess of drunken fury. He set his face resolutely to the front and pummelled the pony to a ragged canter, frightening all the little birds out of the bushes and scattering the rabbits as they went.

The candles were lit in every one of the three-branched candelabra at the end of each pew – an unbelievable expense – yet still the sudden midwinter-darkness pooled in the furthest corners. For a moment the curate could not make out the face of the man standing by the pulpit.

'You are too late, sir, the service is ended,' he said loudly, holding aloft the snuffer to emphasize the point and repeating: 'The service is over.'

The gentleman by the pulpit made no reply. Indeed, he seemed sunk in reverie. Mr Bringloe, a pale, faded, oppressed little man, approached him with caution, much as he might a disagreeable animal discovered in

4

his vestry or behind the choir stalls. He gave a gentle and placatory wave of his snuffer.

'Perhaps you took the wrong road on the Gorse, such a vast wilderness and not a fingerpost upon it, not one. And the storm is about to break, the day has turned to night' – with a shrinking glance up at the windows – 'May I set you on your way? This is the village of High Common . . .'

'No indeed,' said the stranger, moving at last, 'I am not lost – not bodily lost,' in an undertone – 'I am sorry you do not recognize me.'

As he spoke the first rain, brief but heavy, flung up against the glass and a sudden draught made the candles dip and flare. Bringloe gave a little shriek and ran away down the aisle snuffing furiously until at the font he paused to snatch up the one remaining light, a stub burning in an old saucer, and waited courteously to light his guest to the porch.

'Recognize you?' It was scarcely lighter here though the outer door was open and the sky was lively with great flashes. Then, lifting the feeble flame: 'Doctor! Why, what joy to see you, sir! What pleasure! It is almost a year, a whole year, since you were home in High Common.' And what a day to return, he might have added, gazing out a moment at the pelting wet and driving wind. 'Such a great heat,' he continued as his candle was suddenly extinguished. 'It had to come to this sooner or later.'

'It is Nature's temperament,' replied the Doctor, watching as Nature blew with the force of a mild hurricane through the innocent young oaks on the churchyard boundary, 'today a great rain to beat down the barley, tomorrow more unrelenting sun to scorch it all up. But I called on you for news of Lady Gerard. I have received no letters recently, know nothing . . . I met the carrier a mile from the village and he said she had been close to death.'

5

'Oh, that is Pashman all over, the gloomy rogue. How he loves to exaggerate! Though certainly we all believed the dear lady in a desperate state a week ago; a week ago Dr Loder was riding out to Thorn twice a day, three times even. But she is mending now, yes, oh yes. Miss Pennyquick told me only this morning: the improvement is remarkable.'

'How came she to be so ill?'

'She was not ill, not exactly ill, dear Doctor,' and here the wind intervened by slamming shut the outer door, plunging them in darkness. 'Oh! Oh, where is the handle? Hook it back. Wedge it. Quick! Now, what was I saying? Lady Gerard. Yes, a dreadful accident. She was out riding a horse, a very wretch of a horse bought, I believe, from the lady who has taken Blackow Hall, a Mrs M'Cool. I am very much afraid Lady Gerard has a passion for great unruly beasts much as her late husband had, God rest him – I can remember young Sir Harry jumping the gravestones, the very gravestones. Well, this brute ran away with her on the Gorse, carried her into the park at Blackow and tossed her off over a timber rail. Mrs M'Cool found her there unconscious and rode herself for Dr Loder – and on the self-same horse, imagine, oh imagine! – leaving her niece to watch over Lady Gerard. They say no one has ever taken the village street at such a pace and the horse all over foam and half foundered. Dr Loder went out at once but could only prescribe peace and warmth,' and here his tone grew faintly accusing as if he felt medical science might have risen above such a paltry prescription; why, the village wise woman could have given such advice for sixpence. 'She never stirred for four and twenty hours, Babs Pennyquick told me, and Mrs M'Cool sat by her bed all that time, the lady herself and forty dogs – she keeps a whole pack in the house, they say. When Lady Gerard woke and took notice they carried her back to Thorn, it was thought Blackow might hold too many memories.'

6

Memories of Harry Gerard, that charming, unstable boy, of that brief unhappy marriage, of debt and disillusion; of death. Yes, memories enough; and for the Doctor too, who had loved her dearly and still did so, though twenty years and the total indifference of the lady separated them. 'I thank God she is recovered,' he said, his mood lifting as the storm was lifting, blowing away to the north-east. But: I burn for nothing, he reminded himself, she treats me as a harmless eccentric, an old old man.

He had been against her first marriage to Sir Harry Gerard of Blackow Hall but later had helped bring her together with his own friend William Claverden – a truly virtuous act but a horrid war of conscience and inclination. He regretted it deeply now, now she had broken off the engagement. Had she never loved William then? Or had her experience with Harry – a handsome appealing drunkard and a bigamist – made her falter at the last? She had written a brief letter of explanation which had explained nothing, and William, at sea with the Navy, had mentioned it only as fact: '. . . and you will have heard by now Ann and I are not going to marry . . .' Since war had broken out again communication was erratic, but the French Navy and the unpredictable oceans were as nothing compared with William's unshakable reticence. Had they quarrelled then after all? Had she perhaps hoped he might give up the sea?

'See, it is all over,' said Bringloe as a last gust wrenched at the door and flapped his worn skirts. They watched the trees stand up again and the great drops die away. The thunder rumbled into the distance and patches of blue showed between the clouds. In a moment the sun had returned.

'Now I know why I did not recognize you,' cried the curate, darting out over the threshold, 'You have left off your wig, your . . . your . . .' Verminous old rat's nest? 'Your mark of office.'

7

'I am done with wigs. We live in a new age. I am nothing but a plain country sawbones, a surgeon-apothecary even. I am packing my bags for India, for Bombay and service with John Company. Such anti-quated fashions are unhealthy in such heat.'

'But I heard you had been lecturing at the London hospitals, had operated there, had been applauded by great men. Surely . . .' But nothing was sure where the Doctor was concerned. 'And then there are your soldiers; you have spoken so feelingly of them in the past.'

'Oh, I am too old for battlefields, I shall never return to the Army.' And in any case the Army will not have me back, the cross-grained, ill-educated, infernal rats, in spite of my 'well-known eminence in the treatment of the most savage wounds', my 'inestimable contribution to the soldier's welfare'. Who said that? Franck? Surely not. He is an admirable man, candid, sound, above such hypocrisy. 'Twas Howard called me a serpent in their bosom – their skinny ungenerous collective bosom, I suppose he meant – for so constantly opposing the inadequacy of their administration, *ex*posing perhaps I should say. Likewise their bloody pusillanimity. God save us, have they ever cared at all for the man dying for want of a crust or a dry blanket or a decent, humane surgeon? I am proud to have been a serpent in such a bosom, only wish I had bit harder long long ago. Did any one of them know the first rule of running a field hospital? No. Never. They behaved as if cleanliness, warmth, light all fell from Heaven like the quail, like manna . . . 'In general I dislike hospitals,' he said aloud, 'I have lost too many patients in such institutions who would certainly have lived had they been nursed on a pallet in the mud. And then I am set on India. I have been happy in India.'

You have been tolerably happy in High Common, thought Bringloe as he watched the Doctor's slow progress towards the gate, a miserable grey pony in tow, a pony thoroughly drenched and ill disposed; tolerably happy for sure, though you were always a restless dissatisfied soul, a mass of contradiction: disobliging and generous, impatient and painstaking. He sighed and went in, trotting up the aisle until he came to the Gerard pew, a foolishly large box with threadbare silk cushions and straw and footwarmers piled up in one corner. There he sat down a moment to catch his breath in the lingering fog of candlesmoke: he sneezed, coughed, sneezed again. The Gerard monument on the wall above blurred as he looked up at it, his eyes filling with tears. Old Sir Harry, young Sir Harry dead, all dead; no more Gerards to follow them, to sit here on their ancient silk tormenting their chilblains with hot bricks. Little Lady Ann would not stay long at Thorn, every eligible gentleman in the district calling to see how she did after the accident, the house awash with inquiries, good wishes, flowers – and when she remarried the name itself would be lost. The Gerards gone, Blackow gone, gone into the ownership of that mad old woman who wore towels on her head and slept with ten dogs at the foot of her bed, thirty more in the same room.

Another sneeze. So this was indeed the certain end of extravagance, wanton high spirits and moral turpitude: oblivion. Bringloe wheezed and spluttered, wiping his eyes, reading the finely incised words: Henry George Dauncy Gerard, late of Blackow Hall in the County of Norfolk . . . Elizabeth his wife . . . Maria Henrietta, departed this life May 1st 1763 . . . And then the smaller lozenge below: Henry John Dauncy Gerard killed at Copenhagen 1801.

Young Sir Harry dead at Copenhagen, buried at sea; mad young Harry, full of irresistible demonic energy, marrying Ann Mathick on a whim, jumping his grey horse over the gravestones for a wager . . . And how well he had jumped them, and how he had laughed, taking

9

the churchyard gate straight and true. But even Harry Gerard, thought Bringloe, had never galloped through High Common as fast as old Mrs M'Cool.

Perhaps, after all, she was a fitting successor at Blackow. Was it not common knowledge she had only taken the house for its stables, the most commodious, well-planned, well-drained, well-situated stables in the county? And Bringloe suddenly cocked his head and listened, as if he could hear already the beat of approaching hooves, come to jump the graves again.

The Doctor's old house was a tall white ugly building in the very middle of the village. He tied his pony to a branch of the poor wilting bay tree by the front door and set his hand upon the familiar knob.

'Lord!' exclaimed Mrs Turner, hurrying from the back regions to intercept the stranger in the hall and finding herself staring into a shockingly well-remembered face. 'Why, Dr French, we were not expecting you. No, not until next week, sir, the very end of next week.'

'I wrote. I recall that I wrote a letter: the exact time, date, every particular,' was the peevish response.

'But you said the twenty-seventh, Dr Loder told me so, and it is only the . . .'

'Surely not. Perhaps Dr Loder mistook the word, could not read my hand. Where is Dr Loder?'

Dr Loder was in Bungay, dining away from home. There was nothing to eat in the house, Mrs Turner cried out on a rising note of panic, and the kitchen fire was out on account of the faulty chimney, the sweep had been at it all day and still the soot fell, soot and suspicious red dust – they thought the very brickwork was crumbling. 'But you are tired after your journey, such heat . . .' and she drew back a little as any prudent woman might at his malevolent stare. 'I will send young Polly out directly for cheese and ham, for whatever Morrison might have.'

The front parlour at least was unchanged: some few sticks of Indian furniture, a Turkey rug, a coal hod. In the corner was an empty parrot cage and the shell of a giant tortoise. 'Do you not find High Common a little dull?' came Ann's voice from long ago, their very first meeting. 'What can you do here compared with eating tortoise in the middle of a gale?' He remembered her brown eyes lit with laughter, the defiant turn of her head.

'Dr Loder does not use this room, sir. He thought you would like it left as it was . . .' Mrs Turner's voice trailed away as she too looked about: not a comfortable chair, not one cushion, not even a picture on the wall. 'There is nowhere to store any of it,' Loder had said irritably on taking possession. 'Where could I put a tortoise shell that size? Shut up the room, Mrs Turner. Dr French must deal with it when he next visits.'

'Thank you,' Dr French was saying now. 'Thank you, I see. Then perhaps since it is still wholly my own I shall take a dish of tea here. Pray be so good as to bring it in.'

But it appeared that Dr Loder did not care for tea, he was most deeply fond of coffee. The only tea in the house was the bare ounce Dr French himself had left in the box before he had fled to Suffolk, dusty, tasteless stuff by now. He did not care if it were powdered serpents, ground toads, sawdust and alum combined, howled the Doctor, was he to be met with such niggardly hospitality in his own house? Lack of a welcome, lack of courtesy, lack of every staple of civilized life . . . There followed ten minutes of increasingly rancorous accusation and denial while he prowled from room to room in search of Souchong and Congou, a perambulating volcano, not yet spewing flames but trailing unmistakably threatening smoke. There was no tea though, not of any age or pedigree, and finding the heavy hand of Dr Loder on all his other possessions he returned to smoulder with his tortoise shell.

At some point in the next dreary half hour young Jim

Revell came to the window to say he had confined the pony, he had found him up the street with the bay tree dragging behind.

'It was a shrivelled, blighted thing,' remarked the Doctor, for whom no plant grew easily. 'It yearned for hot sun, for southern climes.'

'Love you, sir, the sun shines hot enough this year,' said Jim, an engaging, spotty youth with large teeth, and: 'I hope you have come home to us, Doctor.'

Absurdly, sentimentally, he did not have the heart to deny it. 'Where is the pony now?' he asked by way of a diversion.

'I crammed him in the dickey's hovel. Dr Loder's great hoss fare to kick your stable down. I oont go in there with him though t'other stall's empty.'

The Doctor parted with a penny, all the coin he had, and closed the window with a frown. He had hoped to give Ann the bay tree – was there not something symbolic about bay trees? – along with a few other treasures: his specimens, most of his books. He had no doubt she would keep them safe against his return; he did not intend to return, but that was between him and the tortoise shell.

'Bread and cheese, Doctor,' announced Mrs Turner, sweeping in with a tray and the expression of a patriot compelled to succour the enemy, 'and pickles and a pig's foot. But I cannot make tea, not the smallest pot I can't, there is not a leaf to be had in the village. I could do orange shrub . . .'

He spent the afternoon sorting through his jars and pamphlets, all of which were in what was now Loder's study at the back of the house. A meticulous, careful man, this his substitute, he thought, there was nothing out of place and those few objects on the table were rigidly arranged. Well, he had come highly recommended – no less than Lubbock had given him a testimonial – and in the haste of his own departure last summer Alex French had been willing to sacrifice his patients to any man, so that he was competent and enthusiastic. But such neatness, such order depressed him, he did not know why, and he tried to summon up the memory of Loder's face when he had first met him: a long, pinkish face, thin, sober. Had he been predisposed towards him because he had trained at Alex's own Edinburgh hospital? Or because of Lubbock's unstinted praise? Or because no one else so apparently highly skilled had presented himself at the right moment?

Later, much later, when the half dark of high summer only partly disguised the village, the Doctor sat in miserable contemplation of his wretched, long-ago-devoured tortoise until his limbs seized, his mind running on and on with disjointed, feverish thought: Ann, frustrated desire, age, lack of means, Bombay, incompatibility, Franck apologetic, Howard exultant, Bonaparte, Ann . . . Ann. Loder had not come in by ten so he went to bed, groping his way with a kitchen glim and staring wanly about his old bedroom which, lacking vital pieces of furniture long since appropriated by Loder, appeared unutterably monastic and un-welcoming.

In spite of the heat, the long continuing heat, the bed felt damp. He could not sleep. The opening and closing of the front door at midnight, the shooting home of the bolts and the heavy tread upstairs all sounded pro-prietorial; it was not his house any longer, it was Loder's. When dawn broke he was still awake, writing a letter to his friend Jardine Savage in Jamaica and another to William on his ship. The glim had long since given out but he had found the stump of a candle in the cupboard and blew that out as the dull greyness grew steadily paler and paler until the sun rose in the clearest of skies. 'I shall be glad to leave,' he finished as a flood of yellow washed across the page and he looked up, dazzled, 'I cannot wait to take ship.' No, he could not wait. Perhaps

13

in spirit he had already departed, so that the visible Dr French hunched over his letter-writing was no more the true man than the shell of the tortoise was that comfortable, inquisitive beast he had once known.

He went down to breakfast with a belligerent stubble and on his head a species of turban improvised from two nightcaps.

'Good God!' cried Loder in a low voice, rising from the table. 'Ah. Ah . . . A very good morning to you, sir. I trust you slept?'

'Slept? A little. Have you coffee? And where is Mrs Turner? Where is that woman?' and he moved towards the bell.

'There is fresh coffee in the pot,' said Loder hastily, picking it up and reaching for an empty cup. 'Mrs Turner is not herself this morning.'

He was a tall, serious young man, remarkably thin. He had had no experience of domestic upheaval until this morning. Then to the unwelcome news that Dr French had arrived ten days early was added the threat, the real threat, of his losing an excellent housekeeper. He had risen to find her waiting for him at the foot of the stairs, had been forced to listen to her outpourings: Dr French had a vile rash temper, unspeakable eccentricities, had never been known to keep female servants other than orphans or bastards or pregnant trollops sent him by the overseers . . .

'Will you be staying long?' Loder asked.

'I thought . . .' the Doctor began, pausing to deal with his excellent coffee – he could almost forgive the man for having no tea – 'I thought I would try to be away within the month.'

'A month! Oh! Oh, certainly. A month. But of course it is your home, sir, you may stay as long as you wish.'

We have nothing in common, thought the Doctor, gazing miserably across the table, nothing. Well, he is

14

clearly competent in his profession, inhuman but competent. That must serve.

'I can see why Lubbock recommended him,' he said to Tom Forsie, who called an hour later to welcome him home and stuck his large open smiling face round the door, 'but I pity his patients.'

'We are his patients,' said Tom. 'See what you have left us to – he has no feeling at all, no proper feeling.'

'There is Dr Gray.'

Tom pulled the coffee pot towards him and looked inside. 'You have drunk it all. Dr Gray is eighty at least and never suggests anything but sea bathing.'

'I have nothing against sea bathing.'

'Dr Beevor does not agree with it.'

'I was not aware you and Dr Beevor were acquainted.'

'Oh,' said Tom, grinning, 'he was at Upgate when we dined there last. Lord Barsham knows him.' And calls him in, perhaps, now you have deserted us, said his look. After a little, watching the Doctor finish his toast: 'It is very quiet.'

'That is because there are no women in the house, no busybodying whining arranging women. Mrs Turner has taken herself off to persecute the tradesmen and young Polly has been sent about the parish for tea.'

'Tea?'

'Tea leaves. There is not one – not one! – in this unholy house. But tell me your news. How is Ann? And Thorn?'

Ann was well, pale, shaken, but well, and Thorn continued to prosper. The excitements of the moment were mainly bovine: the newest stock bull – the last proving intractable *and* infertile, an unforgivable combination; the first of their home-bred heifers due to calve; and the oxen, twelve now and beautifully trained, great docile obliging beasts.

The docile obliging beasts had horns a yard wide, the Doctor remembered. Tom's unassailable good humour

15

raised his own spirits too and he smiled across the wreck of the breakfast table. How happy Ann had made this boy by giving him those fifty acres all his own. He was Ann's cousin, the illegitimate son of the disreputable Francis Forsie who had bequeathed her Thorn. She had taken Tom in without regard for the local gossips, the tale-bearers, the strong reek of scandals past and to come, and she had seen to his education – she and Alex French between them – and to establishing a place for him in society. When she had married Harry Gerard she had given Tom enough land for his own farm – a wise precaution – but no house had been built on it yet and he stayed with her at Thorn where she had returned after that brief unhappiness at Blackow.

'And is *Sable Island* still at sea?' asked the Doctor.

'We hope so. We have had no word. In fact, we have had no word since the peace ended, since May.' The *Sable Island* was a privateer, a large and dangerous vessel, which had become Ann's on the death of her husband and which had, with its many prizes, mended her failing fortune and that of her farm.

Sheep and corn occupied the next ten minutes: it was always difficult to keep Tom from agricultural subjects. In time, however, even the glories of the new Leicesters were exhausted and he said abruptly: 'Blackow is sold. Did you know?' Then came an account of the Blackow heifers who had galloped into the yard at Thorn all over mud and lascivious expressions the day the new bull had arrived. 'Scrawny little beasts. They really belong to old Moore at Hall Farm, he rents the grazing in the park. They were wild as deer, ran all over the place moaning and bawling while the bull bawled back. It took us over an hour to drive them home across the Gorse, every time the bull screeched they broke away, the shameless strumpets. Hollin and I did a patch job on the Blackow fence but got no thanks for it, the old lady came by and looked down her nose and said she was not responsible

16

for the cattle. You would have thought we were tinkers by the way she spoke, and all the time prancing about on a horse like Harry's, a great grey, frothing and staring. But she was uncommon civil when Ann was hurt, and her niece was kind. There is a little girl too, Cassandra.'

'But what happened to the Houghtons?'

'Ann thinks we were all too rude and rustic and they feared their morals would be contaminated, what with bastards being accepted in the best drawing rooms and lady farmers and so forth. Anyway, they ran away to Bath – they said it was for Mrs Houghton's health – and put the house up for sale.'

It was not a beautiful house and it was vast, inconvenient and cold. This had not appeared to deter Mrs M'Cool, Tom said, who arrived shortly after the Houghtons had left, careering down the drive in a large antiquated carriage, a carriage commonly claimed to have been stuffed with dogs, peacocks and wild Irishmen besides the lady herself, though no one had actually seen it except Rigby, the groom, and young Annie Thurston in the dairy. Mrs M'Cool, extricating herself from livestock and retainers, had walked round the house with the impatient, elastic stride of someone well used to crossing treacherous country on foot, and then had made a vigorous tour of the stables, the best in the county. Two weeks later she had moved in: more dogs, poultry, Irishmen – and horses.

'It would warm Harry's heart to see them,' said Tom, who had not cared for Harry alive but was willing to concede his expertise in horseflesh now he was dead, 'though Mrs M'Cool is a rare sight. She has red hair and wears odd clothes.'

The slamming of a distant door made the cups rattle. 'The women are returned,' said the Doctor regretfully.

'Perhaps it is Dr Loder,' suggested Tom.

'No. No indeed – ' with a savage look – 'Dr Loder is out harrying a gout, an eye complaint and a diseased ovary to death. Pass me that last cold chop. It would be as well to make merry while we can.'

A little to the left of the gates to Blackow Hall was a miniature Greek temple once inhabited by the gate-keeper and his wife. The Doctor had treated the wife for an ulcerous leg and so had seen at first hand the inconvenience of life in an architectural folly. It certainly looked enchanting, with four pillars flanking the low front door and a classic pediment and frieze in exactly reduced proportion. The gatekeeper had abandoned it long ago, his wife could not endure the isolation and Sir Harry had been behind with wages, the usual sorry tale until Ann had come to Blackow. The Doctor sat quietly contemplating its dilapidated state for five minutes before his pony, growing bored, danced sideways, twirled round twice, dropped a shoulder and shot him on to the drive. With a snort and a knowing look he trotted briskly away between the gates and out on to the Gorse, several score little birds all rising together from the ash scrub to scold him as he passed.

The Doctor stood up and brushed himself off. He had been humiliated by so many horses and ponies across the years it meant very little to him. He walked off to view the gatehouse at close quarters, rubbing his leg absently and muttering. There he found that the sprightly heifers had certainly been at large in the tiny garden and that two of the windows were broken. He was blowing on a dirty pane and ruining his cuff to no effect when the sound of a woman's voice and the clop of small hooves made him look round.

'Is this pony yours, sir?'

'He is, the knave. I salute you for daring to capture him.'

The woman bent to pick up something from the dust. 'Your hat. He has left a pretty hoofmark on it.'

A proud, voluptuous beauty, confident, warm, self-possessed. He gave her a bow and found, as he straightened, that her intense blue gaze was disconcerting. Did she think him a mean and shabby figure, past his prime, obviously poor?

'Are you alone?' he asked, cuffing the pony's long yellow teeth away from his arm.

'Yes, quite alone. Is it any of your business if I choose to walk out unaccompanied?'

'I meant no disrespect. But in my day this place has hosted gipsies, footpads, runaway soldiers and tinkers by the dozen. I was thinking of your safety.'

'I had never looked on Blackow Gorse as such a thieves' kitchen. You astonish me.' Again that steady stare. She was wondering what he was: a cleric, apothecary, lawyer's clerk? She glanced down at his hands. They were long fine hands, carefully tended; there were no ink stains. 'My name is Julia Hawkworth. I live at Blackow Hall.'

'Are you perhaps the niece of Mrs M'Cool?'

'I am. Are we notorious then? What do they say? Have you met those strange women at the Hall, the one old and mad, the other nearly old and nearly mad? And who are you, sir, creeping about my aunt's property and peering through the windows?' And with a sudden wicked delightful laugh: 'Would any gentleman be seen dead on such a pony?'

'I bought him for two pounds. One cannot expect courage and breeding for such a price.'

'One would be a fool to expect anything for such a price.'

She had very fair hair, he noticed, a true blonde, and she was much older than he had first thought, thirty-five perhaps, thirty-five at least. What had she said? One old and mad, the other nearly old and nearly mad.

'I am Dr French of High Common.'

Her face broke into amused surprise. 'Not the Dr Alexander French whose plate is so prominent in the

Street – the tall white awkward-looking house with the bay tree in the tub? Why, you are famous! My aunt is a recluse and I dine out seldom but we have heard your name a score of times, have come to think of you as a strange combination of Diogenes and Apollo, a polymath no less.'

'It is clear I do not live up to your expectations.'

'You do not.'

'Is it not uncivil of you to say so?'

She laughed again and walked off a little way. She had a quick, decisive way of walking and she held her chin very high. There was not so much of grace in it as art, a desire to make an impression. 'How very hot it is,' she said, 'I shall take to the grass and stay under the trees.'

He drew level and looked down the slope of parkland to the house. 'It is a barn of a place for two ladies. I knew it in better days. The Houghtons bought it when Sir Harry Gerard died and began to restore it, I remember. Did they finish?'

'They dug new flowerbeds and dredged the lake and painted the ballroom but by then they had had enough of the rain and snow, mud and cold winds, and galloped away to Bath. The house is nothing to my aunt, she would put up her bed in a pigsty or throw down a blanket in the hayloft.'

All this time he had been following the frantic movements of some creature down near the house. Now there were more: white specks chasing hither and thither.

'There are scores of dogs,' he said at last, 'all running about in the garden.'

'Those are my aunt's hounds. There are forty – and then the terriers and spaniels and the rest. She is hoping to hunt the foxes on the Gorse.'

'There is also a small girl with a whip.'

'That is my daughter, Cassandra. She is trying to train them to do tricks but all in vain, they do nothing but lounge about or hunt. They hunt anything: foxes, hares, cats, other dogs, the poultry, the work-men who came to mend the stable drains. Only my aunt can control them.'

After a while the small girl vanished, the greater part of the pack with her. The oppressive heat of noon burned down and only the occasional swallow skimmed along the park boundary, the occasional pigeon clapped its wings in the great oaks.

'Do you know if your aunt might be willing to let the gatehouse for a month?' asked the Doctor. 'I am on my way to India as soon as I have tied up my affairs and Dr Loder – of course you know Dr Loder – has taken my house. I am only an intruder there. It would suit me to have a place of my own for these last weeks.'

Julia looked back at it, shading her eyes. 'The windows are broken,' she said.

'Only two, and only one pane in each. Should I call upon your aunt?'

'You may call if you like. She may not care to speak to you. Aunt Clodie is as likely to take a whip to you as give you a civil good day. And if she said yes I believe you would regret it, it is a ridiculous little place like a doll's house. Look, it must only have two rooms and the cattle have trampled the garden, the fence is down.'

'An old bachelor does not need more than two rooms – and gardens do not interest me.'

She undid the strings of her bonnet. Her cheeks were flushed with heat. 'What weather! Well, if you are determined on it I suggest you call at the house in the morning, before my aunt has had time to argue with Rigby, or take a toss, or lose her voice screeching at Driscoll.'

With this she began to walk down towards the house, striking off across the grass in the shade of the trees. The Doctor watched her for a long time, watched her until he saw her climb the steps to the front door. Then: 'I wonder what she has done with Mr Hawkworth?' he asked the pony.

21

# 2

'That woman Hawkworth may not have been married at all,' was Lord Barsham's comment, standing with his friend the Doctor in the picture hall at Upgate Place. 'There is something about her . . . Well, there are some women never seem married even when they are. So how is a man to know? She arrived from Paris during the last days of the peace —' and his tone suggested nothing that came out of Paris was wholly without suspicion — 'bringing the child but no husband.'

'A widow then.'

'She may be. Hawkworth's name has never been mentioned.' Barsham sighed, thinking of his own wife, their circumscribed, contented existence. He cared for his family, his house, his acres, liked the orderliness of the county's deeply conservative society. He did not care for handsome unattached women who brought with them the breath of old scandals along with the unsettling, first-hand experience of that wanton, bloody world across the Channel. The damnable thing was, he had rather liked her.

'And Mrs M'Cool? I only ask because I shall shortly have to sue for her favours: I wish to move into her gatehouse.'

'The devil you do. It is a poky hutch of a place. She will most likely send you packing and the dogs in pursuit. She never goes out and don't care for anyone to call. She wears a terrible red wig like old Queen Bess and those hounds of hers hunt anything that moves.'

'And the child?'

'Oh, just an ordinary child, an awkward stumpy little thing. Shy. Neglected perhaps. Whatever else Mrs

22

Hawkworth might be she don't strike a man as maternal.'

The door opened and his eldest daughter Charlotte entered, demanding to know why, the dear Doctor having arrived early for dinner, he had been spirited away to this dingy place to look at dull pictures of people all long since dead. She twitched at the Doctor's drooping neckcloth with motherly concern, smiling up into his face. 'You must come down. Mama has been asking where you are. How different you look with your own hair and such a fine new coat.'

'I would never have recognized you,' was her mother's blunter exclamation as he entered her private sitting room a moment later.

'Have I changed so very much?'

'Well, you are not the man who ran away last summer. You have lost weight,' and then, because she never stood on ceremony with him – he had delivered all her children, how could she preserve a false dignity? – she asked: 'Have you seen Ann yet?'

His expression answered her. He had a remarkably expressionless face except when passionate indignation or simple rage became too much to bear; apparently love too was to have its effect. He must have known it because he walked deliberately to look out of the window at the wide sunburnt lawns. 'Tom Forsie says she is still much shaken, barely convalescent. I thought I would put off a visit until . . . I am only here, after all, to say my farewells.'

'What lies! All lies! What a fool you are, Alex! She frequently asks after you, wonders that you only wrote her three letters in a year, believes you hold it against her that she did not marry William. What are you waiting for? Ask for her hand.'

'She would be astonished.'

'Most probably. Anyway, she would say yes or no. If yes you would be a happy man and if no at least you would be out of this misery, this Hell-on-earth state.'

23

He would not turn round from the window, stood hunched up, a disagreeable rigidity about him. Nonetheless she felt compelled to continue: 'I cannot see you have anything to lose.'

Silence. In the distance the noise of the family gathering for dinner, a raised voice in the hall, the wail of a child, the barking of dogs.

'It is not only Ann,' he said at last with a great effort. 'Do you think I wish to be confined in High Common another twenty years? I must escape for a last time before age and infirmity turn the key. You of all people should understand. You were always sympathetic in the past.'

She looked at him affectionately. 'You were never in love in the past. And I sympathized most with your desire to do right by your poor sacrificed soldiers – in those days you had a regiment. But this vague expedition to India . . .' and the door opened and in came the entire family, including Lord Barsham's formidable mother and Mrs Palmer, Lady Barsham's garrulous sister, Charlotte, a visiting niece whose baby could still be heard howling far off, and also young Mr and Mrs Frayle who had taken the splendid great parsonage, the new parson preferring to live grandly in Cambridge.

'You did meet him,' Louise Barsham told the Doctor, 'very tall and pink. He thinks a great deal of himself too. Thank goodness he will not trouble us much. The last time he came he preached a sermon so clever we none of us understood a word and afterwards, when I dared to suggest he might care to live in his parish he shuddered at the thought of being "buried alive in Norfolk" and said his college could not spare him, in any case, even had he cared for turkeys and turnips. How glad we all are of dear old Bringloe who has more Christian charity in his little finger and who preaches "Love thy neighbour" every Sunday without fail in perfectly comprehensible language.'

Young Mr Frayle, who was as yet undecided whether he too cared to be buried alive at High Common, even with a new, pretty wife to keep him company, found the Doctor something of a puzzle. He seemed on such intimate terms with the family – even the terrible old lady had bestowed on him a species of withered smile – and yet he did not aspire to being an eminent physician, rather the reverse, a country practitioner and sometime Army surgeon, a man to whom the dinner table at Upgate Place ought surely to be barred.

'The Doctor?' cried Mrs Palmer when applied to. 'Why, the Doctor is a genius. There is no other man can sew you up neater. Only recently he has been showing the London surgeons how it should be done. He is an authority on those terrible wounds soldiers so often die from, poor dears, has saved scores of men beyond hope . . .'

The Doctor heard her spirited defence from across the room and moved to destroy her whole effect by coming over with a Mephistophelian gleam to talk about a corpse he was about to dissect, a prize of a corpse – there were so few these days – his friend Menzies had sent a note from the Norwich Hospital only that morning. He might have embarked on the clinical details had they let him but Frayle excused himself, confirmed in his opinion Dr French was an unattractive, uncouth animal, and Mrs Palmer silenced him brusquely with: 'I had almost made you a hero, and now look what you have done,' in a low, irritated tone.

'I was not born to be a hero,' replied the Doctor with a wry smile, 'though I fear I may be called on to act like one when I knock at Mrs M'Cool's door.'

'Call at Blackow? Oh! Oh, dear Doctor, I would not advise it. I called there myself when they were newly arrived – did Louise not mention it? The old woman greeted me in a sort of bed wrapper and a shift, no shoes, no cap, and when I bid her good morning retorted that it was not indeed, it was a foul and bilious morning, the chimneys were smoking, some horse or other was lame and two of the dogs had a distemper – and then she threw a shoe at me and hoped she would never be troubled in her own house again.'

Then followed what gossip reported of Mrs M'Cool's breeding, connections and source of income, of her constant galloping about on large horses, one of which had sunk her in the millpond or jumped the tollgate or both, and of her hounds and peacocks and her tribe of servants, strange shy creatures who spoke a foreign language and were known to be papists.

'Do you know what Mrs Hawkworth said,' Louise broke in, appearing at the Doctor's elbow, 'when I asked her why her aunt did not go about in society? She said . . . Wait a moment, I must remember the very words . . . She said: "She has had a long and uproarious life which has taught her beasts are much to be preferred to human beings." '

'I daresay she is right,' said the Doctor.

'All I wonder,' said Louise, taking his arm to lead him to dinner, 'is what exactly constitutes an "uproarious life"?'

There was a smell of earth and crushed grass, a pleasant coolness after the heat of the day. This was the corner of England he had made his own, where he had assumed he would die and lie in High Common peace. Now he knew he would never do it. On impulse he turned away from the village and rode up to the Gorse in the bright moonlight, the grey pony reluctant and the faint whiff of the tinkers' fires in his nostrils.

Here were the untended acres of rabbit warren and springy turf, the haunt of adders and gold-finches and the wary Norfolk sheep. Here were great sprawling copses of ash and elder and hazel, wild cherry and thorn, now and again the remnants of an ancient forest: vast old oaks, splendidly deformed. It was a mile across between the Blackow gates and the steep lane to Thorn that fell down and down in a long curve to the farm and the watermill – a mile all too quickly covered by Harry Gerard on his thoroughbreds. The Doctor thought of Harry as he rode, for surely Harry's ghost haunted these windy levels, these wild woodlands. If he was anywhere he was here: he had never loved Blackow and had never lived at Thorn.

Thorn. It was there at the foot of Warren Hill, if he stood in his stirrups he could see it quite plain, a great sprawl of barns and cattle yards about the old house with its massive chimneys. He could just make out the apple trees, the half-built hayricks, the carts, kennels, wood-stacks. And beyond them the quiet fields fell away to the flat pale watermeadows and the river.

The fact was inescapable: he had nothing to offer her, or to be more strictly accurate, what little he had she did not want. It was certainly true he had no looks, no money, no career. He had avoided domestic responsibility so long he was quite sure he would avoid it for the rest of his life – what basis was that for a marriage? What basis for a marriage where the woman was still young enough to bear children and no doubt hoped to do so? In any case, he knew what she really wanted, she wanted another Harry Gerard but without Harry's faults, without his selfish impulses, his addiction to drink and gambling and unreliable friends, a man not necessarily monogamous but one who could, in his own fashion, keep sufficient faith.

'But then he would be a paragon,' said the Doctor to his pony. 'Perhaps one man in a million might qualify.'

The pony was no paragon of any kind, however. Once his head was turned for home nothing on earth would have interrupted his racking trot, not the tinkers rising from under his hooves nor the spirit of Harry Gerard cantering from the black pools of shadow beneath the trees.

'I shall sell the pony while I am in Norwich,' the Doctor told Loder at breakfast. 'I hope to make a profit.'

Loder looked sceptical but had the wisdom to remain silent. He passed across the coffee pot. 'So long as you do not sell him to Lady Gerard,' he said after a while, momentarily cheered by the fragrant steam to try a little dour humour. 'She is talking of riding again shortly. I have forbidden it, strictly forbidden it, but I feel she is not a young lady who cares to listen to advice.'

No, thought the Doctor, who had failed to dissuade her from her disastrous marriage though he had camped three days and nights in her house. 'I must confess I sent my old pony up from Suffolk for her to care for,' he said, 'when I believed I was to go abroad this Easter past. He is a chestnut. Perhaps you have seen him.'

'I have. He too is far from suitable for a lady. I suggested a donkey carriage but Lady Gerard only laughed. It is my opinion that Mrs M'Cool will sell her another hard-mouthed brute before long, she is a woman would sell a horse as soon as blink. I put ten stitches in that young woman's scalp and she lay unconscious a day and a night – and she cannot wait to be back in the saddle!'

The Doctor might have said: I admire her for it. Instead he drank his strong coffee and turned his thoughts resolutely to his morning ahead, dissecting Menzies' interesting corpse. He was, in fact, so silent – and he generally looked horribly savage when he was brooding – that Loder struck out into a sticky one-sided conversation about the medical treatment of horses, a subject he knew nothing about. He struck out as a man plunges recklessly into boggy country because he cannot see solid ground in any direction, and the Doctor naturally left him to sink to his ear lobes before rescuing him with a sudden: 'Is that the hour, the very hour? I shall never be in Norwich at the appointed time. Nine miles on that pony! I should never have had a second

28

cup. Pray tell Mrs Turner her muffins are excellent – and I shall not be home for dinner.'

When I told him I should not be home for dinner his face lit up, he thought as he hurried the pony on its way, how he does resent my presence in his house. Yet I have not interfered in any way, I have not mentioned medical matters, have not spoken the name of one patient once mine and now his, nor asked after his impressions of the district, his preferred methods, his relationship with old Parr the chemist who will always cheat a man he does not like. All these topics are perfectly legitimate but I fear to give offence. He is an easy man to offend. Is it because he lacks a sense of humour? How I wish I had left them an open, cheerful character instead of this morose, clever cove with the long face.

'I tell you this,' said Menzies, meeting him at the door and hurrying him through his old Hospital with obvious impatience, 'he will be a rich man in twenty years. He knows how to charge for his services. You never did. What do you think of the new paint, eh? We never see his gloomy countenance here, of course. He doesn'a care for paupers, Alex dear, nor to build his reputation on philanthropic gestures. He thinks only of tending the rich and retiring to a pretty fortune.'

For a moment the two old friends mentally contemplated the pretty fortunes neither of them had made in long careers, perhaps with a certain fleeting regret. Menzies, however, lived very comfortably and had no right to complain; Alex French had none either, having voluntarily squandered his gifts among those with no means to pay him a fee.

'Ah well,' said Menzies as they came to the end of a corridor and turned in to a dismal little room where the sun failed to penetrate, 'there will always be fools to pay his bills. Good luck to him, say I.'

They changed their coats in eager anticipation. Dr French's pockets were found to contain fossils, a fine tortoiseshell lancet, a catapult and a small stuffed squirrel.

'Shall we go in?' asked Menzies, a hand on an inner door.

'Let us do so at once.'

What with the interesting corpse, Menzies' unstinting hospitality – he had bespoke a meal at the King's Head, half a dozen dishes, each one a masterpiece – a self-indulgent hour in his favourite grocer – Wiltshire cheese, tea and cocoa – and the chance meeting of several old acquaintances in the street, the Doctor forgot to dispose of his wicked old pony and set off home to High Common with him slung about with parcels. It was only as they breasted the last gentle rise that brought them to the top of the Gorse that he remembered, remembered too that he had also forgotten to buy Loder the pound of monstrously expensive coffee beans he had intended as a kind of peace offering, and remembered his resolution to tackle this strange old woman M'Cool about the gate-house. Slightly irritated, he pulled the pony's head to the left, clapped in his heels and brought his hat down on its hindquarters. It broke into something resembling the rocking motion of a camel, its ears laid flat with indignation, and so passed through the gates of Blackow and down the long curving drive to the house.

'Well, and come in,' said the being who opened the great front door as he pulled up at the foot of the steps, 'I like to see a man ride with determination. 'Tis a peculiar gait for a pony that, I wonder now where he learnt it.'

The Doctor dismounted and looked about helplessly. There were four peacocks preening themselves on the steps. The vision at the door shrieked 'Rigby!' in much the same tones one of them might have used and immediately a tall wasted figure shuffled round the corner of the house followed by two small spaniels. 'Rigby, take the gentleman's pony now. You, sir, come in.'

The Doctor found himself next to a tall thin woman in gold brocade, in a scarlet petticoat embroidered with roses, in hunting boots – she had kilted up one side of her skirts and they were clearly visible – and in a striped turban perched on top of grizzled red hair.

'I am Claudia M'Cool,' she announced, leading him indoors, 'and you are Dr Alexander French. My niece told me.'

How had she described him, he wondered? He begged Mrs M'Cool's pardon for calling so late, on such a hot day, and unexpectedly, to which she replied that the hours were all alike to her, that there had scarcely been a day since May that had not been hot, and that how else must he have called but unexpectedly unless he had written a letter and she never read letters . . . 'So you are the man they were all clamouring for when young Ann fell over my railings,' she said, turning to look at him as they reached the far side of the wide hall. 'Your replacement is no substitute, they tell me, he likes his patients confined to bed or to mortuary boards, he cannot take them up and running, answering him back, questioning his diagnoses. And I bet you a guinea he has already forbidden Ann Gerard to ride again. Lucy! Lucy!'

There was an all-pervasive smell of dog and cabbage and . . . Something worse? Stewing bones? A small shy figure materialized from the deep shadows by the kitchen passage, bobbed a curtsey and said: 'Please, ma'am, the kitchen chimney's on fire.'

'On fire? Never!' was Mrs M'Cool's surprising response, ''Tis the jackdaw nests burning. Serve 'em right for building in a foolish place. Where's Kitty?'

'Kitty's throwing water up it.'

'Throwing water up a chimney! I never heard the like. I suppose I must go below and set all to rights. Lucy, fetch the Doctor some cordial,' and over her shoulder: ''Tis all we have, that or the Irish whiskey.'

The Doctor waited for some minutes, kicking his heels about the hall, but no cordial appeared and there were shrieks and crashes from the kitchen regions. He went down to investigate, the smell of wet soot and the stewing bones rising to meet him, along with ten or fifteen lemon and white hounds, all very large and all baring their teeth.

'Don't mind them, the rascals,' said their mistress, looking back to see the cause of the commotion. 'Push them away. They've never been known to eat a man yet, Doctor.'

A diminutive girl in a striped dress and apron was standing shaking by the hearth. 'Fetch me a broom, Kate,' came Mrs M'Cool's imperious Irish voice. 'Well and don't stand there, child. There are flames up the chimney and no mistake.'

The girl ran like a hare, returning in a moment with an old yard broom as large as she was herself. Mrs M'Cool thrust it upwards and a vast flaming heap of sticks descended to flare momentarily in the hearth. 'There, what did I tell you? Jackdaws, crows, starlings. Now, where is that Lucy gone and where is the Doctor's cordial?'

Upstairs in the gloom of the hall again she suddenly threw off her turban. The Doctor picked it up off the floor and lodged it on the newel post at the foot of the stairs. Mrs M'Cool had opened the door to the ballroom and disappeared inside. He hesitated a moment – so many memories in this place, more than he had ever expected – and then entered in her wake.

'You have been here before, of course,' she said. 'It has been repainted. Is there an improvement?'

'Certainly.' Certainly, it was almost a new room. Yet here were the six long windows overlooking the terrace and garden, the unsuccessful lake, and here the wall of beautiful mirrors in which he had first been reflected as a young man and might, had he chosen to stay in Norfolk, have been reflected one day as an old one, with a stick and a stoop.

Mrs M'Cool came a little nearer. She had sharp, greenish eyes under carefully plucked brows. He thought, astonished: the red hair is her own. She might have been any age between fifty and ninety and she walked with an athletic, queenly stride.

'You do not look like a man who stands on ceremony,' she remarked. It may have been an oblique reference to his clothes which neither the post mortem nor his epicurean meal had left immaculate, but perhaps she saw beneath the clothes, or beyond them; or not caring for such things herself, had not even noticed them but had read his character accurately in his wrinkles. 'To be sure I do not normally entertain callers in the ballroom – I seldom entertain them at all – but then . . . This is the only room in the house that satisfies my soul. It has noble proportions, does it not? There is nothing mean or cramped about it. One could do a wild jig up such a sweep of floor.'

The Doctor agreed, half afraid she might demonstrate at any moment. But she was right, it was a splendid room. He thought it would be small-minded to remark on the complete lack of chairs. Mrs M'Cool did not give the impression of a woman who cared to sit about much idling her time away. He said: 'I called to speak to you about the gatehouse, the little Greek temple by the front entrance . . .' and hesitated. Was she taking off her petticoat?

Into his abrupt silence she said briskly: 'Quick, hand me up on to the table. Do you see all those flies? That Lucy is the laziest girl ever came out of Galway town.'

The table was delicate, expensive, ornate. Its owner stood braced on its small polished surface swatting the offending insects with a sort of lace apron she had detached somehow and from somewhere amid the rest of her billowing dress. 'I will not have flies in this room,' she said strongly. 'Who knows? One day I may decide to have a ball.'

There was a distant knock and the cordial made its entrance on a tarnished silver tray carried by Lucy herself, who seemed to find nothing odd in the sight of her mistress swaying about in the window. The cordial itself was unmistakably flavoured with bones. The Doctor drank it soberly, like a black draught, trying not to screw up his face, while Mrs M'Cool leapt from her table and swept the flies into a little heap.

'Little Ann Gerard knows how to sit a horse,' was her unexpected announcement as she shook out her piece of lace and folded it.

'I have always thought so. She and her husband made a striking pair.'

'A man after my own heart, she tells me.'

Did she still speak of him with affection? But then, there was no doubting it: she had loved him deeply. 'He lived for his horses,' said the Doctor sourly.

'A bigamist too, I hear. Well. All this – ' and an embracing sweep of her arm – 'and two wives.' A long, penetrating stare. 'Not wanting in courage, I take it, but wanting in sense and discretion. I have met more than a few like that in my time.'

To divert her from the subject of Harry Gerard he asked about her reasons for coming to Norfolk, her arrival at Blackow. She had arrived in the extreme discomfort of her father's ancient coach, she replied, taking him literally, burdened by portmanteaux, hens in sacks, puppies and servants. There had been no room for Julia, who had been forced to follow with Cassandra in a post-chaise, bringing only two trunks and the quartet of terriers in a basket. The truth was there had been no resisting the Blackow stables, or the miles of good riding, acres of uninterrupted heath, nothing enclosed. 'It is a fine wilderness,' she finished with immense satisfaction, her eye gleaming on an inward view of the Gorse, and then: 'Come. Come, have you finished the poisonous mixture? I shall take you to see the horses.'

They were as the Doctor had feared, large and temperamental. And he might as well have been looking at giraffes for all he could judge their finer points – short-tempered, rolling-eyed giraffes.

'They have been abused, poor dears,' said the new mistress of Blackow, 'they have been sadly mistreated. Strong characters mistreated grow vicious or morose,' a close hard look at him again. 'A spirited horse grows vicious, a thinking man morose.'

He looked her in the eye: he was not a coward. But before he could speak she laughed and took his arm, leading him to another stall. 'There, there is my darling. Have you ever seen her like, even you with your dull cold English eye?'

All he knew was that it was a brown mare, perfectly made within the usual standards. Since there was nothing unusual in her colour nor remarkably different in her lovely head from any of the beasts he had just seen, he remained silent, simply staring. 'This is Dido,' said Mrs M'Cool, putting a sinewy brown hand like a monkey's paw down the mare's neck. 'This is my Dido who is going to make our fortune.'

The Doctor had a low opinion of anyone who supposed fortunes could be made on the backs of horses but there was something arresting, even poetic, in the picture of the old woman and the beautiful mare. Then he caught the glint of a greenish eye. Was she laughing at him?

'Ann has not seen her yet,' she said. 'Tommy Strade has only just brought her out of Ireland for me.'

'I thought Lady Gerard would not visit this house, it holds such memories?'

'Memories!' cried the old lady so sharply the mare threw up her head and drew back a step in distress. 'Traitors and blackguards! Nor worth a peck of beans! It

35

don't do to cling to memories, Doctor, nor to let 'em affect you. Come out again into the sunshine. You can see the gardens.'

The clasp of her hand on his arm was too imperious to resist. She propelled him out of the stableyard and into the greenery beyond. And in five minutes he was quite certain she knew everything about gardens, that there was not a plant, however plebeian or retiring, that she could not name, whose habits she knew intimately, whose propagation she could not explain. She visited Sir James Smith in Norwich – the only person on earth she did visit except horse-dealers – had been introduced to him by letter from Sir Joseph Banks with whom she had corresponded for years and years. In the soft south-west of Ireland she had grown as many new species as had come her way, had often been sent strange seed and pages of horticultural instruction. And besides a scientific interest she had a child's unfeigned delight in growing things, a pure enthusiasm, and it was this which charmed the Doctor, led from bush to bush and plant to plant; it was as real and as deep as her passion for horses and hounds, and after a while he wondered if she had taken Blackow for more than its stables, that her glittering eye had seen untold possibilities in the neglected gardens.

'Aunt Clodie! Aunt Clodie!' and a child came jumping over the box hedges, a small, square, stout child with a direct and curious gaze.

'Where are your manners?' demanded Mrs M'Cool. 'And has your mother never told you a lady never shows her legs to a gentleman, leaping about in the air like a brazen creature. Now, say good day to Dr French.'

'How d'you do, sir?' said the child with a commendable curtsey. She was about eight, a cloud of gingery hair about a freckled face.

'Well?' said Mrs M'Cool. 'What is it?'

'The carrier has brought the guinea fowl and they are

36

all in baskets making a horrible noise and Mama says will you come at once nobody knows what to do with them and all the hounds are getting so excited.' She drew breath, her skin a glowing pink beneath the freckles.

'Is there no one with any sense in this house?' asked her great-aunt, sweeping up her skirts and walking away at speed. The child hesitated, looking up at the Doctor.

'I suppose I interrupted,' she said sadly, considering him from head to toe and finding him, apparently, quite harmless.

'Your aunt was talking about plants.'

'Oh, she does. And horses. Do you like horses?'

'Not very much, I fear.'

'I do. Aunt Clodie is teaching me to ride.'

They began to walk back side by side. 'My name is Cassandra,' remarked the child as they turned through an arch in a tall hedge on to the lawns.

'Cass, where have you been?' and Julia Hawkworth was coming down from the terrace, her face protected by an absurdly small sunshade, a scrap of green silk. 'Dr French. I did not know it was you. Has my aunt been showing you the gardens? You cannot guess what a privilege it is. She must like you, you know, else you would have been shown the door within a minute. Cass, run and wash your hands before your meal, Kitty is being kept waiting.'

'I have been round the stables too,' said the Doctor, smiling after the departing child, 'but I very much regret to say I failed to be impressed – and it was noticed. One horse is much like another to me.'

'But did you talk about the gatehouse?'

'I did. She ignored it, and then I dared not mention it again.'

Julia laughed. 'How she makes cowards of everyone!' she cried.

How very fine her skin was, only the faint betraying lines at eyes and mouth telling her age, and that open childlike look, the very blue eyes. Her mouth was a little too large perhaps and now that she turned and began to mount the steps again at his side he thought that when she was not artful – that studied, quite obvious artfulness of movement and manner – she was a little vulgar, a plump overblown beauty that was fading fast.

In the background somewhere was a great noise of guinea fowl and the lesser but more strenuous tone of a furious argument. Mrs Hawkworth listened for a moment and then said: 'We shall all be deaf before long, what with the peacocks and the hounds and now these. Has it occurred to you the gatehouse may be a far from peaceful retreat?'

They were on the same step and as she spoke she turned towards him. He was aware of the warmth of her body though the day was so hot he would have said it was not possible to distinguish heat from heat. He was aware of the gold down on her temples where her hair was swept back.

'There are ten at least stone dead and think what they cost!' exclaimed Mrs M'Cool from the terrace with furious indignation.

'Well, it was sheer extravagance. *I* shall not weep for you,' said Julia.

'Would you deny me my few extravagances?'

'Your *few*? You were always extravagant. You spent two fortunes before you were twenty-five.'

Mrs M'Cool drew breath, put her head on one side, and then smiled. 'Ah well, what is money for if not to spend? And anyway, I have paid in full for all my misdeeds, surely to God.'

'Yes,' said Julia coldly, 'how time brings its revenges.'

'. . . and so I stood there while they lashed their tails and stared each other out,' said the Doctor that evening to Lord Barsham, who was sharing his meagre supper in his bare parlour, 'I had not conceived such ill feeling lay between them. And such a contrast: the old lady in gold brocade at least thirty years old with a tight waist, and the niece in white, the very latest thing – even *I* could tell. So after this what could I do but retreat? The gatehouse was not mentioned. Besides, the fuss about the crates of guinea fowl was still continuing, with little Cassandra gathering up the unfortunate dead for Christian burial in the shrubbery and a melancholy Irish groom prophesying that the white dogs would surely eat every one of the remainder – 'twas not only the gentry partial to them old speckled birds. I ran to the stables to find my pony and there he was, fresh straw to his eyebrows in a great clean stall. I doubt he has ever wallowed in such luxury all his long, ill-spent life.'

Barsham shook his head and eased his gouty leg a little. 'To think what that place has come to after all these years.'

'Harry Gerard would smile to see his stables full. I believe he would approve Mrs M'Cool's taste in horse-flesh.'

They ate their toast in silence for a while. The Doctor, thought Barsham uneasily, had frequently played chess with old Sir Harry, had attended him at his deathbed. Forbidden subjects? Possibly. The Doctor's face was frostily inscrutable. Then there was Ann. Ann too was a difficult subject. He had some vague recollection of Louise's firm warnings about mentioning Ann Gerard in the Doctor's hearing.

'Confusion to Bonaparte,' he said, raising his glass. That, at least, was safe.

'Confusion indeed. How are your Volunteers?'

'Oh, they are all good men and eager to do their best. The point is,' and he sank his kindly florid face into his neckcloth, a sort of subconscious retreat, 'The point is, Alex, well . . . there is no point. What are they to do? March about. What arms are they to carry? A few muskets, pistols, the odd blunderbuss, swords maybe –

and what else? Hatchets, pitchforks, staves? And if this invasion happens tomorrow and Boney lands in the south and east, how are they to be deployed? I don't mind admitting, the whole damn muddle depresses me.'

For so jovial a man he was inordinately depressed, for not only was the real role of the Volunteers currently a mystery – in Whitehall as well as High Common, apparently – but they had fallen to squabbling among themselves which he detested, not only because it was absurd and ungentlemanly conduct but because he felt keenly that it took a parcel of low scrubs to bicker over trifles when their country was in mortal peril. There was no doubt in his mind that the danger was very great. He had no time for the anti-war party, holding out hands for Bonaparte to shake. 'He is more like to cut them off,' he had said to the Doctor before now, 'and their silly heads as well as soon as he can reach them.'

The Doctor rang for more toast but nobody answered the bell. Indeed, both men became aware of a deep brooding silence. 'Why,' said Barsham, consulting his watch, 'it is midnight. Midnight, by God! We are keeping town hours, Alex. No wonder, they are all in bed. More toast at midnight!' and he laughed, all his good humour restored.

'Had it been nine I doubt that contrary woman would have come,' muttered the Doctor, 'and if she had there would have been some excuse why toast was impossible: rats had stolen the bread, the fire out, that sort of thing. I have never known such a disobliging lump of woman-kind.'

'What about your Lascar? Did you not lend him to that doctor in Wymondham while you went to Suffolk?'

'I did, but he is so happy there – *three* old bachelors to look after and a splendid new kitchen entirely his own – that I have no heart to snatch him away for what may be only three or four weeks. In any case, can you see Lal and Mrs Turner good friends? She is a pillar of prejudice, besides which she would not care to dissipate her power: she is queen in the back regions and no one must forget it. That poor kitchen girl leads a miserable life.'

'But will you not need a servant at the gatehouse?'

'I do not see why. I am not incapable. I am not senile and disabled. However, Jim Wells came knocking at my door earlier today and offered himself, so to speak; however I cared to employ him, he said, outside or in. He has fallen on hard times, to be sure.'

Barsham grunted. 'Moore turned him off when he had the accident. He said he had no use for a man with one leg.'

'What a poor feeble lie. I have seen him following a plough with a boot tied on his peg so as not to sink in the ground. He was a fine stockman, a steady, reliable worker. I hate to see him living on the Parish and fetching and carrying at the forge for want of better employment.'

'He is hardly a gentleman's servant.'

'Nor was Lal,' said the Doctor, 'he was a fisherman at home.'

In another part of the house a door opened and closed. It could only be Loder. They listened to the approaching footsteps that came on strongly until just before the door and then stopped, came on again. A loud rap. 'Gentlemen . . .' said Loder, putting in his long face. He said no more, astonished to find it was Lord Barsham rising from the back-breaking wicker chair, his fat red face full of reproof.

'I beg your pardon. I thought . . .'

You thought I was entertaining low company, mused the Doctor, picking up his pipe and peering sadly into its ashy bowl.

'I must bid you good night,' Barsham was saying. 'The hour is late. No, stay where you are, Alex. Dr Loder will see me out.'

When Loder returned the Doctor was apparently

41

asleep, stretched out with his hands folded on his chest. He stirred though when Loder held out a folded paper, sealed and addressed in heavy black writing.

'This came for you earlier this evening. Mrs Turner must have overlooked it, it was on the small table. I shall say good night, Dr French. It is half past midnight and I have a consultation with Dr Clarke in Bungay after breakfast.'

The door closed. The Doctor broke the seal on his letter and unfolded the page, turned it right way up and found two lines only, in a bold, intemperate, educated hand: 'If you think the gatehouse suited to your needs you may do as you please. The key is at the Hall. Yours in haste, C. B. McCool.'

# 3

The heat increased. The dazzling sun and the threat of invasion hung over High Common together but it was the sun caused most consternation. The river was low and the ponds shrinking daily, by noon it was too hot to be abroad. So it was very early in the morning that the hay waggons toiling up Warren Hill passed a wiry figure in black toiling down, the reins of a grey pony in one hand and a brown paper parcel in the other. For a moment Ann Gerard, staring from her bedroom window, did not recognize him – who would expect visitors at such an hour? – and then something in his walk and in the extreme reluctance of the pony to follow him caused her to cry: 'Babs, Babs, look! The Doctor!'

Miss Pennyquick looked. Then she drew Ann firmly away from the window and tucked her into the wing chair by the little table where she had breakfasted every day since her accident.

'Shall I brush your hair? He will think you a fright.'

'Oh Babs, we are such old friends, he and I. What does it matter?'

It was this air of childish defiance she presented to him in person as he stepped through the door: a thin white face all indignation and challenge, as if she dared him to comment on her altered appearance or give any sign of their altered relationship; it *was* altered, they were not as comfortable together any more, though why or how this had come about she could not tell.

'I beg your forgiveness for calling at such an hour,' he began, walking through her door, 'but the days grow so hot and my time is not my own. I pitch and toss between the bank, the attorneys and the Hospital. I have been dissecting . . .' with a gleam of happy recollection.

'We have not breakfasted,' said Ann. 'If you promise not to speak of the dissecting room you may have some coffee and a muffin. Is it true – ' and she leaned forward, the shawl slipping from her shoulders, 'is it true you are going back to India?'

She spoke quietly. A vainer man might have supposed she cared deeply, but the Doctor knew quite well the limits of her caring, they were so well defined.

'I always thought I would be buried in High Common,' he said, walking to the window and looking out at the familiar view, 'I have helped so many into that same ground. But you once said . . . You said: there are more adventures to be had. I thought perhaps there might be a last one, in India, before I grow too old.'

He had already appraised her with a lover's eye, and a doctor's and he knew she was mending. She was wasted and tired and her rich brown curls were dulled and limp – they covered the long wound, the ten stitches, he supposed – but her fine dark eyes were full of life. An extraordinarily painful contraction of some inner part made him assume a dark expression: was that what writers meant by a wringing of the heart? He broke the sudden awkward silence by asking about her fall, forcing himself to smile. A silly great horse, she said strongly, small brain and large feet. Mrs M'Cool had carried her into Blackow unaided, an amazing feat for a woman her age though it was commonly rumoured she was made of iron and whipcord, was not human, and of course Dr Loder had been unrelieved gloom and foreboding, 'like a cormorant' the old lady had said – were cormorants known to be pessimistic and passionately introverted? – and poor Babs had fainted when she heard the news so that Tom had had to dash water in her face.

'And how is my pony?' the Doctor asked at last.

'Your pony!' and she laughed for the first time. 'How

ever do you contrive to stay in the saddle – you, outwitted by the dullest old horse alive? He has no vice, but for cunning I have never known his match. *He* would never have tripped over a simple pole three feet off the ground, though I believe he might have tried to duck beneath it, the rascal he is.'

The tension slackened. Miss Pennyquick returned with coffee and hot rolls and raspberry jam and the information that Hollin had found the Doctor's parcel in the yard. She looked rather anxious as she spoke for the Doctor's ill-wrapped parcels had, in the past, been found to contain strange unsavoury objects, some alive and with teeth, some profoundly dead, some recognizably human: hands, hearts . . .

'It is your present,' said the Doctor to Ann, vanishing at once and returning with the mysterious object, a flat oblong. 'I have carried it carefully all the way from Suffolk. Why, your dogs might have eaten it.'

It was a landscape, small but skilfully done, and there was besides a loving perception of place, a passionate involvement in that intimate sweep of fields, that hedgerow, a hill with trees.

'Oh,' said Ann, holding it out, 'it reminds me of the view from this window.'

'Alas, it is the view from another lady's window.'

'Not the famous Miss Lizzie Rayner? But of course, it was her house I visited by mistake when I called on you in Suffolk. When I met your charming Mr Savage.'

'They are to marry.'

'Are they indeed. Have you been matchmaking?'

'Not I. Only fools interfere in such matters.'

Did she take his words as a reference to herself and William? His good intentions had gone very wide of the mark in that enterprise. She had fallen silent, staring at the painting, while the steam rose from her coffee cup and the little clock on the shelf ticked into the quiet. He thought suddenly that here in this homely old room with its huge oak bed, the clean white linen, the atmosphere of scrupulous housekeeping and necessary intimacy, here was the place, if any perhaps, to say: 'Marry me.'

A shriek from the landing and Miss Pennyquick ran in to say that Mrs M'Cool was cavorting about the watermeadows on a large dark horse, perhaps the Doctor would care to look out of the back passage window: Mrs M'Cool was the lady who had taken Blackow. The Doctor rose and said he would repair to the back passage window at once if Ann gave him leave. She laughed, cried that she would not be left out, a disregarded invalid, and put her small strong hand on his arm. With rather disreputable glee they stooped and peered and saw, far off beyond Hollin's cottage and the birch copse, a spirited brownish thing that dashed up the line of pollarded willows to resolve itself momentarily into a tall furious horse ridden by a tall quiet woman in a flowing green habit. The horse was up to all kinds of antics but the green figure sat perfectly still and in a moment they had flown back the way they had come.

'What I may become in thirty years,' said Ann, walking back to her room. 'Poor woman, she lives for her animals, runs out at humans with a besom. She chased Mrs Palmer away carriage and all, threw gravel at the coachman, I believe. She buys all her horses for a song, broken down or incurably vicious or somehow or other maimed and degraded, and she feeds them and loves them and rides them about quietly and then sells them on at a profit.'

'Rides them about quietly! Well, there are always fools will buy horses who do not know a hoof from a hornet.'

'Indeed there are. You are one yourself. What was that misshapen grey animal you pulled down the hill after you?'

Would he smile? Had they in any way properly re-established their former strong friendship? He seemed changed. She could not decide what kind of change it was, only that it made her long for the old days, the days when he had only taken off his wig to lodge it on her coffee pot and berate her for marrying a man unworthy of her.

'They are turning the hay today,' she said at last when he did not respond. 'Tom has been out since dawn. We have carted half already.'

He poured her more coffee. How well she remembered that long nose, that guarded expression. Perhaps he was not so changed after all, it was only the effect of his newly grown hair – greyer than she had expected – and his good black coat. He had always been slightly shabby, careless of his dress, neckcloth often awry. He said: 'I have taken the Blackow gatehouse for my last few weeks.'

'The temple?'

'Yes. It is a temple to fashion and the impracticality of architects if nothing else, a close, cramped, shady dog-kennel only intended to look the part and without any regard to human comfort. Still, it will do for three weeks or so, and Jim Wells is to come to look after me.'

They finished the last of the hot rolls, talking in a desultory fashion about the gatehouse, about Dr Menzies and his desire to open more beds at the Hospital, about Norwich shawls – she was wearing one – tea, the music shop in the Haymarket, Miss Pennyquick's aching joints and Tom's courting of Charlotte Barsham.

'As to her joints,' said the Doctor, leaning back and wiping jam from his waistcoat, 'she lived in this house for years before you came when it was nothing more than a damp mausoleum, and even now in winter the mists roll up off the river. If she wishes for ease and comfort she must go live in Italy, my dear. And as for Tom – the Barshams may be liberal kindly people but will they truly wish to hand the flower of their house to a bastard son of Francis Frosie?'

She stared at him. 'I thought you were in favour?'

'I am in favour in that the young people seem fond of each other. They are remarkably proper too, they will not go skulking behind the hayricks or down among the sallows, nor will they elope. But do you believe it will ever come to a wedding? That girl will be well provided for and Tom has fifty acres and follows his own plough.'

'I was thinking . . .' She stopped. Where was the genial Doctor of the past, the man whose advice she could ask any time of the day or night, the man who smiled when she flouted convention, being unquestionably unconventional himself?

'You know how we said he would own a thousand acres before he was done,' she said quietly, fiddling with her coffee spoon. 'I believe he might even do better. He has been spending *Sable Island*'s money wisely – you cannot imagine all the improvements – and he has saved a great deal – I let him have some of his own. They smile on him in the bank and rub their hands together.'

'You look tired,' said Tom, coming in at noon with the fragrance of the baking fields all about him. 'Miss P said the Doctor had called. I am sorry I missed him. I wonder he did not ride up to the hayfields. Shall I carry you downstairs?'

She flashed such a look at him that he recoiled slightly. With a sudden irritable movement she threw off her shawl. 'No! No, you shall not! I shall walk downstairs. And tomorrow I will go out in the garden and the day after you may drive me to the village in the gig.'

'You will be shaken to pieces, the lanes are as hard as iron. If you have another tumble it may well be your last. You remember what Dr Loder said. And what about the hay? We shall never carry it all tomorrow, we have only just begun on the water meadows, and the heifers . . .'

She thought perhaps she might scream out damn the hay, damn the heifers, she no longer cared for any of it, for the old rambling house, the demanding land. But she knew it would hurt his feelings, he loved this place so, as she had once, before this strange mood had seized her, the culmination of four years of struggle: with the farm, Harry, William. She had taken stock during these last weeks lying in her bed, her world so pitifully reduced. She had been acutely conscious that life at Thorn went on its familiar round without her, that Tom had become quite naturally the master of the house – that he had been master for some time but she had not noticed it. It seemed to her she was no longer needed, that the *Sable Island* had provided the financial means and Tom the physical to bring the land back into good heart, a process by no means finished but so far advanced they could look with pleasure towards the future, that from now on she would become more and more a decorative object, a social creature, entertaining and entertained.

She could hear Tom going down the stairs; they were wide shallow oak stairs two hundred years old and he sounded like five troopers abreast. It was Tom's house, she thought again, for he was Francis Forsie's son, his very image. She felt she had no moral right to be living here at all. If the Doctor had not been in such a prickly mood she might have told him what she had decided – almost decided; as it was she had begun and then not had the courage: 'I was thinking of renting Thorn to Tom, of moving away.'

'Well, and you look pinched and out of sorts,' said Babs, finding her still in the chair by the bed half an hour later. 'Is it a headache? Shall I fetch anything?'

'No. I think I shall come downstairs and write some letters.'

'Tom is off up to the Ten Acre.'

'What has Tom to do with it? Give me your arm, Babs. I'm so disgracefully weak.'

At the bottom of the stairs she stopped, old Spring coming to thrust a grey muzzle into her hand. Outside

49

the yard dog was barking, a terrible outcry. 'Go and see what it is,' Ann said to Miss Pennyquick.

'Only that old devil of a tinker, I'd wager. Still, I had better see to it or the girls will be running out of the kitchen after his ribbons and lace.'

'No, no,' said Ann, waving away assistance, 'you go.'

Four slow steps brought her to the door of her parlour, the wide old low-ceilinged room where the clock ticked and the old Turkey rug had known the impatient tread of Francis Forsie's large feet. Here was her little writing desk, the one that had followed her to Blackow and come home again; as she looked at it she saw it piled with Harry's bills, Harry's debts. In it she kept the farm ledgers, the day by day account of her battle to rescue the land, the record of every penny spent and received – so few received until these last eighteen months. Since the end of May the entries were in Tom's bold upright hand and the figures were often blotched or crossed out; in the open air among a gang of men, calculating bushels, firkins, perches, shillings per hour, sheep with lambs and without, he would add and subtract in a moment, but neat columns of figures on the virgin white page always bothered him.

'Lie down, Spring,' said Ann, pushing the dog away. She sat down and opened the desk. There were the ledgers, two red and one green for the men's wages. What an ignorant little fool she had been when she had arrived, she thought, turning the pages of this last book and seeing the familiar names, and old Hollin, the only one of Francis's workers left about the place, no help at all, cantankerous and contrary, thwarting her at every turn.

The clock ticked, the house was very quiet. Every window was closed and shuttered against the heat and through the two inches she had opened a bar of piercing gold sunlight fell into the shadowy cool. Had Babs been seduced by the tinker's ribbons? She was a long time returning. Ann leaned on her elbows. What was in the secret drawer? Her wedding ring, the papers proving her the owner of the *Sable Island*, brig, and of Thorn in the parish of High Common in the county of Norfolk, house and two hundred and forty acres, a note from Harry begging her forgiveness for some trifling misdeed, dashed off tongue in cheek no doubt, and a letter from George Neech at the big farm two miles away asking if he might call on her when she was well.

I danced with him at the Assembly in the spring, she might have told the Doctor if the Doctor had proved receptive, and though I had met him a dozen times before, that was the first time he had showed me he admired me, was ridiculously attentive all evening – Mrs Palmer's eyes had never stretched so wide in astonishment and by the time midnight struck she was whispering about wedding breakfasts and how happy Mr Bringloe would be to perform the ceremony. He is an upright, circumspect man, a widower but without children, only thirty-three but behaving like a man of sixty. I like him. I do not wish to encourage him, I cannot think of him as a husband, but I like him. Oh Alex, he has asked permission to call and I have not replied, only sent a message by Tom to say that I was not well enough to think of visits.

And then, hearing distant voices and seeing Spring rise from the rug and cock his head, she leaned in her chair to pull open the shutter another six inches so that the light and heat flooded in and she could see her garden. It was strange, she thought, that she could live in the same house as Tom and own a dozen loving friends and still be lonely.

'Dead Lady Gerard, How grieved I was to hear of your terrible fall . . .' How grave and correct he was! How fundamentally good. I like him, Alex. He is the sort of man who would look for more than ornament in a wife, who must have a companion, a woman with whom he could discuss his affairs. He would be proud of his children too, and indulgent . . .

Alex, what am I to do?

'You will be sunburnt,' cried Babs, coming in with a fistful of lace and a look of horror. 'You will get freckles. See, we would have parted with every penny we had but Tom came home on a load of hay and saw the fellow off. There, I shall fetch you some lemonade and do some sewing while you write your letters.'

'It is sentimentality alone suggests horses can be affectionate creatures,' Loder asserted, having watched the Doctor's fiery little chestnut being confined in the dickey's hovel with a dispassionate eye. 'He remembered past titbits, that was all.' His saturnine face creased into the nearest thing to a true smile possible to such a repressed nature, as if of course he did not mean his words to cause offence but no intelligent being could possibly think otherwise. He was, in fact, absurdly light-hearted and it was entirely owing to the Doctor's imminent departure for the gatehouse. This morning he was disposed to be appreciative of everything and anything: the keen, knowing red head poked out of the lean-to stable, the piles of pamphlets in the hall awaiting collection, the entire contents of the Doctor's parlour piled on a small cart outside; and even the tears of the kitchen girl who had apparently hoped, for some unaccountable reason, that the Doctor had come home to stay, elicited his sympathy. By nightfall, he knew, the house would be entirely his own again. 'You must take a bite to eat before you leave,' he was moved to say at last, almost as cheerful as a normal man.

'That is very kind of you. Bread and cheese would suffice. The cart is leaving at once but I thought I would follow on as soon as possible. Hollin tells me there is a family of bustards on the Gorse, no, not a family, a flock: grandmothers, aunts, remote cousins even. How I would love to meet them! They may, of course, turn out to be something else entirely – Hollin has known for years how I love the bustard – but there is no harm in trying to surprise them in their afternoon dust baths. They are so persecuted, the poor great dears, that they wisely keep to the last wild places.'

'The Gorse is certainly wild,' agreed Loder, leading the way happily to the table. 'It should be enclosed and cultivated. I have had some interesting conversations on the subject with Lady Gerard. I believe she has some plans afoot to improve the place.'

The Doctor raised an eyebrow. 'But without a little wilderness here and there where will the bustards go, sir? Surely it can do no harm to leave a few – wildernesses and bustards – about the world? And where will the tinkers go? They have camped by Bussey's Copse since time immemorial. And Thorn has wheatfields enough, and barley and oats and all the usual ears and roots, not to speak of sheep enough, bleating and moaning all over. In any case, the Gorse belongs to Blackow, I would stake my life on it, and Mrs M'Cool has no stomach for enclosure and improvement: where would her foxes be then?'

The light of dispute flashed in Loder's eye but the ever-present thought that the Doctor would have quit the house in less than an hour had its remarkable soothing effect. He closed his mouth firmly and rang for Mrs Turner.

The Doctor may have declaimed throughout his dish of salad and new bread and pigeon pie on the extraordinary attractiveness of the bustard, of its size, longevity, even its amiable expression, but bustards-in-the-flesh proved infuriatingly elusive. The poor great dears had obviously learnt to lie low at the approach of any interested party, many of whom in the past had proved to be carrying guns. It was galling that anything the size of a large goose should be able to secrete itself so very thoroughly, but it would take weeks to beat the entire Gorse and there was, the Doctor supposed grimly after an hour's fruitless search, always the chance that every last bustard in the district had ended ignominiously in the tinkers' cooking pots.

'So there you are,' said Clodie M'Cool, opening the door to him herself as she had before. 'You are done to a turn, Doctor. What have you been up to to catch the sun so? Away lads, get away! Never mind them, the rogues, it is all gammon.'

The hounds subsided and slunk into the far reaches of the hall where there was still some cool. The Doctor said: 'I have taken the liberty of leaving my pony in an empty stall, I could find no one about.'

'Oh, every man jack about the place is away to a wedding. Rigby's sister. From what I understand they have been waiting twenty years to see her settled so half the countryside is up in celebration. Rigby asked if he could take the servants along to the wedding breakfast and I like a fool said he could, so here we are with a house like a tomb and only yesterday's cold chicken in the pantry. No doubt they will all come home roaring drunk at midnight though I told them to be back by six on pain of death. But come in, come in. What is it you want?'

He wanted the key to the gatehouse, he said, for the cart had arrived to find it shuttered and locked. Just so, said Clodie with satisfaction, for Driscoll and the stable lad had been in with brooms and paint, and Lucy and Annie Thurston with mops and polish. Did he want any Tom, Dick or James walking in to ruin the effect? No, said the Doctor humbly, but the man had left all his furniture in the drive and gone away, had not even bothered to come down to the Hall . . .

'He would have been afraid to,' said Clodie, nodding. 'The whole district knows I abominate visitors.'

They entered the dining room this time, a room the

Doctor remembered with an odd convulsion of his insides, but which he now found extraordinarily bare, ill equipped for anything more formal than a picnic: no table, no chairs, only a knife-box on the floor and a pair of cheap candlesticks. But by the window was a small desk and writing at it, seated on a music stool, was young Cassandra.

'How do you do,' and she rose, bobbed, resumed her seat with a sigh.

'This is all we have by way of a schoolroom,' said Clodie. 'How I dislike women with no education. Julia has none and does not care if her child is as ignorant. God save us, what use is a woman who can do nothing but look pretty?'

Cassandra put down her pen. 'I am not pretty, am I?' she asked but then immediately added: '*Quarante deux, c'est la même chose*,' under her breath, adjusted a figure, blew on the page, and then leaned her chin in her hands and looked out at the view. The view was across the shaven lawns to the lake, a glitter of Mediterranean blue.

'*The Young Lady's New Guide to Arithmetic*,' said the Doctor, looking over her shoulder at her book.

'Aunt Clodie bought it for me,' said Cassandra. 'It tells you how to send parcels and write bills of exchange. I am not sure – ' more hesitantly and with a rather shy look – 'I understand it as well as I ought.'

The Doctor moved to turn a page. 'Yes. Yes, I see.'

'Well and if you don't stick at your sums, Cassie dear, how shall we ever balance the accounts?' demanded Clodie from behind. 'Your mother has never been able to add five and five and as for myself, I have no interest in calculation.' Her bright slanting eyes met the Doctor's, defying contradiction. He did not intend to contradict her; in view of the fact she had disposed of two fortunes in her youth – whose? – he was quite sure she spoke the truth. And besides, he felt it would take a bold man to contradict Clodie M'Cool on any particular whatsoever.

The door opened. Julia stood looking in on them with amusement. 'We do possess chairs, Doctor,' she said, taking in the situation, 'and even a sofa, and carpets, and the means of conventional refreshment. If you would care to step across the hall . . .' and she moved aside, holding the door for him.

'Why would any sensible man want to sit on a sofa at all?' asked Clodie. 'The Doctor has come for his key and I shall fetch it for him.' She departed, Cassandra clinging to one hand, cloaked in disapproval.

'Here,' said Julia, throwing open a door, 'is this not better? Please do sit down. You will be far more comfortable waiting for your key here than standing about in the hall.'

I do not remember this room was ever used, he thought, looking at the windows, their view down a grass walk to what was obviously the walled fruit garden and the hot-houses. Yet it was a charming room, charmingly decorated. Had old Sir Harry kept it locked up? He had lived in the library and one bedroom and his son the same until his marriage. Try as he might the Doctor could not recall Ann in this room. Why not? Whose room had it been? What significance was there in the fact that one of the only pleasant retreats in the house had been ignored? The answer came as he saw the woman seated on the sofa lean forward and smile. A very different woman in his mind's eye leaned forward and smiled with artless joy: Caroline.

'I have not altered this room in the least,' Julia was saying, 'though the Houghtons never touched it, I am sure. It is only a trifle old-fashioned and the silk is very dirty but very pretty too – do you not think so? Surely it was not Lady Gerard decorated it?'

'Not the present Lady Gerard, no.'

'The previous one then, young Harry's mother. I have heard a little about her from Mrs Palmer. She was very young when she died.'

'So she was, no doubt. I know she was unhappy.'

'She ran across the Gorse and bewitched old Mr Forsie, I believe, caused the most terrible scandal and then ran away to London. Is it true?'

'I recall something of the sort.'

She folded her hands in her lap and looked down at them, compressing her mouth. 'I am sorry to stir up old memories. I forget how well you must have known them all.'

After a moment's silence she began to ask him about India, his position with the Company. 'How silly of me,' she said lightly, smiling, 'not to realize how much they must need doctors. Why, they have always had their own troops, have they not? And then there are all the civilians, the clerks and supercargoes or whatever they are called.' She was interrupted here by the arrival of Cassandra, who announced that Clodie had temporarily mislaid the key but she was sure she would find it in a moment. 'That child is scarcely fit for polite company,' said Julia at the closing of the door, 'I am afraid she ran wild in Paris, I left her too much with my maid. It is so difficult to cope with a child when one has a busy social life, regular engagements. I would have liked a good dependable Englishwoman for her but funds would not run to it, we were forced to spend far too much on keeping up the house as it was, my husband's position demanded it though his salary and my poor little income barely stretched. Paul's last words to me were that I must take Cassandra away from France and see she grew up with every advantage. When Clodie offered us a home how could I refuse? But very soon I shall look for my own house, a small quiet place where I can live as I like. In London perhaps.'

He did not like to say: Norwich would be cheaper. He was trying to understand her need to keep up this flow of artificial conversation, this compulsion to speak, this obvious nervousness. If she was trying to make an impression she had failed; he recognized her sudden laugh as entirely false and could not fail to notice the way her eyes avoided his. 'Will London not be expensive?' he asked gently and waited for her reaction.

'Oh, when my money affairs are straightened out – it has been so difficult, you see, because of the war – there should be enough. I do hope so. I could not take such rustic solitude for long.'

'Cassandra will be sorry to leave.'

'Yes.'

Now that was real, thought the Doctor, that clipped, telling syllable. He would have liked to have asked what her life in Paris had been like but he knew in his heart it had been the usual tearing social round, very necessary, he suspected, to a woman of her temper. Perhaps she had occasionally remembered her small daughter but he did not think Cassandra's welfare had been her first concern; the child had been an unbearable inconvenience. But then, he did not want to think ill of her. He had long been starved of her sort of glowing warmth and voluptuousness. He longed for Ann but was not permitted to show it, had not longed for anyone else in ten or fifteen years. He had become a sad old fool, a dry specimen even by his own standards; it occurred to him not for the first time that such rigorous celibacy was unnatural.

'I have your key,' exclaimed Clodie, entering with a breath of the kitchens: ashes, cabbage, bones.

The Doctor received it gratefully and took his leave. Julia gave him her hand. The Doctor bowed over it, wondering at his pitiful capitulation to such obvious charm. A glance at Clodie's face showed him that she was wondering the same, that she had expected better of him. She handed him the big iron key with one of her looks that he was afterwards to hear Driscoll describe as 'A blast from her eyes that would skin the paycocks, mother and son.' Feeling intolerably blasted himself, he bowed again and withdrew.

In the drive he said to himself: I do not care tuppence whether she is a good woman or not, she is a pleasure to look upon. I care even less what the widow M'Cool thinks of my predictable adoration. I am beyond being moved by censure – at least by the censure of a virtual stranger – for it is very many years since any handsome woman looked at me kindly. Mrs Hawkworth looks at me extremely kindly; I am determined to enjoy it while I may. It is not as if I were ignorant of my deficiencies, both physical and otherwise, and she is certainly not a green girl – rather *too* experienced perhaps, a little hard and proud under that charming exterior, unpredictable even. I do not believe she has a constant heart, or whatever organ it is makes one human being affection-ate and another fickle. I do not think I would put my trust in her heart at all but oh, how I like her to smile on me!

He drew nearer to the gatehouse whose windows, newly mended, glittered in the sun. By the pile of furniture stood the melancholy Driscoll, waiting to carry it in, and on the step sat Cassandra in a wide straw hat and bare feet.

'May I come in? I have brought you some flowers.'

'That was very kind. Yes, yes, bring them all,' this to Driscoll who had picked up the tortoise shell and set it back down again almost immediately, 'bring them all in at once out of the sun.'

'How I wish it was my house,' said Cassandra wistfully as she poked in the corners and opened the doors to the cupboard, the cupboard-like bedchamber, and the back kitchen in turn. 'How lucky you are.'

Driscoll brought in the tortoise shell clasped to his bosom, an anxious look in his eyes. It was not natural, he said at last, without its living occupant. Wherefore would the Doctor want to keep a shell with nothing in it? As a footstool, said the Doctor, seeing the man was a chronic superstitious and the tortoise had upset him in some way.

'Is it really a footstool?' asked Cassandra as Driscoll hurried back to the Hall as fast as his legs could carry him.

'No,' said the Doctor.

'Then you told a lie.'

'Yes,' said the Doctor.

'Why is it all right for grown-ups to tell lies but I am not allowed to?'

'It is not all right. I told Driscoll it was a footstool so as not to upset him. He was worrying about the tortoise.'

'He says there is a ghost in the harness room and he wants to go home to Galway. Have you ever been to Galway?'

'No, but I have been not a stone's throw away. Is that where your aunt comes from – Galway?'

'I think so. There used to be a big old house called Russhard but something happened and she had to leave. I remember there were other houses – and lots of horses – but something happened to those and she came to England.' She sat on top of the tortoise shell and drew her knees up so that she could rest her chin on them. 'I like Aunt Clodie. She makes me laugh. She tells me stories about when she was a little girl. She was *very* wicked. She said she never did any sums or read any books. But then, it must have been a long long time ago, she's very old, and perhaps it did not matter in Galway if you did not do any lessons.'

The Doctor's reply was muffled. He was trying to light the kitchen fire and he had his face between the bars, blowing strongly.

'Lord, Doctor,' said a voice and the door behind him opened, 'you are all over ashes and soot. Here, give me the poker, sir, I can see you don't have the knack. Devils they are, these old grates, to anyone unhandy.'

'Jim!' cried the Doctor, standing up and brushing at

his hair with a blackened hand. 'Never has a man been more welcome!'

'If I was you,' said Jim affectionately, looking his new master up and down, 'I would sit quiet a space until I've got the kettle singing and then a bowl of hot water and a dish of tea would do wonders.'

'Yes,' said Cassandra, leading him away, 'you will have to sit very still indeed or you will get soot all over your poor chairs.'

# 4

The small hills rolling north to Norwich were misted with heat day after day. Clodie M'Cool sent Driscoll up to the gatehouse with an ancient garden chair and the Doctor sat out under a canvas awning in his shirt sleeves and a straw hat, writing letters and making notes until the blinding light of noon drove him indoors again. It was unbearably hot even in the deep shade of the oaks and when he went down to the house for butter and eggs he found all the hounds prostrate in the dark of the hall, panting desperately.

The butter sat in ice and both melted. Jim Wells went for more and returned with the news that the two ladies were a-screeching at each other like old hens, he had heard them from the dairy; if the Doctor put out his head he might just hear them for himself. A little while after Cassandra appeared, a flushed and drooping Cassandra, who carried a very small pig cradled in her arms.

'Rigby says it will die,' she announced with vibrant indignation, 'he says it belongs to the parson – but why should it? The parson never calls – Aunt Clodie would chase him away if he did – and Mama says he does not live in the parsonage, Mr Frayle does, so it must belong to Mr Bringloe but Mr Bringloe has nowhere to keep a pig at his little cottage.'

The Doctor said consolingly: 'Perhaps Rigby only meant it was the runt of the litter. I have heard the runt called the parson's pig before now.'

'Oh,' and a moment's silence, a distinct brightening. 'Oh. But will it die?'

The Doctor looked at the piglet with a keen

professional eye, put his head on one side and said: 'I do not see why he should. He has all his faculties and is warm and pink. Go into the kitchen and ask Jim for his advice. He is far more competent at doctoring pigs than I am.'

Cassandra bore the pig away in the crook of her arm and shortly after the Doctor heard a rambling and philosophical conversation on the deep mysteries of pig-rearing going on behind the kitchen door. When Cassandra returned her freckles were glowing.

'Jim says he will feed it for me,' she declared with such intense satisfaction the Doctor was forced to smile. 'He says you will not mind, it is a *very* small pig and is no trouble.'

The Doctor thought of saying that he had never known any living creature, however small, that had not been some trouble, but he hated to diminish her happiness. He said instead: 'You should not be out in such heat, pig or no pig. There is lemonade in the larder, you must drink some before you go home.'

She was perched on the tortoise shell and as she pushed her damp hair back from her forehead he saw her face change, all the cheerfulness draining away. 'I wish this was my house. The Hall is too big. Mama complains because there is no furniture and because Aunt Clodie chases everyone away. And today Mama wants to go to Norwich, she says she must go, it is something to do with the bank, but Aunt Clodie says the horses will get heatstroke, they must stay in the stables.'

'It is the weather makes people irritable. It will soon pass.'

Cassandra bit her lip. 'They are always quarrelling.'

He must change the subject, he thought, but before he could do so she said: 'My father's name was Charles Dixon Hawkworth. Mama has a picture of him.'

'Did you know him?'

She shook her head. He had died when she was a

63

baby. Of course she remembered Monsieur Paul who had lived with them at the big house – they had not always lived in the big house, there had been a poky apartment in an old narrow street – and Monsieur Paul had been a melancholy handsome man with dark hair. She had not seen Mama very much, she had stayed in the nursery or sometimes, when Mama was out, in the kitchens with Marie. A great many people had come to call but she had never met any of them, she had seen them from the stairs, she and Marie had crouched there together, watching. She thought it had been Mama's house and that Monsieur Paul had been Mama's guest because Mama had never consulted him about anything, she had ordered the blue salon changed to green and provided a concert for a hundred people all without asking: Monsieur Paul had been so surprised.

'But he was sad when you left,' remarked the Doctor.

'I think so. He kissed me goodbye. He did not kiss Mama. But then we left in such a hurry and the roads were very busy and Mama was always calling out that we must go faster . . . She said . . . She said we might not get out in time and what would we do if we were left in France?' The child seemed to deflate, crouching down low on her strange stool. In a low, low voice she said: 'I want to stay with Aunt Clodie for ever.'

The Doctor leaned forward and put an arm about her shoulders. He was not naturally demonstrative and she was an unusually dignified child: his embrace, though spontaneous, was almost formal. 'Enough,' he said at once, wiping her eyes clumsily with a large handkerchief. 'Come, I have something to show you.' The something was a trio of young swallows practically howling to be fed.

The next half hour was fully occupied mincing mutton for these three babies, a great deal of raw mutton – 'enough for a kitten,' said Cassandra – and unpleasantly rank because of the heat, and then making minute pills of

64

it to ram down the birds' throats. They proved more difficult to feed than a kitten, gaping and chirruping, and their human foster parents had been bent over the task some time when there was the scrape and jingle of a carriage pulling up outside. It was Julia, and she gave them a long astonished stare as they appeared in the doorway together, the Doctor in a bloody apron and Cassandra apparently bundled in a sheet, something alive and squeaking in one hand.

'Are you engaged in a scientific experiment?' she asked.

'We are feeding the Doctor's swallows, Mama,' said Cassandra.

'You could not have got more smeared and stained had you tried to feed a lion.'

'I am sorry you are displeased,' said the Doctor, stepping forward to the carriage window. 'I did not think there was any harm in her nursing the birds and we swaddled her in a tablecloth to keep her dress clean.'

Julia smiled on him. 'Why should you think I am displeased? I am surprised you stomach being disturbed by an inquisitive child as well as you do. Send her back to the house at once if she is troublesome.'

She was flushed, he noticed, and with more than the heat of the day; with an inner heat, the smouldering of a considerable temper. What a tussle you must have had with the old woman, he thought, and your victory has given you no joy or you would not have that sulky look about your mouth. Well, I would not like to wrestle with Mrs M'Cool for the use of her greys. 'The child is not at all troublesome,' he said. 'She is an interesting little thing, very grave and curious.'

'I have heard children called many things but never "grave and curious". You have an eccentric turn of phrase, Doctor. But the truth is, she is running wild. I must engage a decent, educated woman to take charge of her.' She drew out a small enamelled watch, a pretty thing, and frowned at it. 'I am very much afraid I shall be late. Doctor, good day.'

The Doctor went inside and found the grave and curious child laughing at a swallow on her finger. From the kitchen came a low exclamation of annoyance and Jim appeared in the doorway. 'I made a pint of coffee for you, Doctor, but that there pig has overset it. Will you wait for fresh or is it time you was away?'

'Away where?'

'Bungay, sir. Was it not Bungay? Dr Reeve?'

The Doctor looked confused. 'So it was. Old Reeve, my soul. I had clean forgot. Cassandra dear, you must run home at once. Yes, of course you may feed the swallows again. They will need feeding every hour for a long while yet. Jim, coffee by all means and quick about it. I shall run out to fetch a clean neckcloth.'

'Not off the bushes?' asked Jim in horror, 'Why, Doctor, they were new-washed this morning and . . .'

'In this great heat they will be dried long ago.'
'But there is no time for the iron . . .'

'It will not matter. Who will notice?'

Dr Reeve certainly did not, for even had he not been short-sighted and in any case far too excited by his prize patient, a strange melancholia that exhibited several peculiar symptoms, he would scarcely have picked out a crumpled neckcloth when the man who stood before him was creased and wilted by the heat, and dusty from head to foot. In truth it took him several minutes to recognize this apparition as Alex French and it was only the particular glaring quality of the grey eyes, quite startlingly pale and clear in their grubby setting, that decided him.

'Come in, come in, sir. Perhaps we will open a bottle before stepping along to the madhouse. I thought we might have another storm to lay the dust but it is not to be, not to be,' and as the Doctor passed inside he added: 'How changed you are! I should not have known you.'

This grows tiresome, thought the Doctor, this is like being a spirit returned from the dead. He opened his mouth on a sharp retort but old Reeve, having ushered him into the dim parlour, turned at once and wrung his hand, exclaiming as he did so: 'Why, you are ten years younger! You are a new man!'

'How much better you look,' said Louise Barsham, whose carriage had negotiated the steep lane to Thorn without mishap but in a terrible cloud of dust, amid which the horses still stood, sneezing furiously. 'And how good to see you out and about at last. Come to Upgate the day after tomorrow. Charlotte will be so pleased.'

'I have not been visiting for a month,' said Ann, 'Tom will not let me drive the gig.'

'I should hope not.'

They were in the garden, walking slowly across the burnt grass. All around were roses, lilies, pinks, great clumps of foxgloves, a pretty half moon bed of herbs edged with hyssop. Louise paused every now and then to admire it, remembering its former devastation, the unproductive clearing full of poultry and the shards of broken china.

'When you first came here . . .' she began, turning a full circle and looking up briefly at the house, whose windows were all shut tight against the heat.

'I seem to have been here forty years,' said Ann, taking off her sun hat suddenly and tossing it down on the iron seat.

'It would be quite natural to feel in low spirits, my dear. You have been confined such a long time.'

'I have nothing to do,' was the strange low cry. I have been deprived of a purpose, she meant, among other confused things.

'Well, and nor should you have anything to do until you are quite well. You have Tom,' and then, reflectively: 'Thank goodness you had Tom, how else would you have managed? He copes like a man twice his age, and such tremendous enthusiasm . . . Thorn will rival Holkham in a few short years.'

Ann sat down on the seat and looked up into the boughs of the old apple tree above; a ginger and white kitten crouched on one of the branches looked back at her with satisfaction and presently dropped down to climb on her lap.

'Have you seen the Doctor?' asked Louise, drifting along by the low wall smelling the roses.

'Not for some days. Have you?'

'He has refused every invitation. He said – in a frenzied scribble sent over with Jim Wells on what could only have been the Blackow odd-job pony – that he was involved in certain medical experiments which he hoped to complete before leaving for Bombay, that he and Dr Reeve of Bungay were trying some new . . . something . . . We could not make out what, perhaps it was as well. Then he has been invited to help with some operation at the Hospital and later to dine with Dr Alderson, not to speak of several meetings with the United Friars – he is an honorary member – and so on and so forth. The long and the short of it is he will not be free to see us at Upgate until the week after next when I suppose he will ride up unexpectedly merely to say his goodbyes.'

'I believe he is tired of us and is only waiting to run off to Bombay. Do you remember his mongoose? He was always fond of India. And how dull High Common must seem to him after his adventures in Suffolk, the company of Miss Rayner and his Jamaican friend Mr Savage. I met Mr Savage, a tall amiable handsome man, the opposite of the Doctor in every respect.'

Lady Barsham smiled. 'Poor Alex, he wasn't born with the face of a hero, certainly. But I would rather trust my life to his hands than to the hands of any other man living.' I swore I would not interfere, thought Louise, brushing a hand across the rose petals. 'The truth is, I had so hoped he would come to Charlotte's birthday party – only a small affair, a dozen friends to dinner, some music – but either he did not read my letter or he dropped it, which would be just like him, or he is shy of appearing at my table because he knows full well what I think of this Indian business. Perhaps you might persuade him, impress on him how dejected Charlotte will be if he does not come – that is, if you are strong enough to cross the Gorse to the gatehouse.' There, that was the best she could do with discretion. How difficult it was to bring people together, even perfectly pleasant, mutually affectionate people, without it looking contrived. Louise's romantic nature was tempered by experience but it still lived. She hoped for a happy union, even now at this late hour hoped to hear the High Common bells ring out for her dear old friend Alex and this slight dark courageous girl whom she had come to thoroughly admire.

Ann's fingers caressed the kitten's tiny head. She did not promise to visit the gatehouse. She spoke suddenly of the new tenant at the mill, a painfully shy, hardworking young man, newly married, charged with modest ambition; she had great hopes of him. She spoke of Mr Bringloe's latest adventure with the M'Cool hounds, which only ever strayed, it seemed, in order to bring him to grief – ten at least, ten couple that is, had knocked him off his donkey and raided his pockets.

'The general view,' said Louise, who heard a great deal from her sister, 'is that the bailiffs will soon be in at the Hall, strange raffish men have been seen riding in that direction.'

'They are probably going there to buy horses.'

'Perhaps. Yesterday we had Cassandra to Upgate for the day and she said there is not a stall to spare, the Doctor's pony was relegated to a paddock to make room for the latest purchase.' She had been an engaging little thing, Louise said, though unnaturally self-contained, had been cautioned to stay clean and sent over in her best shoes, so that she was not only stiff and prim for the first hour in an effort to comply with instructions but her feet hurt and tears were the result. After this inauspicious beginning Charlotte had borne her away to wash her face and find some slippers and half an hour later, completely restored, she had run all over the place, played with the dogs in the garden, forgotten her curtseys and eaten enough for two.

The kitten was kneading her claws into Ann's knees, vibrating with ecstasy. 'Oh, I am so glad to see you well . . .' Louise began, watching the sun strike copper out of Ann's soft hair, and then a voice, two voices, Miss Pennyquick's: 'I cannot say if she is receiving visitors,' and a low, gruff reply. Ann rose at once, scooping up the kitten and tucking it, still purring, under one arm.

'Mr Neech is here,' cried Miss Pennyquick in a low urgent voice, coming round the side of the house at a run, 'and wishes to know if he might pay his respects.'

Ann stood irresolute. Then: 'Yes. Yes, I suppose I must. Show him in, Babs. Show him here,' and she sank down again, adding in a soft, pleading voice: 'You will stay? I cannot see him alone.'

'Of course I will stay,' said Louise, coming to sit at her side.

Thus it was that George Neech, striding on to the lawn after the agitated Babs, found two ladies sitting under the apple tree sharing the attentions of an affectionate kitten. He paused, took a firmer grip of his hat, and looked straight at Ann, his face aglow.

So that is the way of it, thought Louise.

Tom had fallen off the hayrick and broken his leg. It was the fourth and last rick and they had worked hard all that sweltering morning to stack it to the eaves, leaning back on their forks in the rare moment's break to gaze up with a growing satisfaction: the last rick, fine hay, and the weather unlikely to break before it was thatched off. At the very peak of their achievement, the moment Jim Knight squared his shoulders, cast a keen glance round and said hoarsely: 'That's all done then,' at that second Tom grinned, raised his weary arms with unutterable relief, stepped back and fell off the rick.

'I never thought I was so near the edge,' he complained as Ann received him in the parlour, carried in by Hollin and young Crow and laid out on her dainty sofa.

'Now you will have to sit still all day and do nothing,' said Ann, undoing the buttons at the knee of his breeches.

'But we shall be harvesting within the month . . .'

'*We* shall, certainly. You may lean on a stick and give orders if you must.'

Jim Knight put in his head to ask respectfully if they would like him to set the bone, but although Ann thanked him profusely – she was fully aware of his skills, had good reason to be thankful for them more than once – she said she felt obliged to send for Dr Loder. Tom, not bearing up particularly well by now under the double onslaught of pain and indignity, mumbled that he would not have Loder touch his leg, Loder was a melancholy ham-fisted baboon.

'You do not know what a baboon is,' remonstrated Ann, thankful to find Babs gliding in with a hot posset containing, if she read Babs' expression correctly, something infinitely soothing and guaranteed to take the strong irritable whine out of Tom's voice.

'I do,' he was protesting now, looking down suddenly at his bloodied stocking as if he had not realized till this moment which bit of his anatomy hurt most, 'the Doctor told me about baboons years ago.'

'The Doctor . . .' began Miss Pennyquick hopefully, her grim expression lifting.

'No, Babs. It must be Dr Loder.'

'But Alex is only a mile away across the Gorse and

Loder is in the village – another two; and no certainty he will be at home,' said Tom, who suspected the posset and was sipping it slowly.

'I will tell the boy,' said Babs with a frosty glance, and went out and down the wide passage to the great kitchen where half the men were gathered on the far side of the room from the fire – a fire in such weather! Though they knew this fire, this fire alone, never went out except in flood, hurricane or at the coming of the French. Mrs McGinley, the cook, a very large and high-coloured woman, was abusing them from the hearth, both for trooping into her kitchen with boots on and for letting Mr Tom fall off the rick, a right pack of boobies and no denying it. She was not a Norfolk woman and her accent was as strange to them as theirs was to her when they protested on both counts: their boots were clean and Mr Tom had aleapt up like a sprite, waving his arms, and had done a back somersault before ever old Jim could catch him – *this* was what came of cavorting about not minding where you put your feet; *and* a piece out of the rick you could stuff a fair-sized calf in, a bugger of a pig's breakfast and no mistake.

If there was anything Mrs McGinley hated more than boots in her kitchen it was foul language. She was about to let fly and drive them all out when Miss Pennyquick intervened, telling young Crow, a square shambling cheerful boy, to take the cob and ride for the Doctor. 'And don't come home without him,' was her final command as he pelted from the room.

He took his duty seriously, hustling the elderly bay mare along in a highly unsympathetic manner, but at the top of Warren Hill he took the Blackow road without hesitation, ramming his heels in her poor sides and hanging on by the reins.

'Is it young Crow?' asked Dr French, coming to his door accompanied by a small girl and a pig on a string,

'Why, Boaz . . . It is Boaz? You have grown a foot since I saw you last.'

Young Crow, his sides heaving as much as the mare's, gasped out his message.

'Are you sure you were sent here?' asked the Doctor when he had made head and tail of it all.

'I was sent to fetch the Doctor, sir,' said young Crow, confused.

'Yes, yes. I daresay you were. Well, give me a moment, I must find my bag and a few odds and ends. Go on, ride back. Say I am coming.'

'They would hev my hide, sir. I was not to goo hum without you.'

Thus it was that Ann, hurrying downstairs with a blanket, found Dr French in possession of her parlour, everyone turned out with harsh words – how could the boy breathe? They should go back to work and leave off this ghoulish staring – and Tom's leg horribly exposed.

'But where is Dr Loder?' Ann demanded.

'Loder?' The Doctor raised a bland inquiring face. 'Did you send for Loder? Perhaps there was some kind of mistake.'

She was in blue, her hair caught up in a ribbon. She was nearly her old self. He thought that if she smiled on him he would declare himself, even in this most cramped undignified position, bent over Tom's leg; but she did not smile, she frowned, coming across to put her blanket on the arm of the sofa and smooth back Tom's damp hair.

'Oh, he will do,' said the Doctor unsympathetically, removing the last of the stocking, 'I have given him some laudanum. Look at that now. It was an unlucky fall to be sure. With so much hay about it seems cruel of Fate to drop him on a ploughshare or whatever it was.'

She shook her head, not looking up. 'Not a ploughshare, the pole of the timber waggon, I think. They had pulled it up to stand on as the rick grew higher.'

'Ah well, we have coped with worse, you and I,' he said, probing deftly and sucking his lower lip. 'This will be no sawing job. Will you renew my water now, my dear, and fetch some clean towels?'

It was so long ago, she thought, hurrying from the room, the evening she had helped him amputate a boy's leg, a gruesome and unbelievably intricate task carried out in an old outhouse. She had not thought about it for a long time and she thought about it now with a sudden pang, for that had been in the days when she was full of hope and energy and fresh plans, when saving Thorn and loving Harry had been equal sources of delight. I had a meal with him afterwards, alone, served by his Lascar; it was highly improper and I did not care.

When she returned with the clean water and the towels he was almost finished and Tom, far down in his laudanum-induced doze, was calling out in a strange deep muffled voice about the oats not being ready, they wanted another week of sun.

'He dreams the farm,' said the Doctor, taking the water from her hands and setting it down by his side. 'I do believe he will never love any woman as much as he loves this place,' and he smiled up, briefly, innocently, knowing how she herself loved it and thinking she would smile in return.

'I was thinking of giving it to him,' in a small voice, not meeting his eyes.

'Giving Thorn to Tom? *Giving* it to him?' He was bent over the leg again but the tone of his voice was chilly.

'He is in charge, you know. I do nothing. I thought . . . He has boundless ambition, aches to own a thousand acres, all the latest machinery. It would be . . . fitting. And I do not mean *give* him Thorn, I mean let him have it at a fair rent until . . . until the day perhaps he can afford to buy me out.'

'I am growing old,' said the Doctor, tying a last knot, 'I am not so quick as once I was. To think I have operated hours at a stretch and all at a tearing rate, one man after another, no time to sit down or drink or even speak except to croak at my assistant for a probe, retractor, dressings. There, it is done. I doubt I have ever taken so long to set a leg. Buy you out, Ann dear? And where shall you be when he so grandly buys you out?'

She blushed, looking away. 'If you think I am contemplating marriage again, you are mistaken. But I cannot see . . . There is nothing for me here,' and she walked jerkily to the window, raising her face in the flood of warm sunlight that broke between the half-closed shutters.

'Perhaps you had better ship aboard your letter of marque,' came the disagreeable admonition from the other side of the room, 'bang off a few guns at the French. You would find enough excitement there without a doubt.'

He rose to his feet, gathering up the bloody rags and the bowl of water. 'If you will excuse me,' he said more gently and with a courteous nod, 'I shall give some instructions in the kitchen. Could Hollin and Crow carry the boy upstairs, d'you think? I shall see him settled and then I must away. It is long long after the time for my swallows' mutton.'

'Your what?' she said, but he had gone, only coming back five minutes later for his coat, which he had tossed over a chair, and bringing with him old Hollin and Crow senior, both in stockinged feet, both creeping in with exaggerated care and seizing Tom with the firm delicacy of a good dog carrying an egg.

'There, mind that leg is held up, do not let it swing. Miss Pennyquick, I shall leave him to your ministrations. He will rouse himself from the laudanum but slowly, I fear, he took so very little but it sent him very deep. In another man it would have had no effect at all worth mentioning.'

At the door he put on his hat and then took it off again. It was too hot, he said, he would keep in the shade of the trees up the hill and only put it on when he reached the baking waste of the Gorse.

'I sent for Dr Loder,' said Ann in a low voice at the gate.

'I know you did.'

'I am glad you came.'

He smiled, the old charming smile she had not seen for a long time now. He said: 'You must not grow sentimental over Tom. He will do very well whether you give him Thorn or no. Before you let it go you must be very sure it is what you want to do.'

She watched him collect his pony from the shade, mount and ride away. In the doorway of the house stood a triumphant Miss Pennyquick, her thin face glowing. 'How lucky Dr French was at home,' she remarked.

And Ann laughed.

The days went by, the demands of the season increased. Ann found out how thoroughly she had abdicated from all her responsibilities. The first week she was profoundly at a loss, she had to ask the men, shamefully humble, what work they had been doing, what work was yet to do. From his bed upstairs Tom issued orders every half hour, sent down lists, requests, complaints and inquiries; in his mood of extreme frustration and irritability he was no help at all but they had no heart to tell him so, carrying up inadequate replies and hasty good wishes. The unthatched ricks cried out for attention – surely this glorious weather must break – the fences along the Gorse needed attention, the tinkers' calves had invaded Pigg's Piece more than once, and there was the butter to take to Norwich, the cheeses to turn.

Ann still felt childishly weak but she would not admit it to anyone. She put on an old muslin dress, stout shoes and a plain hat, and set off to walk the entire farm with a rapidly sinking heart. It was a great distance for someone lately pitched on her head at speed and after a while her temples began to throb and she was obliged to sit down, pale and feeling queer.

'Lady Gerard!' A hooting Scottish voice, the rattle of a gig's wheels on the baked lane, and she looked up unwillingly into the long face of Dr Loder. 'Woman, you look knocked up!'

So this was what he was like when shaken from his rigid sense of protocol, of professional distance. He could not grow very passionate, he was not a passionate man, but within his limits he was striking enough. There was no doubt his concern was deeply felt.

'Take my arm. What do you mean walking so far from home? I have told you and told you not to overdo things. Has Dr French been here again encouraging you in such folly?' He must have been aware as he spoke that this was more than a breach of etiquette, that she and Alex were old friends. He cleared his throat, hurried on before she could reply: 'No, I shall not let you sit here in this sun. I shall take you home at once. At once, Lady Gerard.' With this he helped her up into the gig, and with more feeling than he usually showed his patients, many of whom complained he was an automaton, no heart, no sensitivity at all.

'I have not been round the farm for six weeks,' protested Ann.

'And you must leave it alone for another six, if not for ever. Young Mr Forsie will be sound on his leg, we trust, within three months.'

'Three months! And how is the farm to manage without us both?'

'Is not Jim Knight your bailiff?'

'He goes by no such grand title,' said Ann as the gig began the descent of the hill, the horse jibbing and snorting, held on too tight a rein, 'besides which, I am recovered . . .'

'This is a demonstration of your "recovery", I suppose? No, Lady Gerard, no. You may walk in your garden until you are stronger, and nothing more. Nothing more at all. I hope I make myself clear?'

No reply. The Doctor might have said: watch out for squalls, she has lifted her chin and set her mouth. Loder did not notice, being fully occupied helping his horse to stumble while rating it in a strong disagreeable voice. At the gate in front stood Miss Pennyquick, looking anxious.

'You were gone so long,' she said as they drew alongside, 'and Tom has been threatening to get out of bed unless we sent out a search party.'

'Well, Dr Loder has kindly brought me home.'

Miss Pennyquick was not inclined to give Dr Loder the time of day, having found him early on a hard, solitary, depressed young man, and then she regretted Dr French's absence deeply, they had been on civil terms for years, years when no one else in the neighbourhood would speak to her, thinking her Francis Forsie's mistress as well as his housekeeper. Loder was a usurper in her eyes and as he did not care to make himself agreeable he was resented all the more. Nevertheless she was grateful to him for the return of Ann, who had gone off in a red passion to walk the farm only that tomorrow she could give precise and unequivocal instructions to every man, woman and boy from Jim Knight down to eight-year-old Samuel Crow, the bird-child, old Crow's grandson. Damn that Tom Forsie for falling off a hayrick, she might have said once, though now she was elevated to lady's companion she shut her lips grimly on all such expressions. Her snappish black eyes spoke for her, however, and even Loder, far from being a perceptive man, recognized other emotions besides anxiety in her clipped voice and unbending figure. He would call on the morrow, he said, thinking what a sour old crone she was, he wondered Ann could stand her; he would call on the morrow without fail, both to look at Tom's leg and to make sure Lady Gerard had come to no harm after such exertion. She was pitifully pale. He did not want a relapse: migraines, blackouts. He was really very brutal and all in a drear, discouraging voice, for he quite rightly believed Ann would take little notice of his advice and this was the only way he knew to reinforce it.

'You would think he might have stepped up to see how Tom did today,' said Miss Pennyquick. 'There is no real need, I know, but it would have been pleasant in him. Dr French would never call and run away again in such a manner when one of his patients was abed in the house.'

Ann took her arm. 'Dear Babs. Do you think I did not smoke your trick the day of the accident? The Doctor indeed! You knew full well there was only one Doctor for young Crow.'

Miss Pennyquick pursed up her mouth and looked away. 'Small good it did in the finish,' she said grumpily.

Small good indeed, thought Ann, walking into the house. And as she reached the parlour and shut herself in its cool, familiar comfort, she suddenly wished . . . How she wished Alex would step through the door at this moment, touch her poor mended head with his sure light fingers and say: 'Oh that is nothing. I have seen men lose half their scalps, sustain terrible depressed fractures, splinters of bone in the brain, and still live,' in his dismissive, offhand way, and then sit down the moment after to tea and muffins, talking of voyages he had made, of his soldiers, of his pamphlets on scabies. I must go and see him, she thought; why does he not come to see me again?

'There was a letter sent over by hand,' said Miss Pennyquick, appearing with a tray of tea. 'If you won't go to bed, at least put your feet up, child. That Tom is calling out, face as red as the old man in one of his drunken stupors; I shall have to go up again or he will be down and that leg all to do again.'

Ann was turning over her letter. She knew what it was. Her voice when she spoke was false and light. 'Yes, you had better go up. Perhaps . . . Tell him I shall come and read him the newspaper in a while.'

'He is perfectly capable of reading it for himself, his eyes are not affected.'

'But it may quiet him.'

With the door closed and a dish of tea in her hand she felt better, the slow ticking of the clock the only sound. In a little while she broke open the letter, glancing down once at the lines of close writing and then looking away.

'There is no pacifying him,' said Miss Pennyquick, coming back. 'He says you must go up or he will come down. I told him you were tired out and he said, so much the better, you would not have the strength to argue when he told you what he thought of such a damn foolish expedition. Those were his very words.'

But when Ann went up to his bedroom he said nothing of the kind, was as mild as a lamb, though his face was a dangerous red and all his yellow hair was damp and tumbled. He said gruffly: 'I do not want you to be ill again.'

'I was not ill before.'

'You might have been dead. I thought you would never wake. And you are the only family I have.'

'Well, if you are going to turn sentimental, and find maudlin reasons to keep me in the house . . .'

'No. No, sit down again. Listen . . . You cannot walk about the fields all day, you must simply give orders . . .'

'And who is to see they are carried out?'

'Loder is right, damn him, miserable devil he is: you are not strong enough yet. Jim will see everything is all right. You know he will.'

'I know I am tired of being an invalid.'

He reached out and grasped her hand on the counterpane, and then suddenly laughed, his deep honest irresistible laugh. 'It *would* happen now,' he said, 'with the harvest only a week or two away.'

She smiled, but it was a reserved smile. She said quietly: 'I have had an offer of help from Mr Neech. He says it would be no trouble to oversee our harvest gangs as well as his own, he rides about constantly, two extra miles are nothing. He asks if he may call to discuss it, if I am agreeable.'

Tom's face lost its cheerfulness. 'He is a good sound man,' he conceded at last. 'He has given me a great deal of excellent advice. If anyone has to cast an eye over the men in the fields I would rather it were him than not . . . But . . .'

She sat with bowed head, conscious of the letter in her pocket, of a great dull weight of responsibility – not only for the farm but for Tom's wellbeing and her own happiness. 'I shall write and thank him,' she said at last, 'and say we will manage very well. It is very kind in him, very very kind, but I don't believe we need to trouble him yet. And then I shall call on the Doctor and ask his advice.'

'About the farm?'

'No, of course not. About my head.'

His blue eyes widened a little and a deep furrow appeared between his brows. 'I thought . . . Is that allowed?'

Ann rose, hearing the clatter below that meant Tom's mutton was on the way up. 'I really don't care,' she declared.

'Well!' cried Miss Pennyquick, coming in in advance of Nancy and the dishes, 'I am glad to see you both in such good spirits again. Perhaps today you might eat up your food, Mr Tom, and not dash it on the floor like a baby. Oh, and a basket has come from Upgate, strawberry tarts and the like, jellies and jam and cheesecake: Miss Charlotte, I don't doubt. I have left it in the hall so as not to spoil your appetite for your chops.'

The Doctor was out – out with a spyglass, a drawstring

81

bag and a pocketful of scraps to lure the bustards. Cassandra was on his doorstep, however, trying to teach the piglet to jump over a stick. The piglet was not interested in learning tricks and made sudden dashes for freedom, shrieking furiously when rounded up and brought back to his task. He was plump and energetic now but only wholly tame when he could get his own way, a sad fact of life, Jim Wells had told Cassandra, that applied in his experience to more than piglets.

Ann drove on down to the house where Clodie greeted her with genuine delight, scooped her out of the cart and carried her round the stables to view the latest acquisitions, only leading her indoors when she began to flag. There they met Julia in a gown that was probably, as Ann afterwards told Louise Barsham, the most immodest morning wear ever known in High Common, the very latest style without a doubt, what there was of it to be at all stylish. In Julia's wake came a tall, angular man of about thirty, who bowed over Ann's hand but who had a frank and insolent stare. He was introduced as Captain Morris, a dear friend, Julia had known him for ever, a business acquaintance of her late husband's at the start but soon unquestionably a valued friend . . . Through all this Clodie kept a strict silence and she drew Ann away as soon as possible.

'Friend! Business acquaintance! Ha! Showily dressed young scoundrel. No money and no breeding. Well and she was never discriminating, that fellow Hawkworth was no better. Come. Perhaps you should go home, my dear. You have had enough for one morning. Shall I get Driscoll to drive you?'

Ann declined the offer. It was not her throbbing head, not this deplorable and continuing weakness that had overcome her, it was the memory of Harry, of the little they had shared and the great deal they had quarrelled over, of the ballroom lit by two hundred candles and the desk, her little desk, standing in that room and piled with unpaid bills. She closed her eyes. The bay mare, facing home, trotted on strongly. At the top of the drive the Doctor was just turning in through the gates, his coat over his arm and a weary disappointed look about him. It was damnable, it was absurd, but she was crying. She could not let him see, he would have no sympathy if he guessed she was crying for Harry.

'Ann . . .' he began, standing still and looking hopefully.

She did not even turn her head but raised her whip in a formal salute and set the mare into a canter.

# 5

Though the gatehouse was furnished with the Doctor's few belongings it was Cassandra who decorated it with pots of cow parsley and campion and who arranged everything to her taste. Gradually she brought up all her treasures from the house, as if aware they were not appreciated at Blackow, and these she distributed about the parlour with great care.

They were pitiful treasures when all was said and done; strange stones, some she had painted with faces, feathers, some common birds' eggs, pressed flowers. She did not own a doll, a top, anything of that sort. The Doctor had known cottage children with hardly a rag to their backs who possessed more home-made toys and knick-knacks. He was touched by Cassandra's devotion to his swallows, and to the unrewarding piglet, an ebullient and voracious character without much more than a glimmer of affection in his whole being. She was a thoughtful and introspective child: too little attention had been paid her at every stage of her insignificant life. Just lately she had learned that self-effacement was often the best policy in a house governed by two vivid and excitable women, but she showed a surprising determination too – she wrestled daily with *The Young Lady's Guide to Arithmetic* and daily she spent at least an hour with the Doctor, bringing him weed and greenery from the lake to identify, running across the parched parkland on her plump legs with her dampened skirt hitched above her knees.

'What is the child coming to?' asked Clodie once, stopping at his door on one of her tall, fire-breathing horses. 'Look at the dirt! Look at the tears in her shift.

And where are your shoes, child? Why have you no shoes?'

'My aunt says Cassandra is always on your doorstep,' said Julia, coming by that same morning on one of her infrequent solitary walks across the Gorse. 'If she is any trouble you must send her away.'

'She is no trouble,' replied the Doctor; no trouble, he might have added, compared with an obstreperous piglet and three fledgeling swallows. 'Will you not sit a moment and take some lemonade?'

He did not think she would come in, but she did, untying her bonnet and pulling it off, a rather blundering graceless pulling off as if she could not bear the confinement of it any longer in such a heat. The Doctor found the gesture endearing. She so seldom behaved quite naturally, always careful to only move or speak to some definite effect. He looked on her with something approaching affection and removed a bowl of minced mutton from the chair so that she might sit down.

Lady Barsham, said Julia, arranging herself with difficulty on a seat that encouraged its occupant to sit poker straight, had suggested that Miss Bell, Charlotte's old nurse, might take Cassandra in hand once or twice a week; such a system must surely counterbalance all this running wild at Blackow. All *that* running wild in Paris. Paris over the last ten years, a terrible, extraordinary, delightful city, and during the late war she had moved about quite freely and of course, to a certain extent diplomatic immunity had been hers, a most fortunate state of affairs, her husband being dead ... But the thought of being confined till this present war ended – why, it might be years – and she was not enamoured of Bonaparte, whatever anyone said, whatever good he may have done once or might do again if he could be persuaded to give up these dreams of empire, this had caused her to leave France the moment war looked certain. Her relations in Canterbury – her late husband's relations she should say – so venomous, money so scarce, she had fallen back on Clodie M'Cool.

She did not look as if money had ever been scarce with her. She wore a different bonnet every time he saw her and he had seen her once with rubies in her ears. She had been used to good company, lavish-spending company, and opera, routs, card parties, balls. If Mr Hawkworth had held an obscure diplomatic post he had certainly moved in exalted circles – and why should his widow in any way qualify for diplomatic immunity, such as it had been or ever was? The Doctor listened politely but found his inner picture of Mrs Hawkworth in Paris was of a beautiful and frivolous woman thrown over by one lover and finding refuge eagerly with another. Monsieur Paul? He was not sure he believed in the existence of Hawkworth, not, at least, as a conventional husband and father. But then, did he believe any of it? She had enjoyed a long spell in an atmosphere of vanity, slavish fashion and extravagance, perhaps politically turbulent but otherwise no different from the vain, slavish, extravagant society of London. Beyond this nothing was certain.

She had stopped talking, aware at last that she had only half his attention. She would do better to always talk much less, he thought unkindly. He had heard her at Blackow, distressingly voluble, raising her voice to Clodie M'Cool without a thought anyone might be listening, harsh with Cassandra, always sharp with the servants. And yet . . .

'The lemonade was delightful. Will you walk down to the house with me? I believe I have a patient for you.'

'I am . . . how shall I put it? Hors de combat.'

'But of course I know you are. Only my aunt will never call on Dr Loder nor any other doctor were there six or seven within a mile. She has had a trifling accident to her hand and says fo, it is nothing and binds it up in a grubby bandage, but I think it is unhealthy. Someone I know once had a festering wound just like it and he was dead of poisoning within a month.'

The Doctor said in that case he must come, though he supposed Mrs M'Cool would box his ears and send him away for such presumption. 'Oh, lay it on my head,' said Julia, rising. 'She may rave at me all she likes, I do not mind it.'

Side by side they walked down towards the house, keeping on the grass under the trees. He was conscious of the fact that her eyes were on a level with his own, that they did not avoid his so often, that tendrils of damp hair were clinging to her forehead, that once, in making some gesture, her hand rested briefly on his arm.

'I understand how the Houghtons felt,' she said as they returned to the gravel and crossed the last yards to the steps, 'I am buried alive in this place,' and adding with a sudden perspicacity: 'And you feel the same, I am persuaded of it.'

'I would not have described it as feeling "buried alive".'

'But you ran away to your soldiers all the same and now you are running to India.'

He had opened his mouth to protest but by this time they had stepped in on to the cool black and white tiles of the hall and were instantly surrounded by the suffering hounds. Julia pushed them away impatiently, calling for Lucy, and when the girl came asked where she might find her aunt in just that tone of irritability that the Doctor suspected always overcame her in this house. Mrs M'Cool, bless her and her with a cruel pain in her arm, was in the garden and had been this hour since she had brought that savage brute back, him that had kicked half his stall to kindling sticks and nearly had the ear off Rigby's head.

'I will leave you to find her,' said Julia, mounting the bottom stair and turning to smile. She had taken off her bonnet and she looked flushed and weary. 'Have no fear, she will not eat *you*. She likes you.'

The Doctor was only a few feet away. She suddenly came down off the step and crossed the little space in a moment, hesitating only to look into his face with a look of surprised affection, and then reaching forward to kiss him on the cheek. With that she ran up the stairs like a girl without looking back.

'I saw you and Julia wandering about in the park,' said Clodie when he had run her to earth by the hot-houses. 'You are surely too experienced a man to be taken in by that sort of charm?'

'It would be a sad fellow who did not appreciate her beauty.'

'Ha, beauty! So a pair of blue eyes and a good bosom is all that is needed, eh? Well, well. If that is all an intelligent man wants no wonder poor simpletons take anything to wife so long as it wears a skirt. You disappoint me. I had taken it you were unmarried because your standards were too high, now I see you have none at all, you are simply too lazy.'

He was stung. 'I find your words objectionable,' he said before he could stop himself.

'Play the stiff-necked puritan, would you? Find my words objectionable! Of course they are objectionable. I do not like to see a man of parts give himself over for a pair of blue eyes and a bosom.'

During this forthright speech she waved both hands at him, the one which held a garden trowel and the other swathed in dirty linen. He looked hard at the bandaged one and Clodie, noticing his fixed expression and its cause, nursed the hand a moment, saying: ''Tis a vile cut, a scratch, nothing at all.'

'Mrs Hawkworth has told me of it. In her opinion it has become something more than a scratch.'

'Well, may she be served out for meddling. If you think I will pay you a guinea to look at it you are wrong.'

He had had enough of this, he thought. His old self surfaced, that self which had so frequently left this comfortable place to go about among his soldiers, a choleric, passionate, irascible self, and astonishingly formidable. 'Good day to you, madam,' he said coldly and turned away.

'Oh, look at it if you like then,' said Clodie abruptly. 'It is not a pretty sight but what can a surgeon do for it?'

It had been done by a kitchen knife, she said, unwrapping it in front of his furious eyes. In his opinion – and he told her so – it had been done by teeth, great filthy equine teeth at a guess, and there was damage to the bones. He did not like the look of it and told her that also, and the pain in her arm was another bad sign. Had she lived so long only to neglect a nasty wound and die of avoidable blood poisoning? He led her indoors by the wrist, so completely in charge that she followed as meekly as a small child, and he it was who called for clean water and clean linen and the good Irish whiskey. 'For I shall have to clean it,' he said, 'and a mouthful of spirits may lessen the discomfort.'

Afterwards she told him to pour a glass for himself, did he care for it at all, and she was sorry he had got blood on his shirt front but it was thin poor stuff by now, it would wash out in an instant. What a green and glittering eye she had, to be sure. He could not tell if she were pleased or not. Perhaps she did not know herself. It had been a miserable and messy little job, the pain no doubt considerable. One bone at least had been broken. She was an old woman for all her physical courage and she sat now in an unusual silence, slightly grey and pinched, her eyes sunken, glittering but sunken.

'I am expected at Upgate,' he said at last, consulting his watch and rising to scramble his few instruments together and stow them unceremoniously in a pocket, 'I must go and find my pony.'

'Ring for Lucy,' commanded Clodie harshly, tucking her maimed hand under her breast for a moment and cradling it in the other, and then, looking ashamed of such weakness, sitting up straight and glaring. When Lucy came she ordered the Doctor's pony brought round with an imperiousness the Doctor had seldom heard matched, but he noticed that she still looked grey and that there were beads of perspiration on her upper lip. When he took his leave she gave him her sound hand, her left one, and gripped his heartily as if she too had been a man. Dear Heaven, these women are a mass of contradiction, he thought, now hot, now cold, now shy, now outspoken. Neither of them is happy. Because of the past, the present, each other? He said: 'It must be dressed every day with *clean* dressings. I do not need to tell you. If you trust to luck a second time I will not answer for it, you may live or die as you please. Good day.'

As he crossed the hall he heard galloping hooves but he thought nothing of it till he stood on the steps and watched his pony making good his escape across the park. Rigby slunk up, purplish from a bout of frenzied cursing. 'He's away, Doctor, there's no catching him now.'

'So I see. I shall have to walk then. I cannot ride any other horse in these stables.'

'That you cannot, you queer old cove,' said Rigby under his breath, 'but you'll dirty your fine white stockings tramping it across the Gorse. And that little chestnut devil will be halfway to Suffolk by now and still running, old cock.'

The Doctor stepped out smartly, aware he had very little time and that Upgate was two miles and a half if it was a yard. He had reached the crossroads on the Gorse, fanning his hat and wondering if hurrying in such heat would encourage a congestion of the brain, when a horse and gig heaved into view from the direction of Warren Hill.

'Hi, Hi!' called a familiar voice. 'Hi, Doctor! Your horse is at the farm.'

'My chestnut pony?' He waited for Loder to draw up.

'The very one. He was going flat out down the hill, reins a-dangle. He nearly had us off the road. He knows where he was spoiled, eh?' He offered the seat beside him, astonishingly amiable, but then he had just spent a pleasant half hour at Thorn with his patient, whose headache had gone and whose welcome had been gratifyingly warm. 'Come up, man. I will turn round and take you down. You cannot trudge in the dust in decent stockings. Or have you an appointment? May I set you down somewhere more convenient?'

The Doctor hauled himself up, shaking his head. 'No, no. I must retrieve the pony. I am to dine at Upgate and they will not mind if I am a little late, will not mind dust,' and he brushed a great quantity from around the buckles of his shoes.

The gig was turned. The horse in the shafts ate up the ground at a relentless trot and in only a few minutes they were plunging downhill, the pace only slightly moderated. 'There, there is the cunning laddie,' said Loder, pointing with the whip, and sure enough there was the chestnut pony standing on the lawn, his reins in Ann's own hand. 'He has made the de'il of a mess of the flowerbeds.'

He had. The Doctor gazed about in consternation.

'Oh, never mind it,' said Ann cheerfully as he walked in through the wicket gate, 'I am flattered he should want to come back after being caressed and cosseted at Blackow.' She led the pony out into the lane at the front of the house. 'There. He is quite undamaged anyway and the flowers will stand up again. They stood up again after Tom's heifers went through them.'

For a moment they stood side by side. She felt she should apologize for failing to stop and greet him at Blackow – but how could she do it without confessing the reason? She said instead: 'You have not forgotten Charlotte's party, have you, Alex? It will make her so unhappy if you stay away.'

'I had forgotten it. When is it? Surely not this week?'

'No, next. Lady Barsham wrote to you.'

'Did she? I am at a loss to know what happens to these letters people say they have written to me – why is it, if they have indeed written, that I never seem to read them? My dear, you look a trifle pale again,' and here he dropped his voice, conscious of Loder not ten yards distant. 'Are you doing too much? You are not out in the harvest fields at all hours haranguing the men?'

'They are not cutting yet. I am perfectly well.'

'Shall I keep you company, Doctor,' asked Loder suddenly, breaking in, 'at least as far as the Upgate turn?'

This was hardly a pleasing prospect; in general the Doctor preferred his own company and in particular he disliked that of a man whose professional principles seemed at such variance with his own. It would not be easy to refuse, however, the gig was already turned to face the long hill again and his own pony's bridle was in his hand. He said: 'I would be delighted, sir,' without a tremor and put his foot in the stirrup.

'Do not forget Charlotte,' repeated Ann, her hand on the pony's neck. 'Please do not.'

It seemed to him that there was a note in her voice he had not heard for a long time, years even, perhaps since before her marriage to Harry Gerard. Was she overwhelmed by this setback, this sudden necessity to pick up the reins she had lately thrown down on the horse's neck? To pursue the simile – and here he gathered up his own reins – had she now taken fright at the antics of the horse and could not master him? He had never known her lack courage. On the other hand, a bad fall, an uncertain injury, weeks of inactivity, all thrown on top of her long struggle to establish herself here, to recover from her marriage . . . Who could say? She did look deathly pale, now he came to give her a hard, all-seeing professional stare, and her eyes looked over-large in the drained oval face. He had the fleeting impression as she stood there that if Loder had not been present she might have asked something of him, that Loder combined with diffidence was too much, she would never speak. He said: 'I shall certainly not forget dear Charlotte now. Are you going to be there?'

'I am.'

'Then I shall look forward to it all the more. But now I must hurry along, I must canter. They are blessedly tolerant at Upgate but even so I do not like to strain their patience too far. The dinner hour is come and gone.'

It was true and even at a canter he would be hard put to it to arrive within even Louise's elastic limits – she knew him of old, him and his erratic timekeeping. He reached the Gorse ten yards ahead of the gig, turned to wave with an awkward, crabbed movement and then, clutching his pommel, clapped his heels into the pony and sped away across the heath, a furious cloud of dust. He veered away beyond the tinkers' encampment to take a short cut through the triangular patch of woodland on that extreme corner but either the thickets of hazel and young elms had sprung up wondrously in the year he had been away or he had forgotten the path. The shade was hot and still, the leaves hung limp, the birds were unnaturally silent. The pony saw dragons in the bushes and snorted tremendously, sweat white across his neck. In a little while they emerged through a thin line of thorn and elder and the Doctor found himself half a mile out of his way, the whole chequered countryside spread before him shimmering in heat. He sat there looking out on it with the devouring attention of a man committing it to memory, the long sweep and fall of the fields and woods, the fragrance of the dry meadows, of the thirsty nettles and the drifts of parsley along the side of the wood.

'It is a fine piece of country,' he said aloud. 'Will Bonaparte lay it waste, I wonder? There is High Common on the rise and that other tower is Hilburgh

93

and still further over that is . . . Good God, I am so very late!' and shortly afterwards, leaving hoofmarks gouged deep in the Upgate gravel and a great churned mess where he had pulled up from a gallop: 'Mary and Joseph, as Clodie M'Cool would say, I have never been so late in my life before.'

There was news of a rising in Dublin. The High Common Volunteers, out on the Gorse, cast suspicious looks between the Blackow elms. Was there not a mad old Irishwoman in their very midst?

'I hear Bonaparte is going to bridge the Channel,' the mad old Irishwoman said to the Doctor, 'or failing that, the arrogant soul, is to fly his army over in balloons.'

They were in the old walled garden hunting for the asparagus bed, instead of which there was herb robert, foxgloves and campion in abundance. 'It will have run to seed by now,' said Clodie, parting the jungle with an ancient cricket bat, so ancient it was scarcely recognizable for what it was, 'but I would like to take its bearings. Aha, look at this! So this is where the old grey hen is laying,' and plumb at her feet a nest of a dozen eggs, speckled and clean.

'He would need a great many balloons,' remarked the Doctor thoughtfully, stowing the eggs she handed him in his capacious pocket, 'and supposing he met with a contrary wind? In my experience at sea the wind is invariably wrong for the manoeuvre contemplated, it blows north instead of south or west instead of east, or there is not enough of it or there is too much.'

A mass of tall stuff like dill appeared. Clodie plunged forward in joyful recognition. 'Asparagus! At last!' She turned about to fix the place. 'I do so love asparagus. And peaches. And figs. Did I tell you my father grew the sweetest grapes in the west of Ireland? Did I tell you I was his only daughter?'

'You did not.'

94

'Well, so I was. When he died Russhard – the house and all the land – went to a cousin. But the money came to me. My grandmother, an Englishwoman, a duke's daughter, brought a fortune into the family and that fortune became mine at my father's death. I was the catch of the Galway season four years in a row till it was spent – and then I married M'Cool. Do you raise your brows at me, Alex French, and squint down that long nose? Did you think I married for love?' She let her eye wander over the garden before she shut the gate on it. 'I won't have the hens in my asparagus,' she said, and as an afterthought: 'When I'm dead it will be Cassandra's.'

They walked side by side down the gravel path between the box hedges. A rhythmic swish and sigh came from beyond the shrubbery where Rigby was scything the lower lawn. A smell of hot mown grass wafted to them, of box, of roses. It seemed to the Doctor, looking about, that Blackow was being made beautiful, was being slowly but certainly transformed. He would not have believed it possible, not this uncompromising, plain, foursquare house standing so proud and bleak, but unless his eyes deceived him some plant was already climbing tentatively up the wall by the ballroom windows, and there were new shrubs to break up the long dull view of the lake, a new seat, a pair of stone urns.

'You are making improvements.'

Clodie smiled. 'What do I care for houses? But gardens now . . . Do you see this bush?' and she led him to a tiny wizened stunted thing partially shaded by a straw mat on poles. 'This came from Canton, all the way from Canton, and Heaven knows how many miles it travelled beforehand. Unfortunately the label was lost, it rotted away no doubt in the watering on board ship.'

'Perhaps it is tea,' said the Doctor, walking all round it. 'It does not look very grateful for all your attention.'

'No, it is not tea. It is a mystery, a Chinese mystery. Let us hope it lives to surprise us.'

'Let us hope it is not trampled underfoot when Bonaparte's balloons land in the park,' was the Doctor's dry response.

'Balloons full of soldiers! Can you credit it! And there is even a whisper of a tunnel – to complement the bridge, I suppose.'

They rambled on companionably about the far-fetched reports in the newspapers and the even more far-fetched and hysterical rumours bandied about with obvious glee by Pashman the carrier and those who listened to him or alternatively wished to outdo him in extravagant conjecture. High Common was alive with stories. 'The Arabian Nights are nothing to 'em,' said Clodie, when they had circumambulated the entire garden and arrived back at the Chinese mystery.

'And how do you hear gossip? Nobody calls,' said the Doctor.

'Oh, it would astonish you what comes to our ears. Anyway, Julia is always in Norwich and she has been at cards with Mrs Palmer and to Upgate with Cassandra now they are inviting the child twice a week. By this time tomorrow I shall know which way the wind blows over this Irish business, whether I dare poke my nose out beyond the boundary again. You should see their eyes on stalks when I go into the church.'

'I very much fear it is commonly understood here-abouts that all Irish are papists except those who cry up King Billy.'

'Well, I am not.' She was silent a moment, nursing her injured hand, now newly wrapped in clean bandages and much much easier, and gazing at the pitiful shrub at her feet. 'Have you met the parson?' she demanded suddenly. 'The jumped-up, prating cock-of-the-walk! Do you know what he said to me? "Madam, I must mention – it is my duty to mention – that your dress is unsuitable for Divine Service." Ha! The puritan! Oh, I saw what was in his mind, in his little pop eyes! A scrub and a hypocrite! Is he not a hypocrite? Those pink baby-faced men often are, holding themselves up as morally superior and keeping a mistress in a good little house in town.'

'I have met him once,' said the Doctor, 'when he first came. He honours us with a visit once a year, I believe. Since I do not go to church I manage to avoid him with no great trouble. But he is as virtuous, I trust, as he would have us believe. His wife looked content at any rate.'

'As she would need to be a nincompoop to marry such a man she would hardly have the brains to find him out in infidelity.'

'And was your dress unsuitable?'

'Oh, it was one I had as a girl. Perhaps it was a little low in the bosom but then I have none to speak of and no man is going to be tempted by an old crone. He did it to put me in my place because I had interrupted his sermon. But now, you are not running away? You must see Dido before you go.'

He was ushered to the stableyard and the brown mare was paraded forth. Today she seemed a mysterious creature, dark and splendid, and here, out of her stall, the Doctor could see she was indeed a racing horse. 'Yes,' he said noncommittally, 'she is coming along very nicely.'

They went in for a cold meal and were joined by Julia and Cassandra, Julia in pale blue, strangely elegant and unusually quiet, hardly speaking other than to correct Cassandra's table manners or ask the Doctor whether he would care for more pie or another soused herring. He liked her better in this subdued mood; it suited her to be more grave and self-contained. Afterwards he lingered, talking, and lingered so late he was pressed to a supper of biscuits and coffee, sitting out on the terrace by the ballroom windows. There was a young moon, a token moon as yet, but it did not matter for there was only a diminishing of the daylight, no real darkness. Bats were dipping across the lawns and the owls were hunting along the park railings. What they talked of seemed unimportant, it was enough that tonight Julia had abandoned her disguises, her playing of a part, and seemed to him artless and open, laughing without affectation and not once raising her voice above a low delightful key, one he could listen to for hours.

'There is nothing like good coffee and good company,' she said at some point, and as she turned her head he saw the rubies in her ears again, half hidden by her hair. And later, when Cassandra ran out in her shift, instead of scolding she made as if to take her on to her lap, something Cassandra was not used to for she backed away with a noticeable surprise and came to rest against the Doctor's chair, putting a hand on his for reassurance. Candour, he thought, looking down into her shadowed face, unlimited candour, innocence, uncomplicated affection; in a year or two, in three, all would be gone. Would she cultivate coquetry like her mother perhaps? He did not think so, she had a far different spirit. He hoped not.

'What's all this?' demanded Clodie, returning with more coffee. 'You should be in your bed, Cassie dear.'

She sat down and the child went straight to her, climbing on her bony knees and leaning back happily against her unyielding breast. 'The owls are keeping me awake,' she said.

'Ah well,' replied Clodie, leaning her cheek on the child's head, 'there'll be worse things to keep you awake before you're done. The owls are God's creatures and mean you no harm.'

'If you will excuse me,' said Julia, 'I shall retire.'

The Doctor rose, she touched his hand in passing as an old friend might, a sister, and was gone.

How vulnerable I am, he thought, that a look, a smile, can strike up such an intolerable longing. He sat down again, found Clodie's questioning eyes on him and said for want of anything better: 'I too must be away to my bed.'

'Afraid they will say you have been keeping company with traitors?'

'Traitors?'

'It seems Lord Barsham has received a directive from on high – arrest all suspicious persons. There is not a soul in five miles around not expecting him to arrest *me*.'

'As what? Bonaparte's spy? An Irish rebel?'

'To be sure I believe in Irish independence and don't care who knows it.'

'So do I. So do many right-thinking men, Billy Pitt included. It does not put me in the pay of the French. Besides, what useful information are you to dispatch from High Common? That the hay has been gathered in? That the new miller's wife has a baby? That the tinker children have the ringworm?'

'Oh damn them all!' cried Clodie savagely over Cassandra's head. 'If those few thousand acres of bog and rock were still mine what a rebellion I would raise, and lead it myself – but not with the help of that ambitious Corsican and all his sycophants, not to give Ireland over into the hands of a tyrant.' A pause and the fire died out of her eyes. 'Well, there is no use growing hot for the sake of some bare mountainsides in Galway. Here now, can you carry this child in for me, she is asleep.'

He carried her in. He said good night. She saw him to the door herself, half a dozen of the bitch hounds who were allowed in the house at night padding silently behind. 'It is a kind night,' she said, standing on the top step and sniffing at the faint warm breeze, 'but even so the air makes my bones ache. 'Tis old age, Alex dear. I shall not venture to sit out again in the evening without a flannel wrapper.'

*

99

He walked away up the drive deep in thought about rebellion and patriotism and the nature of politics, 'glum as a newt' as Barsham might have said. A heavy depression settled on him – only the intensifying of what was there before perhaps – and he could not shake it off, nor, on reaching the gatehouse, could he sleep. He unlocked the only trunk to have been packed up and rummaged through his treasures, all those things he had decided to leave behind at Thorn. He did not wonder Clodie M'Cool did not care for her memories: his overwhelmed him. He sat on the cold brick floor a full hour, turning his life over in his hands. The morning found him irritable and red-eyed amid a fog of pipe smoke and raking through the ashes of a fire, a funeral pyre of those very few letters and keepsakes he had not had the heart to destroy until now.

The morning also brought Lady Barsham and Charlotte on their way to Norwich, interrupting his kidneys and bacon, his toast and marmalade to ask if they could run any errands for him, be at all useful? They did not want to stay above a minute, they said, they must not keep the horses waiting and they had an appointment with the dentist.

'Not that terrible old rogue Harper?' cried the Doctor, starting up with a piece of toast in his hand. 'If you let him draw a tooth he will infect your jaw for certain. I have seen his handiwork before and so has Menzies.'

Lady Barsham repressed a shudder and caught Charlotte by the arm. 'If there is nothing we can do for you . . .' she began.

'If you care for my advice – have I ever given you bad advice? – you will avoid Harper like the plagues of Egypt.'

'It is too late. We have an appointment.'

'Then you have an appointment with a murderer.'

'Alex!'

They beat a hurried retreat, he was obviously in a

savage and uncompromising mood. He accompanied them to the carriage, however, his toast still in his hand, in order to see through the common civilities, but his heart was not in it, he looked very dark, and besides ill humour he reeked of tobacco.

'Is that Cassandra?' asked Louise, pausing with her foot on the step. It was, Cassandra in a white dress, diminished by distance to a little toy puppet running and dancing about with a little toy puppet of a pig jerking along behind on a string. What a quiet solitary child she was, said Louise fondly, and how she shrank away when George Barsham swept in, all overpowering good humour and loud voice. Was it right that such a shy impressionable creature should be brought up in that vast old pile with a pair of dubious women, the one mad, the other . . .

'The other Babylonish,' said the Doctor with a snarl.

'Babylonish?' She looked him in the eye but her cheeks were pink and she snapped: 'Yes, indeed, you may be right. But remember it was your word and not mine.'

And why should he desire her to be virtuous, he wondered, watching the carriage turn and roll away through the gates, why hope for a blameless past? It was a pointless desire, a vain hope. He had seen her visitors with his own eyes trotting in and out, ungentlemanlike scrubs for the most part, indistinguishable from the racy grasping types often to be seen in Clodie's stableyard driving a hard bargain. Morris often came, was undeterred by the M'Cool defences: he had seen him walk in at the front door without ringing the bell, showing his whip to the hounds. And there were others. And why did she spend so much time in Norwich? Why did her man of business not come to Blackow? She had said there was some problem about Hawkworth's money, a case in Chancery even. He did not believe it. He did not believe it and hated himself for not believing it.

Why could he not accept her as she was?

Because she was beautiful and such beauty should be virtuous? Why? Why should a beautiful woman be good? It was self-evident she was not evil so could she not be allowed some human failings? Should he be disappointed that she was vain, untruthful, selfish and promiscuous?

'Aunt Clodie wants to know,' said Cassandra at the open window, and then, more shrilly: 'Aunt Clodie wants to know . . .'

'Yes?' said the Doctor.

'Aunt Clodie wants to know if you would like a cucumber.'

'What an extraordinary man you are,' said Julia, finding him reading, three small sleek swallows crouching in the folds of his neckcloth, 'I do believe you like the company of those birds better than anything. You have not called for two days. Can you not think of something to make life here less dull?'

He had struggled up, tipping the birds into their case, throwing down his pamphlet, and now he groped about for his discarded coat. 'My dear, I have seen the carriage go by several times. I assumed you were in Norwich.'

'Oh that,' and she shrugged, bending to poke curiously at some of her daughter's bits and pieces. 'How tiresome it all is. I shall never be free of nasty greasy little legal parasites all wanting me to sign papers and swear oaths, and the worst of it is I shall never have any money – I do not believe I shall ever see a penny of Charles's money, it will stay in France for ever, and in London or wherever it is. The banks are no help and the lawyers squabble. Hoare's will not do this, Gurney's will not do that, the courts must have the proper papers initialled and sealed and the proper papers are not processed, will not be sent till a month on Sunday.' She laughed suddenly, a deep delightful laugh, and swung round with a stone in her hand. She held it out on her palm for him to see.

102

'What is it?'

'Only a common or garden stone, my dear.'

'But it is perfectly round and it has a hole right through.'

'They are tediously common, I assure you, though for all that they are counted lucky, even magical. You would be surprised what everyday objects lend themselves to magic,' and he might have enlightened her, jerking on his coat and sweeping papers and medical instruments off the more comfortable chair of the two, aware of the thump thump of his heart as he came upright to find her beside him, the stone still in her hand. Coherent thought died away, so, temporarily, did the power of speech. To be so smitten by a woman and at my age, he thought, grasping after some ordinary topic of conversation, any topic of conversation.

'I have come,' she said, and he saw that the quiet, reflective mood of two evenings ago was still with her, in spite of her vexations at the banks and attorneys' offices, 'dear Dr French, I have come to ask a favour. Can you use your influence with my aunt to help me to a house in Norwich?' and then, as he raised his brows, 'It is only a very little house, so genteel, so very cheap, and I could entertain my friends there and be a little independent again. You do not know how hard it is after being mistress of my own establishment to be reduced to the position of little more than companion to an eccentric old woman. Oh, oh, you must not think I have anything against her, she has been generous enough, I will not deny it. But we do not suit, we never shall. Her hackles rise when she sees me and mine when I hear her voice praising those eternal horses – do not you think that all this passion for horses is abnormal? I truly believe that if I stay here much longer I shall commit murder.'

'And how may I help?'

'Could you not represent to her how much better it would be if I had my own establishment again? She does not want me here – not that I mean you to say such a thing in her hearing, but it is the truth. A small house in Norwich, a not-too-fashionable district, a low rent, two servants . . . What objection could there be? And when the lawyers are done with Charles's affairs I shall move to London or to Bath. Perhaps Bath.'

He hardly dared ask, although he knew what her answer would be before he spoke. 'My dear, what about Cassandra?'

'Oh, Cassandra,' and she turned away, but not before he had seen her blush. 'Cassie loves the old woman, have you noticed? They would be unhappy without each other and they would neither of them miss me for a moment.'

'You would be happy leaving her here?'

'She will come to no harm, you know. And Clodie has said the estate is to be hers one day. What more could I want for my daughter?' She laughed, a miserable harsh sound this time. 'It is more than I shall ever provide for her.'

The Doctor pressed her to the chair and went to call Jim. He returned in a moment, smiling a politely vacuous smile, but had no sooner advanced four steps into the room than all three swallows launched themselves at him with excited chirrups, thinking he had brought their next meal.

'How they do love you,' said Julia.

'Oh no, I am simply their source of nourishment.' He did not actually believe this, he had raised swallows before and found them touchingly affectionate, but something in the look she gave him made him shy away from discussing it. There was nothing of art, nothing of deliberate flirtation in the look, nothing, he might have said, of the old Julia whose falseness and studied grace had so irritated him, but this gave it all the more force. For a brief moment she reminded him strongly of Cassandra, the same wide blue innocence and earnest entreaty. He coughed and turned away, while the swallows crept up to his neck and chirruped hopefully in his ears.

'I hope you can see your way to speaking to my aunt,' Julia said, and smiled. 'To . . . to putting in a word. She is bound to speak to *you* about me. She does, does she not? I have always suspected she complains to anybody who will listen.'

'No indeed. She has never mentioned you, or certainly not to complain. She tells me you are at home or are in Norwich, nothing more.'

'I am surprised. She can be venomous when she cares . . .'

The door opened and Jim came in with a tray. He put it down by Julia at the Doctor's nod and departed softly, grinning broadly the moment his back was to the room.

'Is it Mama?' whispered Cassandra from her obscure corner by the kitchen hearth.

'It is.'

'Talking to the Doctor?'

'Like a Christian.'

Cassandra put her small dirty feet together and looked down at them. 'I don't like wearing shoes,' she said at last. 'Aunt Clodie says she never wore shoes as a girl though she was ever so rich.'

'Ah well, they have different ways of going on in Ireland for all we know. Or maybe she means she wore riding boots instead.'

Cassandra considered. 'Maybe she does.'

The pig, tied up outside the door, was growing restless and gave a long indignant squeal. It was loud enough to interrupt the Doctor's long explanation of scabies, the scourge of the army, its symptoms, its prevalence in close, crowded conditions . . . It was a subject on which he could talk with ease for a long long time, the greater part of his mind on something else entirely, and he was in

105

full flow, the tea cooling in its dish, when the long-drawn-out shriek penetrated.

'Good Heavens, what was that?' asked Julia, who had been making a spirited pretence of listening, and not only listening but being interested.

'Oh, Cassandra's pig, I expect.'

'Her pig? That dreadful animal. But is she here?'

'If the pig is so is she. They are inseparable.'

Julia rose, said, 'I beg your pardon,' crossed to the kitchen door and opened it. He heard her voice beyond, raised in that unlovely and familiar tone. 'Cass, I will not have you running in and out of . . .' She nearly said 'servants' quarters' but checked herself. 'In and out without shoes. Where are your shoes? And where is your hat? You are filthy. Where have you been?'

There being no sensible answer to so many questions posed in such a manner, such an accusing, high-pitched, unreasonable manner, Cassandra said nothing but allowed herself to be dragged forth into the parlour to stand before the Doctor in all her miserable filth and damnable barefootedness, every freckle subdued and her expression amazingly grave. The Doctor leaned forward and caught, as he did so, a faint whiff of pig.

'Would you like a cup of tea?'

'She would not,' cried Julia, 'she is to come home directly. Alex, you must send her out of the house when she slips in uninvited. I have told you before.'

'She does no harm. My door is always open.'

She gathered her hat and sunshade, taking Cassandra's arm. 'Is it? Yes, it would be. Open to all your friends,' and she gave him another look, less innocent than before, there was no mistaking it. 'Mine would be to you,' she said, 'if I had one; if I had my own, I mean.'

She is not subtle, he thought. For all her airs and stratagems she is not subtle in the least. But he watched her down the drive with a curious expression: affection, amusement, hunger combined. Perhaps after all she was as guileless as a child, that all her obvious flaunting of her attractions was so overdone *because* she was not a practised dissembler: where she cared for someone she must show it naturally and where she did not she found flirtation heavy going. She had too warm and volatile a nature after all to deceive for any length of time with much hope of success. The real Julia must always break through.

The Doctor's heart slowed to its usual measure and he gently picked off the swallows one by one, lowering them into their case yet again and promising them their mutton as soon as the tea things were cleared.

'How his eye do gleam,' said Jim to the piglet, who was now hobbled as well as tied by the neck and who looked as resigned as a pig can look. 'Poor old cove. He ought to be beyond thinking about such things at his age. And a beautiful woman like that. What chance has he? As much chance as I might have was I to ogle her.'

With this still in mind he looked long and attentively at the Doctor when he carried in his supper some hours later and found him with his stockinged feet on the tortoise shell and surrounded by books, papers and the contents of his medical case, among which he had been hunting for a scalpel to use as a letter opener.

'I have been asked to operate at the Hospital again,' he said with understandable satisfaction, 'and privately too. I can fit in both, I believe. I do not leave Norfolk until the thirteenth of August.'

Ho, you have a good stretch yet for her to wring your heart then; but aloud: 'Lookee, Doctor, eat your wittles while they're hot.'

'Tell me,' as he breached the perfect small pie and the gravy ran out steaming, 'you are not a Norfolk man. Do you feel buried alive here?'

'Buried alive, sir? No, sir, not that I knows of. It can be quiet, of course, but I've always been something quiet, sir, being an only child and a shy lad and a bachelor. 'Tis what I'm used to.'

'Yes,' said the Doctor. How some of us long to be so content.

'Will that be all, sir? Oh, and I should tell you, I have put the piglet in the broom cupboard on a blanket. I shall take him down for Miss Cassandra in the morning.'

# 6

The Doctor was crawling about on the Gorse after the bustards, who had all tiptoed away at his approach, when he looked up and there was Cassandra in spotted muslin and a Grecian bonnet two sizes too large.

'I am going to Thorn,' she said, watching him stand up and pick grass seed off his breeches, 'I am going to have tea with Ann.'

The Doctor remonstrated. Should she be alone? Was she not afraid of the charcoal burners, those strange solitary people with blackened skins who spoke a language of their own? No, said Cassandra stoutly, for they all lived over in the woods towards Upgate and besides, when she had met one once walking hurriedly along with a rabbit under his coat he had said a civil good day and had smiled.

'Nevertheless,' said the Doctor, 'I believe I shall escort you.'

She took his arm. She was very small and hung on it a little and he guessed she was already tired. Yes, she had been riding with Aunt Clodie that morning, had jumped two logs and a dry brook, had had a gallop, her very first. This afternoon she had hoed a whole patch of the walled garden, a whole patch that was to be her own, where she could grow whatever she wished. It had been hot work even with her dress tucked up and a straw hat on. Had the Doctor ever had a garden? The Doctor had once, most romantically, had a garden with acacia and banyan and peepul trees, with beds of remarkable lilies and a solitary rose bush, and a stake to tie up an elephant. And had anyone come visiting by elephant and tied him there? Yes indeed, two or three.

They walked slower and slower discussing elephants, the uniform of their mahouts – if any – the difficulties of mounting, the great damage done when they ran amok, and after elephants tigers, and after tigers . . .

From a warm hollow beside the track rose a short, strong, tattered figure, a chain in its hand. The animal at the end of the chain took a moment to shuffle up but in a moment he too was standing, looking at them with an absorbingly expectant expression. It was a bear.

'Oh, he is so hot, the poor thing,' cried Cassandra, who advanced fearlessly, letting go of the Doctor's sleeve.

'He is, Miss, he is. And never a pond in all this cruel hot heath. We have searched an hour or more.'

The Doctor looked at the bear's small eye, at its bulk – it was large for its calling, dancing bears on the whole being small, ill-kept, deprived, ragged beasts – and at its obvious thirst. He said: 'There is water at the farm. Come along with us.'

So it was they reached Thorn in procession, Cassandra running ahead, her clean skirts held up, the Doctor with the bear-keeper and lastly the bear itself, shambling in their wake as docile as a puppy. At last, hot and squalid, he saw the horse pond beyond the gate to the orchard and dragged with pathetic persistence in that direction, tangling his chain momentarily in the Doctor's legs. 'He do so love a bath,' said his keeper, whacking the moth-eaten hide with his stick. Cassandra jumped up and down, holding on to her hat. 'Oh, let him go, let him go! How hot and tired he must be. Look, his paw is bleeding.'

'Ann, Ann,' cried Miss Pennyquick, running into the parlour, 'there is a bear in the pond.'

'A bear?'

'A great brown bear. It is all by itself and frightening the ducks.'

But it was not by itself after all, she found, going to

investigate. It had been played out on the end of a rope provided by Hollin, who stood watching with undisguised interest while it plunged and shook itself. Beside him was the bow-legged little man, its keeper, and beside him the Doctor and Cassandra – not to speak of the bird-boy who had slunk up behind the orchard hedge, the kitchen maid and Mrs McGinley, a wooden spoon still in her hand.

'Well!' said Miss Pennyquick at Ann's elbow.

'I knew you would not mind,' said Cassandra, taking Ann's hand. 'He is a very old bear the man says, and very tired of walking in the heat. He was up on the Gorse sitting in the sun and there is not a pond anywhere.'

'There is a pond by the tinkers' camp. And there is the river,' said Ann.

'The river is too far,' the child replied in a reproving tone. 'You do not mind really? He is a very gentle bear.'

He had had a long strenuous life, he was a cowed bear rather than gentle, and all this Ann saw in an instant, but her fingers tightened reassuringly on Cassandra's wrist and she said softly: 'He looks a kind bear, yes, but do stay well away, he will be all wet when he comes out and you have a clean dress on.'

They walked a little way away. 'The Doctor says I should not walk alone across the Gorse,' said Cassandra after a moment in a small voice.

'He is quite right. I shall speak to your aunt about it. Rigby should have brought you.'

'Mama said it was not necessary. And Driscoll has the stomach ache, Rigby had to drive the carriage.'

The bear was leaving the water, encouraged by shouts and jerks on the rope. He shook himself thoroughly. The Doctor and the bear-leader stepped forward and made the poor beast show his lacerated paw. Remedies were discussed. The Doctor's head bent very low near the muzzled jaws. 'There is an abscess,' they heard him say. The domestic staff glanced round, saw Ann and shuffled

111

away guiltily. The Doctor was examining the bear's other paws, shaking his head. The bear was becoming distressed, he did not like his sore places exposed, he especially did not like them touched. Words were exchanged with his keeper and the note of reproof in them did nothing for his nerves. All the cool bliss of the horse pond was forgotten; he reared up suddenly with a growl.

'Get down, you great booby,' said his keeper amiably, bringing the long stick down across his nose. 'Silly bugger! This gentleman only wants to mend your old sore feet.'

But in another five minutes both bear and man were away, mounting the lane to the Gorse again, the bear hobbling occasionally. Cassandra flew to the Doctor, tears in her eyes. 'Oh, why did you let him go before he had put some salve on the bear's feet? Look, he is limping. I thought you were going to make him better.'

'Alas, his master has never salved his feet in the past and will not bother now, though he agreed to all my suggestions. He will not go to an apothecary, that is the pity of it; he will not go to an apothecary for a bear.'

Cassandra hopped on one leg, unappeased. 'Aunt Clodie would know what to do,' with a long hard look up at the Doctor whose competence was now in some doubt, 'and she would talk to the man and make him go for the ointment. I know she would. Or she would make it up herself, she has lots of bottles in the harness room.'

The Doctor thought this very likely but suggested that the M'Cool hounds would worry the bear unmercifully. 'Oh, the dogs can be shut in,' declared Cassandra, a mass of impatience and indignation, 'they are all shut up when Mama has visitors.'

'She is a determined little thing,' said Ann, drawing closer as Cassandra was borne away by Miss Pennyquick to wash her hands and face, 'I will tell Aunt Clodie' floating back to them as the door opened and closed.

'Even so, I doubt Mrs M'Cool will run about the Gorse after a lame bear. It will be dancing for its supper by now in any case.'

'But where? There are only the tinkers.'

'Their cookpots have bustards bubbling in them. He is dancing so that his keeper may chew on a bustard wing,' replied the Doctor in venomous tones, and he might have said more, either about bustards, bears or tinkers, but he was interrupted by the arrival of a gig, a familiar gig and drawn by a familiar horse. It was Loder, and he climbed down carrying a covered basket, walking up the path to Thorn's front door. It was a massive door, used only for weddings and funerals, though both the Doctor and Ann could recall Harry Gerard leaning from his saddle to rap on it with his whip. Perhaps it was this sudden shared recollection that kept them hanging back by the pond until the door had creaked open and Loder had been admitted, doffing his hat with an unlikely flourish, his deep voice penetrating the summer quiet with 'Pray tell your mistress . . .'

And: 'What is all this I hear about eels?' asked Ann, turning about to face the pond again.

'Eels? Oh, the eels! Did you never go paddling after elvers when you were little?'

'I never did. I was not allowed out without my stockings and shoes. My father was a clergyman, remember, and hoped his only child would set an example.'

'But where did you hear about our fishing?'

'Oh, you know how word gets about. I warn you, you cannot sneeze in your gatehouse without High Common knowing of it an hour later.'

Well, he had been seduced into the adventure, the Doctor said. What man could resist Cassandra in a winning mood? They had stolen to the river bank just below the mill and he had shown her how to scoop up the thin elvers in her hands, a game of hazard in the dappled

113

shadows under the trees. He had not thought about modesty or decorum, only that her small freckled face was supremely happy, that everything else had been forgotten in the joy of the moment: the long hot day, the smell of grass, the clumps of forget-me-not along the bank, and meadowsweet, foxgloves, watermint. There had been cows and calves standing under the alders, tails and ears flicking, and now and again the blue flash of the kingfisher.

'I wish you had called here on your way,' said Ann, 'you could have taught me too.'

'And what would High Common say to Lady Gerard bare-legged in the river?'

Their eyes met. In sudden happiness she put out a hand and touched his, a gesture of intimate friendship, the old intimate friendship she had thought might be lost for ever. 'Did I ever care what High Common said?' and then, hurrying on before he could speak: 'Have you remembered it is nearly Assize week? Oh, I know you have suffered one such week already this year – poor Mr Savage – but that was necessarily grim, this is pleasure. I am getting up a party for the breakfast and concert at the Ranelagh Gardens. Mrs M'Cool is to come, and Cassandra.'

He did not say: Will you be strong enough? He grunted amiably and said instead: 'Strawberries, I suppose, and fireworks?'

'Fireworks certainly. It will be a horrible crush and quite likely not worth the money but Cassandra has never seen fireworks, never been to a concert.'

'This is *your* way of fishing for elvers, I take it.'

'She is a dear child and so neglected. Mrs Hawkworth pleaded a previous engagement, she is always heavily engaged and always with her lawyers. Her husband must have left a great estate and a most complicated will to cause such endless consultations.'

'Perhaps he did not leave a will and that is where the

problem lies. My dear, should you not go in? There is Babs waving her arms by the back door. Mr Loder quite possibly grows impatient.'

She sighed and took his arm, walking slowly towards the house. 'Have you seen the papers?' she asked suddenly. 'Columns of patriotic odes, terrible stuff: no two lines scan and misplaced sentiment at every turn.'

'If the French land we shall have an end to such effusions.'

'Would you welcome them simply to discourage the poor poets in the *Mercury*? I shall tell Tom. He made up his own the other day. He had been watching the volunteers from his window and was carried away with the joy of being a soldier. Babs pointed out that it is pleasant to be a soldier when you know you may go home to your own house for supper and the enemy is still a great way off, even she would take up a musket if that was all there was to it.'

'Good Heavens, that man is pacing the parlour crying woe and damnation!' Miss Pennyquick said now, ushering them in. 'He has brought something for you,' to Ann, 'and when I said you were out by the pond talking to the Doctor he grew uncommon dark and snappish. Doctor, Doctor, your coat is all mud. Let me sponge it for you,' and in a lower voice as she led him away: 'It will not do, doctoring animals in your best coat. Well, if it is not your best coat it is a very fine one . . . A man should be ashamed . . .'

'Dr Loder,' said Ann, opening the door to her parlour. He bowed with extraordinary gallantry, the sour expression rapidly fading from his face to be replaced by a rare affability, a distinct cheerfulness. He looked as if he had taken special care with his dress, his long blue jaw was a startling contrast to his snowy linen, and to her surprise he spoke at random: the weather, the sorry state of many crops, his having seen Tom's face at an upstairs window: he hoped he was not getting about on one leg; while all

115

the time he looked at her, stared and stared quite unabashed, and smiled and smiled. When Miss Pennyquick came in for her sewing basket – the Doctor had torn off a button and loosened another – he talked of head wounds, the sometimes long-lasting effects of head wounds, and he approached to within a few feet as if, any minute, he might call on her to show him her scar, her long tender scar, or to let him examine her eyes.

'Babs,' and she side-stepped, took Miss Pennyquick's long cold skeletal hand. 'Babs, dear, serve the tea as quick as you like. Put it in the old morning room,' and as she turned back, 'Dr Loder, your basket is moving.'

'Oh,' and he dived to the table where he had left it, whipped off the cover and held up a squirming, bad-tempered kitten, furious at being confined for so long. 'This is for you. Miss Pennyquick mentioned your house cat was growing old. I expect you have two score others in the yard but I thought . . .' It was clear he had hoped to make her an acceptable present. She hesitated only a moment and then received it, a bundle of claws, into her hands. When she looked up she found his face full of anxiety, relief and tenderness.

'It was such a kind thought . . .' she began, wondering what she could say.

'Your servant, sir,' said the Doctor, appearing in the doorway and giving an ungracious nod. 'Another kitten? I thought you had a . . .'

'Dr Loder is staying for tea,' said Ann desperately, 'and so must you. Alex . . . Alex, would you take the kitten out to Mrs McGinley and tell her to give it some milk?' Her eyes were brilliant, laughing. She was her old self at last.

She was her old self throughout tea, a most awkward, crabbed, choking sort of meal, Miss Pennyquick on her dignity, Cassandra mulish and still inclined to talk only of the bear, the Doctor preoccupied and silent and Loder unutterably benign. 'How I do dislike that man,' said

Miss Pennyquick, chasing to the back regions for more milk and to berate the parcel of lazy trollops for not answering the bell, only to find Mrs McGinley and the two girls on their hands and knees in the dairy, trying to coax the kitten from behind the butter barrels. 'How I wish the Doctor would wake up and see him off,' she continued, trotting back with her full jug. 'He has not said above three words since he entered the house.'

That man is not a gentleman, said Loder to himself, glancing at the Doctor over his tea cup, he has no manners to speak of, no sense of what is fitting. And his coat is wet. How could he wet his coat on a day as dry as this? Splashing in the pond? How can she bear to have him at her table, a taciturn, disgruntled old devil like that; and call him Alex, as familiar as you like. Alex indeed! And yet Alderson speaks highly of him, and Rigby too. They say he is a Tory if he is anything, most unusual in a medical man, but then on occasion he is more radical than any man alive, prating on about women doctors, reforms in hospital teaching, an entire new regime for the Army. God knows what he is about. He is a United Friar as well, they say, dedicated to scientific learning and philanthropic acts. Well, for my part I find him an obnoxious mixture, a mean sly ill-favoured body if ever there was one.

'Must you go so soon?' asked Ann, accompanying the ill-favoured body to the door.

'I must. If you like I will walk Cassandra home.'

'No. Babs will drive her in the dickey cart. You have grown very solemn over tea. Is there something on your mind? Apart from bustards, I mean. I hope it is not Mr Savage out in Jamaica, I know the French are being very troublesome there.'

'No, my dear, it is not Mr Savage nor yet the French,' and then, stepping out and putting on his hat: 'So Mr Loder is not proof against your charms. He is only cheerful when at Thorn, I find.'

'I hope you do not mean to imply . . . Alex, I have not encouraged him. Alex, he is my doctor. Surely that is not allowed, that a doctor . . . No, it is not. I believe you misinterpret him because you don't like him. All he is is a dull gloomy young man trying to be kind.'

'Because a thing is not allowed does not abolish it. Do single gentlemen refrain from falling in love with married ladies and vice versa simply because it is forbidden? I have known many good doctors tangle themselves in evil webs, all of them "not allowed". Fie, child, if you do not know whether he is overstepping his bounds, his professional bounds, then who may?'

Suddenly he stepped back, put a hand under her chin. 'Do you get headaches still?' and he looked into her eyes with a professional keenness, picked up her wrist and put his thumb against the pulse.

'Hardly at all.'

He parted her hair and looked at the long scar. 'What a fool you were. And I suppose in six months you will give a repeat performance.'

'I never had a fall as bad as that in my life. I shall never have another if I can help it.'

'I seem to remember some catastrophe in the flower-beds at Upgate: Gerard's horse, black outside and in. He shot you over a hedge.'

If he opened old wounds he did not know what they were. Her eyes were bold and shining. 'If he had not I would never have met Louise. Her door was closed to me as Harry's wife.'

'Old history, sour old history. Old wrongs, old slights and old omissions. Do you think she was unaware Harry might have been Barsham's child? *He* believes her ignorant but at one time I thought the guilt, simple overpowering guilt would kill him.'

'Harry had his eyes,' said Ann quietly, looking out over her fields as they rose and rose towards the Gorse.

'Anyway, we have wandered from the point,' more

118

brusquely, 'time and quiet will cure you, not breakfasts, balls and routs.'

'You are a killjoy,' and then, her hand on his arm: 'Will you dance with me at the Assize ball?'

'I was not aware I was attending any balls. In any case, I do not know how.'

'Nonsense! I have seen you glide about the room with Louise Barsham like Noverre himself. I had never thought of you as a graceful man until that moment.'

'But my dear, I have not bought a ticket. They will be uncommon difficult to get. The entire county crams into Norwich for Assize week.'

'I will buy one for you. There will be no trouble about it. Mrs M'Cool knows a surprising number of people, would ask Croesus himself for the loan of a bar of gold if she had need of one; a ticket to a provincial ball will be nothing.'

He picked up her hand and kissed it, all professional disinterest vanished. 'I cannot refuse then. But now . . . I shall go in again and talk to young Tom for a while. Is there any reason he cannot be helped down to sit in the parlour? He could have shared our tea.'

'Dr Loder said . . .'

'Bah!' said the Doctor.

'What a surprise!' said Tom, heaving himself on to an elbow, 'I thought you had gone home.'

'Do you call that shrunken, diminished Greek temple home? I had hoped you were up. It would do no harm to sit in the parlour with the leg on a gout stool.'

Tom's face grew dark. 'So I told Ann but she would not have it. Loder says I must stay abed another week at least. What can I do? They are cutting the barley tomorrow in the Ten Acre and I had sworn I would . . . Oh well. How do you think Ann is? How do you find her?'

'Well. She is looking very fine, colour in her cheeks again and her old quick walk returned.'

119

'But what about her head? Did you look at her head?'

'I did, though I can in no way justify such behaviour. I have trespassed on Loder's province. But the flesh wound is nothing, is healed to perfection: it was the blow did the damage.'

Tom sank back among his pillows with some ill-considered remarks on uncontrollable horses and head-strong women. He was not taking his captivity well, the Doctor could see. A genuine concern for Ann was overlaid by a constant irritation at lying idle while the great work of harvest was all to do, two harvest gangs to supervise this year and one of the waggons out of action already with a splintered axle.

'Neech has offered help,' he said wearily, his hand fretting at the bedcover. 'Ann sent to say that we could manage for the time being. He is a steady old-fashioned man, always very kind, but . . .' Another long pause. He bit his lip and looked towards the window above which the house martins came and went, came and went, feeding their brood, their wings sometimes brushing the panes. 'Well, I have thought once or twice he would not be so eager to oversee our reapers if he did not believe it would put him well with Ann. Perhaps . . . Perhaps he already sees himself as master of Thorn.'

'Tomorrow,' declared the Doctor, 'you must get up come what may. Anything is better than lying here imagining such nonsense. Is there any question of marriage? Does she care for him?'

He had everything to recommend him, said Tom, he was quite young, was wealthy, popular with his tenants and his men, and not so dull he would not take his wife to Norwich now and then or entertain at home as frequently as she wished. He thought . . . He had thought once or twice that Ann would have liked children, she was fond of children, took them on her knee always in the cottages and spent a great deal of time with that Cassandra. There might come a time in a woman's life when she felt such a need particularly strongly, felt it above and beyond all the rest; and along with a kindly, well-ordered house, affection, comfort, George Neech might be supposed to offer the hope of a family, a family before it was too late.

'It is far from too late,' said the Doctor at this point as his heart constricted more painfully than ever, 'I have known ladies bring forth paragons of babies at a very advanced age, and Ann is not thirty yet, not thirty for a year or two. I reject your theory utterly. She will not marry Neech simply because he is suitable and can give her a child. Why, any man might do that.'

The Doctor pulled out his pipe and filled it and lit it, puffing smoke among the bed hangings. He began to speak of India, quietly and without much conviction, as if it had become a little unreal to him these last weeks and that, the start of his journey having been so long delayed, all his hopes and desires had grown shadowy too. Lately he had come to feel dispossessed. He did not belong anywhere. Though if he had been asked on the far side of the world where was his home he would have said without a second's hesitation 'Norfolk', here in Norfolk itself he was nothing more than a bird of passage, sitting at friends' tables, operating in his old Hospital, meeting former patients all with a strange sense of remove, of no longer belonging. He was needed in Bombay, there was no doubt of it, but then there was a case for his being needed in Norwich. And if the French did come . . .

'You do not believe they will,' said Tom.

'No, I do not. But that is a feeling in my bones, I cannot make out a rational argument.'

Tom pleated his sheets and unpleated them. 'I do wish you would stay.'

A small face looked round the door. 'I am to go home,' said Cassandra, 'I came up to say goodbye.'

She advanced to the bed and sneezed in the smoke. Tom took both her hands in one of his and said: 'I am to

121

get up tomorrow. With luck I shall get to the Ranelagh breakfast on crutches.'

'Will you? Will you?' and her face beamed. She ran round to the Doctor. 'You must come too.'

'Not I.'

'Why not? There is going to be music as well as things to eat. You have not forgotten the bear,' in a lower voice, 'I shall tell Aunt Clodie about the bear so we can rescue him.'

'But what have you done with the piglet?'

'He chewed his string and ran away this morning. Driscoll caught him in the stables and he says he must go in the sty and be fattened. I think Mama has said I should not play with him any longer.'

The Doctor said gently: 'He was a very disobliging pig.'

'I could get you another,' said Tom cheerfully.

'Mama would make them put it in the sty, but . . .' and she looked with hopeful eyes at the Doctor behind his smoke screen. 'But I would love a mongoose.'

A thin rain had fallen in the night, enough to damp the hot streets but not enough to cool the air. The Doctor paid a perfunctory visit to the Hospital because visiting the Hospital was second nature after so many years and he was always sure of a welcome. Menzies was there and told him bluntly he looked wan and costive, a shadow of his former self, he would never stand the rigours of the voyage and the climate of Bombay.

'You won't forget the Benefit Sermon now, Alex? In the cathedral as ever, and a concert as well of course. And there's the dinner afterwards at the King's Head.'

'But the dinner is seven and six a ticket!' protested the Doctor, who could be mean over certain trifles: he did not much care for official dinners.

'Man, 'tis for the Hospital. We need every penny we can get. If everybody was as mean as you that would be an end of free treatment.'

122

The Doctor hurried away and into the city, leaving his chestnut pony at the Grey Cock and making his way to his bank. His bank was pleased to see him, an unusual state of affairs. He had rarely owned any great amount of money and his meagre savings frequently dwindled to nothing, but a year of living in Suffolk almost entirely at Jary Savage's expense and no kind of extravagances, no new surgical instruments, no great number of medical pamphlets, no pounds of tea, Parma hams, Turkish tobacco, had left a healthy sum in hand. This healthy sum was rapidly depleted by the purchase of a ticket for the Benefit dinner – it seemed exceedingly tightfisted to avoid it now – half a dozen new shirts, smallclothes, silk stockings and nightcaps. He passed a sign advertising haircuts in the latest styles, hesitated and turned back. Half an hour later he reappeared a new man, tamed and trimmed, close-shaved.

'Mrs Badcock dear, I will have my chop at two,' he said at the Cock, depositing his many parcels.

'Two on the stroke,' replied the landlady, well used to his unreliability in spite of the fact that his fine French watch kept perfect time and there were a dozen bells in Norwich to ring out the hour notwithstanding. 'And I have a piece of excellent veal, and to follow all a gooseberry pie.' She was a large, rather slatternly woman but she was a capable cook and had looked after the Doctor since she was a slender young thing, a pink and white country girl, very newly married. Now she watched with a fond smile as he ran out again, remarked under her breath that these medical men were all of them wholly strange though she would never say a word against Dr French, he had always paid his bills and treated her like a duchess, and retired to her kitchen to see to his meal.

The Doctor was hurrying along with an anxious expression, intent on his finest Souchong, when by the Rampant Horse he was held up while two screeching

123

women, a small boy and a jibbing pony caused a temporary jam. He looked up in time to see a face he knew on the far side of the street, a face and figure he knew well. It was Julia Hawkworth and with a gentleman, a tall black-haired high-cheeked foreign-looking man. He walked close beside her, touching her elbow as he spoke to emphasize a point, and she looked up and laughed as if he had been the dearest creature in the world.

'Now that is no banker,' said the Doctor to himself. He watched until she was out of sight and disappointment burned through him: was she shamelessly parading her lover through the streets? At a pinch, he thought, it might have been her attorney, he had a disagreeable, sharp-witted air.

'God damn these crowds! Alex!' and he looked up, bemused, to find Barsham's carriage drawing with difficulty towards the side. 'Alex, good day. Step up. Step up to the window. Have you ever seen such traffic and in a cursed narrow thoroughfare.'

The Doctor stood obediently while his friend sorted a pile of papers beside him on the seat. Such high colour, such perspiration . . . 'Your digestion is disturbed,' he remarked as if he had been called over for a consultation. 'You should eat less meat and try to deny yourself cucumber. I know it is one of your delights but I must tell you cucumber is . . .'

'If 'twas only cucumber, good Lord, Alex, I believe I could be a happy man. No, far worse – all these,' and he pointed to his papers. 'I am like some Whitehall clerk, forever running up and down for orders, lists – oh, quite five dozen lists since yesterday morning - and consultations, though everything is decided before we meet to consult as far as I can see. But what I wanted to say was this: every man between fifteen and sixty must now turn out with the Volunteers. Or find a substitute. Unless you leave for India at this minute, unless you pack and are

124

away within a very few days, I must compel you to one or the other.'

The Doctor said something very low, mostly drowned by the hubbub in the street, in which the words 'officious magistrates' and 'needless panic' rose clear to sting Barsham's ears. 'There is no point in growling away like an old dog,' he said snappishly, 'the government . . .'

'Government! Ha!' cried the Doctor, stepping back into the crowd which instantly swallowed him entire. But even at the Grey Cock they read the newspaper, and his chops and his excellent veal came in on a blast of patriotic fervour, the pot-boy declaring: 'We 'on't half warm their backsides do they land up the coast,' and going on for some time in condemnation of Bonaparte, his flat-bottomed boats and his unseemly tantrums up and down Europe. Mrs Badcock brought in the gooseberry pie herself and asked if he had heard that there were to be a dozen big guns at the castle, there were soldiers from the barracks running up and down the castle mound giving advice and, she hoped, all their spare cannon balls, while others had been told to guard every gate into the city.

'How they must regret having the gates demolished, else they could have put a gun on every tower,' was the sardonic comment from the table. 'Do not fret yourself, Mrs B. The French will never come.'

'Do you not think so, sir? Every knife in the house is sharpened a-purpose and Mr Badcock sleeps with his pistol under the pillow.'

The Doctor looked up from his pie. 'My dear woman, tell him to desist. Surely he is not so foolish as to put a *loaded* – loaded! – pistol within an inch of his brain? Tell me it is not loaded, Mrs Badcock.'

She blushed to say it but she had seen him prime it with her own eyes and though she had remonstrated he had overruled her, calling her a great many names no husband should use to a woman who had shared his bed these fifteen years and borne him seven children. Come to that, she might sleep in the guest chamber tonight, in case of accidents.

'Do so,' said the Doctor, 'leave Mr Badcock to blow himself up without let or hindrance. But now, my dear, I must send out for the pony. I must take my shopping home.'

Home to the diminished Greek temple and at a good pace, such a good pace that the pony dripped in the heat and his reins were white with lather. Only at the lower reaches of the Gorse did the Doctor ease the pace, asking the animal's pardon, so that they trotted gently between the bushes and over the first wide expanse of grass. Whether his improving mood was because this ancient, uncultivated land, loud with larks and plovers and the distant bleating of the half wild sheep, soothed him by some natural process, or whether because his heart beat faster at the thought of finding – if his luck had turned – twenty bustards in a row all come out to sun themselves, there was no telling. Whatever it was he felt his bad humour melt away and he wore the nearest he could come to a cheerful expression as he rode down the long drive to Blackow. The sight of the house did not fill him with the usual anguish; indeed, it might have been another house entirely. He looked benignly at it and at its gardens and, taking it all in in one long sweeping glance, at the lake that had cost old Sir Harry so dear in time and money and barrowloads of stinking silt. The lake was blue, had been blue these many weeks because no stretch of water, however turgid, could fail to reflect such burningly blue skies. Beside it Clodie M'Cool was walking under a green sunshade and looking into a small book.

'You are the picture of delight,' she said, stopping for a brief moment and looking him over. 'Have you had good news, Doctor?'

'Oh, it was my jog across the Gorse restored me. I hope I do not interrupt?'

'Interrupt? There is nothing to interrupt.' She was in white muslin, appropriate for once to the current fashion and the current year, but not perhaps to her age, and spoiled somewhat by being gathered in by a wide sash and uplifted at the back by a distinct false bottom. 'What is three hundred and twenty-two added to four hundred and nine?'

'Seven hundred and thirty-one,' he told her after a moment's reflection.

'Yes,' and she consulted her little book, 'I thought so.' And after a while, shutting it and thrusting it under her arm: 'The figures are as damnable as usual, add them up how I will. Dido must make our fortunes or we shall be off to join the tinkers. But now, come and see the horses with me, I feel I need an arm to lean on.'

Anyone less in need of an arm to lean on could not have been found between Norwich and Bungay but the Doctor willingly offered his and walked her along to the yard. There she seated herself on a mounting block while Rigby led out a bay mare and foal, a very young, skittish, hide-and-seekish foal, dodging about its mother's legs and making a great to-do about the cobbles. Clodie tilted her sunshade and grinned.

'By True Briton by Brigand by Badsticks,' she said promptly. 'I need not ask if you know anything about horse breeding.'

'I know nothing. The foal will be grey though, by the looks of him.'

'Badsticks was a grey, they tell me, stood in Bungay many a long year ago. Tell me, did my niece mention a house in Norwich?'

'She spoke of moving there when her affairs were settled.'

'Did she so. Ah well. How discreet you are, Doctor. I am sure she said a great deal more.'

The mare was led away. A chestnut stallion took her place, a small self-important beast given to shrieking.

Clodie watched him a moment and then shrugged. 'He is very worried by his stones, always prancing here and there, showing away. But he was so cheap I wonder if he has not done his duty; in spite of all they said I still wonder, and some of the youngsters they paraded for my benefit may not have been his at all. Have you not met men like that, Doctor, all noise and no performance?'

The Doctor cleared his throat, hesitating, then said weakly: 'Is he any use to you then?'

'Oh, sensible treatment and better food might work wonders. If not he must resign himself to becoming a gelding like his brothers. Put him away, Rigby, he will deafen us. But there, he is a splendid creature really and amazing well bred.'

A small shape flitted into view. Cassandra ran up, her face scarlet. 'I have run all round the lake twice,' and she bent a little, nursing the stitch in her side. 'Did Aunt Clodie tell you, Doctor – there are to be fireworks at the breakfast.'

Clodie looked down her nose. 'Fireworks, pooh!' she said, 'you will have fireworks enough if the French get across the Channel.' She rose, a little stiffly, and indeed she caught the Doctor's eye and gave a grin. 'I was pitched into a gorse bush yesterday and my old bones are sore.'

'It was the horse that threw Ann off,' Cassandra informed him guilelessly.

'Sure there's no harm in him, he's a clumsy brute, no more. Now come into the garden a moment, Doctor, and admire our progress.'

There was a weedy pimpled lad in the walled garden whom Clodie commanded to 'show the Doctor the figgery' and who, cautiously at first and then with growing confidence, led the way past the restored glasshouses to the warmest corner, expounding the nurture of exotic fruits as he went. As well as the figgery there seemed to be a grapery and pinery, a peachery and melon ground. All was in a state of remarkable neatness and order, everything flourishing or set to flourish next year when loving care had overcome the last vestiges of neglect. The Doctor gave the boy his sincere congratulations.

'You must look at mine now,' cried Cassandra, tugging at his coat.

Through the wooden gate and into the smaller garden where the asparagus was, and here were still rank weeds and heaps of spoil. A small patch six by six was all there was of good clean earth and Cassandra stood looking at it with understandable pride. 'There, that is mine.'

A round, rather vacant face appeared above the wall. 'If that is you, Jack Mussett, get down before I pull the ladder from under you,' said Clodie, shying up a clod of earth. 'If you had no manners before you can learn some now.'

There was a terrified squeak and the face withdrew. 'Where do you find them?' the Doctor inquired. 'All your gardening boys.'

'All? All two. From the Parish. I went to old Bringloe a few weeks back and said I needed a pair of able-bodied youngsters to dig and prune. They sleep above the stables and Rigby keeps them in order.'

They walked back to the front of the house in time to see a carriage pulling up by the steps. 'That old rogue Barsham,' said Clodie sharply, 'what a roast beef clodpole he is, to be sure. How can that clever woman stand him for more than an hour a sennight? Good day to you, sir, and a hot journey you have had, I see.'

Barsham mopped his brow. He found her rude, contrary and often incomprehensible. Several times she had flown off at him unprovoked, tilting at his politics and his duties as magistrate, his dress, the paintwork of his carriage and the health of his dogs. He was the most hospitable of men and yet he dreaded her crossing the Upgate threshold; he was also bluff and patronizing with women and where this approach would not serve was always at a loss. He was at a loss now, standing abjectly on her gravel, his hat in his hand.

'Run away?' Clodie demanded, when he had explained his business. 'Why should we run away?'

'I do not call it running away, madam. The government has given orders . . . I have to find out how many women and children in the parish would be ready to move at short notice, how many elderly bedridden . . .'

'I am not bedridden yet, thank the Lord, nor am I leaving this house without being turned out of it. How is this grand retreat to take place, tell me that? And where do we go? To Scotland? To Wales? Where else would be safe except on the top of some bleak mountain? I tell you, the first Frenchman through my gates will receive a musket ball with my curses – I have a few terrible curses in the dear Irish that will do well – and musket balls we have in plenty and willing hands to fire 'em.'

'Madam . . . Madam, I admire you for it. I do indeed. But I have to make the returns, I have to count . . .'

'Yes, and look how hot and flustered it makes you, gadding about in this heat counting old crones. I can offer you lemonade or sherbet and there is still ice in the ice house, thank God, in spite of this wicked summer.'

He only wished to get home. He would not step inside her house for anything, not if she thought him an ill-mannered fool for it. He mumbled that he would not stop for refreshment, time was passing, and he shuffled uneasily by his carriage door, but she said: 'Cassie, run in and fetch a glass of iced lemon for Lord Barsham,' so that he had to stand and suffer, pulling irritably at his neckcloth. There was the parish constable, the overseers, any number of minions to count heads and compile the returns; he had simply thought, with his natural generosity, that it would be more congenial and neighbourly to visit her himself. 'I have been in Norwich all morning,' he said, 'and a vast pile of business still to do before this evening. To think that in the old days I rarely went to town above six times a year and now it is in and out, in and out . . . Alex, you will not forget what I said to you? You will not forget the Volunteers?'

'The Doctor to be a Volunteer?' began Clodie, but then her eye was caught by the pair of grey carriage horses raking holes in her gravel and she moved across to speak to the man at their heads.

'God save us,' murmured Barsham, 'she is going to interrogate Dyball. Can you do nothing? She is a meddlesome old witch. And why does she look so odd? Damned odd.'

'I believe the sash she has tied round her middle is part of a bed hanging. The overall effect is strangely romantic, even Eastern.'

'Good God, she is telling him the amount of oats they are to have to the last ounce. He will throw a fit if she keeps on in that vein. He has been groom and coachman thirty years at Upgate. Alex . . .'

'Lady Gerard is in the drive,' said Cassandra, trotting up with the lemonade.

They craned to see, and sure enough she was, a small figure on the old brown mare momentarily surrounded by masses of noisy greyish shapes: the guinea fowl.

'Your first ride,' said Barsham, approving, as she came near enough, and he beamed at her: how fine she had always looked in the saddle.

'I crept out like a felon,' she replied smiling, 'in case Babs or Tom should see me. I thought I would be safer at Blackow. You do not mind?' This to Clodie, who left off tormenting Dyball to give the mare a critical stare and to say very low: 'Her feet are not a pair,' before remarking: 'You look a decent pink at last. Why should I mind? If I were you I would snap my fingers at them all at Thorn, what should you care what they think?'

She had not cared once, galloping about the Gorse on Harry's horses, wrestling with the unforgiving land in some of the worst years for farming in living memory, coping with local prejudice, flagrant gossip, censure, scandal. She had taken in Tom Forsie and made a gentleman of him against all advice and expectation; she had married Harry Gerard and kept her inheritance and, apparently, her sanity. Now she was a wealthy, desirable widow must she be reduced to jogging secretly round Blackow park for fear of being seen? She sat very straight in the saddle but she was biting her bottom lip in the way she did when not quite at ease. It was perhaps her only nervous habit. The Doctor saw it, knew all her doubts and frustrations by it, and looked up lovingly.

She saw a face she knew full of affection and amused sympathy, but it was an out-of-the-ordinary affection and a very intimate sympathy. Then the mare moved, and by the time she was quiet again the Doctor had looked away, everyone was talking at once, about the harvest, the Assize breakfast, the ball, the guinea fowl. I was mistaken, she thought; in any other man I might have said . . . No, no, not in him. She cast about for something to say and found only: 'Will you not come with us to the breakfast?'

'Go voluntarily to a great crush like that?' he asked, 'an ill-prepared greasy meal and some low-class fiddle-scraping?'

'How unkind you are. We are all determined to enjoy ourselves; Tom is defying Dr Loder at every turn, he is so determined to be there, and Cassandra has been looking forward to it for days.'

'Forgive me, but I have my own crush to attend in the cathedral: a sermon for the benefit of the Hospital, and some Handel, I believe. Then I dine at the King's Head with the Governors and a rowdy concourse of medical brethren and benefactors.'

'Let us hope there is no low-class fiddle-scraping in the cathedral then,' with a challenging look.

He took a step back and Barsham caught his arm.

'Alex, have a ride to the gate. Get in, get in. Mrs M'Cool, your servant. I have seldom tasted such lemonade.' ('And that was true, it had a fishy taste, by God,' he said afterwards in the confines of the carriage.) 'Ann, my dear, will you ride by the coach as far as the crossroads?'

She rode one side while Cassandra ran on the other, her skirt lifted up, her whole face shining with the bursting energy of the young.

'What a boyish little thing,' exclaimed Barsham, turning to see her. 'Why, she has no shoes on. Where is that mother of hers I would like to know?'

His loud voice carried in both directions through the open windows and while Ann said 'Hush!' Cassandra cried out cheerfully: 'Mama has taken a house in Norwich and is going to live in it, but I am staying here.'

'Bless me!' said Barsham.

# 7

The clock ticked. Ann had twice been upstairs to hold a candle over Cassandra, strangely moved to find she was asleep after all, a small, curled-up body in the vast feather bed. All her new clothes for the breakfast were laid out ready along with a stuffed squirrel the Doctor had given her and sixpence from Miss Pennyquick. Ann smiled, tweaked the sheet straight and crept out, dragging old Spring off the threshold and down the stairs.

It was a quarter past ten. 'Why are you not in bed?' asked Tom, stifling a huge yawn and reaching for his crutches. 'How are we to be up for this early start if we are not abed till midnight?'

'I have a letter to write.'

'To Neech?' It came out before he could stop himself and it sounded harsh: Neech had been much on his mind lately, he had watched him patrolling the barley fields on his dark, long-tailed horse, watched and watched from his window and yesterday from the garden, and had even spoken to him when he had ridden up – working clothes, dusty boots, old hat, but clean linen and a new-shaved chin – had had immense shameful delight in informing him that Anne was out, was out walking.

'Why should I write to Mr Neech? I shall see him at the breakfast. In fact, he may call here on his way and ride with us.'

'I hope not,' under his breath. 'He is always here. The whole parish is asking when the wedding will be. I suppose he has not asked you yet, that is all.'

She blushed and bent over her little desk. 'I wish you would not mention it again. And if you must know, I am writing to Mr Bridger about the farm. There is some business I need to discuss at – ' and she dipped the quill and scratched on quickly – 'at his earliest convenience. There, now he will come running, poor little man, summoned so boldly.'

'But why an attorney?' Tom turned and searched her face. 'You are not thinking of raising a mortgage on Thorn simply because we have had no word from the *Sable Island*? No, surely . . .'

'No. I am not so mad as to put us back in debt only the year after we finally won clear. Though it would be as well to think seriously on what we shall do if *Sable Island* is captured or sunk.'

'Captured or sunk! Impossible!' with all the strong disbelief of a cheerful nature. 'But why Bridger?'

'I will discuss it with you,' she said firmly, 'when I have spoken to Mr Bridger. I have . . . I have been thinking something over, but it is to be a surprise. You must not ask me anything more. Please, Tom. Now, do you want some help upstairs?'

The wind was stirring the curtains at the still open window, and it stirred tendrils of dark hair against her brow. He smiled sheepishly, holding out one large, blunt-fingered hand. 'Not money to build a house on my fifty acres? You must not do it, Ann.'

'No, not that.'

She stood a moment with her hand in his. 'I am sorry I spoke so gruffly about Neech,' he said, 'but it rankles so seeing him striding about the fields as if . . .' He stopped, flushing a bright pink, aware he was about to fling himself into the morass again. 'Ann, you did tell him we could manage alone? I only ask because . . .' Another pause. Tact, she knew, had never been his strong point.

'Because poor Jim Knight came to you to complain that Mr Neech was impatient with the harvest gang, telling them they rested too long and that the barley should be finished by now, the wheat was waiting.'

'How do you know? I told Babs not to mention it after Jim had left.'

'It was not Babs. Jim came to me late yesterday and said that Mr Neech was talking about reorganizing the gang,' and at this point her eyes met Tom's furious blue ones: it was an unheard-of, intolerable interference to challenge the composition of a gang. 'He begged me to intervene, he thought some of the men might resent it.'

'Resent it! We shall be left with half the corn standing and no reapers! Ann . . .'

'So I said there was no question of Mr Neech altering the status quo, he had no authority. I thought I might have a private word with him tomorrow, just a brief word,' and here Tom felt her fingers contract, 'while we are all being pleasant with one another. But you – ' and she gazed down at him fondly with a sudden mischievous smile, 'you must restrain yourself from bursting out and spoiling the effect. He really thinks he is doing us a good turn, poor man, has no idea how offensive the men find it.'

'But you did ask him . . . You did tell him we could manage without his help?' he repeated.

'I did. Oh Tom, I did. It is just that he has become,' and here she sank down and put her head on his arm, 'possessive. I am not sure that is the right word, perhaps it is too strong, yet he has grown so familiar lately – oh, always polite, always the gentleman, but not so restrained as he used to be and always telling me what would be best for the farm or for my head or for your leg until I could cry out. I thought that tomorrow I would try to make it clear I have no wish to . . . no desire to take it further, to . . .'

'Marry him. Thank God. I thought for a moment . . . At least, I have thought on and off these last weeks that it was inevitable, you have done nothing to discourage him.'

'I have certainly done nothing to encourage him

136

either. Now, are you going to try the stairs or stay here all night?'

In her room she opened the casement and leaned out. The breeze was stronger, yes, but it was as hot and dry as in the day. Cassandra had turned on her back and flung off the covers, one leg stuck out over the side of the bed. Mrs Hawkworth has a child and does not care for her, thought Ann, and I have none and would care for one very much. She moved the leg gently back into place, pulled down the rumpled night-shift and then retired herself, listening to Cassandra's quiet breathing. Spring listened too, in his place by the door, but he heard the flight of the owls and the snuffling of the hedgepigs on the lawn and once the far far distant howl of one of Clodie M'Cool's hounds, and he was the first to rise and stretch himself as the dawn broke, thumping his old tail as he caught the low murmurings of the reapers arriving and, for the first time in many days, the stronger murmur that was Tom's voice as he greeted them.

The music lifted him, enfolded him; the vast building reverberated with Handel. The Doctor dropped his head into his hands and let himself be carried away. Later, opening his eyes during a silence all the more profound because of the preceding sound and the great press of people, he saw the sunlight chequering the massive pillars and up, up to where the stone ribs of the roof sprang out, a prayer themselves. Music often moved him, architecture seldom, but this place had drawn him from a very young man: this space, this strength, this incredible vitality in stone.

The sunlight outside, however, hot and dusty, was a shock.

'A creditable sermon,' said Menzies, who met him in the porch, 'and a goodly congregation. You are coming to the dinner, Alex? You are not absconding?'

They walked along together in amiable conversation;

137

at least, the Doctor hummed Handel and Menzies kept up a flow of comment and inconsequential chit-chat, bowing and nodding to acquaintances every few yards. Through the Close and into Tombland. 'Such fine weather and still the farmers grumble,' said Menzies as they turned up towards London Lane in step. He spoke to air, for the Doctor had lingered to look in at the French confectioner, a shop he had long patronized for Gorgona anchovies and Westphalia ham. 'Come, come,' and Menzies darted back for him, prising him from the doorway, 'we shall be late.'

The official dinner was rowdy and unbearably hot. The Doctor was separated from Menzies by a loud clutch of fellow medical men: Cooper, Fulcher, Burrows, Fredericks; and as he ate, conversing very little, he had the opportunity to study his friend with more than usual keenness, a hard disinterested keenness he thought it was, as if he were looking at a stranger and not a man he had known fifteen years. It was partly the presence of the young man on Menzies' left that drew his eye, for he was a very beautiful young man, perhaps the most beautiful young man the Doctor had ever seen in Norwich, and he well knew Menzies' preferences. The young man was blissfully unaware of being favoured, unaware even of his own beauty, and talked away with total good humour, stabbing his knife in the air and laughing. Menzies watched him with a starved, desperate look that could not fail to pass unnoticed. The Doctor's right-hand neighbour, lowering his fork, said in a hushed voice: 'The young fool, always going on about these electrical experiments of his. 'Tis unbecoming, prating on and on, drawing attention to himself.' After a while as the food came and went, remove after remove it seemed, and the wine flowed, conversation grew more of a serious business, a physical effort, and the whole tone of the dinner went down a key, the pudding reducing them to near stupefaction. Through it all the young man kept up an unwearying description of his apparent discoveries, far far in advance of Galvanic theory, and only slightly muted by over-indulgence; and through it all Menzies inclined towards him, smiling, agreeing and hungering. How he does expose himself, the Doctor thought sadly, expose himself to ridicule more than the other – there are few men in his immediate vicinity do not know his proclivities and turn the fabled blind eye. It is sad to see a grown man so struck, like a green girl, almost gaping. Oh well, there is nothing I can do, six places down, and no doubt he has behaved thus before.

'Galvani, Galvani,' muttered his right-hand neighbour at this moment, 'nothing but Galvani. If his discoveries are so much more important than those of his everlasting Galvani why does he not publish them, eh? What it is to be young and foolish,' and then, sitting back and undoing several buttons, his face a dangerous purple, he asked: 'Are you returning to the Army, sir?'

'They will not have me. I am bound for Bombay. I have been promised employment by the Company if I present myself in Bombay.'

'Surely the Army will reconsider now we are at war again?'

'I shall not ask them.'

'Nevertheless, you may be recalled. They have raised this great body of volunteers without the least idea what to do with them. For what has their stirring of patriotic fervour called forth? Not an army, a disciplined regular army, but an untrained rabble lorded over by every petty tyrant the country can produce. Have you seen the fools swaggering about the Walk in their frogged jackets pretending to be cavalry officers? I hear old Page the military tailor has made his fortune and intends to retire to be a country gentleman. But Bombay. Bombay? We shall be needing every good surgeon here before the year is out. If this invasion happens . . .'

'If. If. Always if.'

139

'So you are set on India. Well, it would not be my choice, but then I have domestic responsibilities, five children now, a sixth on the way, not to speak of having to give house room to my wife's sister and an elderly uncle. There is no saying, were I a bachelor again, I would not up and run to Bombay and a Company salary.'

And: 'I saw you glowering away down the table. Was yon fellow troublesome?' asked Menzies as they left the inn.

At the elegant house off St Giles belonging to a cousin of Louise Barsham where he called to inquire the success of the breakfast party, he found Cassandra in a state of wild excitement, so wild and so continuous it seemed four walls could never contain it, she would be altogether safer in the garden. Ann looked tired, the result, she told him, of having to sit through an hour of dreadful squawking and howling – by which she meant, the Doctor assumed, the Ranelagh concert complete with renowned opera singer.

'What can you expect for one and sixpence?' he demanded. 'I did venture to suggest a public breakfast was no place for a lady. Mr Neech, your servant, sir,' as George Neech came in, tall, grave, pleasant.

'There were hundreds there,' said Neech. 'We are about to revive ourselves with strong coffee. Will you take a cup, Doctor?'

'Gladly. And Mrs M'Cool? Did she enjoy herself?'

'She has gone to lie down,' said Ann. 'She told me that she had not felt her age until today. Since Mrs Carey has so kindly allowed us all the use of her house for tonight so that we may stay for the ball she declared she would not budge from her bed until the dressing hour.'

Cassandra burst in, Mrs Carey behind with Tom. She had loved everything, everything, she cried, especially the small spotted dog with a large red bow which might or might not have belonged to the famous opera singer but certainly ran about in an amusing way. She could not remember what they had eaten, but it had been lovely; she could not remember what anyone had said but they had all been happy and friendly; and Aunt Clodie had looked magnificent.

'Indeed she did,' said Mrs Carey, smiling fondly at the Doctor as he bid her good day and asked politely after her health. 'Thank God we are all well, bless you. Oh, it is an age since you were here. We miss you extremely, you know, we speak of you often. No, Cassandra, I think it would be better for you to go outside, you cannot dance about like that where there are coffee cups.'

'She can come and sit with me,' said Tom, carefully lowering himself into a chair and patting his good knee. 'You will not fidget, will you, Cassie? Or you will hurt my poor leg.'

'Mrs M'Cool was a picture,' put in Mrs Carey, sitting next to Ann and smiling round at the gentlemen.

'She caused a sensation,' remarked Neech. 'She sat at the very front and told off this poor suffering cellist who was always somehow half a beat behind. He shrank with horror and bowed away feverishly more and more out of time until his nearest neighbour actually took away his bow.'

The coffee pot went round again. Mrs Carey apologized for the absence of Mr Carey who was away on official business to do with the rituals of Assize week, something to do with the sheriffs, the judges, the mayor. 'I will take you to see the Lord Mayor in his coach this afternoon,' she told Cassandra, who had subsided inelegantly but finally silent on Tom's knee. 'Doctor – oh, how strange it is to see you without a wig! – Louise says you are to leave for India before the summer is over. India again, all that heat, disease and dreadful battle, I suppose, though I can never understand who is fighting whom or why. Now Bonaparte is another matter: why, he is only just across the sea – such narrow seas – waiting to launch himself upon us. But India. It is very mysterious why anyone should care to fight in India.'

The Doctor smiled and suffered her to run down naturally, reminded of how Louise had once, long ago, referred to her cousin as 'that feather-headed puss, no style, no wit'. But Mrs Carey loved her dull husband dearly, adored her children and was never known to be disagreeable. So the Doctor smiled and when she had finished, run out of breath rather than words, he said: 'If you will excuse me, my dear, I must see to this young man's leg,' and moved his chair to Tom's side, saying quietly: 'You have overdone it. So few weeks mending and you hammer it over Norwich without a thought. I hope you do not mean to attend the ball?'

'Of course I do. I must for Ann's sake.'

'Can she not manage without you? Is she in need of a chaperon at her age, a widow too. She will have Mrs M'Cool one step behind, dear boy.'

'And Mr Neech,' said Tom in a low rumble and with a meaning look.

The Doctor laughed, drawing attention to them, so was forced to bring out some story of his attending an auction, a prize cargo up for sale at Yarmouth.

'Medical instruments?' asked Mrs Carey.

'No, not at all. Madder, I believe, damask tablecloths and nutmegs, and one hundred and seventy-three elephants' teeth.'

Ann leaned forward. 'Teeth?'

'I have never yet possessed an elephant's tooth. I do not see what is so very humorous.'

'I should be careful,' struck in Neech, 'you may find that buying the one means buying them all, and one hundred and seventy-three seems an embarrassment of teeth for one man. Are they very large?'

'Oh indeed, the teeth of . . .' and the Doctor began a wandering commentary, an encyclopedic account of

142

elephant dentition: growth, function, value. As she listened Ann watched his face, only animated when speaking of subjects close to his heart and now hardly moved – and yet she knew he cared a great deal for elephants, had once talked of them lovingly to her. Very soon, she thought, I will hear his voice for the last time.

He stopped speaking suddenly, finding her eye fixed on him with a strange unhappy intensity as if she had just become aware of something that displeased her. 'But I am boring you,' he finished lamely, standing up, 'and I must leave you now, I must run back to the Cock to see if they have baited my pony and taken delivery of my stockings and my coat.'

Neech rose and shook his hand, assuring him they must meet again at the Assembly; Tom grinned over the head of the sleeping Cassandra; Ann looked up and said: 'You have not forgotten your promise?'

'A promise!' cried Mrs Carey, showing him to the door herself in her kindly way. 'How romantic!' And then, almost in a whisper and with a guilty look back at the parlour door: 'What a pleasant couple they would make, I mean, of course, was they to . . . you know, come to an understanding. He is just right for her, such a steady sober gentleman – not at all like you know who – and so deeply interested in his land, just what she approves of, and money too – his mother was an heiress from somewhere in the West country, a charming woman, exceedingly well bred. Oh how I wish it may come off!'

'Madam, I must run. My stockings . . . My coat . . .'

'Did you leave them behind? How you were used to forget things in the old days. You left a whole set of those surgeon's knives here once, dreadful wicked things, quite as sharp as razors, and we had to send a servant to the Hospital with them. And there was I thinking you had changed such a great deal – but not at all, not at all.'

It is the pity of the world, thought the Doctor,

stepping out into the street, that most men change so very little, come what may.

'Here is your parcel, sir, at last,' and the door opened to admit it, carried by a short meagre girl, perpetually harassed.

'Thank you, Mary. Put it on the bed, child.'

In the parcel were his coat, a newly pressed shirt and a pair of his best silk stockings. He had no sooner laid out all these articles on the counterpane and loosened his neckcloth, calculating how long it would take to make himself presentable, when Mrs Badcock knocked, demanding to know if he would take anything to eat or drink, he surely could not dance on an empty stomach and *she* knew the sort of supper he might expect: creams and jellies or a sliver of chicken breast. As she spoke she seized his coat and hung it up and brushed it, remarking as she stood back to scrutinize the results that it had been folded by a fool and if that shirt had been shown an iron in the last four and twenty hours she was Nancy Dawson.

'A slice of pie would not go unappreciated,' said the Doctor when she had finished giving her opinion. 'For all I know there will only be bread and butter and tea.'

Half a rabbit pie duly appeared, and cheese, new bread; shortly after in came the boot boy to shave him, grinning broadly and tying on a fresh white apron. By this time the candles were lit, for though the Doctor's room was up under the eaves the Grey Cock was an old inn and was overshadowed by newer neighbours on every side, not a glimmer of the soft pale evening light entered. In a while the noise of revelry from the crowded taproom rose to a staggering pitch and when Mary came up to clear away her cap was off and her hair hanging down.

'Lord how they do drink,' she said. 'Why, Doctor, how fine you look.'

He squinted in the mirror, a small dark ancient mirror, given to distortion. 'I must set out, I suppose. I shall stroll gently up the hill. Where is my hat? Mary dear, where is my hat?'

'Behind you, sir. Wait till I brush it off,' and she did so with a pink forearm, blowing on it as a finishing touch.

'Tell Dixon not to let any of that drunken crowd steal my pony,' he said, and then leaned to touch her cheek, 'or steal anything of you.'

A flushed Mrs Badcock whom he met in the low entrance obligingly cleared the doorway of loungers and saw him into the street, calling after him to mind his stockings, the alley was unsavoury. He minded them, gaining the bottom of the hill in a minute and stopping to look about. Night air, cool and fresh, the moon in a clear sky; all the way up carriages one behind the other, lamps, link-boys, chairs and a continuous noise: hooves, talking, muffled shouts, cries of 'Make way there! Make way if you please!' as the chairs passed the almost stationary coaches. The Doctor, guarding his stockings with exaggerated care, made his way behind, joining in the thick crowd of pedestrians, ball-goers and oglers, climbing towards their goal. As he passed through the gates he saw a carriage he recognized draw up at the door, and as he reached the steps and took his first breath of candle-wax, musk, tight-pressed bodies, hair lotion and hungary water, Louise Barsham was handed out by a lackey in tight satin breeches and a ludicrous wig.

'Alex, is it you?' and she drew back a little, admiring him.

'Always like this,' grumbled Barsham, ducking from under the noses of the horses next in line, 'intolerable crush outside and worse inside. Look at 'em! And scarcely a woman decently dressed.'

'It is the new fashion, dear,' said Louise, taking his arm. 'But look at Alex. Have you ever seen him so? He is a new man.'

On this Barsham passed no comment until they had been received by the surging crowd within and torn asunder from the Doctor in spite of their best endeavours, washed relentlessly away towards the inner room. Then he said: 'He looks like a quaker, a plain unadorned old quaker. What do you mean "a new man"? A clean coat and a shaven chin don't make a new man. Look, there is that odd friend of his, that Menzies. To think they find it pleasant chopping up corpses together. Good Lord, who is that?'

It was Clodie M'Cool, red curls adorned by a white silk turban with two vast and sweeping feathers kept in place by a diamond brooch, a crescent of enormous stones. There was a great undercurrent of speculation as to the brooch being real or paste and an ill-natured general agreement that anyway it was vulgar to sport such eccentric headgear. Clodie knew perfectly well what was being said but as she whispered in an aside to Ann, she had been seven times tried in the fire, thank God, and did not give a Sligo pig for any of them. Ann laughed, turned round, stared, said: 'Alex!' with gratifying surprise, and held out her hand. He was a slender, puritan figure, very nearly unrecognizable. Clodie finished making a complete circle, bending her glittering head with stunning condescension to complete strangers, and saw him too. 'Doctor, my dear, how truly elegant you look. And how welcome you are. We are standing here waiting to be rescued, there is not a familiar face in the room and they are all jealous of my diamonds.'

'But where is Tom?' and he gazed about, gazed anywhere but at Ann, fragile and lovely in rose pink.

'He was afraid for his leg in such a crush so he is staying out in the hall with the other invalids and the chaperons and old dames.' Plain but spirited, he had thought her once, but now, real pink roses at her bosom and in her hair, no cap, no sign of widowhood, and a striking, eager face like a girl's . . .

'Lady Gerard, how charming you look,' and George Neech smiled on her, giving the Doctor the merest nod and a perfunctory bow to Clodie that made her eyes flash.

Louise Barsham sailed by. 'Alex. Alex, why are you alone and so . . .' Grim? 'I thought I saw Ann a moment ago.'

'You did. She has been captured by Mr Neech and borne away to the dance floor.'

'And you let it happen? Shame on you! And where is Mrs M'Cool? I have heard nothing but talk about some diamonds she is wearing since I set foot inside the door and half a dozen people have told me to my face she is a fanatic, an Irish patriot of the first order come to stir up an insurrection or shoot the King or both. I swear they are agog to see her draw a pistol in the supper room and murder the Lord Lieutenant. Oh, there she is. And a splendid bauble after all. It makes everyone else's jewels look second rate, as indeed they are, I suppose. I give her this, she has unimpeachable style. You would think to look at her she has been used to receiving royal princes every day of the week.'

'You do not fault her dress? Those plumes?'

'Oh, there is nothing to object to there. It is the first stare of fashion and entirely suitable for a great lady past her prime. The turban is only a little eccentric and she carries it off so well that it scarcely matters.'

There were only latecomers being shown in now and the young people had drifted away to the dancing. The Doctor watched for a while but the sudden sight of Ann on Neech's arm sent him back to the outer hall where the elderly and infirm, the grandmothers and aunts sat about on dainty little chairs. There he found Mrs Palmer talking at Tom in an invalid chair, his leg propped up and his red face amazingly cheerful. He was having the time of his life, he assured the Doctor, for when old Slocombe had purloined the chair and pushed him in it

147

to this particular spot he was immediately surrounded by young women and old all desperately anxious to ask after his health and commiserate over his accident. It was true he looked strikingly handsome even with his height disguised by being stretched out and one leg in splints, and in the course of five minutes four different ladies, none of whom he had met more than once before, came up to tell him what a loss he was to the dance floor. The Doctor remained at his side, talking amiably, for some time, and at last, when he felt he must return to the ballroom or look conspicuous, he caught sight of a very old friend, a retired surgeon, whom he had not seen for years. His delight at their reunion was strengthened by the shameful thought that now he could avoid the dance a little longer, and he was expounding a long-held theory on the best treatment of stumps when the old man's sudden smile, an astonished smile of extreme pleasure, made him look round.

'Doctor, forgive me, I did not mean to interrupt,' said Julia, 'I was looking for my aunt.'

She was in blue, a deep jewel-like colour that stood out among the pale muslins, the pure white of the younger women, and drew every eye in the room. She was disgracefully late, running up the steps like a girl, alone and laughing. Her face had not yet lost the glow that was the aftermath of her laughter and was extremely beautiful. Old Goring struggled to rise, giving her the sort of salutation current at the Assembly thirty years before, and she smiled, begged him to sit again, she could see he had been ill, and all as if he were not ancient and feeble and indescribably withered but quite the reverse.

'What a dear old man,' she said a moment later as the Doctor led her away in search of Clodie. 'Why is it all the most sympathetic doctors are retired? But I am not sure I would care for a ball if I were confined to a wheeled carriage.'

'It does not seem to have inhibited Tom Forsie. There

are ladies vying with each other to carry him his supper.
But old Goring is only here because his granddaughters
insisted: their father is abroad and their mother would
not come without a gentleman to escort her. He says he
will play cards shortly, will be quite content. He lives in
Bungay, came there half a century ago in connection
with the cold bath.'

'How I would like a cold bath at this very moment.
There are twice as many people here as there is room
for.' And then, looking about: 'And a great many
undistinguished dresses.'

The ballroom was much more crowded than the hall
and the colour as well as the heat was more intense,
every corner crammed with officers from the barracks or
the sons of the Norfolk gentry in their Volunteer
uniforms. The dancers looked very young, hardly more
than children, and were very energetic, perspiring up
and down the rows and in and out with much laughter
and good-natured muddle.

'Can't abide country dances,' said Clodie, meeting the
Doctor and Julia near the poor, desperate musicians,
parboiled by the heat. 'No elegance to 'em. Look at that!
Only fit for children, and children they are; half those
boys are incapable of growing whiskers and the girls out
of the nursery.'

Julia plied her fan as best she could. 'I have been
looking for you. The Doctor kindly put his shoulder to
the crowd. How can you bear it? There is no room to
breathe.'

'Looking for me?' said Clodie in some disbelief.

'How is Cassandra? Did she enjoy her breakfast?'

This seemed a natural sort of inquiry in the circumstances and showed perhaps a measure of maternal
feeling, but Clodie tossed her plumes and drew herself
up to her full height, which was considerable. 'Why
should you care? Snug in that house, quit of your
responsibilities – what would you do if *I* said I could not

keep her? Take her back with you and neglect her as you did in Paris? If you want to know how she is come out to Blackow and see for yourself.'

'How she despises me,' said Julia as Clodie vanished into the press, and putting a hand on the Doctor's arm: 'Quick, or I shall never be rid of him all evening. He is a bully and a bore.' And as he turned to see that man he had seen her with by the Rampant Horse: 'Come, Dr French. Come and dance.'

'The Doctor is dancing with Mrs Hawkworth,' said Lord Barsham to his wife, peering above several white caps and Clodie M'Cool's tremendous plumes, 'he has the luck of the devil. Why should she want to prance about with a strait-laced black-coated cove like him? If he were not my friend I would cut in and . . .'

'You shall do no such thing. But why has every one of you only eyes for her? There are a score of women here can match her in looks, surpass her even,' said Louise, casting about doubtfully for them. 'She has an over-blown beauty. It must be because she is available then, because you suspect that were you handsome enough or witty enough or clever enough she would be yours for the asking.'

Barsham did not remember her speaking like this before, but his conscience was not so clear that he could take a great deal of it. He allowed himself to be led away meekly to the fruit cup and the supper table, saying: 'You know, I believe Alex is more than a little under her spell, and I always thought it was Ann he admired. They could not be more different.'

'Perhaps that is the reason.'

The dance had ended. Julia still hung upon the Doctor's arm. They were in the supper room together – 'Oh pray, keep me company a little longer. Mr Conway will not force his attentions if you are with me' – when Ann and George Neech, Clodie and Mrs Palmer came in.

'I shall eat a little and then go,' said Julia. 'What a gathering of country louts. The Doctor is the only man I dare trust not to tread all over my feet and tear my train. Mr Neech, how very delightful to see you again. I take back what I said. *You* would not trample my toes or lose your way in the middle of a figure.'

'And I would be honoured to stand up with you for any dance you care to name,' replied Neech, a dull brick red, 'I suspect you have none free, however.'

'They are all free, sir. For I did truly intend to run away after swallowing a bite of supper.'

'Then before you do perhaps we might return to the ballroom,' and he offered her his arm.

'Very prettily done,' said Clodie, casting up and down for things to fill her plate. 'She is in a rare mood tonight. I wonder why? Doctor, what is that yellow stuff with the almonds? Boy, what is this curdle with nuts?'

The Doctor said suddenly: 'Ann, my dear, come out for some air. You look pale.'

'I knew I should not touch the punch. At least, it was the dancing and the punch together.'

There was a green garden outside hung about with a great number of lights, more than enough to reveal all to the watching chaperons. In a haze of gold and red and blue they walked up and down between the small bushes, completely silent, while giggling girls and hopeful young men came and went on either side. The music was a distant tinkling, occasionally lifted by a drawn-out scrape of the fiddles, some high tremulous notes that dashed off immediately into another jolly tune, another of what Clodie so aptly called 'hop, step and canter'.

They reached the furthest point from the building, a patch of shadow beyond the last lantern, and under the wall they stopped and looked back. The Doctor said quietly: 'Ann, will you marry me?'

The look on her face told him everything, including

151

the answer he expected: a piercing surprise, confusion, even horror. Nevertheless he put his hands over hers and stood facing her, saying: 'I mean it. I have loved you a long time. There is nothing in the world I want so much as to have you for my wife.' He felt her disbelief, her resistance as strongly as if she had tried to pull away. He added: 'I am quite sure, my dear, you do not love me. You must forgive me . . . But I could not bear to leave, after all, without letting you know my feelings.'

She stepped back and he let her go. 'You would hate it, you know – marriage,' she said softly, 'you have been a bachelor far too long.'

'We could live apart as much as you like. I am not a man to care about convention and you have Thorn, I would not ask you to leave.'

The old delightful smile, but she was looking down and even in that unsatisfactory romantic light he could see she was troubled with memories. 'Harry spent most of his time away leading his own life. Oh, not that you would run about the country with other women, or gamble, or drink to excess, but that arrangement would not suit me. Not now.'

If she had not mentioned Harry Gerard they might have parted with regrets, regrets certainly but also undiminished affection, even laughter, gentle healing laughter. But the Doctor had been understandably jealous of Gerard when alive and even more so after his death when it appeared that for all his reckless cruelty Ann still loved him. The dull cold ache of disappointment, only a very little less acute for being expected, gave way to a deep and mounting fury. 'I suppose Neech suits you now,' he said, 'and that is where I shall look for you if ever I return from India: in Neech's bed, half a dozen young Neeches in the nursery.'

She put up her hands to her hot cheeks. 'Alex . . .'

'I have never minced words with you. I never shall. Tom is convinced you will marry Neech. Well, why not?

He is so suitable. And what an ornament you would be to him, you and Thorn.'

'Tom is to have Thorn.'

'Make sure then that Neech understands that point before you marry.'

A wild look, resentment at last, her eyes full of anger. 'You mean he would not take me without Thorn? That was what you said about Harry.'

'I believe I was right about Harry. My dear girl, I would take you in your shift without a penny.'

'So might he.'

'So might he, but I doubt it.'

She turned abruptly and began to walk back towards the people, the open doors. When she reached there she was running and he saw her lift her skirts to fly up the steps, the brief pink glow of her dress in the lights.

'Alex French, upon my soul, what a to-do.' Clodie met him as he walked in. 'Ann and the talkative Mrs Carey have gone home to bed. I had promised a dance to Colonel Wodehouse, only the second I have danced this evening, and would not be done out of it, not for an attack of muleygrubs and a sham headache. They are sending the carriage back for me.'

The Doctor bowed. He scarcely saw her; he might have been dead. He said with an automatic politeness: 'If that wailing is the prelude to something slow and stately such as I danced in my youth perhaps you would do me the honour?'

She danced well, regal and tireless. Her face was lit by a deep satisfaction, a pleasure in the steps and the music, and in him, in a competent partner. They were mismatched in height, in temperament, in everything, yet as the last bars were played and their hands were joined for the finish she said: 'How well you point your toe. I would never have thought of you as a good dancer. What a shame we are thrown back upon each other, too crabbed and dry to be wanted by anyone else. Oh, how I loved dancing when I was young!' And as they passed out into the hall and the general bustle of departure: 'Of course she refused you.'

His smile went awry. 'Of course.'

'I thought it was something like that when you took her out. You know, marriage to that young wastrel has made her long for a quiet life and safety. She may get over it. She had great spirit once and perhaps she will again.'

'But would I not offer her a quiet life? I am not a tempestuous soul.'

'But you would require her to be completely independent, would make demands infrequently, would neglect her. And that is what she does not want yet; she wants security, dependence, no responsibilities. What you offer is romantic and uncomfortable. You are an uncomfortable sort of man. She could not trifle with you, could not ignore you, but half the time you would be elsewhere and half your affections would be given to your patients. But I tell you this, if I were forty years younger I would run away with you tomorrow.'

The carriage had returned. She stooped to kiss him on the cheek before she entered it, the plumes brushing his shoulder.


'A beautiful woman,' nodded Goring, being wheeled away by a plump self-satisfied creature of no more than seventeen, 'the finest female I have seen in a long time, French.'

'To whom does he refer?' asked Menzies with his usual vulgar curiosity.

'To Mrs Hawkworth, I believe.'

Menzies did not know Mrs Hawkworth but he did know the man Conway, a smooth unctuous rogue, he said, an adventurer, but who had nevertheless brought him a packet from Paris – letters from French colleagues, medical pamphlets, two books – and had apologized most charmingly for its late arrival.

'So he was in Paris,' said the Doctor.

'Apparently. Fousson used him as a postman – you remember Fousson of the Académie? – and glad I am he did, though what kind of acquaintance they had is a mystery.'

'Well, Mrs Hawkworth knows him – she too was in Paris until war broke out – and by all accounts she moved in the highest circles.'

And there she was, and on Conway's arm too, walking out into the hall. She looked grave, looked for the briefest of seconds just like Cassandra when things were not quite right for her, and gravely she looked round, scanning the faces, until her eyes met the Doctor's and she broke away from Conway and ran forward.

'Dr French, I thought you would be gone already, that you would have grown tired of waiting. Robert,' and she turned to Conway as he hurried up, 'this is Dr French from Blackow who so kindly asked to see me home.'

The Doctor inclined his head, introduced Menzies, decided he liked Conway no better close to than he had liked him at a distance, wondered momentarily why such a woman should keep up an acquaintance with such a man, and asked her if she was ready to leave.

Outside: 'You know I have no carriage. Do we need a link? My little house is down by Charing Cross.'

'A link certainly. The poor boys need employment.'

They began to walk. Dawn would break soon and the city wake but in the shadow of the old houses the link was a comforting brightness a few yards ahead.

'You have not remarked on my behaviour,' she said after a long silence. 'You would have every right to be disgusted. I dashed up like some foolish young girl. And what lies!'

'My dear, I do not mind it, though it puzzles me you should be so pursued by Mr Conway. Would it not do if you told him . . .'

'Tell him! I knew him in Paris. He followed me about there and he has come to follow me about here.'

They were descending the hill to Charing Cross. Julia called back the link-boy. 'We will not need him now,' she said, 'unless you want him to light you back to your inn?'

He thrust a hand into his pocket and pulled out some change along with the usual trophies. 'No,' he said, very low, 'no, I shall not want a light.'

The boy looked at the coins, grinned and was gone. In the soft smoky dark Julia's face was a blur but her hair attracted all the light there was: he saw the glint of gold under her silk hood. A few more yards, a right-hand turn, and here was Lydd's Row: a narrow opening, a green door at the far end, a small gracious old house with baskets and tubs and urns of flowers about it in the tiny court. Julia parted the leaves at the side of the nearest urn, drew out a large key and fitted it in the lock.

'The servants are in bed,' she said. 'They are only young girls. I could not have them waiting up till dawn.'

He stood with his hat in his hand. How the lock grated in the silence. The door swung back and she stepped in; in another minute the rasp and click of the flint and a candle bloomed in the cool dark. She turned, holding it up.

'Will you not come in?'

# 8

Though Mrs Palmer could be relied on to know most things that passed between the Gorse, Upgate, High Common and Priddy's Barns, the four outposts, so to speak, of the parish, there were a few secrets still intact, a very few. One of these was Ann's long, involved, troubled meeting with Mr Bridger who had a true lawyer's distrust of hurry, ill-considered clauses, generous terms and any sense of moral obligation rather than legal: no, he would have no truck with moral duty, come what may. That Ann emerged triumphant was due to the battle being fought almost entirely on her terms, for she wished to lease Thorn to Tom Forsie lock, stock and barrel and lease it she would, she was resolved. Not all his postulating, mental bludgeoning or shameful entreaty could shake this resolve, as eccentric and absurd a piece of female fancy as he had ever come across, and so, with the most extreme, *extreme* reluctance, he was brought to pick up his pen at last.

'I will have the document drawn up at once,' he said after another painful half hour, gazing down in horror at the notes he had made. 'You must bring the young man to sign, of course. Or would it be more convenient if I called?'

'Mr Bridger is to call tomorrow,' said Ann that evening, sitting with her feet tucked up on her sofa and eating her supper of bread and butter and milk.

'Oh?' Tom was scratching away at accounts in the corner.

'He has drawn up a lease, a very favourable lease – or so he constantly tells me – and it but needs your name to it to finish it off.'

157

'Finish it off? Can you multiply forty coombs by sixteen shillings in your head? No, on second thoughts let us call it a pound which makes forty pounds take away forty four-shillingses . . .' He sighed, bending low over the book. He was a poor hand with numbers on a page and the columns balanced only after great mental and even physical effort: the perspiration had beaded his forehead now and his quill was bowing ominously. He dwarfed her little desk, a frail lady's thing, and looked all the more awkward with his broken leg thrust out sideways and propped on the gout stool. He said: 'I wish I could put all the corn money into a safe venture and double it overnight,' and then, seeing that seven and nine would never make eighteen and scratching it out with another grunt of exasperation: 'What did you see Bridger about anyway?' and looking up at last: 'Lease? What lease?'

The long-case clock in the corner struck the hour. Old Spring stood up, shook himself and lay down again. The smell of roses and pinks drifted in through the open window.

'What lease?' he repeated, and she saw that his face had lost its colour, that those bright blue eyes were dull with sudden anxiety.

'I am giving Thorn to you, the house, the buildings, the land. I am afraid poor Mr Bridger nearly choked himself to death over the rent, he cried out against it so long and turned such a very dark red I thought I would be obliged to run out for a doctor . . . Tom, do stop scowling so. Do you not want the farm?'

He threw down the pen and heaved himself to his feet, knocking over the sand-box as he did so and scattering odd pages on the floor. At full height he was a formidable figure, filled out from the lanky boy she had first brought here, and his face too had shaped to maturity: strong nose, strong chin, an honest, patient, bullish look. The men would do anything for him, young though he still was, but they did not care to cross him. He is a true Forsie in a rage, remembered Ann, who was half a Forsie herself and knew all about such a temper.

'Want the farm?'

'Must you repeat everything? Yes, do you not want the farm? You told me once you were determined to own a thousand acres.'

'What have you done?' he cried, a loud, deep cry that brought Miss Pennyquick to pull off her nightcap and run to put her ear to a crack in her door upstairs.

She told him what she had done and all the time he stood watching her, his face the most unlikely mask of rage, his mouth harder than she had ever seen it. He did not interrupt but stood there rigid, leaning on her desk for support, the gout stool kicked away. At last when she fell silent he bent awkwardly to pick up his ruined accounts, crammed the sheets willy-nilly into the book, snapped it shut, groped behind for his crutches and made for the door. 'Tell Bridger to tear up his lease, I want none of it. Thorn is yours. Thorn will always be yours. Unless, of course, you are going to marry Neech after all. If you spoke to him at all about not interfering with the reapers you spoke to little effect: he was up here this morning riding up and down and poking his nose in. If you do not warn him off I shall.'

'Warn him off! Tom, now you are being ridiculous . . . He has not asked me to marry him.'

'And what was all that nonsense the night before last then? Running away in the middle of supper because you had a headache. I do not believe it was a headache at all. You never used to get headaches, not till you had that fall, and now they are so convenient. I thought he must have asked you . . .'

'No,' and she shook her head, looking down.

'But that is why you have done this, isn't it? You were wise enough before you married Gerard to give me my

159

fifty acres and now you think to safeguard Thorn entirely by leasing it to me before you marry Neech.'

She did not reply. The look she gave him was white and desperate. Were all her good intentions to run so far astray? There was no point in protest: he was implacable. Her only hope was that this red-hot anger would have cooled sufficiently by the morning to make him listen, if not to her, to Bridger when he came. Perhaps too when he had read the lease . . .

But Mr Bridger brought his documents to Thorn in vain and was not even required to take them from their leather bag, ushered into the small garden to find Lady Gerard seated under the apple tree with several papers in her lap and a pale, shattered look about her as if she had just received bad news. Bad news it was, though in his opinion – which he naturally did not voice, not being entirely devoid of tact – inevitable news, inevitable sooner or later, the state of the war being what it was, the French more ardent, rapacious and wily than had formerly been the case.

'Good day to you, sir, I trust you are well?' said Tom Forsie whom he met in the hall on his way out. 'And Mrs Bridger? Have you seen Lady Gerard?'

'She is in the garden, poor lady. It is a grievous loss indeed. I can tell you, Mr Forsie, since you will understand me without prejudice – it is seldom so with ladies, I fear – that I had long expected something of this kind. The sea is such a dangerous element and privateers so given to taking risks, but to blow up . . . No, sir, that was a cruel calamity.'

'The French are all bottled up in port,' said Tom, who had regained his usual composure with the arrival at breakfast of the news that *Sable Island* was no more and who was now facing the thought of all her seamen dying: her dear, cunning, elderly master, the men he had once met and talked to, happy men and tolerably rich, for the *Sable Island* had always been a lucky ship – and dying one death, one mighty and explosive death – with the patient calm which was the other side of his usually exuberant nature.

'They may be so,' said Bridger. 'At least, it is what we are told. But there are doubtless French ships at sea still plying in trade back and forth across the oceans, and may they not all carry guns in self-defence? Our Indiamen have always done so. A lucky shot, Mr Forsie, from even the smallest gun or a fire on board . . . The *Sable Island* carried a great store of ammunition, I daresay.'

Tom could not deny it, he knew nothing of ships, contrived to be seasick on the placid Yare, but however the *Sable Island* had met her end it was a terrible thing, and a terrible blow for Ann who had vowed to keep her as long as she could afford to – and what a prodigious amount of money was needed to keep even a small two-masted vessel afloat – in memory of her husband, in order to satisfy some deep inner need for excitement, in order to clear Thorn of debt and in order, of course, to contribute to the harassment of French shipping.

'Well,' said Bridger pompously, 'the farm is clear of debt, she would not have contemplated leasing it to you, sir, had it still been encumbered. And about this lease . . .'

'You may put it in a drawer,' said Tom, 'it will not be needed for some time.'

'Oh, I am so glad to hear it, so very glad. I told Lady Gerard her terms were too generous, so generous indeed that I am not averse to saying it to your face, Mr Forsie: the farm would have been yours for a song, and in a very few years perhaps the freehold yours for yet another song. I did not like it and I told Lady Gerard so. I have the honour to act for you also, sir, upon occasion and though this document – ' and he touched his leather bag – 'is unquestionably in your favour I must say that were I an honourable man – in the circumstances, Lady Gerard my only kin, mutual affection and all that – I

161

could not sign such a paper and thereafter hold up my head.'

'He told me to my face he thought I would be ungentlemanly to put my name to it,' Tom said, hauling himself across the grass to the apple tree. 'It has so upset him he goes cross-eyed when he speaks of it and blows out his cheeks like this . . .' and when Ann smiled, added: 'It cannot be helped. She has blown up. We shall never know how. But there are two independent reports of it, one from an Irish fisherman who has no cause to love us – he need not have said a word.'

'Has Bridger gone?' and she stirred, gathering her papers. 'Tom, run and fetch him in again if he is still by the door. I have just thought . . . There are all the families of the crew, the wives and children, some on Guernsey, some in Devon . . .'

'But Lady Gerard,' protested Bridger, persuaded back reluctantly, leather bag and all, 'such generosity is commendable indeed but it is my duty to remind you that the *Sable Island* had undertaken several successful voyages, that prize money had been plentiful, that it is more than likely these unknown wives and no doubt numerous offspring are already adequately provided for. I really do not think . . .'

'I see we are to be at odds again,' and she rose, smiling, as lovely and dignified as she had ever looked as Lady Gerard of Blackow Hall, dancing in the light of those several hundred candles. 'Come, Mr Bridger, don't let us quarrel. How am I to cope without you? Tom, dear, tell them in the kitchen we need a pot of coffee and some cakes. Mr Bridger and I shall be in the parlour.'

Bridger took a deep breath, met her dark smiling eyes, dropped his own modestly, swore inwardly with unusual vehemence, and followed her into the house.

They could see the blaze of candles, every downstairs window aglow, as the chaise turned in at the gate.

'What extravagance!' said Miss Pennyquick, who had known Thorn lit by tallow dips and who still sometimes shuddered at profligacy.

'Well, it is Charlotte's birthday,' said Tom, whose leg was impeding both the ladies, propped up as it was on the seat opposite. 'What can you expect?'

As the chaise pulled up – a hired chaise and four, commendably clean for its calling, though undeniably shabby – the light fell over its occupants and revealed them in remarkable finery for 'just a few friends, dinner, a little music'. Ann was in a dress of cream silk, so plain, so thin that she would have looked like a child but for the double row of pearls about her neck and the pearl ornament in her brown hair which had belonged to her mother and which had survived her marriage, double-wrapped in velvet and tissue paper and hidden away in a hollow figurine. Babs Pennyquick was in sumptuous brown, not so plain, certainly not bordering on the transparent, and her snowy and respectable cap was a model of its kind.

'Damn this leg,' said Tom, manhandling it through the door.

'Be careful. Here, take your crutches,' and Ann waited while the postillion, an elderly obliging man, had lent his shoulder and a strong arm to extricate Tom from the carriage and set him on his sound foot. The steps were another hazard but he was used to steps by now and gained the top with a flush of triumph, even offering an arm – such as he could spare – to Ann as they reached the threshold.

The 'few friends' seemed a great many, and most of them already arrived and talking cheerfully in expectation of a good meal and pleasant entertainment. Several came over at once to ask Tom how he did and to murmur how sorry they were at the loss of the *Sable Island* – such news as that invariably escaped and travelled the length of the parish in twenty-four hours or even less. And then

163

Charlotte was there, a slight figure in white, receiving congratulations and good wishes with all her usual smiling modesty, embracing Ann, saying how glad she was they could come . . .

But: 'Is the Doctor come?' asked Tom, and her face fell in an instant, he wished he had not spoken.

'Perhaps he has forgotten the day,' put in Miss Pennyquick valiantly. 'How he was used to forget what day it was,' and adding thoughtfully: 'I suppose in a battle time is of little importance.'

Less charitable observations were made in other parts of the room – had they not all suffered at one time or another by the Doctor's inability to read the hour? – but the moment before they were called in to dinner he arrived, hurrying through the door in some distress, all profuse apologies: the pony had run away with him on the Gorse, had run halfway to High Common before he could be turned round. He had frequently been run away with in the old days, a succession of perfectly decent, unexceptional horses having the mastery over him in the blink of an eye, and there was some good-natured laughter, happy bantering, the inevitable 'Do you remember when . . .' and old old hares chased up and about for a considerable length of time, long after they had sat down to eat and far into the splendid offerings, even unto the puddings and after, only with the port domestic anecdotes taking over, and serious talk of the war, commerce, Addington's old-womanish indecision. By the time the gentlemen rejoined the ladies the Doctor's foibles had been mercifully forgotten. Bonaparte and his misdeeds were on everyone's lips, and it was only Lady Barsham reminding them all quite sternly that this was, after all, a birthday party, that restored them to a shamefaced silence and then, gradually, to their former merriment.

The short concert was very fine; some accomplished players from Norwich, some excellent modern pieces.

During the last movement of all the Doctor, sitting at the back, lifted his head at last to study the woman in cream silk who sat, holding Charlotte's hand, on a small sofa to one side. Had what he had heard been the truth? Had the *Sable Island* sunk with all hands? Ann looked more alive tonight than he had seen her for weeks, all these long hot idle weeks. He saw her turn her head, catch Tom's shining blue eye and smile. That leg would never heal satisfactorily, dragged about regardless, thumped in and out of carriages . . . Did he know yet that she was giving him the farm? He should be overjoyed; this irrational, bitter jealousy of Neech was only because he could not bear the thought of Thorn in Neech's hands. Or was there more to it? Had he grown over-protective, not of the farm, but Ann? After all, how many years separated them? Not so many. Six, seven . . . You are jealous yourself, Alex French, and just as much now when all your hopes are dashed as before you spoke to her, those few short days ago when ridiculous unfounded hope still lived.

'How lovely Ann looks,' Mrs Palmer said to him as they waited to say their farewells. 'I am quite surprised to find her so full of life, so obviously enjoying herself after such mournful news. And that Tom Forsie . . . He always did have a vulgar great laugh. Are you not glad to see her so well though, Doctor?'

'I am indeed.'

'And how are you all at Blackow? How I miss Mrs Hawkworth, such a fashionable lady, an ornament to any drawing room. She has begged me to visit her in Norwich but you know how seldom I go to the city . . . I own I am curious to see her "little" house. I suppose it is the equivalent of her "poor" trinkets: rubies as large as my thumbnail, Doctor, a whole necklace of them. Upon my word, I have never seen such splendid things. How I would like them for my own!'

The hired chaise had rolled up to the steps. Tom

hopped across all smiles to wring the Doctor's hand, and there was Ann behind him; the first time he had seen her since the Assembly and he had not spoken to her either during dinner or after, separated from her by accident or design every single moment.

'I was sorry to hear about *Sable Island*. Was there nothing to be done, no one saved? Captain Saufret? That dear boy Brandt?' And at her look of distress: 'Forgive me. It is a damnable business.'

'Yes, it is, but most damnable because she blew up, because it was so very final. If she had been captured or even sunk then of course there would have been survivors, even if only a few. But we are doing what we can. Mr Bridger is posting to Exeter to try to obtain an up-to-date record of all the men who signed on for her last voyage; a great many will be Guernseymen, I think, as Saufret was.'

'You cannot support the dependants of the entire crew.'

'That is what Bridger says, growing more cross-eyed, poor man, at every moment. But I must do what I can, what little I can.'

He was not to know how little that little was, for she and Tom had not spared themselves to restore the farm and funds had sunk low, very low. She had received an anxious letter from the bank only this morning. It did not worry her though; she, like Clodie, had been seven times tried in the fire. She had been up at five to juggle the hard black figures, to come at the unpalatable truth, had breakfasted at six on black coffee and toast, still writing, and by eight sat with a pile of letters in front of her: to the agent Shaw, to Luke Brandt's family, to an attorney in Portsmouth through whom a great part of *Sable Island*'s crew remitted their wages and their prize money. At half past eight Tom had come in from his round of the harvest fields – the men had rigged him a litter of canvas and poles on which he sat somewhat like an Eastern potentate and was carried by young Crow and Jim Knight with frequent pauses for breath – and had found her leaning back and looking out of the window at the long sweep of Warren Hill where the large red waggon was slowly climbing for the first of the barley sheaves. He had expected her to be pale and tired, instead she was pink and full of energy, saying as he entered: 'I have quite worn out two pens this morning. How are the reapers?'

'They have begun on the last field. I have never known a harvest so fine.'

'You had better rouse Mrs McGinley then: tell her her pies will soon be needed for the harvest supper. There, those are for the post. Thank Heaven they are finished.'

'If there is anything I can do,' said the Doctor, 'do not hesitate to ask. I shall most likely have to post to London next week – there may be some errand I can run for you there.' And in a lower tone, turning his back on the room: 'The Army Board.'

'Alex . . .'

To his surprise she put a hand on his arm and walked back towards the inner room. Peace and warmth; she closed the door on Charlotte's departing guests. 'Alex?'

'You are the first to know. I have written again to the Army Board and have received an encouraging reply.'

'But before . . .'

'Ah, before was in peacetime and this is war.'

'And is it truly what you want?'

'If they take me back I have every reason to suppose they will send me to India, so my plans are not changed so very much. As for whether it is what I truly want – I cannot answer that.'

'Oh!' cried Mrs Palmer, putting her head round the door, 'I hope I do not interrupt. Young Tom is in the coach, my dear, and Miss Pennyquick running about looking for you.'

Ann said quietly the moment she had gone: 'What

167

must you think of me, running away at the ball . . . I never thanked you. Why did we have to quarrel?'

'There is no need to speak of it, my dear. It is all over and forgotten.'

It is all over and forgotten, he had said, which was an ardent lie: his love had not diminished and her look of shock at his proposal not forgotten; but he had lain with another woman since that night, and gladly, only too grateful for passion willingly returned. He had thought of it as lust in action, but tempered perhaps by that strange inconstant fondness he felt for Julia which was strongest when she reminded him most of Cassandra and weakest when she put on the airs of a shallow, consequential, garrulous woman of fashion. It had been strong enough though, those few hours at Lydd's Row.

He had not intended to call there again but one morning a post-chaise drew up outside the gatehouse and in she flew, a glowing, excited Julia: she had presents on the seat for Cassandra and a present for him, dearest Alex, a snuff box, such a little snuff box worth nothing . . . He must not protest. She had money in the bank at last, a moderate amount, a very very moderate amount, but oh, the relief after having none, after having to petition Clodie for every penny, after even contemplating pawning her rings . . .

She drew him away from the window, kissed him. 'Do not neglect me,' she said and then, at some noise from the kitchen, the warning rattle of cups: 'How I must dash, I should have been here hours ago. Cass will think I am not coming.'

He saw her into the chaise: remembered perfume, that soft pale hair. Leaning out she said: 'You must come,' and immediately: 'Drive on,' and she was borne away down the long drive.

No, he had not intended to call at Lydd's Row again but he had dined with Menzies and perhaps the wine had made him bold. A brief shower of rain had fallen, enough to make the desiccated population wish for more, and the inconsiderable drizzle that followed, growing less and less, fell softly on his shoulders as he stood waiting at the door.

'Why, you are quite wet,' as he was shown in. 'My poor Alex. Have you no umbrella?'

'I meant to take a chair but then it seemed such a short step from Chapel Field, and it was only a shower, a very meagre shower.'

'It is all of half a mile to Chapel Field. Your shoes are wet too. I shall ring for a cloth and a towel.'

She was dressed to dine out herself, or perhaps, the hour being so late, to attend some private party: cards, dancing. She wore the rubies in her ears and a matching ruby necklace, an extraordinarily beautiful thing. The door opened at last. 'Fanny,' said Julia, 'bring the Doctor a clean damp cloth and a towel, he has had the misfortune to step in a puddle.'

'I am sorry you are going out,' he said when they came, taking off his damp shoes and rubbing at his splashed stockings.

'Going out? No, I am not going out,' and as if to give credit to her words she removed the stones from her ears and dropped them into a small china bowl on the mantelshelf. Then she took the towel from him when he had finished, folded it, rang the bell again. 'Fanny, take these away. And whoever calls, I am indisposed, regretfully indisposed.'

Not fifteen minutes later a noise outside, a carriage drawing up in the road at the mouth of the Row perhaps, and then footsteps and a long long peal of the bell. There was a murmur of voices, the sharp click of the door closing, and silence.

'My dear, did you not want to go?'

'Not now that you have come.' And turning her back

to him, bending her head: 'Undo the clasp, Alex. Help me take off this necklace.'

What Mrs Palmer did know was that little Ann Gerard had twice driven herself in the gig to Norwich, that Mr Bridger of Bridger, Stevens and Bower had been in and out of Thorn like a jack-in-the-box, the last time careering down the hill in a post-chaise and four, and that Dr Loder had been to remonstrate, insisting on rest, rest and no excitement whatsoever, and had been ignored. Indeed, the last time he had come, by an unfortunate piece of timing meeting the post-chaise departing and having, the lane being so narrow, to back up a considerable distance, he had found the house loud with the noise of merriment, loud guffaws and high-pitched squeaks issuing from the old parlour and all the dogs barking in sympathy. Since no one had answered his knock and he had walked in unannounced he rapped on this door rather sharply and opened it as he did so. Utter silence had fallen. He looked round, bewildered.

It was a room he had not entered before, the heart of the original house, large, square, panelled floor to ceiling, a beautiful, dark old room with polished floors and ancient oak furniture. Tom Forsie was lounging on a great settle, his leg on a joint stool, and on a small red rug Cassandra, a scatter of playing cards all about her. They both turned slightly guilty faces on the intruder but they said nothing, and in the quiet Loder was conscious of raucous shouting in the distant kitchen and the un-mistakable soft murmur of Ann's own voice across the passage in her parlour.

'Good morning,' he said, 'I have called to see Lady Gerard.'

'Oh,' Tom replied, easing his leg a little and reaching down to ruffle Cassandra's hair, 'she is in her little sitting room with Miss Barsham. I think you had better ring the bell. No, Cassie, you do it.'

Since no mechanical bell had ever been fitted in this room Cassandra went to the door with a brass handbell and rang it some long time, but no one came, only, if anything, the shrieks from the kitchen rose in volume and a rhythmic thumping began, accompanied by cheering.

'We are celebrating the harvest the day after tomorrow,' said Tom, seeing Loder's eyebrows climb and his expression darken considerably, 'the kitchen is in an uproar. They have been baking for two days. Cassandra, go to Ann's room, will you, and knock and say politely that Dr Loder is here and waiting to see her.'

In a minute Cassandra returned: would Dr Loder care to step along to the parlour? Lady Gerard would see him there. She curtseyed, mindful of her manners. He nodded without smiling and went out. And there at her little desk, a desk piled once more with accounts, correspondence, bills, legal documents, sat Ann in a charming sprigged muslin dress and a ribbon in her short dark curls, and on the sofa Charlotte, playing with two kittens, one of which was the one he had brought over all those weeks ago.

'Ladies . . .' and he bowed stiffly. 'I thought I ordered peace and quiet?' in a more harsh and disagreeable tone than he had intended.

'We are very peaceful,' said Charlotte boldly, blushing. 'We have only sat here talking. And Ann is quite well. I believe she is quite quite well.'

He could not dispute it: her face had colour and her eyes shone. Perhaps they shone now with too much of a challenge, too much boldness. He had never seen her ferocious, had never imagined her roused to anger, only stirred to the petulant outbursts of the invalid, a perfectly understandable reaction. Miss Pennyquick brought in tea and Cassandra together, saying that Mr Tom had been carried away in his 'chair', he wanted to see the men and what remained to be done for the morrow.

171

'Oh, I wish I could come,' cried Cassandra, 'I do wish I could. I would like to ride back on the waggon with the sheaves.'

'You will be at Upgate,' said Miss Pennyquick, 'learning to be a lady.'

'I go twice a week,' Cassandra informed Dr Loder, 'and always on the same day, and I have lessons and dancing – I practise the dancing with Aunt Clodie when I go home – and sometimes I read to Charlotte . . . to Miss Barsham, and I have tea. I ride there and back on my pony. He is only a very little pony and Rigby leads him,' and proudly, with the arch look of Clodie M'Cool: 'I have never fallen off.'

Today, however, she managed to spill her tea and was led away by Miss Pennyquick, almost in tears, to be sponged down. Dr Loder seemed disinclined to leave even after one of the kittens had knocked over the milk jug and splashed his sleeve and the other had scratched him. At last Ann rose, saying: 'I must see what is happening in the kitchen. And I do not want to keep you, Dr Loder. I am sure you have a great deal to do.'

As a dismissal it was blunt enough but he was a man with a thick skin: where another would have been mortified he felt very little, was quite prepared to accept she was needed in the kitchen if that dreadful prolonged shrieking was any indication of the chaos there, and indeed, he did have a great deal to do. But still he hesitated, and in the hall he said in a low urgent voice: 'May I speak to you alone a moment? Could we step into the garden?'

She said at once: 'Of course. I am sorry, I had no idea this was a . . . a professional visit.'

'I assure you, it is not,' and he followed her out on to the lawn, adding: 'Perhaps this was foolish of me. The heat is so intense. You should have a hat, you know.'

'There is shade under the apple tree,' and she walked there and sat down on the bench, looking up at him.

'I thought I might find you alone,' he began awkwardly, and because standing there gazing down on her seemed to give him an advantage which he found, in these circumstances, he did not care for, he came to sit hesitantly on the very end of the bench. 'I had hoped to find you alone. When a man has a . . . I wanted to speak to you about your future.'

'My future?' and she turned a look on him so full of gentle surprise he did not see the stiffening of her interlaced fingers, the very perfect stillness of her whole body.

'As you know, I have a large practice, a very handsome practice. Indeed, I have been thinking of moving to set up my plate in Hilborough, the house in High Common is not ideal, rather cramped and shabby, and I have a great number of patients in Hilborough.' He paused, seeing something like consternation in her face, so he hurried on: 'Hilborough is only two miles from High Common.'

'I know that. But since Dr French came . . . There has always been a doctor in High Common.'

'Hilborough is a larger village, and I have made inquiries about a suitable property, a good big modern house standing back from the road. And then there is only one thing to make my happiness complete,' and he reached and took one of her hands, took it with difficulty because it seemed wedded to its fellow. 'Dear Lady Gerard, will you do me the honour of becoming my wife?'

'Well,' said Tom, seeing the sprigged muslin advancing up the cart rut, 'what brings you up here and nearly the dinner hour?'

'I might ask why you are sitting on a tree stump with only one crutch to hand and a quarter-mile walk to the farm. Why did you send the litter back without a message of any kind? When I asked Jim Knight he said he did not know why but you wanted to sit on the hill, you were not yourself.'

He said: 'If this stump was larger I would share it with you. As it is . . . Look at the view. I have always thought this was the finest view.'

Ann obediently turned about, shaded her eyes, and stared down across Thorn's chimneys to the drought-browned ollands, the green loop of the river, the far hill – so far it was a faint insubstantial blur of gold. The dismal calling of a newly calved cow, separated temporarily from her child, rose on the still air.

'I think my father would have been glad you have undone all his mischief; by all accounts, he loved this place too.'

'*We* have undone it.'

It was hot and quiet in the lee of the deep old hedgerow and in the nearest field the last of the corn stooks bleached in the sun, row on row. Not long ago all this had been tares and thistles. Ann found a flat place on the bank and sat down. 'Do you remember,' she said, 'the best barley in Norfolk.'

'We have not grown it yet. But we shall.'

So they fell to talking of country matters: shrews, so very fierce, wells, ponds, the new Fifeshire oxen who had revealed themselves more wily than the old Norfolk ones, the pair of setter puppies awaiting collection at Blackow – 'called Pitt and Fox because they squabble so' – the partridges, the owls, the Doctor's family of swallows. After a long time, and into a pause when they both looked down on Thorn, the blue smoke from the re-fired oven rising suddenly in a long spiral from the greatest of its chimneys, Ann remarked quietly: 'What would you say if I told you I was to marry Dr Loder?'

'Loder?' a huge squawk of surprise. 'I would say Hell and damnation no, not while I still breathe.'

'I do not believe you have any right to stop me.'

'What, see you – and Thorn – in the hands of that sour, self-absorbed . . .'

'He is not interested in Thorn. He thinks perhaps the wisest course would be to sell and to invest the capital, but of course these things could not interest me, being a woman, and he would naturally consult his man of business, he has always depended on his advice. There is a large modern house on the edge of Hilborough which he intends to fit up for his bride.'

Tom stared. 'You are serious. Do you mean he said all that? Do you mean he asked you? He asked you to be his wife?'

She leaned back into the hedge and laughed. Her laughter was particularly happy and free, and presently he joined in, his red, mulish look quite vanished, and after a long while, pressing his aching ribs, he gasped: 'He asked you?'

'In the garden.'

'And what did you say?' He wiped his eyes on his sleeve and pressed harder under his ribs.

'I said thank you but no. Oh Tom, we ought not to laugh. He was so very serious and so very put about when I refused him, and we did not part on the best of terms for he did not take defeat very graciously and asked if I was to marry George Neech. I am afraid I told him he was ungentlemanly to ask such a thing and then compounded his misery by saying that I must beg leave to seek the advice of another doctor, I could not possibly continue as his patient in the circumstances. Oh Tom!' and she laughed again, but this time her hands covered her eyes and he wondered if she was near to tears.

'It will not do to sit on top of this hill any longer,' he told her, 'I believe I see Babs in the garden. She is out with a spyglass. It must be the dinner hour.'

There was the smallest twinkle of light. 'You're right. It *is* a spyglass,' said Ann, helping him to his feet. 'Now where did she get it?'

175

'From a chest in the attics. She keeps it in her room.'

They made slow and uncertain progress down the hill, for Tom could not get along well with only one crutch and though Ann lent her shoulder she was so much shorter it made little difference to him. 'Of course,' he said as they drew near the house and saw Miss Pennyquick darting out, 'you might regret refusing him, the dog, he will be disgracefully rich one day, living on old men's over-indulgence and Mrs Palmer's hypochondria.'

'But I shall have the rent you will pay me for Thorn.'

'I told you never to speak of that again.'

'But I shall. And you shall sign that lease.'

'And what will you live on? There is no *Sable Island* now. And where will you go? This is your home.'

For a moment he stopped, leaning on her rather heavily, breathing hard. He was more than fourteen stone and it was a considerable effort to hop a quarter of a mile on a hot day.

'All I know is, you must have Thorn,' was all she said in reply and that in the lowest of voices, he was not sure he had heard her clearly, but it was too late, for there was Miss Pennyquick tearing up and showing a good deal of stocking as she did so, crying out that Mr Neech had called, had sat a long time patiently waiting, had gone away again a disappointed man.

'But surely you told him I had only walked up the hill?'

'But you had walked up the hill after *Tom*,' stated Miss Pennyquick with heavy emphasis, 'and it was perfectly clear to anyone with an ounce of knowing that he wished to speak to you alone.'

Menzies had been to the gatehouse, stumping in and out in total disbelief, glaring at the pillars, the extraordinarily narrow windows, the miniature kitchen. Surprise having taken away his power of speech, he allowed himself a pint and a half of strong coffee and half a duck pie before he passed any comment of any kind, and then it was only: "Tis a strange wee place for a human being – a normal-sized human being.' With a certain air of resignation he agreed to store such of the Doctor's belongings as were not portable – the tortoise shell for instance and the fifty specimen jars with their gruesome contents. He hoped, he said, the three swallows would have flown by the time the Doctor departed, *if* the Doctor departed – had he heard again from the Army Board? The wheels of officialdom turned painfully slow, everyone knew that, but if they were not careful, writing it all up in triplicate, stamping every page, signing and counter-signing, old Boney would be turning them from their cosy offices at swordpoint and then how they may wish they had not lost a minute, the scoundrels.

There was the sound of running feet, of laboured breath. Driscoll was on the doorstep heaving air into his lungs and harsh disjointed words out all at the same time.

'Calm yourself,' said the Doctor, 'come in. Sit. Take long steady breaths, not great gulps.'

'Sir, the mistress has asked me to fetch you. Could you come down to the house at once? The little girl is gone missing, taken, sir, snatched away . . .'

'What are you saying, Henry Driscoll? That the child has been stolen?'

The man nodded vehemently, still sucking in air with a grating, wheezing noise. Lungs affected by years of horse dust, hay dust, straw dust, thought the Doctor. He patted the man's shoulder. 'Stay here. My colleague, Dr Menzies will stay with you. No, do not get up. I shall go to the Hall directly.'

Driscoll raised bloodshot eyes. 'She said you was to take your bag, Doctor. They have broken Rigby's head for him.'

# 9

The drive to Blackow had not been scored by the passing of so many carriages for years and for once Clodie kept the hounds confined and flung open the door to all comers. The rumour was all over High Common that she would give the better part of a fortune to have the child back, and she had paid every shiftless scavenger and barrow boy and jobless clerk in Norwich to find her, that being Irish she had no confidence in the abilities of the constables or even the Militia and was preparing to ride the lanes of Norfolk herself calling Cassandra by name. As for Mrs Hawkworth, that unnatural mother, she had been seen at Blackow in the dawn of the day following, in evening dress and piled with jewels, but had left within half an hour and at a tremendous pace.

'She runs in crying out against us all,' said Clodie furiously to the Doctor when he stepped in at noon to examine his patient, 'saying it is all our fault, that she should never have left her child, that she always had doubts and look what has come of it. I tell you, I was sorely tempted to shake her.'

The Doctor repaired to the clean bare room above the stables where Rigby kept to his narrow bed, a strikingly large white bandage wound about his head that had been put there, he croaked with a mixture of awe and surprise, by the old lady herself. She was a rare bird, he added shyly, a rare bird indeed. He doubted he could be looked after better in the King's own palace, Lucy running up and down with possets and caudles and gruel and this morning beef soup and at long last a bite of good bread. He felt able to get up. Did the Doctor not think he ought to get up? That Driscoll was a good man, had been brought up in stables – born in one most likely – but sometimes his ways were foreign and the horses were not used to it. Did the Doctor not think he ought to get up for an hour or two, do the blood congeal with lying struck rigid so long?

'Poor man,' said Clodie, who was waiting in the yard. 'He wept when he woke and told me how it had happened. I looked away, did my best not to see, but he is mortified, unconsolable. He must get back to his horses before they too are snatched from under his nose.' She drew herself up but it was a great effort. She had not slept the previous night and since returning from Norwich this morning had not sat down or ceased to answer questions and give out orders. She looked magnificent and worn out and old.

'Come in here,' she said, plucking at the Doctor's sleeve. He followed a little reluctantly. She had nothing in her stables that could interest him, a man with no particular love of horses.

Every stall and loose box was full, all the inmates undeniably handsome but some of them unpleasant company for unprotected human beings on foot. 'In here,' said Clodie, leading him along the passage to the far end, the last stall. The Doctor caught a glimpse of the furious face – nose wrinkled, ears laid – of the occupant of the last stall but one and hurried past, thankful for the bars. There he found Clodie in a commodious, clean, deep-strawed square of utter privacy.

'I need your advice,' she said. 'Oh, I have sore need of a sober man's advice.'

It came to him that she had led him to the stable not because she feared they would be overheard – she could have taken him to any part of the garden, the park, the far side of the lake – but because a stable was her natural refuge. Close on this thought another: what was his own natural refuge? The battlefield? Why had he periodically returned to his cold, uncomfortable, high-smelling, invariably unwaterproof tent, in which he was not only supposed to sleep but eat, hold social intercourse and operate on the wounded?

'I am not sure . . .' he began diffidently.

'But who else is my friend in all this godforsaken country?'

In the next stall the horse had ceased his restless scraping and stood with his ears pricked, listening to Clodie's voice, an alert and anxious look about him. She would ask her horses what to do, the Doctor thought, if there was the remotest chance one of them might reply.

'Would you ride to Norwich for me,' she said, 'and ask after a man called Conway? He was staying at the King's Head, I believe.'

'The tall dark solemn man at the Assembly.'

'That is the fellow. He is an acquaintance of my niece.'

'Do you connect him with Cassandra's disappearance?'

She hesitated, though whether it was a natural reluctance to tell him some salient fact she possessed or else an equally natural disinclination to show him how desperately, how very very desperately she was clutching at straws, he could not tell.

There was the rasp of nailed boots on the bricks. 'Mistress, are you there at all?' and Driscoll came slowly up the row of stalls.

'And what if I am?' Clodie demanded, stepping out.

'There is a gentleman in the drive and all in a lather, him and his horses.'

They hurried out. There stood a post-chaise, the horses sweating pitifully. Barsham was on the steps, fretting and grumbling, pacing up and down. At the sight of Clodie he gave a bellow and plunged down towards her, and from the open door of the house sped a large, young, jolly man – at least, he was normally jolly but his face was a perfect blob of anxiety now, flushed and shining.

'Mr Tobin,' said Clodie. 'How do you do yet again. Is there news? Mr Tobin is my man of business, my advisor,' she explained to the Doctor, 'he belongs to the bank. Mr Tobin, Dr French of High Common. Well, is there news? Lord Barsham – ' with an imperious nod – 'have you travelled together?'

'I took the liberty, madam, of calling for Lord Barsham on my way.' He was painfully conscious Upgate had not been on his way from Norwich and that to accomplish this intention the chaise had passed Blackow and returned; though the horses had been sent along at an alarming rate and he had surely lost no more than half an hour, rousing Barsham from a quagmire of official paperwork and bustling him away with scarcely a civil word to Lady Barsham or any of the other females who had cluttered the door, he was unsure how Mrs M'Cool would take any kind of delay once she knew the news he brought. Besides, in common decency he had felt obliged to visit Lydd's Row before leaving Norwich, though the contents of the letter he had received made no mention of Mrs Hawkworth. It was with a trembling hand that he gave it to Clodie, therefore, and with a guilty overcast look that he watched her walk into the house, unfolding it as she went.

'I have seldom met a woman with stranger manners,' murmured Barsham, banging his hat against his leg with a sudden spurt of irritability. 'What are we to do now? I'm damned if I'll stand about on her steps till she comes out again.'

'Then we had best go in,' said the Doctor, and led the way.

He was instantly at a loss where to lead them, and settled on the ballroom with misgivings. He hung upon the bell till Lucy appeared, her apron and her fingers bloodied, her hair down on her shoulders, her eyes red with weeping, and told her to let her mistress know the gentlemen were waiting on her in the ballroom. While they waited, standing about, a confusion of sounds penetrated: dogs barking, raised voices – vehemently raised and in the Irish – a heavy bang as if someone had dropped a copper pan, the echo rolling on and on. Once feet ran lightly across the tiles outside, and once a crowd of guinea fowl passed along the terrace looking to right and left and all talking away without pause. Two peacocks sat two yards apart on the balustrade and occasionally exchanged malevolent looks, but all the peahens were in the thickets beyond the lake keeping to the shade and paying no attention.

'Perhaps you could tell me,' the Doctor said to Tobin after ten minutes of this, 'what is in the letter? Strictly speaking, it is not my business, I know, but Mrs M'Cool calls me her friend and if there is anything . . .'

'Oh dear me,' said Tobin, looking distraught, 'I doubt there is much anyone can do save pay up and pray. I do not mean any disrespect, sir, I do not indeed. Needless to say the letter was anonymous and delivered by hand: the child safe, the ransom ten thousand pounds in gold – gold sent in a box to Suffolk, child returned by same coach.'

'There was a direction in Suffolk, an inn, a house?'

'Oh yes, sir. A house. My own opinion is it is fictitious. Or perhaps it is empty, uninhabited, a ruin. In any case I do not think I would risk keeping an appointment at a definite spot upon the map – how if it were surrounded with parish constables, thief-takers and soldiers? No sir, rest assured the coach will never reach that place but will be waylaid upon the road. There are great tracts of lonely country in those parts, especially towards the sea. But whether the little girl will be returned . . . I cannot say. I would not like to say. I have never had to do with a child-stealing before, only a sad case of a deranged woman who had lost her baby and absconded with another's.'

'Ten thousand pounds is a very great deal of money.'

'It troubles me indeed.' But Tobin naturally refrained from saying why it troubled him so very deeply. 'I might have expected a common ruffian to ask a thousand. A thousand pounds is a cheering heap of money for most men,' and he looked sadly at the Doctor for a moment, thinking what a cheering heap of money it would be for himself.

'This is no common ruffian,' put in Barsham, turning impatiently from the long window where he had been staring out at the peacocks – there were another two approaching slowly along the gravel. 'He has laid his plans carefully. He knew what hour Rigby would set out for Upgate, left a valuable cob and the child's pony tied to a stump, and had the wit to send his demand to Tobin, a busy office, notes handed in every moment, no possibility of its being traced.'

'Even a common ruffian,' said the Doctor mildly, 'cannot run about stealing children on a whim, not if he hopes for success, for Mr Tobin's cheering heap of money. It would be a sad fool who had not made discreet inquiries or lain in watch meditating on the trap he might set. But on the whole I must agree: ten thousand pounds is a vast amount of money and will need a large strong awkward box.'

'I hope Rigby is ashamed of himself,' Barsham continued with some warmth, 'falling for an old trick: "Sir, my horse is lame. I have picked up his foot but can see no injury. Please to look yourself, I can tell you are a man with great experience." Pah! A quick knock on the head and the fellow's away.'

'I do not think Rigby will forget it a long and painful while,' said the Doctor. 'But come, should we not rouse out Mrs M'Cool? I suppose you are of the opinion the money should be raised?'

'If it can be raised,' murmured Tobin.

'I do not see what else can be done,' said Barsham. 'Our only hope is to catch the devil when he takes

183

delivery. And even that,' morosely, 'is easier said than done, gentlemen.'

They turned in a concerted movement towards the door, but as they did so it opened, it and its twin together, so that the whole grand entrance stood wide as if to admit a double row of dancers. Clodie stood there, as proud an old woman as one might hope to meet on the hill of Tara itself, and she said that of course she would pay the ten thousand pounds and to the devil with anyone who tried to prevent her. In the hall behind her two favourite hounds, infected by her mood, rose from the cool tiles and growled.

'Madam,' said Tobin, amiable and anxious, 'may I consult you in private?'

She put up her chin ominously but led him away without comment and Barsham and the Doctor heard the shutting of a distant door. 'He is gone to tell her that ten thousand pounds in gold pieces is a hellish difficult undertaking, that she would do better to have it in two-pound notes. On the other hand – ' and he rubbed his bulbous red nose a while – 'on the other hand, she may not have ten thousand pounds. This place may be mortgaged to the attics the way it always was in the Gerards' time. Why is there no furniture? She spends on the gardens – a wholesale replanting – and nothing is too good for her horses, but apart from those what sign is there of any real wealth? We have only her word for it she is related to the O'Neills or the Fitzgeralds or whoever it is, and as to M'Cool having owned tens of thousands of acres well, all I can say is: Irish acres are not at all the same as English ones. 'Tis almost like saying a man has vast estates in Egypt without taking account of the desert.'

'I have been in pleasant fertile places and all of them in Ireland. It is not an absolute certainty M'Cool's acres were sparse and barren.'

Footsteps echoed in the hall. 'Gentlemen,' said Tobin,

'I suggest we depart. Doctor, if you would be so good . . . Mrs M'Cool has an errand for you. Perhaps I could explain in the chaise?'

'The Doctor has two errands,' said a firm voice behind and Clodie stood in the shadows, 'but one of them is strictly between him and myself.'

In the confines of the chaise Tobin said: 'Mrs M'Cool has charged you and I, sir, with the heavy responsibility of all those gold pieces, a proper chest for them and the hiring of a suitable carriage . . . It did occur to me the carriage might be driven by a volunteer, pledged to save the money as well as the child – but I cannot see how it is to be done without arousing suspicion and who knows how many rogues are involved? Why, one might be faced with two dozen. And besides, Mrs M'Cool will not countenance it, says Cassandra must come before anything, God damn the money,' and he coughed, embarrassed, looking down at the buttons on his waistcoat.

'Quite right,' said Barsham. 'What good are heroics? Alex, do you want to get out, to put up a bag of necessaries? You may be in Norwich some long time. Tobin can call for you after leaving me at Upgate.'

The Doctor got out and walked miserably into his gatehouse. He stood a moment undecided.

'It is you, sir. Should I bring some coffee?' and Jim came in, looking him over with an almost motherly concern.

'Yes . . . Yes, perhaps there is time. Indeed, there must be time. The carriage will still be half a mile from Blackow and now there is no need to drive like the wind. Not that there was before, poor fools. It was a cruelty, a thoughtless cruelty to flog those horses along in such a heat. I am going to Norwich, how long for I do not know – Mr Tobin will call shortly.'

'I shall have a bag ready before he comes, Doctor. And the coffee too. And you are not to be anxious about the birds – I shall feed them regular.'

Instantly, as if they had heard, the swallows left their glass case and flew across the room making loving noises. They did not fly to Jim though but to the Doctor, their dear parent, and nestled into his collar. This led to several unsightly messes on his good brown coat, vigorous sponging and Jim tight-lipped, reduced – after several frantic minutes, the rattle of a carriage already a faint faint sound under and behind the stop-start of the woodpigeons, the chatter of the sparrows in the roof and the constant happy chirrupings of the swallows – to crying out: 'This will not do, Doctor. You will have to wear the old green. Or the new black.'

Tobin too was not in the best of moods. For a mild and amiable man he had had a trying morning. He did his best to master himself, to achieve a pleasant look as the Doctor climbed into the carriage and the weary horses were turned round. Privately he thought the Doctor looked worn, grey and savage but since they must necessarily cooperate he only remarked that it was a wearisome business, he hoped it might have a happy ending. After this they rode in silence until the city was less than a mile away when the Doctor said, rousing himself from his lethargy: 'May I ask you how you found Mrs Hawkworth?'

'The mother? I beg your pardon, Doctor, of course you must know her well. Mrs Hawkworth was . . .' He paused, a conflict plainly visible. 'Very beautiful,' he finished, looking distinctly ashamed. 'I do not think . . . I do not think she had been weeping but she was certainly upset. She thanked me and thanked me for bringing her the news, and then she cried out that the old lady might refuse to pay and she herself without the means – how was she to get her daughter back? I did my best to calm her but I am not used to hysteria – I am a bachelor and a retiring man – and I was never so glad as when her maid ran in with handkerchiefs and a smelling bottle so that I could decently leave.' He was silent a

186

moment, staring out as the chaise slowed to a walk in the traffic of St Stephen's: a score of anxious bullocks, a huge hog driven by an old man and a company of Dragoons. 'There is no love lost between the aunt and niece,' he remarked in dull tones. 'There is no question of them comforting each other like Christian women.'

'No indeed. They are temperamentally unsuited and what is more, I believe there is something in the family history which adds fuel to their dislike. I do not know what it is: jealousy, a runaway marriage, a dispute over a will – who can say? But I feel it is there and that, on the whole, Mrs Hawkworth is more conscious of it than her aunt – though it is a bitter thing to live upon charity, to be the fabled "poor relation". I suppose you know nothing of Mrs Hawkworth's past, her marriage, her life in Paris?'

Tobin shook his head. 'I know only that she arrived in England during the last week of the peace, was given the cold shoulder by relatives in Kent – I believe it was Kent – I suppose I should say relatives of Hawkworth for she has none apart from Mrs M'Cool; and after that she made herself known to the old lady and came to Norfolk with her. I cannot discuss Mrs M'Cool's affairs of course but you are correct to call the niece a poor relation, most unfortunately accurate.'

'Yet she has jewels, quite magnificent jewels.'

'Has she? I have only met her twice before this morning and both times she was unadorned, not even a ring – not even a wedding ring. I remarked it particularly, for many widows like to keep it on, an indication of status perhaps if nothing else. But jewels . . . No, Doctor. Without divulging secrets I may say that "magnificent jewels" are most unlikely – perhaps the ones you saw were paste, coloured glass?'

The Doctor sank back in his corner feeling a scrub, yet still those rubies troubled him. A gift perhaps? Conway's gift?

'You do not know a Mr Conway?' he hazarded as they pulled in to the side and he prepared to alight.

'Conway? No, I don't believe I do.'

'I thought not,' said the Doctor. 'It would have been too happy a coincidence. Now, I shall run and leave my bag with Mrs Badcock and then I shall join you at the bank.'

'I am afraid we have a much more delicate mission before we can approach the Bank,' said Tobin gravely, and he reached into his coat pocket and pulled out a largish square of velvet, a velvet parcel. He flicked it open: dark blue velvet, very dark blue, and there in the middle, balanced on his palm, the great crescent of diamonds that had flashed in Clodie's turban at the Assembly.

'Good God!' said the Doctor. 'And are they real?'

'I assure you they are. At least, Mrs M'Cool tells me so, tells me this extraordinary bauble belonged to her grandmother who had it of a king. Which king, I wonder?'

'I hope she is not mistaken.'

'Oh so do I!' cried Tobin earnestly, wrapping up the diamonds with feverish haste and stowing them away again, 'for this must purchase part of Miss Cassandra's freedom, this and a few other trinkets I have in my inner pockets. I am charged with their disposal – and a heavy burden it is,' and his fresh young face clouded as he contemplated such a responsibility. 'I little thought when I woke this morning that I would come to selling precious stones before the day was out.'

The Grey Cock was very quiet for it was past two in the morning and the door had long been locked. The Doctor's candle had burned down to a stump and by its feeble light he had re-counted the gold and put it gently back into its little leather bags, stowing them in turn in the moderate-sized iron box that stood at his feet. At

188

length he closed the lid and struggled a few moments with the double locks: 'I am not used to this work,' he said out loud, pausing to suck a skinned finger. When he had finished he stared down with considerable dislike, wishing he could at the very least slide the thing across the floor to a less conspicuous resting place, but it was too heavy, it had taken two giant wrestlers in respectable subfusc suits – employed by the bank – to carry it to the Cock by chariot and the inn's sagging floor sagged all the lower for its weight. He had been reduced to telling Mrs Badcock that it came from the Hospital and was full of bones and she had glanced at it in horror, supposing a small corpse to be cut up and packed inside. She had brought up a pot of coffee with an anxious inquiry as to how long it was to remain in his room and when the Doctor replied only the night was as obviously happy as himself at the thought of hurrying it away in the morning. Had his bachelor quarters not been up an ancient spiral stair at the very top of a house full of busybodies Tobin could have kept it himself and welcome: 'Though to be sure he was comically reluctant,' said the Doctor to himself, pulling on his nightshirt, and on blowing out the candle: 'Since the famous crescent was not paste at all we must conclude it was, quite truthfully, the gift of a king. In view of its value the services rendered must have been far beyond the usual.' But the last thing he thought of before he slept was Julia's ruby necklace and why it should trouble him so.

The chaise hired from the King's Head drew into the small yard at the Cock at eight o'clock followed by the two large silent men from the bank and Mr Tobin, all three in good brown coats and small-clothes, the very picture of respectability. They made short work of carrying down the box and stowing it on the floor of the carriage, shaking the Doctor's hand and allowing themselves the faintest smile of satisfaction before departing as mutely as they had come. The Doctor and Tobin spoke briefly to the postillion, a weedy middle-aged man who had already received copious and strict instructions and a substantial lump sum in cash. He was a volunteer, and counting over his guineas he had been congratulating himself on such easy money. Now, repeatedly exhorted not to stop on the road by the young flustered cove and stared at silently and coldly by the sinister-looking one in the bottle-green coat, he felt his first qualms.

'How are you to get home?' Tobin asked when the chaise had rocked out of sight and then, harking back to his main worry: 'How I hope that man is honest. He is to change horses in Bungay and Lord Barsham will meet him and speed him on his way again, but what a responsibility, what a load on my mind – what if the wretched box never reaches Bungay, say? Or is waylaid, or has an accident?'

'Come,' said the Doctor, putting on his hat, 'let us walk to the King's Head and make a leisurely breakfast.'

'But I have already breakfasted – ' though it was a scrap of toast and thin watery coffee – 'and there is the bank . . .'

'I too have breakfasted, but to tell you the truth it sits uncomfortably: I could not eat and enjoy it until I had discharged my duty to that box,' and lower, to himself: 'That damn box. I would think it friendly of you to be my guest at the King's Head. I will make it right with the bank.'

Good strong coffee, muffins, kidneys, sausages, and a fresh-faced cheerful little boy running in and out attending to their every need. 'To the best inn in Norwich,' said Tobin, raising his cup, all his good humour restored and a pink flush in his plump cheeks. 'Perhaps I shall have just one more sausage. It seems a shame to leave them. How about you, Doctor? Can you manage another?'

'No, no. Mrs Badcock brought me porridge at six thirty this morning and I was forced to eat it for fear of offending her if I refused. I have already eaten three excellent sausages, a plate of kidneys and a small mountain of toast: it is hypocritical in a man who goes about warning others of self-indulgence. In any case, I must leave you a moment – I have some small business with the landlord. Pray excuse me,' and he got up, threw down his napkin and went out.

But it was not the landlord he sought, it was old Dibden, an elderly stooping man whom he had known for years, who had waited on him at many and many a Benefit dinner and whose toothless smile greeted him now as he waylaid him outside the public dining room.

'A Mr Conway, sir? Oh yes, I remember him: a tall dark foreign sort of gentleman. Was he a friend, sir?'

'No, but I have been asked to get news of him if I can.'

'Dishonoured bills, sir? He paid up here, you know – Mrs Cracknell mentioned it when she come in the kitchen – and he tipped liberal, sir, no doubt about it. But old Joe in the yard, who says he can tell a real gentleman at twenty yards, he said that the horse was better bred than the man. But then again, he was foreign, sir, perhaps it was to be expected.'

'Was he so? I did not know that.'

'Not his name but his manner, and some of his clothes, and Joe heard him talking foreign to his horse one time so that was that as far as Joe was concerned, sir; talking foreign like a true foreigner, he said. After that he would have it Mr Conway was old Boney's spy but I said what, Boney's spy going to the Assembly? How would they let him in?'

'Could you tell me when he left?'

'That would have been the Tuesday, Tuesday this week.'

'Not bad news?' asked Tobin, hastily putting the lid back on the dish to conceal the fact that he had devoured every last sausage, 'I do hope not.'

'Only what I expected. At least . . . But tell me, are

you walking back to the bank when you have drunk up the coffee? May I walk along with you? I shall occupy myself at the bookseller's for an hour and then call on a friend.'

Tobin wiped his greasy chin, so restored by good food and sympathetic company he only sounded a very little anxious as he said: 'I wonder where that box is got to? I hope to God it is not lying in a ditch halfway to Bungay.'

The Doctor consulted his watch. 'No, no. With such good horses he will have reached Bungay by now, will be setting out on the last part of his journey.'

'Is that the time? The real time? Oh Doctor, would you mind if we hurried along? I was expected in the office at nine.'

The Doctor smiled. 'I should not hurry along too furiously, Mr Tobin. It wants but ten minutes to eleven: they will most assuredly have given you up for dead.'

It was not to be hoped that the almost monastic seclusion of Blackow or its distance from the village would lessen the gossip. News was not easy to extinguish once Mrs Palmer had carried it round every house of consequence and lit a dozen small conflagrations of curiosity and surmise. It was commonly held that Mrs Hawkworth, prostrate with grief, was attended by two or even three of the most distinguished doctors Norwich could provide while her aunt fulminated about the gardens at Blackow, only speaking civilly to Alex French. There was still a considerable coming and going, Lord Barsham dashing to the house every hour and every hour the reports from the continent more grave so that he was ground between the millstones of Clodie M'Cool and Bonaparte. It was also supposed that the old lady was now penniless, having paid an extortionate sum for Cassandra's return, and that some if not all of the secretive dark coves trotting past the gatehouse were not thief-takers at all but bums and tipstaffs.

'What is all this about, this cock-and-bull story of Mrs M'Cool piling her furniture – what furniture, by God? – piling it on a cart and putting the house up for sale?' Barsham demanded, finding the Doctor at home as he came from another brief but gruelling interview. 'Who starts these rumours?' Well may he ask, his own house being full of shrill energetic women talking scandal.

'I have no idea.'

'You were always a close cove, damnit. I only ask because I have always had an eye on those outlying acres beyond Lubbock's Hole – you know the stretch – a grand enclosure of land, the only land on the entire Blackow estate that was ever in anything like good heart. If the place was to come up for sale again it would do the old lady no harm to let me buy them, they are a quarter of a mile from all the rest and right on my own boundary.'

'I am disappointed in you. I did not think you were a vulture, like all the rest.'

It was late afternoon and the day had turned thundery, had several times promised rain and had delivered none, but now the sky had cleared, the hot sun shone again over the parched earth. From the window of his tiny parlour the Doctor could see the swallows skimming low over the grass, two of them apparently quartering all the area between the gatehouse and the first two oaks along the drive, back and forth, back and forth, an effortless exhibition of purpose, speed, agility. The shadows of the trees lay long and black and beyond, beyond the park itself, were small hills lost in a pale blue mist.

'All that money,' said Barsham, taking three paces across the room and three back. 'Alex, this place is nothing more than a doll's house. How I did dislike waving goodbye to that money, seeing it out onto the Halesworth road; and how I wish we had hired a competent man to follow it, some old rogue who'd been working the roads all his life and would never be noticed.'

'To be sure he would be noticed. A man who seriously expects ten thousand pounds would have considered such a possibility. And the note said, did it not: let it be unaccompanied.'

'But 'tis a long straight road, flat land . . . Alex, where are you going? Are you listening?'

The Doctor's head had vanished round the kitchen door. The low growling sound of question, answer, mild dispute and submission wafted through the gap along with the essense of a vegetable curry. The Doctor, however, withdrew himself only to turn round with a tray in his hand, a tray on which was coffee, anchovy toast, ham sandwiches and pickled onions.

'What meal is this, pray?' asked Barsham with a quick glance at the clock.

'Call it a demi-supper.'

'And what suppers we have shared!' exclaimed his friend, settling on a spindly chair with a sigh and staring resentfully at the Doctor's miserably thin person. 'Do you remember . . .' But he stopped, closed his mouth, sensibly refusing to open it again except to admit a pickled onion, and then, looking up with watering eyes, murmured: 'What is all this about the Army Board?'

'Did you receive my note? It did not seem the time or place to mention it at Blackow yesterday and I did not think you would mind a hurried explanation in a letter . . .'

'A letter! A scrap of paper folded over. Not even sealed. Why, that man of yours must have read it as he came along.'

'If he did I am sorry for it, though perhaps it would only be human. And he is very discreet.'

'So you are going before the Army Board again? Back to war, Alex. And to hell with discretion: what does Ann Gerard think of it?'

The Doctor looked confused. 'Listen,' he said, 'I cannot stay here. I have my reasons, foolish and muddled as they would sound to you, no doubt.'

'Hmm. Well, I shall say nothing. You know what I thought of your India caper. Louise said . . . I know I am not supposed to mention it, but what is the difficulty about proposing to Ann Gerard? She is free to marry you, and affectionate – she spoke of you often when you were skulking in Suffolk. If it is age – Louise's other sister married a man twenty-five years older than herself, bore him seven children and died before he did.'

'I am not entirely surprised; men can have no idea the strain on the female constitution of repeated confinements.' And he looked out again at the swallows, munching his toast.

'If you set up your plate again patients will flock in. We would think it kindly of you was you to put it up again in High Common. Loder don't suit us at all. And you are still spry, good for a few years yet. I don't say you have looks, you never had any even when you was a youngster – and that only seems like yesterday,' with another sigh, for he had been a handsome youngster himself. 'But looks are nothing, not when it comes to the point.'

'The point?' The swallows had risen, apparently kissed in midair and shifted their ground a little, hunting the edge of the drive.

'The point is . . . Ask her to marry you.'

The Doctor noted that the two swallows had been joined by several more. He said nothing but put down his plate and stepped over to the corner where the glass case sat upon a little table.

'Alex, what are you doing?'

'I am going to let my swallows fly,' and the Doctor picked up the case and went to the door.

At the foot-high hedge that surrounded his little wrecked garden he stopped, put down his burden, brought out one bird after another. They flew from his finger with a chirrup of astonishment and winged away at speed up and up into the great deep blue bowl of the

195

sky. 'There,' said Barsham, who had come to the door to watch, a sandwich in his hand, 'they are away over the oaks. Now . . .' But he had scarcely formed the word before two small birds alighted on the Doctor's shoulder and stole lovingly against his neck. 'Good God, they are come back! Alex, Alex – they are come back.'

'I am afraid so. I am all their family now, you see. I have found this before with hirundae. It is evening, they are very young, they are not used to being out so late and catching their own supper: they wish to go to bed. Have you not noticed how they cram themselves in their nests at night, it is wonder such frail mud baskets hold them all – well, I am their mother and father and nest together.'

'But you aint a swallow.'

'To them perhaps I am.' It was too obviously true. It took him some minutes to detach them from his collar and relaunch them, flapping his arms.

He and Barsham went in again, leaving the door open. 'I suppose I must go,' said Barsham gloomily. 'I have a meeting with Captain Exton. They are putting up a signal post on Yarmouth church tower, you know, to let the country know when the French come. I saw Wodehouse yesterday and he said Norwich would be well prepared but for my part . . .' He shook his head, his pleasant broad red face thoroughly miserable. 'For my part I do not see how we are to stop them.'

'Natural forces will stop them – these are the best anchovies I have tasted in a long while – wind and water will stop them. I would not care to be embarked on a flat-bottomed boat in the grip of the Channel. I have been on such a craft with a few hundred sick and sorry soldiers and I tell you, it is no joke. I do not believe Bonaparte understands the sea or he would not be so sanguine of success.'

'But he has able men who do.'

'But does he listen to them? And do you listen to your

physician's advice, my dear friend? You are fat and high-coloured. It will be the gout stool and abstinence if you do not take care. Have I not explained the damage to your liver could . . .'

'Yes, yes. Loder charged me three guineas for the same lecture.'

Here they were interrupted by the return of one of the swallows, who gave a contented chirrup and plunged into his glass case. 'I shall go,' said Barsham. 'Your family returns.'

'Unfortunately yes. Pray give my regards to Lady Barsham. If there is any news of the chaise, of Cassandra, I shall make sure they send a boy over to Upgate at once.'

He had a heavy, a leaden premonition that there would be no news or that what news came would be grim and unpalatable. He supposed vaguely that he must walk down to the Hall to report to Clodie M'Cool, to tell her that Conway had left Norwich. By the time he had done so it was twilight; when he looked up there were stars. He came into the gatehouse with a heavy step, thinking only of the old, old, haggard face, her soft cry of: 'Well, there's no help for it. Of course he has gone. I knew it all along,' and a little later something else along the same lines and almost incoherent, but a rustle in the corner of the room called for investigation and there, crouched affectionately cheek to cheek, were all three of his swallows.

'That's twice you have put them out and they've come back, Doctor,' said Jim Wells, coming in to light the candles. 'Will you want negus? A glass of the good red?'

'No, nothing tonight. Twice is it? Yes, twice. They are more trouble than human children to launch into the world. Oh well, I must try again tomorrow. I will take them down to the Hall and put them in an old nest in the stables.'

'Cassandra would have liked that,' said Jim.

197

*

She had been asleep, she said, running into the room, just fallen asleep after hours and hours of torment awake, but her face was pale and composed, she might never have wept at all. She had on a blue silk wrapper, absurd little blue slippers, and her hair had been pinned up hastily, escaping in fronds. She had looked as lovely as ever, and tragic, dropping her head once to his shoulder as if she could not bear its weight or the weight of her grief any longer.

'I came to say how sorry I am . . .' he began.

'Don't speak of it. Not now. I could not bear it. Come,' and she put both hands on his arm, 'Come. Sit down. Take a glass of wine with me.'

But he had refused. Though he kissed her cheek and her neck with tenderness and though the solid warmth of her in his arms moved his heart, he would not stay. He did not like to see her voluble and false – instinct whispered it was false, this attitude of hers. He did not know how or why but it was so, he had witnessed grief enough, deprivation, cruel reversals, pain, uncomplaining suffering, and though he could not put it into words he knew her sorrow to be unreal.

'My dear, I shall visit you again,' he had said, and when she would have clung to him put her away gently, going to the door.

I hope I am wrong, he said to himself, sitting in the dark with one candle and his feet on the tortoise shell; oh, how I hope I am wrong.

# 10

The Doctor was dining at Thorn. It is all over and forgotten, he repeated to himself as he walked into the parlour and saw her sitting at her little desk, Spring at her feet, and as she rose: 'My dear Ann, I am early,' and held out his hands.

She did not hesitate but stepped forward to take them, smiling. A moment ago she had been hot and bothered, finishing off yet another letter about *Sable Island*, consulting her columns of figures. How happy she was to see him, she said, how very happy – and she *did* sound happy and the grip of her hands was unusually strong.

'You are in good looks and good spirits,' he remarked as she turned back to shovel her correspondence into a heap, pens, wax, seals and all.

'Because I am glad to see you. I thought . . . I was afraid you might refuse the invitation.'

'My dear, that is simple foolishness. Now tell me, how is Tom's leg?'

'Shall we say: as well as can be expected? He sat up most of the night for the harvest supper, ate like three men, grew very drunk and broke one of his crutches. Do not ask me what he was doing, I had long been abed and thought it better not to inquire. Hollin has made him another. I would be obliged if you could look him over, I have . . . Dr Loder no longer attends at Thorn.'

He put his head on one side and studied her. 'Dear me. Do not tell me you met him while out riding, the poor man, and snapped your fingers at his good advice? No, no. I am only teasing. It would be highly improper were you to tell me of any complaint.'

It was highly improbable she would ever tell him the

true reason for Loder's dismissal. She swallowed the truth down firmly and went to the door. 'I can hear Tom on the stairs. Sit down, Alex, sit down. I must go and wash my hands.'

'And your cheek. Have you been wrestling hard with the accounts?'

'Not the farm accounts. I have been arranging for the last of *Sable Island*'s prize money to be distributed to the widows and children. There is not so very much after all. I had hoped . . . Mr Bridger is very sour about the whole affair, he calls it reckless philanthropy – "I must warn you, Lady Gerard, such reckless philanthropy will not do, will not do at all. Do you wish to be reduced to begging in the street, madam?" But Alex, tell me – Cassandra. Have you heard anything?'

'Nothing.'

'Mrs M'Cool called this morning. She was riding Dido. She said that if she did not hear today she would surely run mad, that the ransom was paid and still no word . . .'

'Doctor!' and Tom burst through the door. 'Why, you are early. Now you can come out and see the oxen, give me your opinion.'

'I would not be so rash,' said the Doctor, who had unhappy memories of certain opinions he had passed in Suffolk on a gentleman's stock bull.

'Tom, you are not to go out in the yard ten minutes before dinner. You will come in smelling of the cattle sheds. Call for Babs, do, and forget all about the oxen.'

The oxen were not forgotten however, they made their presence felt at the dinner table, along with oats, beans, clover, preferred methods of making cheese, the latest thing in seed drills and the eating qualities of some type of new pig. The Doctor was not much interested in agriculture but he felt the necessity of a flow of cheerful conversation and Tom, who was an optimist and wholly convinced Cassandra would be found, was the least affected by the continuing absence of news. It was only agriculture on which he would talk freely though, he was disillusioned with the Volunteers – 'too much creeping about in the hedgerows and no proper weapons' – and oddly reticent on the subject of Dr Loder whose name was mentioned in connection with his leg. The harvest home, Thorn's bacchanalia, provided the only spontaneous smiles of the meal.

The cheese came in and the dessert. The Doctor talked on at random: the Frayles, the Moores, Mr Bringloe's donkey. Miss Pennyquick remarked that it was only a matter of time before Mrs M'Cool appropriated the donkey for her hounds, poor mangy ancient creature. Thus, for all his care, they were brought back to Blackow.

'Of course they will find Cass,' declared Tom. 'Why, what would the old lady do without her?'

'She would never recover,' said Ann, 'never.'

'At the moment she survives on action, on directing operations,' said the Doctor. 'She has hired every wastrel and tinker and professional thief-taker this side of Ipswich – the Lord knows what it is costing her – and they are scouring the countryside from the Waveney to the Orwell.'

A heavy silence followed: the issue he had been at pains to avoid all evening rose and confronted them in all its horror. Where was Cassandra and was she still alive?

There was a knock. Mrs McGinley herself, aproned and majestic, opened the door. There was a *gentleman* without, come banging on the kitchen door yelling out for Dr French, sent from Norwich and a Mr Tobin, given the wrong direction off the turnpike, nearly drowned in the river – an impossibility, the ford was so shallow with the drought – and carrying on so in *her* kitchen: would the Doctor oblige by stepping along at once? The *gentleman* was not dressed for the dining room.

He was a sullen, weary, brutish man in a shabby

uniform coat and huge boots and he spoke in resentful tones – a most reluctant messenger. The Doctor took him outside, down towards the horse pond, a colourless, magical stretch of water in the last of the daylight. There he unfolded Tobin's letter and read it, tilting the page towards the paler west.

'And was there any verbal message?' he asked at last, crumpling what was in his hand as he gazed out across the pond, watching a lone coot creeping about the reeds on the far side. It was late, he thought, for a coot to be about.

'No, sir.'

Miss Pennyquick was in the parlour door with a kitten in each hand. 'Little devils,' she said, 'running up the curtain and knocking over the roses.'

'Is Ann here?'

She was, pouring tea. 'My dear, Mr Tobin says the chaise is found, and the driver – tied up but unharmed – in a barn on the Essex border. But no money of course. And no Cassandra.'

'We must tell Mrs M'Cool,' she said, rising with a little clatter of dishes. 'Wait till I change my shoes and fetch a cloak.'

'Ann, Ann, there is no need for you to come . . .'

'I think I would like to. I think perhaps I would like to stay the night at Blackow. What a lonely place it must be without Cassandra.'

Ann's dashing gig being temporarily in pieces at the coach-builders, a trap was brought out of retirement, the cob hustled between the shafts. 'Mind,' said Hollin ominously as the Doctor got up, 'them's phaeton reins,' and he gently disentangled the Doctor's feet, and: 'There you are,' as Ann appeared, shod, cloaked and carrying a small bag, Mrs McGinley behind with some spoils from Thorn's dairy packed in a basket of hay. ''Tis only a bit of old dust.'

'So it is,' said Ann, climbing in, 'and who ever cared for a bit of old dust?'

The Doctor gave the command, the mare went into her collar, the bit of old dust rose about them in a small cloud. The trap was so indescribably ancient – once pulled by Hollin's notorious pony, a local byword for all that was wicked in the equine race – that it had a brittle quality, giving its occupants a sense of impending disintegration. The mare went splendidly – all horses ran away with the Doctor – but such springs as there were groaned horribly and as they crossed the Gorse, bumping in the ruts, something detached itself from the well and fell away into the dust.

'What was that?' asked the Doctor.

'I cannot say,' said Ann, clutching at her seat with both hands and not bothering to look back. 'It was not vital.'

'Then we shall think no more about it.'

He did not speak again until they passed his gatehouse, calling 'Ho, hola!' to Jim and waving a hand, a falsely cheerful gesture. At the gentle bend where the whole front of the house came in sight Ann said: 'Poor Blackow, never loved, always neglected. The Gerards did not care for it – why did they build it? Harry said even his father called it expensive and inconvenient and he was the fondest of them all. Do mind, Alex, Molly is taking charge.'

'Such understatements you horse-coping folk employ – taking charge! She took charge at the outset and is now charging us down to our deaths. Haul on that, if you please, and I will haul on this.'

'These are phaeton reins,' cried Ann, grovelling at her feet, 'Alex – yard on yard – they are phaeton reins. No, no, pull on them both together. Oh, here, give them to me! No, the reins . . . To me. Put the whip in the socket. Molly, whoa old lady.'

They swept past the front door and veered towards the stableyard. Clodie was there, giving titbits to her favourites.

'Is this an experiment? 'Tis not the safest way to get along, my dears. It is customary for one person to do the driving. Good evening to you both and welcome. Are you staying at all? Shall Driscoll put up the mare?'

Inside she fended off the hounds and strode on ahead. 'What do you mean?' came her carrying voice from afar. 'Is there food and drink in the house or not? It will not do, this constant 'twas the dogs, ma'am, 'twas the dogs. Well may you hang your head, Kitty Lynch. Bring up the port and be quick about it.' Returning to the ballroom she said: 'I have port in your honour, Doctor. You will take a glass, I hope.'

The Doctor did so and while he drank it she read Tobin's letter and grew visibly thinner, older and more grey. Silence stretched out and out, and it was too late for the quarrelling of the guinea fowl or even raised voices from the servants, all the dogs mute and the house settling down to sleep. Deep deep silence then, Ann looking at her hands clasped in her lap and the Doctor lifting his glass to the light to admire the colour.

'God save us,' said Clodie harshly after this age, 'I must be growing old. I cannot bear the thought of it, of that child dead. What was the harm in putting Cassie in the coach and turning it round? He has the money, the devil, sure he can't want the child as well.'

'I believe I should have cried the next moment,' Ann said to the Doctor afterwards, long afterwards, 'but then that sluttish little thing came in with the letter, saying that the man was waiting for a reply.'

'What man?' asked Clodie sharply.

'The one who stands on the step. Mr Driscoll has just asked him did he want a bucket of water thrown over his poor horse.'

They saw the colour leave Clodie's face and her hand shake a little as she turned the paper. 'Pooh, get out, go on with you,' she said, 'give the fellow a mug of ale and a

204

piece of pie. I have to read it again in case my eyes deceive me.'

Her eyes did not deceive her: her colour returned and with it her old poise. There is news after all, thought the Doctor, good news too. 'Read it,' she said, tossing him the letter, and in spite of all her tremendous self-control he saw the flicker of a triumphant smile. 'She is alive, Alex. She is alive.'

'Conway,' said the Doctor, reading, 'Conway again. Who is this Conway?'

'Except that he is known to Julia, I cannot say. They became acquainted long ago, in France.'

A message was sent at once to Upgate: one of Mrs M'Cool's thief-takers had discovered a tall dark man calling himself Conway in a low house in the back alleys of Woodbridge – and with him was a child, a sick child, it was said, who kept to the room upstairs. Driscoll called at Thorn on his return journey and Tom rode back to Blackow with him on a green, leggy youngster well up to his weight and frothing with excitement as they clattered into the stableyard, a stableyard frantic with activity, the garden boys and Rigby dragging forth a huge old carriage and Clodie's greys, aristocrats to a whisker, plunging and trampling in confusion. Tom choked, said 'Good God!' in his deep voice and dismounted.

'We are going to Suffolk,' said Ann, running from the shadows.

'We?' and he handed his reins to Driscoll, watched his horse led away and the greys put to, watched Rigby checking buckles and traces, turning a twisted rein, settling a browband more comfortably.

'The Doctor and myself.'

'And the old lady?'

'She says she would rather stay here.'

The lanterns had been lit, the lanterns that had shown three generations of Gerards the way home, great flickering lanterns on each side of the yard. One or two yellow-white hounds slunk about, and Clodie's terriers, and once a peacock ran from the darkness into the flood of gold and out again, roused from sleep by the endless noise and activity. Ann put up her hood and in its shelter her face was pale. 'Oh Tom, I hope she is alive.'

'Come,' and the Doctor was at her side, 'if we are to be in Woodbridge for breakfast we must start now. Tom, you are just the person. Where is that Rigby? Ah . . . Rigby, Mr Forsie travels with Lady Gerard and myself. See that his horse goes back to Thorn and send word with it that Miss Pennyquick is not to worry, not to worry in the least.'

Tom's face was all smiles. But: 'I have never been to Woodbridge,' was all he could produce to express his sudden joy.

'It occurred to me,' said the Doctor to Ann, 'that he is much more than six feet tall and is no stranger to a gun, two things that would recommend him in any cutting-out party. He also has a handsome cheerful innocent face, which is more than I can say for myself, and doors might open for him where they would remain close-bolted for me.'

The horses plunged and were straightened with a harsh word from Rigby.

'You have not passed any comment on my extra-ordinary feat,' said Tom, 'you have not congratulated me on riding from Thorn. I have just sent into the house for a walking stick as I had to leave the crutches behind.'

The Doctor looked him up and down. 'If you want my opinion I would say, you are a fool, Tom Forsie, but then I suppose you were born one and cannot be altered now. I do not know how they got you in the saddle – Hollin and Driscoll together, no doubt, the well-meaning brainless dogs – but I saw you get out of it; I saw your face and the jar you gave the leg, the way you hung upon the stirrup leather. Do not think to pull wool over my eyes. And I will add this – ' in a low ferocious voice the more shocking because it was the one he reserved for private reflections upon the Army Board and for chastising ignorant lumps of surgeons' assistants on the battlefield – 'if you put that leg to the ground before the agreed number of weeks is up, if you treat it in this light-hearted and criminal way, I will not answer for its mending, for its being a sound limb again – *ever* again, Tom Forsie. You will go a cripple to your grave.'

Speed, unconsidered speed: the miles fell away and no thought of personal comforts, Rigby on the box, Driscoll up behind, the horses . . . After a while it seemed they had always lived with the incessant growl of the wheels and the clatter of hooves, interrupted only by the demands, exclamations and commonplace remarks at the two tollgates before Bungay, by Rigby's voice as he spoke to his horses, and by another vehicle that met them on a narrow bend and pulled over with a sudden uproar, the driver shouting out, the horses neighing. It was not midnight yet, Ann thought, though at least a day and a half seemed to have passed since she and the Doctor had taken the drive to Blackow at the gallop.

The old coach, swaying on its vast springs, turned in at an innyard. 'I dare not drive them further,' said Rigby apologetically at the window, 'they are done up already pulling this blasted old coach and the near leader has taken a knock. I shall ask for their best horses to take us on a stage.' And in a husky conspiratorial whisper: 'I hev a bag of gold in my pocket, Doctor.'

'Do what you think best,' said the Doctor, adding under his breath: 'Damn that woman, scattering gold coins from here to the ends of the earth.' Then: 'Is it worth while changing to a lighter carriage?'

'There is nothing to suit,' said Rigby sourly, 'only that there, and that there will only carry two.' He nodded over his shoulder at a very old post-chaise from which two screws had just been unharnessed, two pitifully nervous beasts, all skin and bone. 'This here great ark needs six to get it along sprightly, but howsomever we shall do our best.'

Mile after mile, the familiar road to Halesworth, straight and true; Halesworth itself, mostly sleeping, Driscoll at the reins and the coach pulling over because of some obstruction, over, over, the whole vehicle on the slant, a cry of, 'Hold up, you buggers,' a dreadful slide of hooves and then the level again, 'Good lads, get on then,' from the box, and cool air coming in at the window as the Doctor peered out in satisfaction, cool air and smelling of the fields.

Saxmundham. How many hours had they been on the road? Not so many. Driscoll nursed the horses in through a splendid archway and drew up. 'Breakfast,' said Tom, smelling bacon cooking.

'Breakfast in the middle of the night?' asked Ann, roused from her stupor in the corner and looking out of her concealing hood to find the Doctor's lean and savage face illuminated by a half dozen blazing lanterns.

'It is morning,' he said, opening the door and climbing down stiffly.

Would the lady step in, there was tea and toast, hot rolls, pie, anything she liked, said the landlord, hurrying out on being told a carriage with a coat of arms stood in his yard. Ann got down to a low hum of speculation and keen eyes watched the Bungay chestnuts led away, the sweat thick under their collars and dust up to their saddles. They had gone two stages like the good'uns they were, Rigby told the head stableman, they were to be cooled down before they were watered and later they were to be fed royally, no tainted oats or sawdust.

The Doctor paused on the threshold of the inn and looked back at Clodie's remarkable carriage. 'Do you know its history?' he asked Ann as they stepped in.

'No. Do you?'

'She told me it was made so that her father might

travel across Europe in comfort. That is why it is so very large and high-sprung: the French roads of fifty years ago were atrocious, I believe. There is also that hooded seat behind, roomy and cushioned, for a servant. Yes, landlord, coffee, toast, a muffin for the lady – we must be away in fifteen minutes, no more, not a minute more.'

Driscoll looked in to the small private room. 'Beg pardon, sir, but Mr Rigby would consult with you.'

'Very well. Did you get any sleep at all in the back?'

'Not what you might call Christian sleep, your honour, but I nodded away for a mile or two between the gates. We were nearly run off the road once, the b . . . the rogue held to the middle, drunker than a lord and one of his lights on the dim.'

'Coffee will set you up,' said the Doctor, watching him knuckle his red-rimmed eyes. 'Now, where is Rigby?'

'He wanted to give me the bag of guineas,' he told Ann on his return. 'The novelty of riches has worn off and he disliked the responsibility. Mrs M'Cool only gave them to him to bribe the stable lads and pay the tolls but he has handed them over with a grin of relief. How is the muffin?'

'A little burnt but not enough to complain of. Where is Tom?'

'Hobbling in with his walking stick. He is in some considerable pain. I warned him of it, I warned him repeatedly . . . He has been pig-headed and must now stew in his own gravy.'

'That is a very odd figure of speech. Oh Tom, there you are. Come and sit down and eat before it grows cold or the Doctor hustles us all out again.'

He sat and ate, but in unusual silence. The Doctor's threats had subdued him – and the pain. The toast stuck in his throat and although the coffee washed it down in the end he looked rather pale and weary. 'That coach,' he said at last, 'they are all clustered round it in the yard, gaping and exclaiming. It is as good as a fairground exhibit.'

'The Doctor tells me it was made to travel Europe,' said Ann, crumbling the last of her muffin on to the plate and reaching for the coffee pot.

'It reached Rome,' he told her now, 'and only two accidents and something unlikely – oh, I remember: an axle setting on fire. Apparently Mrs M'Cool's father had a man called Box sitting up behind him with a blunder-buss. He sat there almost without a break from Calais to Rome, refused to come down except out of necessity or when the stop was longer than two days because he had a mortal horror of all things foreign – and that to Box was anywhere east of Galway town – so he kept a hamper up there with him full of bread and water and cheese as well as enough shot to slaughter the whole of a moderate village. Mrs M'Cool said he did not even condescend to speak until they were homeward bound and a mile out of Cork harbour and then it was only to say that the Irish Sea could never make a man as sick as that old devil of a carriage.'

The Doctor's companions laughed, as he intended they should, but Ann's dark eye was thoughtful and Tom was still not his cheerful self. Alex hurried out, found a small boy in a grubby apron and asked: 'Where is the nearest apothecary? Is it far?'

'A step, sir. Two doors down this very street.'

The Doctor pulled out a scrap of paper and the stub of an old crayon, wrote a few words, wrapped a coin in his message, handed it to the staring child saying: 'Now run to this apothecary and tell him to give you what is on this paper.'

'He will be abed, sir.'

'Then knock him up. If you are not back in ten minutes it will be the worse for you.'

In the yard three bays and a grey were being backed up to the coach. 'They look a likely bunch,' said Rigby to the Doctor as he stepped out. 'High steppers though, trotting horses. I don't know as how we'll get along so quick.'

Tom and Ann emerged. 'Good, now we can leave,' said the Doctor, and as he put his foot on the step of the coach the boy ran in, tears in his eyes and his lungs bursting, two bottles in his hand, one large, one small.

The carriage was turned, a considerable feat in itself, and the horses erupted into the road. They were fresh and inclined to break out of step at the least hint of a check, but they could trot as fast as many of their brothers could run and once out of the town they proceeded to demonstrate their prowess.

'These old hosses take a bit of holding,' said Rigby at the first toll, 'blast them, so they do. We shall be in Woodbridge afore you know it, Doctor, or even Ipswich do they rush past, the beggars.'

Woodbridge; a stealthy entry, the horses sobered at last, and a stealthier drawing-up at a back entrance, a private house with a large weedy stableyard.

'Is this the place?' asked Ann, looking out.

'According to Porton's letter, yes. See, there is the name: Old Brewery House.'

Fifteen minutes slipped away; the sun had risen. The coach was conspicuous. The Doctor took out his watch and turned it over in his hand, the finest French workmanship, his only treasure. It had visited some strange places in his company, he thought, had been stolen once and returned, had been lost twice and found, and now lay on his palm and ticked out the minutes of Porton's non-arrival.

'Good morning, gentlemen, madam,' and a small wiry man in a brown coat looked in at the window. 'Do you have a letter for me now, I wonder?'

The Doctor pulled out Clodie's single sheet of boldly scrawled recommendation. Porton looked it over, raising his blue-tinted spectacles to his forehead to do so. He had a mean, reduced look about him and though his clothes were clean his skin was ingrained with dirt – long

211

years of inadequate washing or no washing at all, thought the Doctor – and he had a large mole at the corner of his mouth that quite obviously bled every time he shaved, it was in such a sorry state.

'This coach is something,' he said, pocketing his letter, 'not easy to hide, is it? Could you not have come in a nice black ordinary post-shay with a couple of dull brown screws? A bright blue Noah's Ark and three horses with white stockings and one white all over – love you, gentlemen, there's no disguising you at all. Still, we must do what we can. My suggestion is your man takes it back up the road a mile or so, finds a decent inn off the highway and lies up for the day. There would be no difficulty in that, I hope. If questions are asked, they needn't be answered. As for you, Dr French, you must come with me, sir. And the young gentleman. And the lady.'

A good inn, a private snug and a second breakfast. There was sun pouring in through the windows now, a fine breezy morning, noise, bustle, interest. But: would the lady like to go upstairs, asked the good-natured florid woman in the doorway, hot water could be provided, a mirror, a quiet room with a sofa, a bed, anything the lady required. Ann rose and followed her out, her stomach recoiling at food steaming by, at a clutch of fashionable people who stared at her rudely as if she had been some kind of drab. But that is what I look like, she thought in surprise, staring in the promised mirror as she took off her bonnet: crushed, shabby, miserably tired. She was wearing a simple blue dress in which she had sat down to dinner with the Doctor, an old dress, neither very fashionable nor very remarkable, and half covered by her second-best, much-loved, much-worn grey cloak. Well, she thought, I am not any kind of heiress now, though I was once, and every penny of my capital is spent, no more to come until next year's harvest; no *Sable Island*.

The hot water came. She was horrified to find it turned a cloudy grey with dust from the road.

Downstairs again she found that Porton had 'stepped out to see what was afoot' – he had watchers, number unspecified, all about the house where Conway was staying. The Doctor had ordered coffee but now it had come sat looking at the pot, mortally tired, while Tom had fallen asleep on the settle, his leg propped on a chair. 'Is there any plan?' asked Ann. 'And who is this Conway?'

'Mrs Hawkworth knew him in France.' And at her astonished frown: 'Yes, perhaps in the biblical sense too. It scarcely matters. They met again in Norwich recently – she told me he annoyed her, followed her, importuned, that he had done so in France, that he would not be shaken off. I have it on reliable authority that he is a foreigner but that might mean, after all, that he is only an Englishman long-domiciled in France or Italy and become by degrees almost a native of those countries. I have known a man, a man fluent in the Spanish, return from a two-year stay in that country and swear at his servant for six months in that language before he reverted fully to his own tongue.'

'But why steal Mrs Hawkworth's child and keep her? He has his ransom. Is that not all he wanted?'

'Presumably not. But who can say what their relationship has been, what scandal, jealousy, quarrels, bitterness, foolish threats, violence even. Perhaps he uses the child to bargain for something, something from her mother not from Clodie M'Cool. Who knows, my dear.'

They sat drinking coffee together, saying no more, until Driscoll knocked and came in with news of Rigby, safely installed in a respectable tavern a little off the road two miles back, the carriage filling the yard entirely. He, Driscoll, had ridden in to Woodbridge again on one of the wheelers, now with his white blaze in a bucket of oats outside. 'Yes, stay,' said the Doctor wearily, 'we may need you.' Driscoll sat in the corner on a small chair, ill at ease. Ann could not tempt him to a coffee and he said outright suddenly that he would prefer to go out and cast his eye about the horse, he would faint with shame if any harm came to the beast.

'What harm can come to him here?' asked Ann, finding as she turned with his coffee in her hand that the Doctor had fallen asleep and was crumpled in his chair, his head tilted forward. After a little Driscoll, drawn out by her quiet questioning, began to talk about Ireland, about Galway and about Russhard. He had grown up there but it had gone to ruin when the old man died – Mrs M'Cool's father – and a cousin had inherited, a depraved soul who cared nothing for it, who doubled the rents and sold the stock and the little fertile land, who sold the tiles off the stable roofs . . . 'Dear, how th'old lady did weep. She was not an old lady then, sure, but how she wept, wept and swore and raged at once. Ah, she was a fine figure of a girl, I never saw a woman sit so well on a horse, and ride straight across a mountain if need be, clapping in her heel. "Go on with you now, Henry," I heard her say to me once when I was follying a terrible steep path on a mountain pony – her father would not let her ride out alone – "Go on with you, 'tis only a bit of a hill." Bit of a hill! It had sides like the slant of a steeple, great rocks breaking out all over, my own pony scrabbling up with his eyes closed and herself riding her half-bred at it like it was a flat old meadow. There is never a one like her at Russhard now, they say, and the people wrung with the high rents and the good land neglected. Was she to go back the half of Galway would turn out to wave her on and welcome her to her own.' His eye glittered with the thought, with the hope.

Porton returned. 'Yes, I will take a cup. A kind thought, Lady Gerard. I passed a long night of it myself.'

Driscoll said: 'I shall see the horse is comfortable,' and slipped out.

'What a strange melancholy fellow. But this is a good brew. In my opinion, madam, we should take this Conway in the house. The back entrance can be covered, there is no chance of his going over the roofs and though he is a tall wiry sort of man he does not look nimble with his fists, not a bruiser as you might say.'

'Does he never go out?'

'Yes, indeed, but for ten minutes' exercise up and down the street, never out of sight of the house though it is tucked in a filthy little yard, a hogs' wallow of a place. It's in my mind he is waiting for something, or someone, and that at a certain hour he will fly, Lady Gerard, fly so quick he leaves us standing gaping after. Not a bruiser, no, but a cunning cove. Though I have his bolt-hole watched night and day still I would not wager on catching him as he slips away – if I am not there, for instance, the boys will not dare to touch him. The Doctor must decide at any rate. But tell me, what is this Mrs M'Cool like? I have heard she is a present day substitute for the Queen of Sheba: racehorses, diamonds, packs of hounds . . .'

'She is a great lady,' said Ann, 'and the little girl is all she has to love apart from her horses and dogs. You must put your case forcefully to the Doctor when he wakes. If we lose Cassandra now Mrs M'Cool will never forgive us. Perhaps you could ring for fresh coffee – I can rouse the gentlemen when it comes.'

215

## 11

'Driscoll, what is that under your coat?'

'It is a pistol, Doctor, Mrs M'Cool give it me. "Henry," she said, "be sure the Doctor needs you as his bodyguard." But 'tis an awkward heavy piece, sir.'

'Since it is the size of a small musket I am not surprised. Put it away. Hide it. Does it fire true at all?'

'It did, sir, but that was many a year ago.'

It was doubtful if two more desperate-looking men had ever been seen in that Suffolk town, for the Doctor's face, scored with tiredness and anxiety, looked positively criminal above his travel-crumpled clothes and Driscoll wore a cloak although the night was so warm, a peculiarly sinister sight. Luckily they met no one, save one young boy in a doorway most pitifully drunk, and crept on in a most suspicious manner to the opening where Porton waited, furious and impatient.

'I said we should have gone in for him,' he said angrily into the Doctor's ear. 'Alerting the constable, turning out the watch, waiting for bloody magistrates . . . Beg your pardon, Doctor, but villains don't wait upon events, don't hang about nice and cheerful while other folk wait for the ink to dry on warrants and suchlike. He is gone. Soon as it grew dark – out he came, child and all. There was a horse in the rathole they are pleased to call a stable . . . Not ten minutes since, and he rode by me smiling, the . . . But never mind, what's done's done. What are my orders?'

'Which road did he take?'

'The road to Sutton and the sea, sir. Like as not he has a boat waiting somewhere down river.'

'Then we had better follow. I do not like the sound of a boat. Where would he be going in a boat?'

'Why, anywhere, sir. They are all amphibious here-abouts. If he knows he is watched by land what better than the sea, sir? He could be back in Norwich by water before we had smoked his intentions.'

Two minutes. Three squat ill-bred horses put in an appearance led by a gap-toothed child with boils. Porton, holding the dark lantern, looked irritated, as well he might considering they had ignored his advice and now faced a long ride – probably for nothing – into the wilderness of field and marsh towards the Deben's mouth. The Doctor gave sixpence to the erupting boy and said: 'Tell the young man at the inn, the large yellow-haired young man, Mr Forsie, where I have gone, and give him this,' and he produced the larger of his two medicine bottles, handing it over with a fierce minatory stare. 'Tell him to take ten drops in a glass if the pain is bad but no more, no more if he values his constitution. Do not drop it, I beg you. And do not try it yourself, you will regret it extremely.' He hauled himself into the saddle. 'Lead on, Mr Porton. Lead on.'

Night: black, soft, fragrant; the watcher on the road, barefoot and breathless, told them Conway had passed twenty minutes ago, the child in the crook of his arm, a packhorse behind. Night: no moon but a clear sky and, as the human eye adapted, a thinning of the black to indigo, to blue, to the division of earth from heaven, the recognition of trees, hedges, buildings, sleeping animals. There was no horseman, however, to be picked out against the quiet country. Was he concealed behind those trees watching them ride by, laughing? wondered the Doctor. Was he already waterborne, slipping down the Deben on the turning tide?

'Where are we?' he asked Porton ten minutes later, 'I can smell the sea.'

'You can smell the river. The sea is a good way off.'

They rode on, quickening the pace. Was there any point to it? The man might have doubled back, might have cut across the intervening country to the river, or might have turned north leaving them to this wild-goose chase into untamed and silent heaths and marshes. A village: only one light and that doused as they passed. This was smuggling country where everything was noticed and nothing seen. A hundred small craft could be found within three miles of this peaceful place to carry a man or his goods anywhere and at any time for the right price.

'Hold up,' said Porton, drawing rein and putting his nightglass to his eye. 'There he goes. See? Over beyond that copse, turned off the road somewhere, damn him, and pushing on. Perhaps he has wind of us.'

Off the road, Ramsholt away to the right, a feeble light and no more, the sea smell strong and the ground soft underfoot, long grasses brushing the horses' sides, reeds, a great dyke. 'What is he at?' whispered Porton, thrusting ahead. 'He has a boat for sure, a boat hidden up and waiting.'

'He will need help with the gold,' said the Doctor. 'He cannot manage the child and the gold together.'

The first sight of water, an inky calm. Were those boats? Two, three, half a dozen, crab-boats and other fishermen, all shadows among other shadows, slate, blue, pitchy black. There were the horses, the horseman gone. 'Quickly,' cried Porton with all the urgency of a man committed to a battle. 'Down there. See. A ship is out in the river.'

The Doctor looked at the open water with undisguised dislike. He had spent so much time afloat and generally in leaking, crank troop carriers. This was a small ship though, a ketch, something like: two masts, running bowsprit, figures on her deck. As he gazed a rowing boat pushed off from the bank a hundred yards away.

'Follow me,' cried Porton. Had he had a sword, the Doctor thought, tumbling from his saddle, he would have drawn it. But an enthusiastic leader, as he well

218

knew, is irresistible. He ran in Porton's footsteps, Driscoll at his back. A quagmire, grass, rushes, shingle; a splash as Porton boldly waded for the nearest mooring rope, up to his waist in a moment, cutting her loose without hesitation, leaping in, a surprisingly agile little man, drifting away on the ebb before he could lift out the oars. What if there are no oars? was the Doctor's only coherent thought as he plunged after, and: 'Pull yourself in, man. Where's that Irish fellow? God damn him, he's staying on the bank. Where are they? Has she moved?'

The ship had moved: though there was scarcely a breath of wind yet the tide was setting seawards, carrying her down with it, and besides, she was impatient, there were cross and constantly raised voices on deck as the rowing boat ceased to gain on her and for a moment, a long anxious moment, let her open an apparently unassailable lead.

'We shall have him yet,' said Porton, a mad light in his eye, and he bent to his oars with a strength the Doctor was well used to in the midst of battle, an inhuman, unrelenting, furious strength. A man of stone must have been moved, and the Doctor was not stone. He gripped the gunwale, not even conscious of his soaked breeches, his feet in two inches of water, the remarkable distance they had already travelled. He was worried that he could not see Cassandra, and even through Porton's nightglass made out only Conway in the stern and the large dumb hatless man who rowed him. Then the ship turned a little, setting a sail of some kind, and in that pause Conway's boat shot alongside to a chorus of oaths: distinct voices now across the small stretch of intervening water, one naturally harsh, one softer, the true Suffolk, but capable of tremendously inventive swearing. And there, there at last, a dark huddled shape, then a sack, two sacks, three, all obviously heavy, passed up the side.

'Cassandra,' said the Doctor aloud, snapping his glass

shut. 'Stretch out, Mr Porton, we are almost there,' and as he spoke a dull crack and a little spurt of flame. That takes me back, he thought, surprised at his own calmness, but this is better than a duel, better than standing in some draughty spot pointing a gun in cold blood ... They were sheeting home another sail but what wind there was was fickle, there was only the tide to help her still. In another minute, another minute ... Her mainsail rose at last. A long-forgotten phrase resurrected itself in the Doctor's memory, heard many times in his younger days in many a foreign harbour. He leaned forward, straining his eyes. She was only yards ahead and not gaining yet, not in this infinitesimal moment in time. No orders now, no hurry, no shouting ... Conway had no intention of shooting again though he stood there still, gun in hand.

'Mr Porton, you are a hero,' yelled the Doctor. 'Lay us alongside that ship.'

The familiar creak and groan of hull and rigging came and went. He supposed he had passed out from the blow to the side of his head. A voice said: 'Here, Jo, he's awake,' and someone stooped over him with a lantern.

'Count yourself lucky to be alive,' said the unseen, 'leaping out of a small boat flapping your arms ... Did you think you would fly aboard? I thought you must be drownded, seeing you go under like a stone. If our Luke hadn't of grabbed your ears and Patterson clapped on with the boat hook you would have been long gone.'

The Doctor became aware that his clothes were wringing wet, that the cloak someone had thoughtfully wrapped about him only gave an illusion of warmth, that his teeth were beginning to chatter and that his head was bleeding. It took a distinct effort to recall the immediate past, a dreamlike sequence of events ending in that bold frantic jump across two yards of swift water: he could feel the harsh damp rope in his hand now – and when he looked down his palm was sorely skinned – the rope hanging from the ketch's side on which he had fastened his eye. But as for the bang on his head, the boat hook, the bundling on deck . . . Nothing. But he had kept his grasp of the rope, they had had to prise his fingers open to make him let go.

'Where are we?'

'At sea, sir. Where else?' and the little ship, changing course slightly, skipped a little, shivering her sails. 'This here all about us is the ocean.'

'But where is Suffolk?' and the Doctor struggled to sit up.

'Suffolk? Ho, Patterson, the gentleman wants to know where Suffolk is?' over his shoulder, and an invisible body at the tiller replied to the effect that he might climb the bleedin' mast and see it if he cared to, but the light at the mouth of the Orwell was fading astern, he would have to look sharpish. 'You will have to bear with us, sir,' said the voice behind the lantern, 'for we have business across the water.'

'Holland?'

'France.'

The Doctor stood up with difficulty. Though the sea was calm and the light breeze steady the ketch had a disconcerting twist and waggle as she pushed on through the fading dark. It was a long time too since he had walked upon a sloping deck. He straightened carefully, exploring his head wound.

'Better to leave well alone,' said the voice and then the lantern rose a little and revealed a short square man with a creased good-natured face and a pigtail. 'Young Edward will bring you a kid of water and a towel below.'

'Sir,' said the Doctor, putting out a hand, 'do you have a child on board? A girl.'

'And if I do?'

'She is stolen. The tall dark gentleman stole her in Norfolk.'

A wary look, confusion too, a mental struggle. 'Is that so? Well, you and the gentleman must fight it out as you can. *I* thought you was a bum-bailiff and him firing warning shots across your bows . . . And *he* says he is the youngster's father. But come below and clap a towel to that bleeding, it don't do a man good to stand bleeding in the dawn air. What's more, 'tis unlucky, splashing gore about my holy deck.'

If the shambles below was any indication of the habitual state of the deck above, holy was a ten-times-unsuitable word to describe it. She was a small smuggling ketch and what accommodation she had was in her bowels, bowels that smelled not only of tar and vermin but of fish: her very planks reeked of old and decayed fish. It was nothing, however, to a man once confined for six weeks to the lower deck of a troop carrier, bad weather and a virulent fever sealing hatches and doors alike. Imprisoned in his sickbay, sending up fifteen corpses a day to be hurried over the side with a short prayer and although in theory so isolated yet breathing in the terrible fetid unhealthy fug of the hundreds of men only the other side of a six-inch piece of wood, he had learnt, for all time, to cope with smells. That was not to say he cared much for the ketch's peculiarly strong odour of rotten fish.

A grinning, well-intentioned idiot brought him dry clothes: duck trousers and a knitted guernsey, and brought the promised kid of water and an old old towel. He backed out of the tiny space still grinning and still mute, but returned with a corner of mirror which he set down near the lantern. 'Thank you,' said the Doctor. The boy waved a hand towards the stern, made some gestures, an extraordinary mime, and left. I suppose that means the others are back there, the Doctor thought, lifting the mirror closer to the hanging lantern and peering at his wound: nothing very much, a long clean gash, bruising, the usual copious bleeding. Blood had run down his forehead and cheek, soaked his stock, one whole shoulder – a spectacular amount. The water in the kid turned pink, then red, the towel might have come from one of his field hospitals. He mopped and dried, put on his dry clothes, and then sat abruptly on the edge of the locker until the nausea passed. Head wounds, he thought, remembering Ann, damn head wounds.

'Here you are, sir. Dried off at last. Not in danger of a congestion. That was a wicked leap and the old girl gathering way like the racehorse she is . . . Come in. This is the gentleman who fired at you; but at sea, land quarrels must be given over. And this – ' and the man jerked his chin over his shoulder – 'this is as to say the gentleman who fired at you's daughter.'

The Doctor took a step forward. A small pointed face, very white, very frightened, gloriously freckled.

'Cassandra,' he said and 'Oh!' she cried, leaping up, taking a plunge sideways as the deck lifted gently and then running down the long slow fall into his arms.

'How very touching,' said Conway, 'but she is still my daughter and I have every right to take her where I please.'

'There is the unfortunate question of the money though,' said the Doctor, 'the money is surely Mrs M'Cool's.'

There was nothing of this man in Cassandra, thought the Doctor a moment later, watching the light play on the sallow skin and high cheekbones: a handsome but discontented face, a long, narrow, unattractive chin. I would not question the truth of his statement though: I have known ugly, low-bred parents produce the most beautiful offspring and the reverse – Clodie M'Cool finds the same in her careful breeding policies, she has complained of it occasionally; her precious Dido's last foal was knock-kneed, goose-rumped and a nincompoop, she said, yet the stallion was if anything handsomer than the mare. So this is Cassandra's father, we must believe it, and Charles Dixon Hawkworth as fictional as once I suspected, or at least, if not fictional, irrelevant. Or does she not know whose child it is? Did she live upon the baby for a while, throwing blame for it on the most open-handed of her lovers, the one most likely to succour her? Yet Conway is far from open-handed, the very opposite of a generous spirit, a man who would be too fly to take upon himself the responsibility of another man's child. Or even his own.

The Doctor sat down, Cassandra on his knee. She said nothing but held on to the front of his guernsey much as he had held on to that blessed rope, and looking down at her after a moment, aware of the dead weight, he found her asleep: deep sleep, total exhaustion. She had been crying for hours by the look of her eyes and her whole blotched puffy face. He eased her a little on his arm and asked mildly in his deep, agreeable voice: 'Are you a Frenchman, sir?'

'I am not, but I have lived there all my life which might amount to the same thing. My mother was from Naples.'

'And what prompted you to take the child? Do not misunderstand me, Mr Conway, I have no reason to suppose you are not her father or that you do not care for her – but what kind of caring is it that snatches her from a happy house, from an old woman who loves her, and from her mother . . . The money I can well understand, but this hurrying the child away to France – what is it about, sir?'

'And what business is it of yours? Why should you damn near kill yourself for Julia's child? Are you in love with her? You would not be the first to bleed for her, I assure you – ' with a sardonic look. 'There was a subaltern once . . . Ah well. Have you ever fought a duel, Dr French? It is Dr French, is it not?'

'In my youth.'

'Well, the subaltern bled to death on account of Julia. I tell you, she is not worth your spilling a drop.'

224

'To be sure you must dislike her heartily to steal her child away – it is *her* child as well as your own. Yet you and she seemed perfectly at ease, even happy together.' She complained of your attentions yet she smiled up at you . . . how? That moment near the Rampant Horse: a speaking glance, as fond as any I have ever seen a woman give a man. Did she only speak out against you to make me think I and I alone was her current choice? Did she see it would appeal to me, a sort of proof that she too could be continent? And yet what did it really matter? The sexual act is of small account with her, a momentary pleasure as ordinary as eating buns: she might sleep with any man for friendship's sake, gratitude, curiosity, simple high spirits.

Conway had risen and was opening the door behind him. 'Is there nothing to drink in this damn ship? Wine, coffee, anything. The Doctor and I have an appetite for breakfast too.'

And then, in answer to the Doctor's remark – the remark he half repeated by saying, turning Cassandra gently so that he could stretch out his numbing leg: 'You steal the child . . . and yet seem happy together' – in a low voice, half to himself, he said quietly: 'But it was Julia who asked me to do it.'

I am not shocked, thought the Doctor; have I known it all along? No. No, of course not. But that false grief did not deceive me and I could not forget it.

'You are shocked,' said Conway easily, sitting down again. 'Did it seem to you she was a fond mother? If so, you must indeed have been in love. A cat has more maternal feelings.'

'Some women make little of motherhood, appear to find no joy in it, and yet they would not subject their child to kidnap, a long and frightening journey in the company of a stranger. And in general too even the most selfish and neglectful woman has her limits.'

Conway's thin black brows rose up and his mouth

curled in a smile of pure delight. Then he laughed, leaning back and slapping his thigh, just as the door opened to a kick and the idiot entered, chuckling himself and bearing a tray of ham and eggs. 'Surely you knew – no, how could you know? Who would have told you? That woman lived in my house in Paris for three years, and such a fashionable expensive woman . . . And the child lived there too. Well, where else would she live? I am no stranger to little Miss Cassandra.'

'Ah no,' said the Doctor, 'of course you are not. You are Monsieur Paul.'

The *Katherine* was a brisk cunning foxy smuggler and slipped away on the summer wind leaving the green coast of England far behind and bringing the green coast of France into view without the least trouble, a journey she had made many and many a time, for years and years, tobacco and brandy beneath her fishy bottom boards or in the secret places here and there about her stout Suffolk hull. Once or twice she had smuggled men, this way and that, wanted men across and French aristocrats back, spies out and in, anonymous men of no certain nation with money belts and hidden papers, run seamen, several Irishmen in 98 . . . It was with something of a swagger – that strange idiosyncratic griping motion she had – that she set Dr French, Conway, Cassandra and ten thousand pounds in gold upon a French beach that moonless, damp midnight, her boat not even grating on the shingle but standing off in two feet of water and the splash the Doctor made – he was carrying Cassandra – drawing a hoarse muttered oath and a 'That's right, tell the bloody French we're here. Strike a light, why don't you, and huzzah.'

'Will you not reconsider?' the Doctor said, wading on to dry land – a relative term, he found, for the stony sand was criss-crossed with rivulets of fresh water streaming seawards and inch, three-inch, six-inch deep lagoons left by the retreating tide.

'Julia asked me to bring the child to France. Why ask the same old questions? We have talked hours on that filthy Orford smuggler. There is no more to say.' And turning round, staring out to sea: 'You had best run for it, Doctor. The boat is shoving off.'

And shoving off it was, a blacker blob in the blackness, but most definitely a moving blob, though the muffled oars made no sound above the suck and hiss of the quiet sea and the *Katherine*, all her lights doused, was wholly invisible.

The Doctor was no coward. Under fire and under the extreme stress of operating in the field he had shown a remarkably cold and steady sort of courage, wielding his instruments with grim single-mindedness though all about was chaos. Storm, war, shipwreck, he had seen them all. But it seemed to him, on that long flat alien beach, that he had never put his courage to the test: he had never, for instance, picked up a musket and shot at the enemy, and it had not been him who had command of the open boat in which he had spent three miserable days of sunstroke and starvation. Though his makeshift operating theatre shook with explosions it was still, in the main, a safer place to be than in a square of infantry advancing on an old experienced enemy. So now, when the thought came to him, his heart beat faster instantly, he felt his hands grow damp . . .

'I will carry the child to the dunes. They have orders to wait for me.'

'On your head be it. I would not trust them myself. After all, you have paid them nothing and have cost them dear in coffee and ham and bandages. But as you will. If you are left here I will not lift a finger to help you escape, let me make that plain. I have friends waiting a little inland to deal with this.' And he stirred the oilcloth bags of gold with his foot. 'Once I give the word they will be here in minutes. It would be only natural for them to think you are an English spy.'

The first gentle hump, dry sand, deep and awkward, especially deep and awkward with a weight to carry. 'Wait a moment. My arms . . . Why could you not have carried her from the boat?'

'She clings to you. She flies out at me and cries.'

'You will have a pleasant time of it then, in Paris.'

'The maid that looked after her is still in my house, and in a few days Julia will join me. She should have joined me in Woodbridge but she did not come. No matter. She was always unsure she could get away without suspicion and by the time you get home, Doctor, she will already be on her way.'

Dunes all round now, coarse stinging grass. It was difficult to see where the steep falls were, the pits and hollows. The Doctor fell further and further behind, panting loudly, staggering often. Conway said: 'Give her to me now. They will have given you up.' He was perhaps twenty-five feet away, a voice in the darkness. 'Where are you? Come up closer. How do you expect me to pick the child up if I can't see her?'

The Doctor said amiably: 'I wonder she is still asleep. I have nearly dropped her twice . . .' and ducked sideways just as the pistol fired. A little flash of yellow-red, a report. Meant for me as I walked towards him, not such a risky shot for a man with a true aim, a good pistol and nerve. Well, he has failed, and as he stumbled down a long soft incline, hampered by having no hands and the child an intolerable sagging weight: shall I?

His plan had been to dodge among the dunes, regain the beach and run. Had they indeed shoved off and left him? The idea had come to him only during that long silent row to the shore and having it in mind he had caught young Patterson by the shoulder as he stepped out of the boat, whispering: 'Remember, you must wait for me,' in a particularly urgent way. But then, why should they wait for him? Save that he was English, penniless and unarmed, and was in the country of his enemies, what other consideration was there? He had paid them nothing: it was irrefutable. Nor would he till they returned to the coast of Suffolk where, for all they knew, instead of his gratitude they might expect to be inmates of Ipswich gaol. 'A bird in the hand is worth a whole rookery,' Clodie M'Cool had once said to him with her hooting laugh: they would want to see his money now and not risk landing him in England where they might never see the colour of it and be betrayed into the bargain.

Wait for me, wait, he cried out in his inner being, reaching the beach in a last scramble, such a desperate painful scramble that Cassandra woke, cried out – and Conway, only a little behind, swung a little lefthanded to cut them off.

Firm sand, then bog, water, solid ground again and the black heap that was Clodie's money. Where was the boat? Was there any boat? Nothing, nothing. A long long stretch of whispering dark, the hush of the shingle down near the water, an occasional gleam. The Doctor put Cassandra down, took her hand, said 'Run!' and pelted across the wide wide emptiness to the sea, his lungs so painful, his heart so noisy that when he halted, abruptly, swinging about in desperation, he could hear nothing but the pounding in his ears. Then: 'Here, sir. A little to the right,' and there he supposed it was, lifting and falling on that gentle swell, but he could not hear it nor see it, and he took hold of Cassandra and thrust her out into the water.

'Damn you. Do you want me to shoot the child?' shouted Conway, and once again the crack of the pistol – so that was why there had been a breathing space: he had crouched down to reload – followed by a howl from the boat, a sharp: 'Look lively, Doctor. Are you hit, Patterson? I have the little girl. Get in, Doctor, get in.'

A brisk cunning foxy smuggler, well used to danger, to ambush and hot receptions on hostile shores; perhaps the *Katherine*'s Jo Harris was bolder and more experienced than most, or perhaps all Suffolk men were as daring in pursuit of profit; certainly his ancestors had moored their dragonprowed boats in his home creek with an eye on the main chance. As an exhibition of neat ship-handling, silent communication, every man in his place without a word and the sails up and drawing almost before the Doctor had been pushed aboard, it was unsurpassed.

And when the Doctor began his thanks he was cut short very briskly, bundled below, told to see to his head, the bandage was adrift and he was bleeding again, bleeding again and all over the deck.

The homeward journey was pleasant enough but much slower than the outward one on account of their hurrying away towards the coast of Holland – 'and don't I wish we may not fall in with a Dutch bugger of the line, Doctor' – to avoid two bomb ketches and a frigate tearing along out of Yarmouth. If the crew of the *Katherine* were safe from impressment nevertheless they had an instinctive horror of ships carrying guns, ships with authority, ships who could and very well might ask them to heave to in order to rummage their hold. The same was especially so with Revenue cutters but even an ugly wallowing transport had them scuttling about trying to look like a fisherman, an innocent hard-working fisherman out of the Orwell. To this end they danced about hove-to under bare poles – the tiniest scrap of sail like a dishcloth set with a smirk while a vast acreage of canvas was furled in a twinkling – pretending to draw a net through the sublimely blue sea, and the transport passed far to starboard with no sign that she had even condescended a second glance, a dull half-witted ship, like so many, who could not tell the difference between the fastest, most questionable vessel on the East coast and a slow old fishing boat catching cod.

Once the horizon was clear – and it was seldom clear in this busy sea – the *Katherine* shook out her large and distinctive wings and skimmed away into that intense blue. 'Light airs and variable,' said Jo Harris, combing his hair and tying it again with a fresh ribbon, 'but they will take us home, never you worry, Doctor.' It was pleasant on deck. The Doctor and Cassandra sat on the warm boards in the bow, silent more often than not. She had felt sick, but he suspected it was more the sickness of exhaustion and relief combined. Now that there was apparent safety, now that Conway had been left behind, reaction was setting in: she was more quiet and timid than ever, clinging on to him. Oh for a good stolid motherly woman to deal with this crisis, he thought, looking down on the limp dirty curls drooping against his chest; I am inadequate for this role.

'Look,' he said, 'my breeches still blow shamelessly in the wind, my stockings too. I shall have to put them on shortly and try to make myself respectable.'

'I like you in your trousers.'

He felt a first faint hope: was shock ebbing at last? 'Look at all the gulls,' he went on, and she looked up dutifully to where half a dozen gulls kept pace with them, one or two so close the yellow of their greedy eyes was extraordinarily vivid.

'Aunt Clodie says she has eaten seagull,' came the small voice, 'she says papists are allowed seagulls on Fridays because they are a kind of fish.'

'Is that so?' and he looked up into the wondering eye of the avian fish. 'What curious sophists men are indeed. But I have eaten them myself. They are pleasant enough when one is hungry, and at the time I was very hungry, so hungry I believe I would cheerfully have devoured feathers and all.'

231

Cassandra lifted her head and gave him a long stare in which was the very faintest glimmer of curiosity. '*Where* did you eat seagulls? Were you shipwrecked? Have you eaten penguins?'

He told her yes, he had eaten penguin, salted, smoked and dried. He talked on, gently and monotonously, about his voyages, some quite unintentional, and about diet – the importance of eating up one's cabbage, for instance. Quite soon her head dropped again and she slept, her ear to the comforting thump of his heart, but in half an hour the sun was so high there was no shade at all on deck and he staggered up, cramped and stiff, to carry her below. She woke at once, gazed about in fright, gripped at him frantically. He set her on her feet, making soothing noises, and as he did so Patterson, who was look-out, gave a strange hoot and roared 'Sail!' and in the tone the Doctor understood that, whatever ship it was, it was an unwelcome sight. Harris came up, climbed with his glass to where he could see for himself, looked at his wake, at his sails, at the miles of sea in every direction and then again at the stranger.

'Is it pirates?' asked Cassandra, hanging on to the Doctor and standing on tiptoe.

'No, my dear, not pirates. At least . . .' He stared away into the dazzling noon but could see nothing, nothing yet, unless that tiny whitish smudge . . .

Patterson had descended, paused near them, said genially: 'Brig-of-war, Doctor. She will be up with us in half an hour on her present course, maybe a little more. And there is something I don't like about her . . .'

'Not an enemy?'

'Ha, that we shan't know till she come closer. I doubt it.'

'And how is your arm, Amos Patterson? I saw you climbing one-handed. Does it trouble you?'

'Not so much. 'Twas a lucky shot of his, the devil, shooting blind.'

'You will not miss a half inch of flesh. But later, when you have outrun your brig-of-war, come and let me dress it again.'

An hour passed. Though the *Katherine* nonchalantly turned away and fled, trying not to appear as if she did so, the brig changed course and followed, and it was true the winds were light and variable, whistle as they might they remained so most subbornly, and try what ruse they could there was no progress without wind. The Doctor took Cassandra below and fed her a hard roll and a cup of water, all there was, the galley stove being out. Her face had lost its dead-white fixed look but she still gave the impression of a perfectly articulated doll, rigid and inhuman. Above their heads feet ran up and down. 'What are they doing?' she asked. 'Is that other ship going to catch us?'

He did not know, he said, but all this difficult manoeuvring was pointless, strictly speaking, for the *Katherine* carried no contraband that he knew of, her men, all carrying papers to say they were fishermen, could not be impressed, and so her swooping here and there to avoid the brig was simply the automatic reaction of a guilty conscience. He hoped they would soon see Suffolk again and give up this nonsense.

Feet again: the way fell off the *Katherine* with a suddenness that caught him by surprise. 'We've stopped,' said Cassandra with a decided gleam of excitement, anxious excitement it was true, but excitement nonetheless. The Doctor climbed the companion and poked out his head.

'You may come and see her if you like,' said Harris, standing a yard away with his hands in his pockets. 'Bring up the little girl if you like.'

The brig was so close the ragged edges of her elderly signal flags were clearly visible. 'She is one of ours then,' said the Doctor.

'So she says. I thought at first she was a Dutchman.'

233

'Why are we stopped?' asked Cassandra, shading her eyes to look over the short stretch of water to where the brig rose and fell, rose and fell.

'We are hove to, dearies, 'cos she asked us to hove to and Jo Harris won't argue with wicked old guns like those.'

'Are they pointing at us?' and she stared in fascination at the open ports, the figures behind them.

The Doctor, leaning on the rail, recognized naval efficiency in the lowering of the boat, and familiar naval language came clear and crisp to his ears. The officer in the stern was a large tough solid fellow with fair hair.

'There are some ladies on deck,' said Cassandra, squinting.

'We knew it was you,' Ann said afterwards, 'because Tom recognized your coat and breeches on the washing line.'

Though the brig was more roomy than the ketch – a mere insignificant brig and yet a floating palace compared with the *Katherine* – and though all her crew seemed pleased to welcome him aboard, her captain wrung his hand heartily and Ann, his ideal Ann, was there on deck, the Doctor regretted parting from the smuggler. To everyone's amazement his first act, before he had done more than nod to the assembled officers, was to run straight up to Tom Forsie and demand money, any money, all the money he had. This resulted in a small leather bag, chinking prettily, being sent across in the boat, though it did not contain the half of what was due, the Doctor said; perhaps Clodie M'Cool, having scattered guineas like rice throughout the county, might make up the difference.

The rest of the afternoon was taken up with the recounting of adventures, the Doctor reticent about his own but Tom loud in condemnation of his underhand desertion at Woodbridge, his sneaking off with Driscoll.

And what about poor Driscoll, left on the bank in confusion, sworn at quite horribly by Porton when he returned to shore in great mental and physical distress convinced that the Doctor was dead, drowned for certain, he had seen him leap, fall against the side, go under . . . 'Imagine how we felt,' said Tom, 'knocked up in the night by these two, Driscoll like a ghost, Porton's hands in a terrible state . . . And then to be told that not only was Cassandra gone but you were dead.' The only cheering news, if it could be called that, was that Porton had recognized the *Katherine*, a famous ship in those parts and to a seaman unmistakable. Porton was not a seaman but one of his watchers was.

'And so we galloped to Ipswich,' said Tom. 'It was Ann's idea. She could not get Porton to say for sure that he had seen you drowned, he kept repeating he had seen you go under as the smuggler turned but it was dark and he was looking over his shoulder. So we knocked up His Majesty's Customs and told them the tale but they said human beings carried no duty and in any case they would only be interested in a smuggler coming home not going out, but if we cared to step along to where some boat or other was tied up by the steps, we might find we could interest His Majesty's Navy in apprehending a Bonapartist spy returning to his own country. So we did, double quick, and it was the gig or jolly boat or whatever term they use, and Captain Hammond in it just about to say "Shove off" or the like, and when we said "Frenchman" his face lit up like a beacon – and so here we are.'

The Doctor was examining his beautiful watch, ruined by seawater. 'My dear Tom, it was very noble of you to rouse out a warship for my sake, but you look ten years older, a walking corpse. Have you still kept the medicine I sent? We must . . .'

'I left it at the inn. I could not help it, Ann ran down with her bonnet on, said "Come!" and flew out of the door. I am not sure that poor fat red woman from the inn wanted to join us but Ann clapped on her cloak and hat, pushed her in the boat and that was that. It was a very dirty inn too, hard by the harbour, but Ann said she was a perfectly decent woman and William had once warned her about sailing away with six hundred sailors and no female companion – not that this cockle has a crew of six hundred but anyway, it comes to the same thing. Captain Hammond has met William by the way, and two of his officers have served with him, so that we are counted part of one big family, it seems. Anyway, they could not do enough for Ann, asking every ten seconds if she was comfortable, were even polite to Mrs Robins though she speaks such broad Ipswich no one can tell a word she says. And then after sailing up and down – we saw France quite clear. France! – we spotted you. "Now that is the *Katherine*," says some cove with a pigtail down to his waist, and they all get out their glasses and watch, and alter course a little and watch again. "She is running away from us, the saucy whore," says the First Lieutenant, and so they put up some more sails and change direction – and here you are. We saw Cassandra first and then the washing and Ann said, "He is alive." I never saw her so happy since Dr Loder asked her to marry him.'

The Doctor put down his watch with a trembling hand. 'Since when?'

'Oh,' said Tom, turning red. 'Oh. I am not supposed to mention it. Ann said . . .'

'So she is going to marry Dr Loder? I had thought there was a strong possibility of her accepting George Neech . . .'

'Neech!' cried Tom, who had not forgiven the man for his disastrous interference with the harvest gang. 'By God, I do not think I could stand that.'

'My dear, he is a decent man, unobjectionable. He will give her a happy home, children, companionship. I am surprised she should even consider Loder, I thought she disliked him – mildly perhaps, but disliked is certainly the word – and I did not think her judgement so at fault.'

'Oh but she is not going to marry him. I only meant . . . I mean, when she told me how he had asked her, well, we laughed about something, I forget what, and she was the old Ann, full of life. But of course she turned him down. Why, the miserable long-faced so-and-so, he asked her – no, he told her – to sell the farm.'

'Yes, I see,' said the Doctor, who had sat down and reopened his watch, puzzling at its internal injury. 'That was a terrible mistake on his part. To be sure the dear girl would give it away tomorrow but she will never sell. Now I wonder if there is a man aboard who was a watchmaker before he was a sailor? And while I am about it, I shall seek out the surgeon – if there is one – and his inadequate medicine chest – it is bound to be inadequate unless he has supplemented it privately – and see if I cannot find you something to make you sleep until we touch land. Are you over the worst of your sickness? The waves are very little, the motion very slight. But still you are Methuselah and a dead dog combined . . . You must take a strong dose and immobilize that leg.'

Voices outside and a knock: Mrs Robins to say Cassandra was asleep at last, such a sobbing and for so long she had never heard. Lady Gerard thought the Doctor might like to know.

'And where is Lady Gerard?'

'She is gone up the deck, sir, to take the air. She is quite worn out, the lamb.'

The surgeon, a very young, ill-trained, enthusiastic boy, gave him the run of his medicine chest with the greatest good will in the world and said that not only would he be glad to carry a draught to Mr Forsie with his own hand but that if Dr French would permit, he would re-splint the leg, he had whiled away many hours devising new methods of total immobilization, a warship saw so many fractures in a nasty blow, deck plunging, masts whipping about, ratlines frozen sometimes. 'Pox and more pox and broken bones,' he said mournfully, comparing his watery existence with that of a land surgeon, 'and scurvy when we were in the southern latitudes, provisions running low, no greenstuff and adulterated juice . . . And I have seen gaol fever in some quota men. That was unpleasant. And hernias . . . scores of those. Boils. Lice. But I have never been in action yet, sir. I cannot say how I would tackle such damage as I would see then. Sometimes . . . I am not very sure of my skill at all.'

He hurried off to settle Tom and the Doctor climbed the short way to daylight and fresh air, coming out into a flood of evening gold, Hammond walking up at once saying: 'The coast is in sight, Doctor, and the tide setting just right. I believe I may say that you will sleep in a feather bed tonight on the solid land.'

'The solid land would be very welcome.'

'Is your head very painful, sir?'

'Oh this. No, not in the least now. And your excellent young Mr Brown has put this dressing on, a sort of elegant wisp,' and he raised his hat for Hammond to see. 'He is clever with a bandage, young Mr Brown. But pray, Captain Hammond, might I have a word with Lady Gerard? I have not spoken to her since I came aboard and there is something I must tell her about the little girl.'

'Can you not take an hour's sleep before we reach land?' was his question when they came face to face by the rail, the blue water slipping by below.

'Perhaps. Alex, that poor child . . .'

'I know, my dear. But perhaps the crisis is past. We must hope so. I was never so pleased as when she howled, seeing you there; she has been so deathly quiet. But listen . . . Conway claims to be her father . . .'

'So that is what she meant. I could not understand her.'

'Wait. This is between the two of us. Conway claimed to be her father, told me that Julia Hawkworth was to join him in France. Do you understand? Yes, I thought you would. They are to begin a new life together on Clodie M'Cool's money.'

'But neither of them want Cassandra' – a fierce low voice, looking down into the water.

'You may be wrong. Conway certainly went to a great deal of trouble to get her to France – he could so easily have abandoned her and run away with the money, abandoned Cassandra and her mother. But he is a strange, difficult man, perhaps in the last resort even a little weak. He speaks ill of Mrs Hawkworth, calls her names, yet I believe he looked forward to her joining him, that ten thousand pounds *and* Mrs Hawkworth was nearly all he could desire. I say "nearly all" because his life with her was never wholly satisfactory and never will be and he knows it. It is why he rails at her yet does her bidding. All this escapade was her idea, I have no doubt. You see, though he deceives her with other women he cannot reconcile himself to her deceiving him with other men. I am sure they have rowed mightily. It rankles fiercely, he never ceases to allude to her amours . . . All the names he calls her, the little stories he tells. He is not even sure Cassandra is truly his child and still he wants to believe it. It took me some time to realize why he repeated the fact so often: "You cannot interfere, *I* am her father . . . If her father does not have the right to decide his daughter's future who does," etc. etc. If he had not been so bold with that pistol I might have come to pity him: he pursues a dream and knows it.'

'And will she join him now?'

'I believe so. After all, he has ten thousand pounds.'

They had stood side by side speaking into the emptiness of sea, their voices lowered. Now Ann sighed, turned to face him: 'I must go below. Cassandra might wake.' Her eyes travelled over him. 'Alex, how tired you look. Does your head hurt you?'

'Thank you, no. It is only tender to the touch.'

'Pardon the intrusion,' said the First Lieutenant, stepping up, 'but Mr Brown would be much obliged was you to go below to admire his handiwork, Doctor. He has devised a new splint for Mr Forsie and is uncommon pleased with it. I hope you will be encouraging, sir,' in a lower voice, 'for he is a kindly young man and though ignorant – he could not function, he said, without his well-thumbed book – he means well and tries hard. The hands are very fond of him.'

'I am glad to hear it. But tell me, did you see Mr Forsie for yourself? Does he sleep?'

'Like an ox, sir. Oh, I beg your pardon . . . What I mean to say is yes, he is as fast asleep as any man I have ever seen, you would think he was in a coma.'

'Good,' said the Doctor. 'If we can keep that leg still half an hour I shall consider it an achievement.'

# 12

Here was Lydd's Row, the narrow opening, the green door at the far end. The Doctor heard the bell clanging far off, and light footsteps approached, the girl he knew opening the door and saying she did not know if her mistress was at home. She showed him into the parlour, however, and left him: he could hear her climbing the stairs.

'Alex, Alex, oh how glad I am to see you!' and Julia ran in, fragrant, stylish, dressed in white.

'I did not see you at Blackow so I thought I must call when I came to the city. How well you look. How very well you look.'

'It is joy. Cassandra returned . . . And all because of you, because of your courage. I might have known. I always did know. You are one of those men who hides your light under the bushel or whatever. How can I ever thank you?' She was agitated, walked to the window and back, turned the little gold rings in her ears. 'You have not come to scold me for staying at Blackow such a little time? No, you are not a scolding man. I could not do any good there, Alex. Clodie and Cassandra are happy in each other and I . . . I am superfluous. I thought that in a little, when she is more grown up, she might like to come and live with me again, but I see now she will never do so of her own free will . . . No, never. She is quite at home in that dull old house, riding her pony and digging her garden. I am no asset to her and she would be none to me. I can see that now. "You should not have been a mother," Clodie says. Well, and so I should not, I never wanted to be.'

She ran forward suddenly, taking his hands, kissing

241

his mouth. He thought: yes, yes . . . And then: I am grown very cold after all. It is seeing Cassandra in that extreme state . . . Cling to him as she would he was all resistance, a resistance begun in his mind and slowly overcoming every last vestige of lust. He allowed her to kiss him. While she did so his thoughts remained quite clear, quite coherent: she is doing this for a purpose, she has no immediate sexual desire, this glow is something else entirely, this warm happiness. Is she glad because her lover is free and in France, the richer by ten thousand pounds? Is she to join him shortly?

'You judge me after all,' she said suddenly, stepping back. 'You do. It is in your face. And you are quite unmoved. Alex, you were not always unmoved.'

'Dear Julia, I . . .'

'You think I am no kind of mother, a selfish foolish fashionable neglectful woman, encouraging men like Conway . . . How could I know he had designs upon the child? Men expect such standards yet have none themselves. Cassandra's father refused to own her, never asked me how I did, never cared if the baby lived or died – and no one accused him of failing in paternal instinct.'

'Conway is not Cassandra's father then?'

She stood perfectly still, her breath coming quickly. 'He thinks he is. I suppose he was taking Cass to France in the hope I would follow him there, live with him . . .' Her clear blue eyes were raised to the Doctor's face. She is trying to gauge what I know, he thought with that awful clarity, she is trying to decide if Conway told me anything, spoke of her . . . She knows, poor woman, that if Conway spoke of her part in all this she is lost. 'Cassandra's father . . .' and she shook her head, turned away. 'I loved Charles Hawkworth and I married him, but he was young and penniless and died of a consumption within a year. After that I was inconsolable for a long while and . . . and indiscriminate. I do not know Cassandra's father.'

242

'Then I think perhaps you must be brave and tell her so. Or tell her it is Hawkworth after all, the lie is in the best of causes. The child thinks she is Conway's and she hates and fears him. He was not unkind to her; in fact, I believe he was kind enough in his own fashion, but he snatched her away from all she knew and loved. I believe she had some small fondness for him when she knew him as Monsieur Paul and believe me, hate and fear and the dregs of affection are too much at one time when one is only eight years old. She does not want him to be her father, she had imagined her father a different sort of man. It would be kind in you to convince her he is not.'

Julia turned her back on him, her head bent: a delicate ear, fair curls at the nape of her neck . . . Had she planned her daughter's kidnap with naive delight, never seeing the effect it might have? Or had she planned in cold blood, deliberately discounting such certain pain, eager only for ten thousand pounds and a resumption of her old carefree life?

'What lies you believe I have told you,' she said quietly. 'I told you Conway was an old friend, I did not mention that I lived in his house for three and a half years . . .'

'My dear, I am not an inexperienced boy.'

'But you will think I lied and lied, that nothing I ever said to you was true.'

'But perhaps I never set much store by what you said so I can never be so disillusioned. Lies come most easily when we wish to give a good account of ourselves, or to avoid a hurt . . . Would you have believed me if I had said I loved you? No. You would have smiled and passed over it, would have taken it as lightly as it deserved. Men say such things in bed, you would have said. And you would not have counted it an outright wicked lie.'

She said softly: 'You never said such a thing. After all you are too honest.'

'And we both grow too melancholy. You were in such

243

spirits when I arrived, Cassandra restored, Conway far far away . . .'

'I was fond of him once.' Was this to serve as an excuse when she ran away to join him?

'I never doubted it. But you will speak to Cassandra? Whatever else, you will do that?'

She turned, looked up smiling. He thought he had never seen her so lovely except that evening, sitting in the garden at Blackow, and that night, her hair falling over his hands. No falseness, no pretence, an innocent serenity that only lacked the freckles to be Cassandra.

'Bless you, Alex. I will do it straight away.'

The *Norwich Mercury* carried an advertisement: A convenient mansion house . . . a spacious hall, ballroom, withdrawing rooms, library, extensive domestic offices, eight large commodious bedchambers . . . coach house, stabling for twenty, purpose-built kennels, two walled gardens, glass-houses . . . set in a delightful park with large lake, temple and folly.

'I did not know there was a folly,' said the Doctor eating his supper at Thorn, he and Tom snug in Ann's parlour with Spring and the puppies in a hopeful press about their feet.

'Nor did I. I asked Ann and she said there was a sort of ruin in the copse on the far side of the lake. She had always thought it was another ice house or a pigsty.'

'I am sorry the old lady is so hard pushed. I never thought it would come to this. And all the time . . .' And all the time Conway sitting on her box of gold and waiting for Julia to join him. But he could not speak of that so he bit off his words and a piece of his sausage together, reflecting on the difference between lies and half truths, mortal and venial sin. It was two days since he had been to Lydd's Row and true to her word Julia had come to Blackow and taken Cassandra for a long walk through the park, through the park and up on to the Gorse over the broken-down fence. The child had come home rather quiet but filled, he had thought when they called at the gatehouse to bid him good afternoon, with a new confidence, and she and her mother had been almost pleased with each other in a muted way, perhaps as close as they had ever been. What had Julia said, up there in the wilderness, walking the sheep paths? I shall never know, thought the Doctor, but then it hardly matters . . . And when Julia took his hand to say goodbye he kissed her cheek with more affection than he had ever felt for her, said quietly: 'Thank you, my dear. I wish you every happiness.'

'I think you do. But how solemn. You speak as if I am going away,' and she avoided his eye, gazed down on Blackow through the trees. 'I could never come to love a place like this, so much country . . . And in winter how could one stand it?'

The Doctor ate steadily through his sausage, three pairs of keen brown eyes watching his every movement. Tom, his leg now packed in a Thompson's splint purloined from the Norwich Hospital, said: 'Shut them out, the rogues. They are dribbling on my slipper.' Afterwards, when the Doctor came back, he said: 'Have you heard any more about the Army?'

'There was a letter waiting. I am to present myself in London next Monday.'

For a while they spoke of committees, the endless chat, the too frequent straying from the point – far from the point, halfway round the world, metaphorically speaking – and how, sometimes, one prayed for a benevolent tyrant, a man who could not only take command but accept responsibility, who did not say at every turn: it will not do, it must be referred to another department . . . From this they came to Ann's desire to go to a harpsichord concerto – Tom groaned at musical evenings – the excellence of the Bungay theatre, the travelling fire-eater, snake man and conjuror met on the

Upgate road, the Leicester rams on view at Swannington the next week, the Cook's drill machine he intended to buy at the Michaelmas farm sales, gardens . . . Yesterday when he had called at Blackow with a cheese and a gallon of cream Clodie M'Cool had taken him on a tour of the gardens. He was aware it was a signal honour, said Tom, but for himself he did not care for gardens, for the inescapable bother, for their always growing weeds by the thousand while all the interesting things went into a wilt – and one only had to turn one's back between May and September and anything of a lawn took on the appearance of a badly grazed common.

The clock struck the half hour with a choleric whirring, sudden rattle and a dry clicking. Two other clocks elsewhere could be heard dinging simultaneously. The dogs sniffed at the bottom of the door.

'It grows late,' said the Doctor, 'I shall help you upstairs and then hurry home. I suppose you are invited to Cassandra's picnic?'

'We all are. Babs says nothing on earth will induce her to get in a punt on the lake but she will not miss the rest for the world. There is some French confectioner engaged, incredibly expensive, and judging by the way those garden boys were going at the drive when I was there not a blade of grass will be out of place on the day. I would like to know how she is paying for it. The way I am going to pay for my Cook's drill, I suppose – with fresh air.'

'Is it that bad?' asked the Doctor. 'I knew the loss of the *Sable Island* would make a great difference but I never thought it would mean – what was it Ann called it once, that dreadful time? Retrenchment?'

'Oh, we shall not starve. We are out of debt, the harvest has been good . . . Though I do wish – it may be an unChristian thought, I cannot help it – I do wish she had not distributed *all* our capital to the widows and children. It was a noble gesture but it leaves us the shorn

246

lamb, and who knows what winter winds to blow? Besides which it leaves the farm her only possession, her only material asset, and George Neech treats it already as if it were his own.'

'He has not asked her to marry him?'

'Not yet. Well, since coming home from Suffolk she has been at Blackow and now Mrs Palmer's for the night, some more wailing I suppose, and a greasy Italian sobbing on a fiddle. I am sure he will be here the minute she returns, putting the question with a loving look when all he loves is Thorn.'

'You have grown excitable, I see, on the subject of Mr Neech. You fear you will be supplanted? Has it occurred to you he may at this very moment be putting the question with a loving look to the romantic accompaniment of wailing and sobbing on the fiddle?'

'Good God!' cried Tom, starting up and then sinking back, anchored by his splint. 'Alex, you don't believe he is? At Mrs Palmer's? Oh never. Never!'

And outside the door, hearing the note of anguish in his voice, Spring and the puppies began to bark in sympathy.


'I am obliged to you, sir, for being the harbinger of great joy,' said the small cowed man in Menzies' front parlour, bowing low, a man who had just learnt that the lump in his wife's side was almost certainly benign, was operable, was hardly to be thought of.

'Not at all,' said Alex French warmly, 'but you must mind and bring Mrs Hollett to the surgeons soon, nothing is to be gained by putting off what must be done. She will bear it nobly, I am sure, and you may look forward to many more years together.'

'What rot you talk, man,' Menzies burst out as soon as the front door closed and the footsteps died away along the street. 'What odds do you give 'tis malignant after all? *I* was not sure of it, that was why I asked for your opinion. In any case it is grave, a difficult site for one thing, and she is fat . . . She is prone to histrionics too, damn talkative and steeped in self-pity. She will never survive the operation.'

'When you talk like this you remind me of Loder. I shall continue to believe, and you shall not shake me from it, that the physician's first duty is to cheer his patient. Often no more is required, time and Nature work to effect a cure. In this particular case we need a docile, willing, courageous body upon the table, one trusting the surgeons implicitly and optimistic of full recovery. I did not lie to her, Menzies, nor to the husband.'

'Bah! You did not tell the whole truth either. You have led them, in effect, to expect a miracle.'

'And by the way, I have bought two tickets in the Lottery, almost my last money in Gurney's and as ill spent as any I have ever thrown away on cocks, or dogs, or the black beetles the men used to race in the troop ships.'

Menzies gave a series of grunts which Dr French took for laughter and said it was a cavalier way to treat with a dwindling fortune. He understood there was a first prize of twenty thousand pounds – what he could not do with such a sum, what the Hospital could not do with it; and he grew steadily more excited over the possibilities of such wealth until, having agreed to swap a fresh liver – female, young – for a pot of superior anchovy paste, he spoke aloud the sudden thought: 'But when did you ever meet a man who had ever won more than ten pounds on the Lottery?' and all his enthusiasm drained away.

The Doctor's pocket, capacious though it was, was not large enough for the liver which, wrapped and double-wrapped, he was forced to carry awkwardly in both hands. He was hurrying down past St Peter Mancroft in a complete dream, intent on his morbid treasure, when a large hand fell on his shoulder. 'Alex, I say . . . Alex,'

248

and Barsham's heavy eager face swam into focus above his own.

'Where are you hurrying to? I have scarcely exchanged half a dozen words with you since you came back from that extraordinary adventure in Suffolk. May I walk along with you? Is the parcel something special?'

'Oh, oh this. 'Tis just a liver. I must gallop it home directly, it cannot wait. At least, I must *walk* it home, my pony has been injured.'

'Injured?'

'Shockingly injured. He ran away with Dr Loder early this morning – there was a small box overlooked, he had sent a note for me to collect it.' The mean-spirited dog, he might have added, not to have brought it to the gatehouse himself, the Lord knows how often he crossed the Gorse on the Norwich road. 'While I was in High Common he was called away, some kind of seizure, but his horse is lame and he begged the loan of mine. I told him I had never had him in harness, I would not advise it, but he is an obdurate sort of man and ignorant too, more ignorant than I am perhaps on the subject of horses – I believe he thinks them quasi-mechanical. So there it was: harness clapped on, trap brought round, and away he went.'

'He did not jib then? He went into his collar?' asked Barsham, whose memories of watching colts broken to the plough suggested that an unwieldy dead weight and the combined pulling power of four men could not hold a horse when he took it into his head to bolt.

'He certainly went forward and at a tremendous rate. It was fortunate Dr Loder fell out at the first bend. The pony fled to Thorn but the place was full of hogs about to go to market, and like many of his kind, he does not like hogs. He dashed on through the river, struck over some fields somehow, came on to the turnpike and jumped the tollgate.'

'With the trap behind.'

'I fear so. He cut his legs about, I fear. The moment they had cut him from the wreckage the fools let go of the bridle and he was away again. He came to his old stable at the Grey Cock and stands there most forlorn. I have cleaned the wounds but there is gravel deeply embedded in his knees, I am sure of it. I have only stitched the gash upon his shoulder, it is inadvisable to stitch the knee . . .' and he ran on a little, walking along at Barsham's side to the Cock, complaining of Loder: 'A shabby thing to snatch a man's pony from under his nose, shabby, unmannerly, foolhardy besides,' and asking how an intelligent man – even a moderately intelligent man, even an idiot – could think of driving a saddle horse. One might as well tie a can to a cat's tail. At the Cock he grew very gentle and mild, talking soothingly to the pony in the dark and ancient stable. 'Now, this will not hurt much, my dear. Stand very still for me. What a difference in this patient and my other this morning. I ran up to Menzies' house when I had seen this – ' and he waved a hand down at the pony's legs – 'and borrowed some few instruments from him, probes and the like, and was about to run back when he asked me to give my opinion of . . . Well, I shall not say of what. I may say it was a lady, middle-aged, querulous and very scared, also difficult to examine, contradictory in her replies to my questions, and unusually, disgracefully fat. I do not mind a talkative patient in general, one can learn a lot by listening, even to nonsense, but she was such a very tiresome mixture of self-importance and prudery. And here stands this dumb beast, in considerable pain, lets me poke about without complaint . . .' He poked too deep this time, however, and the pony staggered back. 'Oh,' said the Doctor, 'what I would not give for Clodie M'Cool to be here.'

'Does she use such wicked-looking instruments on her horses then?'

'I have seen her rasp their teeth. I wager she could sew

all four legs back on were they to fall off – if it could be done there is no doubt that she would do it.'

'She is to sell the horses, all but two and the child's pony. I never thought I would feel a pang for that old witch, Alex, but think of it . . . Sell her horses. It will break her heart.'

'I believe she has sold whole stablefuls before – should that be stablesful? But where is she to move once the house is sold?'

'Moore told me she had asked about Hoyley's Lodge, that isolated old place the other side of Hilborough. It would fit in the stableyard at Blackow. It has been empty four years, the rent must be practically nothing . . . Alex, what is all this about Ann Gerard giving away all her money?'

The Doctor rose from his knees, brushed straw from his coat and fixed him with a steely eye. 'I know nothing of it. If you are so interested in the gossip of the district why do you not attend one of Lady Barsham's tea parties or charity meetings and discuss these things with people of like mind? Pray, mind where you put your feet – my liver is down there. Are you handy with bridles at all? Put this one on him please while I pay Mrs Badcock for the oats. I shall lead him home slowly, the poor brute, and give him into Mrs M'Cool's safekeeping.'

'I left him walking the beast away up St Stephen's,' reported Barsham to his wife two hours later as he walked in to dinner at Upgate. 'He is still on the road no doubt. He did not look himself, Louise, he had that foul-weather scowl, but then some fat old woman patient of Menzies had upset him, I think, and the state of his pony's knees.'

'Perhaps his head troubles him. There is going to be a dreadful scar, almost to his eyebrow.' Her husband, she judged, wore his own version of the Doctor's foul-weather scowl, a milder look for certain but still a danger

251

signal. Should she ask how his meeting had gone? She knew he was not on the best of terms with the Lord Lieutenant and that any discussion of general policy – and this had been one, an attempt, she suspected, to make every petty commander believe in the efficiency, omniscience and boldness of his overlords – would turn up old grievances, old omissions and worse: old family differences going back five generations. She leaned over to ring the bell. 'Oh Nancy. Tell Miss Charlotte dinner is ready.'

'What is wrong with the gong?' demanded Barsham. It was a gong the Doctor had carried back from India and he was strangely fond of it.

'The stick has been lost. You know, the striker with the knob. Charlotte thinks one of the dogs must have chewed it. She was out earlier searching the places where they hide their bones.'

'Damn foolery. You could strike it with a spoon, come to that.'

Louise took a breath, said gently: 'I see you have had a difficult morning,' and moved towards the door.

He had endured a difficult week. Two parish meetings to discuss the impending invasion had somehow degenerated into an inter-village squabble about whose responsibility it was to ring the bells when the moment came. That the moment was bound to come, signalled from Yarmouth church tower across the miles of quiet and prosperous land, was not in doubt. But they were peevish and inflamed – this threat had been with them all this long hot summer – and they longed to be in action at last. The mood had been unquestionably bellicose, but they had taken out their passions on the sexton, the curate and the obdurate churchwardens. This had been followed by trouble among the High Common Volunteers, the Captain being an officious and unsympathetic man and falling out with all his immediate subordinates, one of whom, nominally a Lieutenant, was an intelligent elderly man who had once served in the regular Army. The quarrelling between these two having reached a certain pitch and the troopers laying down pitchfork and blunderbuss every half hour to listen to the latest row, Barsham had been forced to step between them. His natural authority was not great, however, and his military duties clashed horribly with his social ones: these were both men who frequently dined at his table and whose families had lived next door to his own for years.

'They were at it again today at the meeting,' he told Louise, smelling the mutton being carried in next door but not moving from his chair. 'I wish I had not had to take them there, but Clarke was invited and Collinge is related to the Mayor so got himself invited, and it was damnably embarrassing, I can tell you, both of them sounding off, nobody else getting a word in, shouting even, and all in public, in Norwich, in front of greater men. Save bawling them out there was nothing I could do, they would not take hints. Afterwards Harmer said a bucket of water might have done it, like fighting dogs . . .'

Charlotte came in. 'I have found it, but Tod has eaten down to the ball on the end,' and she showed them a sad object, almost unrecognizable.

'You look very charming, my dear,' said her father, bending to kiss her, the greater part of his irritation draining away as he did so.

'Well, I am going to Thorn this afternoon.'

'Not to see that Tom Forsie alone, by God!'

'No, Papa. Cissie Petersfield is coming with me and Ann will be there. And Miss Pennyquick. And even the Doctor.'

'Oh,' said her father, mollified. 'You may not look for the Doctor until this time tomorrow. He is walking his pony home from Norwich.'

*

The familiar lanes, deeply rutted and choked with dust, the familiar pattern of fields, the curve of the small hills with their clinging oak woods, the solitary cottages, the out-of-the-way hamlets, the lonely churches: they all griped at his heart. He had made this country his own, was safe in the affection of its people; he was not a sociable man and he had never courted popularity, but he knew that this was so. It was in a sombre mood that he turned the last bend that brought him to the foot of the Gorse, and in a sombre reflective mood he led his hobbling pony up and up between the great outcrops of the plant that gave it its name.

There were cattle standing together swishing their tails, herded by a little girl in a red dress; there were swallows skimming the short turf. A sense of peace and wellbeing overtook him somewhere where the road lifted to the level and grew and grew, so that he tied his pony to a bush and wandered a little in search of those elusive bustards, meeting instead the charcoal burners on some errand, pacing along in single file, all of them pitchy black. Then there was a sunwarmed hollow and a tinker child with two geese, and half a dozen sheep panting in the shade, and an old mare and her well-grown foal; and permeating heat and quiet and blessed wilderness on all sides. It was true he had been in other places that had given him this kind of repose; jungles sometimes, the desert always, wide ribbed Atlantic beaches, the vast oceans; but here especially, where no danger threatened, no job cried out to be done, no guns spoke, no orders were given, he felt a remarkable limitless joy, a perfect freedom.

Or did the knowledge that home comforts were less than a mile away add to his content, or the familiar unchanging sounds, the familiar view, the very smell of the familiar earth?

But I have no ties of blood to this place, he thought, coming round a bush to surprise a bustard and surprising instead a whole family of rabbits from great-grandparents to fourth cousins; of the twenty years I have called myself Dr French of High Common ten I have spent in far-distant places, in other worlds, one might argue, where hardship and danger have darker meanings than here on this old Norfolk heath. Yet I do indeed belong here, there is an undefinable, tenuous link. Why should the smell of the gorse move me so? The gorse smells the same in any part of England, in the Low Countries, in France . . . The smell of gorse, crackling dry in the sun: if he were thrown into space and returned blinded he would know where he was in an instant.

'There is a wasps' nest under this roof,' said Clodie, who was standing on the mounting block in the yard poking at something under the tiles.

'My pony has met with an accident,' said the Doctor.

'So he has, the poor soul. That will teach him to jump a great gate with a trap behind him. Hand me up that broom, Doctor. I shall stir them up, the buzzards.'

'I would not recommend it.'

'Holy Mary,' whispered Driscoll as he came to lead away the pony.

'You will be stung,' said the Doctor, handing up the instrument of doom.

'Ha, frightened of wasps, d'you think I am? Look at the little vermin now, going in and out.'

He looked. A stream of angry orange bodies poured forth, circled, tried to re-enter. Clodie lifted a tile. The stream was enlarged. 'Perhaps not,' she said, brushing her face and then her arms. 'We shall have to smoke them out or drown them. Rigby! Rigby. Do you know anything about wasps?'

He knew enough, said his expression, not to ginger them up with a broom handle. He stood well away, looking up politely but muttering under his breath. Clodie jumped down off the stone, shook out her skirt, threw down the broom, cried: 'Oh! Oh, they are in my hair!' and ran away round the corner with the agility of a ten-year-old.

'I have run them off me,' she said a little later, returning to look at the pony's knees. 'They gave up the chase when I jumped the lavender. Yes, well . . . I have seen worse. 'Tis the bruising causes the problem. See? The bruising and the grit driven in with such force. If we are not careful there will be proud flesh.'

'But how did you hear about him?'

'That Barsham called on his way home from Norwich, did not get out, thank God, but poked his head through the window. It was something to do with weapons and church bells. I could not understand a word. I like a man to take a job seriously, but how can such an ox – I beg pardon, he is your friend, I know – cope with this grievous muddle? The truth is the government has called this Volunteer Force into being and now don't know what to do with it, and meanwhile never-ending bureaucratic muddle and deception, pikes offered and rejected, muskets in short supply, false alarms every other week . . . Go in to the house, my dear. You will find a letter in the library. Yes, for you. A letter for you. Never mind the pony, Rigby and I will tend the pony. Go in, Alex, go in.'

The library, she had assured him once, contained four travel books, a novel entitled *The Depraved Husband and the Philosophic Wife* and a Bible. ''Tis a striking sight,' said the Doctor to himself, gazing at shelf upon empty shelf. On the great old oak table in the middle of the room were some sheets of blank paper, a writing stand, a little pile of spilled sand, and a letter with his name on it. He opened the shutters a fraction, letting in the sun, and then he sat in the only chair, deep, comfortable, worn and with a pile of cushions, a slim book stuffed into its vitals; he pulled it out and found it was a traveller's phrase book.

A dashing hand, but the letters not well formed and inclined to suddenly stand upright and then lean back as if the pen followed the train of thought so exactly that where thought ceased or grappled with difficulties the words shied and reared up in their turn. The Doctor read it through once, laid it down, walked to the window. From this window he had first seen Ann Gerard, walking in the park; no, not walking, running, young Harry at her heels. She had not worn any kind of hat, he remembered, and she might have been the boy's sister, turning to grasp his hand and laugh, and run on. He went back to the chair, picked up his letter.

'My dear Alex – when you read this I shall be on my way to Paris. There is a packet leaves Dover regularly for France, an unofficial packet of course, but mutually convenient, and this time in three days when she reaches Calais I shall step ashore to be married to Paul in a church hard by the harbour. *You* will not say: what romantic nonsense; you will say: how they deserve each other. For you have guessed my part in all this, have you not? I was always afraid you saw too clearly and now I find out from Paul he told you so much, almost everything. How like you to have pretended otherwise at our last meeting, so courteous and so kind, and all, I suppose, because you knew Cassandra was safe, that I would relinquish her to Clodie. It was not what I intended, I meant to hurt her heart as well as her pocket. She suspected Paul from the first – had she spies in Norwich? Had someone pointed him out at the Assembly? I told him not to go, not to be so foolish, and I was furious when I found him there. Sometimes he is a little reckless, perhaps it is his Neapolitan blood, but he is very fond of me, very very fond. By marrying him I become a French citizen as he has been one years and years and so shortly I shall become your enemy, dear Doctor, but only on paper, believe me for I remain your affectionate Julia Hawkworth. P.S. I beg you as a man of honour to burn this and tell no one. The package is for Cassandra.'

Naive, absurd, he thought angrily, she has been reading Mrs Bonhote and that Fanny Burney. My affectionate Julia Hawkworth! And: burn this and tell no one. After she has told me at the top of the page that she hurried me from the Assembly to her bed so that I might forget I had ever seen Conway. But no, that is hardly fair: I followed her willingly and being given the choice, chose to enter her house with all alacrity, a very lustful dog indeed. No, no. She is a touching combination of studied guile and blundering innocence, but I must not lay my own sins on her head. A marriage in a church hard by the harbour. I hope so, for her sake, or she will pass a sorry and uncomfortable war; however well he stands in Parisian society he will find it difficult to pass off an English mistress. If his protection fails she will be interned. But what is this package? And where is it? There is no package here.

The bar of sunlight on the floor altered its angle. For once the house was silent, not a dog raised its voice, not a shriek rose from the kitchens, and all the guinea fowl were patrolling the far side of the lake. The Doctor sat in his chair, the letter and the phrase book on his knee, and after a while he opened the book at random and read how to complain to the landlord at third-rate hostelries, what coin to offer, how to address sluggish waiters, postillions who galloped too fast or trotted too slowly and those who refused to supply tea and toast, decently roasted beef, horseradish and milk. One could also, it seemed, ask for more dangerous commodities: 'Sir, I pray you, where might I find a woman of the town?'

What a singular word they suggest as translation of that delicate phrase. Now how among the many did he hit on that? It might procure something far different . . . Where I have met with it among the deluded, poxed sailors of Martinique and St Pierre it had a most specific meaning: the wrong sex entirely. Perhaps it has come to be corrupted in the Indies, is still respectable in France.

Still, I would hesitate to use it in Marseilles, or Nice, or even Paris, for fear of being misunderstood. And what is this: 'Monsieur, I require some tincture of laudanum, some balm of . . . rhubarb . . . ginseng . . .' You would do well to find ginseng in the wilds of Piedmont, my friend. You wish me to look discreetly away, my affectionate Julia Hawkworth, while you post to your Dover packet and set sail for that church hard by the harbour. Your Conway tried to kill me – a wild, ineffectual, undisciplined shot, I believe he was afraid of his gun – and he might have killed your child by chance; I give him this, he would never have killed her by design. I must keep to myself then the miserable tale of your deceit, of how you are not only a liar but a thief, for it was you who robbed Clodie M'Cool of her ten thousand pounds, you who planned each detail. I know enough to hang you, you are wise to flee the country . . . My enemy on paper.

The anger left him again, this time for good. He stood up, groping for his tinderbox.

'I smell burning,' said Clodie, coming in a moment later. 'Or is it soot? They will have to put a goose up these chimneys if they cannot find me a decent sweep, lumps of soot the size of my fist rattle down every hour.'

'Tell me,' said the Doctor, picking up the poker to stir the mess of ashes, 'was there any package with my letter?'

'Package? I believe there was. Is it not on the table? Perhaps that Lucy has run off with it to the dining room where she lays out my post. No, look . . .' and she stooped, peering. 'There it is beneath the table.'

It was a small slight thing, not many inches square, tied with string and sealed. 'It is for Cassandra,' he said.

'Well, Cassandra is away to Thorn, best dress, best slippers, hair crimped up as well as Kitty can do it; taking tea with Ann Gerard and that Barsham girl, the pretty one with the big blue eyes.' She looked down at the parcel in his hand. 'Perhaps you should open it. Julia would not mind. If it contains what I think it does it must be locked away; 'tis not a present for a child.'

He hesitated, fiddling with the loose knot of the string. 'She has left Norwich,' he said at last.

'Well of course she has. What did you expect? She has gone into keeping with that Morris, I suppose, or that gross profligate ancient man Warner. He has an estate in the north of the county, somewhere by Cromer. She threatened to run off with him once – he sent her jewels, paid the rent on that house in Lydd's Row. Why, Doctor, you did not think *I* furnished her with the money? I would not. Had I done so it would not have ended there, all her debts would have piled at my door, and debts there would have been, she has always lived expensively. When I would not budge she called me names and galloped away to try her fat corrupt old man who wanted, so she said, to marry her. Let us hope he does, if that is where she has gone. In ten years she will not find it so easy to coax sapphires from lewd fools.'

'I did not know of Warner.'

'Did you not? You look a little pale and ill, my dear. You have the sunstroke from that long walk with the pony. I shall ring for ice-packs, thank God there is still ice, though we have dug so deep it is twenty-year-old vintage stuff, laid down in the year eighty at the very least. But come, humour me a little – open the package. It will not be dishonourable in us, or did she insist Cassandra see it first?'

He shook his head, pulled the string, smoothed out the paper. The rubies Mrs Palmer coveted slid out upon the table.

'Ah,' said Clodie and smiled. 'I thought as much. Well, bless her then for one good deed at least. The earrings and the necklace . . . Yes. I saw my mother wear these once. It is fitting they should come to Cassandra, though to be sure I asked Julia for them when Tobin and

260

I were struggling to come by the ransom. "Give me the rubies," I said, "help raise the price of your own child." But no. "These are the Russhard rubies," says she, "and will never leave me while I live." She liked a dramatic phrase, did Julia.'

'I believe your pleasure is too exultant for my taste, madam. It savours of triumph and . . .'

'Alex, my dear,' and she scooped up the jewels, thrust them in their wrapping and put all into his hand, closing his fingers tightly. 'You must forgive an old woman a little triumph, it is not what you think. It is relief. Do you not see what these jewels mean? They mean she has given up her claim on Cassandra. They mean she is not coming back.'

'Shall I tell you about the Russhard rubies?' said Clodie half an hour later as they sat on an iron seat on the lower terrace looking down on the lake. 'They are not worth a very great deal, after all, but the necklace is a pretty thing, a pretty thing to keep. My father's youngest sister was Julia's grandmother – we are cousins at some remove. This youngest sister ran away with a military man, an Englishman, but he did not marry her and Julia's mother was born in a London lodging house. She was brought up on tales of Russhard, the great house and the fine relations. "When you grow up," she was told, "and tell them who you are, they will welcome you home." When she grew up and put it to the test that stiff old man my father would have none of her. It had cost him dear to bar his door to a sister he loved and part of the price he paid was that there was no softness in him ever after, he had brought himself to be hard by locking up his heart and it was never unlocked, not to anyone. So Russhard did not welcome her home, and in a while she married a schoolmaster, too poor to spare a penny in the Sunday collection, and she brought up her daughter to hate the name of Russhard and all who belonged to it.

261

My father was dead by then and I had spent his money – a mortal pile of money, Alex – but though I was young when he died I had gone into his affairs with the lawyers, I knew my Aunt Julia had run off with a soldier, that there was a child my own age or thereabouts; I did not know then that she had knocked upon my father's door the year before he died and that he had sent her away. Oh, it was nothing to me to be generous, not then, not with that heap of riches, so I picked out the rubies and set them aside and instructed the lawyers to find Julia and Julia's child. It took them many months but they did so, found the child only, though, for Julia was dead, a fact my father knew and I did not. That was how the rubies came to Marianne, and after Marianne to Julia her daughter. Though they ate crusts and wanted clothes to their backs that woman would not sell the rubies. Of what they were the symbol, God in his mercy knows. And then one day I receive a letter saying: "My name is Julia Hawkworth, I am your cousin. Will you do me the kindness of righting the sins and omissions of fifty years." I did not know what manner of woman she was then, but she seemed in distress and she had the child with her. And you know the rest.'

'Ten thousand pounds was a high price for the sins and omissions of others.'

'Perhaps. Or perhaps it was her due after all. Ten thousand pounds was nothing to me once. What it means now is that we shall have to leave Blackow and draw in our horns a little. But with the money from the sale of the estate ... Never fear, Doctor. We shall survive. And it was a pitiful small sum to pay for Cassandra and no money better spent in my life. Now, your colour is a little better. There is nothing like being out in a garden for reviving the spirit. Do you think you are strong enough to walk? I have a surprise for you. The Chinese mystery is in flower.'

# 13

Down by the river the new young miller looked on with a grin of sympathy as the old flat-bottomed boat turned round and round on the mill pond. The mill owner herself, looking unperturbed, sat in the stern under a sunshade and he distinctly heard her say that this was the ideal way to see the country. Little Miss Cassandra, grappling with the heavy old oars, could only squeak in reply: she had no breath left.

'Here,' said Ann at last, 'perhaps if we take an oar each. After all, we shall be rowing against the current and two will be far better than one.' She put down her sunshade and came to take up her new position.

The boat turned once more but this time remained with its bluff bow pointed upstream and the valiant rowers bent over their task. 'We shall row up to the ford,' said Ann, 'and then drift back.'

The river had shrunk to a quarter of its normal width, a process which had left wide expanses of mud exposed on either side, mud that in its turn baked and cracked, mud on which the gasping cattle now walked with slow and painful steps, it was cooked into such bone-hard ridges. The flow of the current scarcely troubled them and after a little Cassandra said: 'I can do it. I can do it,' watching her own oar dip in and out, in and out. Fifty yards was enough though, she was panting and her face was scarlet.

'We shall go on a little,' said Ann. 'Let me have both oars and sit there in the stern and navigate.' The blades scraped the paved bottom of the ford so she reversed one oar and poled them over, dropping into a comfortable rhythm on the other side, the willows slipping past and the alder scrub on the bend just before the place where the cattle drank . . . They rounded the shallow bend at a splendid speed and ran straight into Tom's young shorthorns, all standing knee-deep in the cool shade. Long streams of silt drifted downriver; in the silence that followed the comic scramble Ann said: 'They must never have seen a boat before,' and dabbed one oar urgently to stop them going aground.

Moored beneath the trees they shared the sandwiches and afterwards Cassandra leaned out, staring into the water. 'Is there anything left alive?'

'Very little, I should think. The poor fish are all up by the mill arches trying to keep cool.'

Cassandra trailed her fingers and poked experiment-ally at the soft weed. A small weary bird piped from an elder and the sound of trickling water was very loud. Then several finches alighted on some hogweed, made a sudden great chatter and flew away again. Ann slipped the knot that made them fast and the boat swung gently round on the current and drifted, only needing the lightest touch to guide her. 'Oh,' said Cassandra, 'oh, how quiet it is without the oars.'

So quiet that they came down to the ford before the horseman there could gather his reins. Ann swung her oar, turned the boat, and grounded.

'Perhaps, sir, you would be so good as to push us off again,' she said, adding indignantly but very low: 'Instead of standing there like a pudding.' The man rode to the bank and dismounted but was obviously anxious about his horse – a short-tailed chestnut she did not recognize – and cast about for a place to secure him. It was only when he came delicately over the hard mud that she saw he was elegantly dressed: a very fine brown coat, the whitest cravat, boots boned and polished to a mirror finish; she saw also that it was George Neech.

'I cannot come any nearer,' he said suddenly, 'I shall

264

get wet. If you could hand me one of your oars I might push you off from here.'

He does not recognize me, thought Ann.

'It is Mr Neech,' said Cassandra. 'Good afternoon.'

'Good God!' and then, recovering: 'Lady Gerard. Forgive me, I did not know . . . But surely this old boat . . .' and taking a bold step nearer: 'It leaks.'

'Only a little, and we can only sink six inches if we sink at all.' If he cannot push us off I must, thought Ann. She stood up and stepped out over the stern by Cassandra.

The water might have been shallow but the mud was soft and yielding. She sank to her knees laughing, her skirts, her old cotton skirts, floating out like the weed. She leaned her weight on the bow and the graceless old tub ground back obediently.

'Lady Gerard . . .' began George Neech in an admonishing tone. She had gained the stones of the ford by now, walking along by the boat, and he could see not only her bare slender white feet but a length of elegant leg outlined in her wet skirts. Such behaviour – and that young fool at the mill ogling from behind his floury windows . . . 'Lady Gerard, I had ridden over to call on you.'

She saw him looking at her ankles as she climbed back in. 'Then I am sorry I was not at home.'

'May I wait for you? Can you spare me a quarter of an hour?'

The boat was already ten feet away, ten yards . . . 'Perhaps . . .' she said and the rest was lost as she was carried away round the last bend to the mill pond. When he walked the horse along the track to the mill and met her there, seated on a flat stone and putting on her shoes, she said quietly: 'You are the first to know – I did not mean to tell anyone yet but you have been such a good friend – Tom is to have the whole of Thorn. There, it is out. Is it not a splendid idea? Maybe the match with Charlotte will come off after all, for the only objection now is his birth: "only half a gentleman" as he puts it.'

'But . . .' said Neech, obvious dismay in his face, 'but, dear Lady Gerard, I cannot help thinking it is a lamentable step. Why, you have been so involved with Thorn and . . .' The mental effort of adjustment was too great; he fell silent. His ability to keep up a flow of talk for civility's sake being small at most times, and her revelation having left him bewildered, they walked the small distance to the farm without speaking, Cassandra running on in front. In the gateway, when Ann turned to say: 'Please do step in. I shall run up to change my dress, it will only take a moment,' he shook his head, pleading a prior engagement and riding away on his new horse with a grim look.

'Tom,' she said, marching in and throwing her straw hat on the sofa. Tom was propped up by her desk and was making lists. Since he had been so closely confined – 'like a gaolbird' he complained – he passed a great part of the day making lists and worrying anyone who passed by and asked him how he did to add to them or alter them. Now he said, without looking up: 'They should have begun harvesting the beans. Why am I not allowed out on my litter? Look, these are all the things we need and do not have – there is a mark by each one we might easily come by second-hand: the troughs and mangers for the new cowhouses, for instance. There is no problem there. But this Cook's drill. Ann, I had set my heart on a decent drill at last.'

'But we have a drill. In fact, we have two. We are the only farm in the district with two and now you are proposing to make it three . . . But Tom dear, please listen.'

He gave her his grudging attention and found her flushed and oddly nervous, standing looking out over his head into the garden.

'I have told George Neech that you are to have Thorn.'

'You have done what?' in a bellow and then, a little lower: 'Why? Why? Women are all alike, speaking out, no thought for the consequences. Why should you tell that man our business? In any case, I will not sign the documents. You have told him a lie.'

'Then you should sign them and make it the truth.'

'Suppose he tells someone else?' he rushed on, ignoring her. 'He has his old mother staying with him, Babs says, and everyone knows old women have nothing to do but squawk among themselves. It will be blab blab all over the parish before we have eaten our supper tonight.'

Now he looked at her more closely he thought perhaps her agitation stemmed from anger, but it was a deep bitter difficult sort of anger, not at all obvious. He saw that her skirts were very damp, here and there a smear of green and round the hems a low tide mark of mud. Then he heard Cassandra's highpitched laughter in another part of the house and he remembered. 'Of course, you were out on the river. Did you manage the boat all right?' and with a sudden suspicion: 'I hope you and Cass did not fall in. Ann . . .' and when she suddenly looked down, biting her lip: 'Ann, what have you done?'

That well-known lift of her chin. 'I believe,' she said, 'that I have just cured Mr Neech of his ill-considered passion. The Doctor told me how long long ago but I would not listen, and there I have been all these weeks fending him off, avoiding him, keeping such a distance, when all the time . . . When all the time . . .' Her voice died.

'He has not insulted you?'

'No, of course not,' and she smiled gently, put a hand on his shoulder. 'He called to ask me to marry him, I am sure of it.'

'Babs told me he knocked. I thought it odd he did not stay, just sent in his compliments. Rum time of day to propose . . . I thought he might have done it at Mrs

267

Palmer's musical evening: I am sure a musical evening is more the place than a river bank.' He took her small cool hand in his large warm one. 'But why did you tell him a lie?'

'I do want you to have Thorn, you know,' and she brushed the damp fair curls back from his forehead. 'I suppose I wanted to know if he would still take me in my shift without a penny.'

Tom gave a wry smile. 'I take it he will not.'

'Apparently not.'

Silence. The clock ticked, thought about striking the hour, ticked on, struck. The chimes were echoed by those other clocks about the house, all fifteen seconds behind.

'Do you mind very much?'

'Mind?' It seemed to her a mild word for such cruel disappointment, the sudden breaking open of old wounds. She had liked and respected the man, had thought seriously about marriage. Until the Doctor had proposed . . . 'Of course I mind that he only likes me for my land. Or perhaps it was my paddling in the river – ' with a grim smile and an attempt at cheerful lightness. 'He is rather quiet and strict. He would not care for any wife of his taking off her shoes and stockings and running about in the mud.'

'Nor would I. Nor would most men,' and he grinned, pulled her closer so that she could read his writing, pages of writing, some neatly underlined. 'Look, I believe I can see how to do it. If we left the troughs . . . See. We would save enough to buy the drill.'

'Dr French! Dr French!' cried a breathless Bringloe, appearing round a thicket of brambles nine feet high, 'I have been searching for you, sir. That charming child Cassandra climbed a tree by the Blackow gate and said she saw you coming but then you vanished and did not reappear. I ran out at once, having hurried back and forth,' and so he had, but rather less like one of Clodie's hounds and more like a senseless puppy, bounding in all directions at once. 'I have brought you some news from Norwich.'

The Doctor stood a moment, brought back only by degrees from another world: a long, elegant and high-ceilinged room in Whitehall full of great men, medical and military, to whom he was giving an impassioned speech on the proper treatment of the soldier both at home and on the battlefield.

'Bonaparte is dead?'

'What? Oh no, no! I am afraid it is nothing of a political nature. It is domestic for sure.'

'But what could be more domestic? Are not young women and old instructed how to drive all the beasts west and north if he comes, their babes and grand-mothers hanging on their arms? Do we not weekly ruin our dinners and even our breakfasts in order to march and countermarch with pike and musket – if pike and musket are available? I would to God he would either die or get himself and his army into his much-vaunted flat-bottomed boats and come over here where we may give him a bloody head.'

'Oh, what fighting talk!' cried Bringloe, fanning himself with his hat. 'But I see you are weary, sir. Surely you have not walked from Norwich?'

'I came by Pashman's cart to the foot of the hill there.'

'But then I passed you! I passed you on the turnpike, flogging my poor donkey along as fast as he could go. Had I known . . . Why, had I caught you so few miles out of the town you could have turned back at once.'

'But why should I turn back, sir? What is this news?'

'Oh yes, well of course . . . I took Noah Briton to the Hospital this morning for an operation on his eye – he cannot see at all well so I undertook to lead him there – and I met a Dr Menzies, your colleague, your old especial colleague. He saw that I came from here, asked

269

if I knew you, grew very agitated, said you had been in London and that there was an urgent message waiting your return. Then he said he would write a note, would I deliver it? But he had no sooner written the first word than he was called away – an accident, a terrible accident – and cried out in his hurrying off along the corridor that I was to tell you to check your Lottery numbers, to check them against the tickets drawn. Oh Doctor, could it mean you have won a handsome prize?'

There were larks directly overhead, an unbelievable intensity of sound. 'He did not say which prize?'

'Oh,' said Bringloe, 'surely that would be indiscreet? But he repeated that you were to check the tickets, repeated it several times.'

'Well, if it is five guineas you may give it to old Briton with my blessing,' said the Doctor.

The Doctor told himself he preferred Bombay to Norwich, though Norwich was built on charming small hills and in the crook of a charming river. He told himself that it might be a prosperous and elegant city with a great many beautiful gardens and a splendid cathedral but it could not compare with that other place on the far side of the world: it did not compare in excitement or interest or in smells. It did however, this fine morning in early September, hold a surprise which even Bombay would be hard put to match.

'Oh,' said the Doctor when informed of the fortunes of one of his Lottery tickets. 'Oh. Is that so? I had not expected it. I had not expected even a tenth part of it.'

It was a beautiful morning, yet another in a long succession of beautiful mornings they had had this year, on every one of which they had confidently expected an invasion and on every one of which they had been disappointed. The sky was its customary unsullied blue above the jumbled roofs and there were small boys on the river paddling rafts between the keels, or fishing, or plunging in and out. From St Peter came a sudden bell, silenced almost before it had begun, and from the Cathedral another, muffled and distant. No, there would be no invasion today. And through this pleasant sunlit city the Doctor walked without conscious thought, following a route imprinted in his brain, so that in fifteen minutes when St Peter's full peal rang out over the heads of the market traders he was already in the meadows by the river, stared at by the placid cows and a flock of distressed sheep – distressed because the grass was all burnt away and the only green was on the river bank, out of bounds beyond their fence.

The Doctor climbed this fence and went to the edge of the water, and sat down and took off his hat. Then he unfolded his newspaper and looked into it, but apart from the usual patriotic poem asserting that all Norfolk men were ready to teach the French what liberty, fraternity and equality were really about, the only words to catch his eye were those lauding Spilsbury's Anti-scorbutic Drops, an advertisement that appeared in every edition and always made him grind his teeth, for he had written two learned papers on scabies and could not stand a quack, even a well-meaning one.

Beside him the river slipped quietly by towards the sea, towards Yarmouth where several warships waited for the French as they had done a long while now, where Lord Nelson was used to come and go, his home port, and where in the past the Doctor had sent a patient or two for sea bathing. He thought of his friend William Claverden on a ship keeping watch over Toulon, and of Jardine Savage of Jamaica . . . Perhaps Jary is the only man I have ever met, he thought, not affected by his wealth in any way. He would be as liberal with sixpence as with sixty thousand pounds and he cares nothing for social standing. Not affected by wealth, no, but then he had been brought up among poor black fishermen, only snatched back to the bosom of his wealthy family for

271

fleeting visits. The Doctor pondered the effect of this double life, the probable effect of it on a man's attitude to money; he pondered on the differences between wealth inherited and wealth earned by toil or invention or business acumen, by fraud or luck. Luck. Now there was an unfathomable thing: luck.

'Good day to you, Doctor,' said a hearty voice above and there was Paine, one of Menzies' assistants, leering down at him.

The leer was occasioned by the sunshine, by this time a full steady blaze. 'I must give you joy of your good fortune,' Paine continued as the Doctor got to his feet and folded his newspaper. 'Of course I do not know the sum involved – *you* may not think it a fortune – but I do know the prizes appeared substantial to a man of my means. I would give a great deal to be in your shoes this morning.'

'I am sure you would, you ill-mannered young cub,' said the Doctor under his breath, walking away down the path. 'And how is Dr Menzies' cardiac distortion? Has the treatment answered? What is your opinion of Spilsbury's Drops and Spinluff's Cordial and Welch's Female Pills?'

'Ah,' said Paine, who did not know which question to answer first. He did not know anything about a cardiac distortion and he suspected this Drops and Cordial nonsense a piece of eccentric gammon – he had been warned about Dr French, an awkward, testy character. 'Ah,' he said again with a knowing look when the Doctor turned in at his bank, but he hurried away thinking that it could not have been a very substantial prize after all for the Doctor's face had given no sign of joy, not the least human hint of it.

The bank, however, was charmed to have charge of Dr French's money, it had seen so little, so very little money belonging to that gentleman in the past, for he had existed entirely on a combination of his Army pay when

272

he was a regular regimental surgeon and a small inheritance left him by his foster mother, plus, at long intervals, the miserable fees for his doctoring High Common. Since he did not attend very many rich men and undercharged those he did it had often been a wonder to the bank how he kept body and soul together, especially since when money was to hand he was rashly extravagant in the matter of new surgical instruments and the most expensive tea, and – or so they always suspected – in giving away small sums to the needy. It was a blessing he rented the house in High Common from Barsham, a kindly and long-suffering landlord, and at an exceedingly low rent; and also that many of his patients, perhaps the majority, paid him in kind, so that he never lacked a hen for his poultry coop or a rasher of bacon for his breakfast.

'I would advise investment,' said Mr Harborn, deciding privately that first of all his client might care to invest in a new razor and a hat brush, 'otherwise you might find the sum frittered away on this and that. It is surprising what a very little way such a huge sum may go in unwise hands: a classic case of here today and gone tomorrow. But make a wise investment and the sum will grow, d'you see? You may live handsomely on the interest.'

'Unless the bells ring for the invasion.'

'Doctor! Never think of it! Besides, I believe that rapacious fellow has missed his tide as they say in the Navy, that he ought to have come in the spring. For my part I cannot see the point of delaying all this perfect summer and then taking to small boats when gales are expected. In another month the weather will be against him. And then there is Nelson . . .'

The Doctor knew that to get a Norfolk man to drop the subject of Nelson was not easy, but by interrupting quite flagrantly with a series of shrewd questions – or fairly shrewd for an amateur in the financial world – he turned

Harborn from the Admiral to safe funds and compound interest.

'I had it in mind,' he said at last, when Harborn's flow had diminished a little, 'to invest in some property.'

'Property?' A long, furious look. 'What kind of property, sir? Property is always a difficult thing on which to give advice. I really think you would do well to leave it alone.'

'A modern, convenient mansion house, a park, a few dozen acres?'

'No, no,' and Harborn shook his grey head violently. 'Not a good time to buy. And there is your imminent return to the Army to consider . . .'

'Irrelevant, sir.'

'I assure you it is not irrelevant, Doctor, not at all. You cannot buy a property in Norfolk and then tear away to the ends of the earth without another thought. Who will tend your few dozen acres, for instance? You will have to appoint an agent. Buildings deteriorate, gardens go to ruin, pasture must be maintained. If you let you must make sure you receive the rent, that repairs are carried out, that the lease is not abused, that the insurance is paid . . . Oh no, a property is usually a very great bother and seldom makes a satisfactory return.'

'I have a property in mind,' continued the Doctor firmly, 'but I hope to purchase anonymously, otherwise there would be difficulties thrown in the way: the owner is a friend and might jib at being made to feel the object of, how shall we say, charity? It is a delicate situation, you understand.'

Mr Harborn looked gloomier and gloomier. 'I do, of course. And of course if you are set on this transaction, if it is a question of helping a friend . . . Yes indeed. I shall say no more. Our Mr Arbuthnot can act for you, can remain your agent if you so wish and settle any leases, rent monies and so forth. I will impress on him your desire for secrecy, absolute secrecy. You may certainly

274

trust his discretion. I have never employed so discreet a young man.'

The Doctor said he would be happy to do business with Mr Arbuthnot on Mr Harborn's recommendation, asked if he might draw a little against his fortune for immediate expenses and left with several crisp notes in an inside pocket. The sun was less strong now and the gold, dusty light slanted across the city. By any standards – ordinary standards – I am a rich man, he thought. He did not find it cheered his soul. But he found the French confectioner's open as he went up Queen Street and succumbed to the urgent temptation and went in, emerging after a long while with the usual anchovy paste and some pickled mushrooms and half a Dutch sausage. This purchase lifted his spirits. He thought suddenly that he had not had twenty thousand pounds yesterday and it would not materially affect him if he did not have twenty thousand pounds tomorrow, but he had made sure of his anchovy paste today. This made him smile, and surely he ought to enjoy good fortune when it came his way.

He hummed a few notes of a complicated piece of Bach, too complicated for his mental state, his vocal chords and his imperfect ear. He tried it again, nearly run down by a waggon as he crossed the road by the market, and again, so absorbed in remembering the true sequence of notes that he walked blindly, in danger of losing his parcel if not his life. 'And then the cello joins, dum-dum-dummm. *Was* it a cello? Such ages since I listened to the piece, a year perhaps, more . . . Why should it come back into my head today? Twenty thousand pounds, dear God! I shall make an anonymous donation to the Hospital of course . . . dum-dum-dum-dum . . . No, that is not right. What will Ann say?'

'Mind that cove with the parcel,' cried the boy at the entrance to the King's Head to the driver of a departing chaise, and the horses pulled up, shaking their heads.

'Mrs Badcock, my dear, here is some money for a shawl, one of those shawls you have always so admired,' as he ran into the Grey Cock.

'My goodness, Doctor, what a terrible heap of money. No, no. How could I accept it? Are you all right, dear? You have not been with those rascally medical gents who delight in the bottle?'

'Not at all. It is for you.'

''Tis not corpse money?' In the dim past the Doctor had once sold on a newly purchased corpse at a profit thus enabling him to treat his friends to Mrs Badcock's cooking. She had never forgotten it, not least perhaps because the corpse had occupied her stable while the gentlemen were striking the bargain.

'Corpse money? I beg your pardon. I had thought – ' in a low and offended voice – 'that you had always wanted a silk shawl.'

'Oh my dear, I do! I shall run out for one directly. It is just,' and she looked down with a wondering eye, 'that it is such a very great deal of money.'

On September 10th it was announced that all aliens were to leave the country – alien French that is – and were to have assisted passage across the Channel. Barsham called at Blackow to explain that this in no way affected Cassandra even if she was – and it had not been proved – the child of a French citizen. He choked dreadfully over this for he found, having started, that he could not say it and keep within the bounds of polite convention: he could not say it and fail to cast aspersions at Mrs Hawkworth's morals. He managed to stumble on, redder and redder, to the end and luckily Clodie's sardonic smile was lost on him in his confusion.

'Better half French than undiluted English,' she snapped, wicked enough to enjoy the sight of him reduced to incoherence and tied hand and foot by the double cords of manners and good nature. He might kick off the bonds of good nature but manners would hold him fast. But then she took pity on his distress and had Lucy bring him a bottle of cold white Spanish wine, a sort he had never drunk before – 'Oh, a case of them fell my way a while ago. I know nothing of wine. I never have' – and it was wonderfully refreshing, extraordinarily good. Accompanying it was a large pasty: solid meat, pints of gravy. He had never expected anything half as good from an Irish kitchen and he ate up half his prejudices along with it. Clodie left him alone saying that she had to see to her horses, she never sat about making conversation, he was welcome to finish the bottle and call for another and there were a score of pasties in the larder.

'Damn strange house this has become,' he said to himself a little later, brushing the crumbs of the second pasty from his lapels and stamping into the hall where he found his hat decorating the stair post.

The Irish, he thought, getting into his carriage, were passionate and irresponsible. Who else would behave so oddly? He lowered the sash to ask Dyball why they had not moved and found it was because Dyball was discussing bog spavins with Clodie M'Cool.

''Twas a kind thought you had,' she said unexpectedly, riding up to the window. She had a high colour but she did not look passionate. She sat at ease on a tall chestnut horse quite up to his weight and to which she must have seemed as nothing: an irritation, a faint tension on the reins. For a moment he seriously wondered how she would get back in the saddle supposing she were to come out of it far from assistance. 'Give my regards to your wife,' she continued merrily, edging the chestnut closer to the window and bending low – painfully low, her bosom colliding with the saddle horn – to look in on him. 'Tell her I am to leave at the end of the month, the house is sold – or will be when the lawyers have ceased their bickerings – so there will be no hunting in this country the coming season, she may keep her husband at home.'

'I am sorry to hear it,' he said and found that he was, he had not hunted in a long while and some inner part of him warmed at the thought.

'I shall not sell Dido. No, I shall not, not until bailiffs come hammering on the door.' Here the chestnut snorted, pretending he saw a lion in the interior of the carriage. 'Go on, get up! What manners!' cried Clodie, bringing him back to his former position with precision. His rolling eye was on a level with Barsham's own and perhaps they shared an equal anxiety as to the true disposition of the lady in the saddle; neither of them, certainly, would ever get the better of her. 'Ha,' she said, bending down again, 'I am a tough old nut. I don't crack at a small reverse nor do a pack of legal boobies put me down. Has it crossed your mind, has it now, that this horse would carry you all day and never turn a hair, not one, though you asked him to jump every hedge and beck between here and Scole? A fine tall man like you needs a fine tall horse to show him off. You could not go wrong with him – he has a stout heart and gentleman's manners.'

He kept a good stable and she knew it. She also knew that he had always curbed his enthusiasm in the interests of common sense, good housekeeping and a natural anxiety – as a family man – for his neck. He did his best but he could not convincingly disguise his interest. He went a deep crimson and cleared his throat uneasily, while both Clodie and the chestnut looked in on him.

'I do not need another horse, Mrs M'Cool,' he got out at last.

'But your old white hunter is past his best, hardly up to your weight. If Cooper buys my hounds there will be some hunting after all and then you will wish you had bought this nonpareil for the sixpence I am asking. You would scour the country and not find an animal with a bigger jump in him.'

He did not doubt this: all Clodie's horses were of a fast, leaping variety. He turned redder still in an unholy state of indecision.

'Well, think it over,' she said, straightening. 'Good day to you now,' and she let the chestnut walk on with a proud, elastic stride. Barsham watched them go with a leaden feeling of opportunity missed.

'Home,' he said dully, 'drive home.'

As he trotted up the long drive he looked out to see Clodie cantering easily among the great trees by the boundary. She seemed so small and the horse so big it was impossible to believe she was not an ineffectual passenger, but he saw her check him, change leg and start off again, as neat a little display as he had seen. That it was for his own benefit he never guessed, thinking her too far away and quite unaware of him.

But Clodie M'Cool had been selling horses all her life.

'I tell you I am tempted,' Barsham told the Doctor later, finding him unexpectedly at Upgate in a shabby and debauched state, unshaved, ill-shod and hollow-eyed.

'Tempted by the horse – or the hounds?'

'Well, it would break my heart to see Cooper have them, he is a wild extravagant cub, much like Harry Gerard used to be. But there is absolutely no question . . . What would Louise say? Do you know what they cost per annum?'

'I do not. I am not interested in dogs at all and keeping three swallows for a sennight taught me the expense involved . . . Imagine it: if we say that twenty swallows are the equivalent of one small dog, one would have to provide for a thousand . . .'

'Are you quite well? How can twenty swallows equal a dog? Are you drunk?'

'Why do people keep asking if I am quite well? Lady

279

Barsham was kind enough to give me a glass of sherry wine when I arrived but I do not think I am in much danger from one glass. Listen . . . Listen, I have come here for your candid opinion, your advice, even perhaps a favour, but I will not discuss it while you prowl about in this agitated state. And I know what you are at: you are computing the cost of keeping all those dogs in your own kennels.'

'I am not. I am wondering what that old witch would let the chestnut go for. Sixpence she said! Now what could she have meant by that?'

'She meant as much as she could tempt you to pay. Oh, but you are ripe fruit for the Clodie M'Cools of this world, dangling into their very hands.'

For a while the conversation ran away on horses, a one-sided conversation and increasingly technical, so that when Barsham reached strangles and glanders the Doctor called a halt, rising to refill his glass and one for his friend, saying: 'I have won a first prize in the Lottery, the not inconsiderable sum of twenty thousand pounds . . .'

'Alex!'

'. . .and I have taken the bank's advice on investment, dry tedious advice that it was: ordinary shares, government stock, three per cents – no, perhaps not three per cent: five? No, do not interrupt. I need your help and would be obliged if you would listen with proper attention and not fidget all over the room wringing your hands and thinking about hounds.'

'I am not thinking about hounds. I am thinking about your fortune – your very good fortune. Lord, it is not every day a man receives that kind of sum gratis.'

'It was not gratis, I paid thirty-six pounds for the tickets, all the spare cash I had in the world. Listen – we are old old friends. I have to tell you that I am buying Blackow.'

Barsham sat down suddenly in a chair by the cold

fireplace. 'Blackow. By God you are! The old lady told me the place was sold.'

'She does not know yet who it is. Now my problem is this: what am I to do with the land?'

'Well, Moore has it in hand now but he gives it up come Michaelmas, he is aged, poor fellow and almost incapable . . . But they will have told you all this. How much is there altogether?'

'Something above six hundred acres including the Gorse, the whole of the Gorse, which I believe amounts to nearly three hundred acres, and of course there are the odd roods and perches tacked on, tacked on to every sum, would you credit it, and I have not wrestled with such measures since I was a boy, a very little boy. I had thought – ' and the Doctor looked at his wine for a moment, then swallowed it – 'I thought of retaining the park and the Gorse. As you had spoken to me some time ago about the outlying acres on the Upgate side I wondered . . . I wondered if you would care to relieve me of the rest.'

Barsham drew in a long breath and let it out again quickly. 'The rest,' he said slowly.

'It would not amount to much, say three hundred and thirty acres and a perch or two.'

Not much. The Doctor studied his nails. Barsham puffed and blew over his sherry. 'What about the old lady?' he asked at last.

'I hoped she might stay on. I will fix a fair rent. Indeed there are half a dozen able gentlemen on fire to tell me what fair rent to fix.'

'She may not relish you as her landlord. Alex, why are you buying the place?'

'Oh, I wish to preserve the Gorse. I wish the bustards to find eternal sactuary there.'

'Bah, bustards! I have not seen one there for years.' He saw the Doctor's gaunt face darken and added quickly: 'Who is acting for you?'

'Chapel of Chapel and Hick, and Arbuthnot at the bank is my agent. I do not wish it to be known I am involved.'

Barsham scratched his chin. 'Have you mentioned it to Ann?'

'I have mentioned it to no one. It is between you and me. I have spent two days and nights in Norwich closeted with cautious lawyers and glum bankers, was asked to a dinner with the United Friars which I could not with decency refuse, assisted Menzies in a very tricky operation – a very large faint-hearted lady, what one might truthfully call the surgeon's nightmare – and the minute I return home you suggest . . .'

'I suggest nothing. But, Alex, if I were to refuse your offer – apart from those odd fifty acres – Ann may care to snap up the rest for young Tom.'

She no longer has the means, said the Doctor to himself. But: 'Perhaps so. But I must impress on you that for the moment no one must know anything of this matter save you and I, the bank and Mr Chapel. Menzies knows of course, but I have sworn him to an oath and he will keep it or die, that is his temperament. Apart from not wishing it generally known I have set up for a gentleman – which I have not – the bird would be out of the bush and my good intentions with it the moment the news reached Blackow.'

'What bird? What bush? Oh, I see what you mean. Alex, why *are* you buying Blackow? You! What do you want with a mansion and a park?'

'A mansion and a park?' said Louise, hurrying in to shoo her husband away to change for dinner. 'Has someone shown an interest in Blackow?' She was aware of a guilty silence, a general looking away. 'Alex, you will stay to eat. My sister is here, and George Neech and his mother. Have you met his mother? A very elderly lady, looks so frail a puff of wind would carry her off, but quite mentally sound, quite talkative. *He* looks very melancholy and has hardly spoken since they arrived.

And there is some strange story about Ann giving up Thorn and running off with a rich old man.'

'I regret I cannot stay,' and the Doctor bowed, his expression remote, his eyes quite cold. 'I have been absent two days and there is such a very great deal to do. I have to report on the tenth of next month for my papers and my surgeon's coat; they have restored me, grudgingly, to a regiment. My dear, goodbye. You must dine with me before I leave – Mrs M'Cool has kindly offered me Blackow and its dining room for the evening.'

'Ha ha,' croaked Barsham, 'ha, ha, ha,' and then he caught the Doctor's burning eye and coughed himself silent.

In the hall, Charlotte with a small dog under one arm: 'Are you really going?' She put down the dog and came to brush at the Doctor's coat. 'We shall miss you. *I* shall miss you.'

'But my dear, I have been absent half your short life; I have been absent the whole of the past year, come to that. You did not miss me then.'

'I did, I did. And it is unkind of you to smile on me that way, to be so condescending, as if I were six again and had the snuffles. Life is much more dull without you. There is no one else like you in High Common.'

He was moved, she was so obviously sincere: moved and flattered. 'Oh come now, I shall return in time, a weathered ancient, burned very brown and full of strange habits.'

Her eyes met his. They were of a height now; he could not dismiss her with a kiss on top of her head as he had used to long ago. 'No, you will not,' she said, 'you will not come back.'

'She told my fortune,' said Ann, coming home to find the great front door open and Tom in a wicker chair on the step, the dogs about him. 'She said I would have a long life and great troubles.'

'You mean you consulted the gipsies? I know you have been in a wild mood these last days but galloping up to the Gorse to ask the future of the gipsies . . .'

'Something must be done about the Gorse,' she said, thinking aloud. 'It is a great waste of good land.'

'You will never persuade Clodie M'Cool to enclose.'

'The new owner may hold advanced ideas. Who knows?'

His bright blue eyes were no longer smiling and there was a perceptible hardening of all his features. 'Leave the Gorse alone. The Doctor loves the Gorse – and so did Harry. In any case, where would the cottagers go for grazing? Where would the tinkers live?'

'What you mean is: you do not want it enclosed.' It took her a moment to recover from his deliberate use of Harry's name, Harry whom he had never mentioned before without calling him 'Harry Gerard' with obvious dislike.

'Yes, *I* do not want it enclosed,' and now there was a spark of fury in his eye and his chin thrust forward. 'My father would not have wanted it enclosed. There are families in High Common have had rights on that land since . . . since . . .' His history was not strong. 'Since Canute.'

'There is no escaping the fact that it belongs to Blackow.'

Tom's face blazed, he grew larger as she watched. All the frustration and anxiety of the last weeks, his fears for the farm, his fears for her, his concealed but very real grief for the *Sable Island*, his sorrow at losing the Doctor . . . All rose up and exploded in a tremendous display of temper. He went scarlet. His voice roared. 'It belongs to all of us. Hell and damnation, it belongs to the tinkers and the bustards and the sheep.'

'Ah ha,' said Hollin in the kitchen, tipping back his chair so that he looked up at the row of great hams along the beam. 'Do I hear the master exercising of his lungs?' He grinned, wider and wider.

'Like old times,' he added.

# 14

Young Mr Arbuthnot, that paragon of probity and
discretion, sat on the Doctor's frail chair and fanned
himself with a large legal document fringed with
dangling seals.

'I am sorry, Doctor, but the lady says she must know
your name or she will refuse to sell. I received her note
this morning, sent over by hand. In view of this, I
suggest we have no option but to reveal all.'

'She would do it too –' in a low, resigned tone –
'though Heaven knows she is not in a position to refuse to
sell. Refuse to sell! I cannot pretend that I am not
disappointed: my appointment with Mr Chapel
tomorrow was, as you know, to sign the final document.'

'Until that is done, all monies paid, the house is not
yours,' said Arbuthnot slowly, stressing the words
heavily as to a foreigner or an idiot. His round pink face
was shiny with heat and anxiety.

'I see I must tell her the truth then, tell her it is
Alexander French putting up the money for her graceless heap of bricks and mortar, miserable unlucky house
it has always been.'

'I am sorry to hear that, Doctor. It is a constant
surprise to me how pleasant some homes can be, cheerful
and well loved, and how, without any obvious reason,
the very opposite is true of others: draughts, brooding
atmospheres, broken lives, even spirits wandering
abroad. But I had not suspected Blackow of being a
house of ill omen, it seemed perfectly charming to a
stranger's eye. Shall you visit the lady in person, sir, or
shall I reply by letter?'

'I shall call this afternoon. There is no merit in delay.

'"Twere well it were done quickly," as that inhospitable Scot says in the play.'

Arbuthnot nodded, mopped his brow, resumed his fanning with a sigh. 'She is a very difficult lady, if I may say so, a very difficult lady. If it is any comfort to you I doubt very much that she will withdraw from the sale. Why, the money is on the table, so to speak. Cheer up, Doctor. Tomorrow or the day after you will own this very gatehouse – ' with a polite, wondering look and an automatic smile. 'All this will be yours.'

'I hear what you say,' said the Doctor. For a man newly possessed of a fortune and about to set up his carriage he looked uncommon dark and gloomy.

'Then I shall leave you,' said Arbuthnot. 'I shall assume a happy outcome of your meeting with the lady this afternoon, and I shall look forward to meeting you again at Mr Chapel's office tomorrow at four o'clock.'

He had no sooner departed than Barsham arrived on his old white horse, a horse with a bone-breaking trot, the equivalent of the grinding of some monstrous machinery; he was exhausted, a dark purple, sweat running under his collar and down his backbone.

'Mr Lubbock has written a great deal of sense about apoplexy,' said the Doctor encouragingly, leading him to that single, insufficient chair in the naked parlour. 'Sit down at once, loosen your neckcloth and take off your boots. Have you been galloping to get yourself in this dangerous state? Wait one moment . . . Jim! Ho, Jim!'

Jim Wells' intelligent face at the door almost at once. 'Bring the jug standing on the slate and the large bottle next the asafoetida. Now – ' as the face vanished – 'I said take off your boots. Here, let me do it. And hold this to your head. The water is from the well outside, the coldest available, though a good way down now, a horrible way down. I believe you would be easier for being bled a little. Yes, I shall bleed you when you have recovered your composure.'

Barsham disliked being bled and said so, said that nothing was more likely to upset his composure and how did the Doctor justify interfering with another man's patient? Was he not always pratting on about etiquette, professional mores? That was irrelevant in the present case, said the Doctor, producing an instrument from his pocket the size of a horse fleam and testing its edge with an experienced finger. 'It is new,' he announced with intense satisfaction.

'Damn you, Alex, you are not coming near my veins with that. They are my veins after all.'

The fruit juice came, and the bottle. Jim said: 'I have the kettle on the boil, Doctor, should you be wanting tea in a little while,' with a significant look.

'How he runs about on that peg leg,' said Barsham, drinking his juice gratefully. 'This is good, very good indeed. 'Tis all I need to set me up again.'

'I am glad you find it pleasant, glad it tastes quite normal.'

'Good God!' said Barsham, peering suspiciously into the glass. 'I never saw you touch it. What was in that bottle?' When the Doctor smiled and made no answer he went on: 'What would Loder say if he knew you were dosing me up?'

'As I said, etiquette is irrelevant to the present case: you were expiring on my doorstep. I was obliged by my oath if not by common humanity to do my utmost to preserve you.'

'You may think differently when you have heard what I have to say.'

'That you are not going to buy the land.'

'How did you know?'

'Oh, call it a sixth sense.'

'But I will gladly take the fifty acres by Lubbock's Hole.'

'And welcome to them – if they are ever mine to sell. Now, we shall fetch the basin and towels and Jim will be

288

my assistant. No, no, my dear, sit back. You will be much better for it. You will feel a new man.'

Halfway down the drive he turned aside to sit on a fallen oak. There were a few red leaves at his feet. Was it autumn after all? But the park lay in the usual flood of sunshine and all the heifers were bunched up in the shade, flicking at the flies and feeling miserable. A pheasant clucked away into the undergrowth and down at the house there was a sudden chorus from the guinea fowl and the frenzied yapping of a dog. There are six peacocks in a row on the front steps, he thought, shading his eyes.

'You think I am in my dotage,' said Clodie, pulling off her gardening gloves and looking him up and down. 'Well, I am not yet, by the grace of St Michael and all the angels. Hand me that trowel. For a clever man you are uncommon clumsy trying to buy the roof over my head and offer it back at a peppercorn rent. I'll have none of it.'

'It would not be a peppercorn rent. Mr Arbuthnot has strict views on . . .'

'This was to be Cassandra's house,' she said, ignoring him. 'I had hoped, in time, she might inherit it along with what little else I had. There is little else indeed, my jewels gone and her mother . . . No, I must not say it. Heaven knows, I hope I shall never grow a hard uncharitable old hag. Alex, my dear, I will not take your money.'

'Your debts are very great.'

'Who says so?'

'Indeed they are. We are not children to play at make believe.'

She strode to the seat, flung down trowel and gloves, sat there as sulky as a child. Then she patted the warm slats beside her, looked up and smiled.

What were you like as a girl? he wondered. He sat

beside her looking away across the lawns. 'I am buying this house for one reason, one reason only.'

'Oh, and what is that, Dr French?' and she cocked a gleaming eye at him.

'I want to own the Gorse.'

She made no reply but turned to stare across the burnt ground to where two figures walked, one tall, one small. All of a sudden the tall one embraced the smaller, knocking off her hat.

'Ann Gerard and Cassandra,' said Clodie. 'They have been looking for the best place to put the wicket. The picnic party . . . It is in three days. Have you forgot? Yes, I see you have. Someone has asked for a game of cricket. Rigby said the top lawn was always the cricket field in the old days but now it has all those new beds . . . Look at that child run. You will not miss our picnic, Alex?' Silence. She put out a hand and gripped his arm, an old hand but immensely strong. 'That Hoyley's Lodge is a terrible small hole and the ground cold cold clay – the Chinese mystery will wither away there for sure. And so shall I. If you fix a fair rent I will pay it. Here, let me lean on your arm. Walk me back to the house.'

She looked down at him as they paced back along the path, found his eyes the darkest grey imaginable, his mouth a long hard line.

'I might say bless you, Alex French, you are a staunch friend,' she said, 'but I will not. I am not a sentimental woman, thank God. Now tell me, do you play cricket?'

'You mean, the house is mine?'

'Oh, I have the strangest feeling the house is Cassandra's, but the Gorse is yours and all the neglected land. So long as I can hunt my hounds across it you may do with it what you will.'

'So long as they do not chase my bustards,' he said.

The King's Head was never less than busy, tonight it was in uproar. The huge dining room was full, the private rooms all booked for clubs, societies, the officers of the Something Light Horse – the Doctor could not catch the name as he was hurried along the passage by the howling servant – and of course, the medical gentlemen. 'Here you are, sir,' and a door was flung open to reveal Menzies and a dozen others already well into second helpings of goose and all its accompanying dishes.

'Alex! Well, man, but we had given you up,' shouted Menzies above the din. 'Sit down, sit down. Richards, send up a plate. We were saying only a moment ago, were we not, gentlemen, that old Alex had forgot our party. But better late than never, as they say.'

There was a chorus of agreement, genuine agreement, for the Doctor had been a valued colleague to some of these men, three of them close friends for many years. Two of the others he did not know at all, young men and somewhat addicted to the rather childish jokes of their student days. One was a tall golden youth, a near Adonis, and though he had little to say for himself he graced the table remarkably well and Menzies smiled on him with a particular affection; one was a botanist, a very learned man, and since he had spent his whole childhood in India of great interest to the Doctor, who was seated next to him. But after two and a half hours, the total demolition of the goose, several pies, a shoulder of mutton, a whole kitchen garden of vegetables, three sorts of pudding and cheese and fruit, the Doctor rose, excused himself, and went out. 'He is a man of nice habits,' whispered Menzies to his nearest neighbour, who had also taken too much claret for the safety of his liver, 'he will not use the pot in the cupboard.'

'Did you call, sir?' asked the hot, wretched boy who had served them all evening, flying along the passage with yet another tray.

'No, no I did not call. Carry on. I have seldom seen the place so crowded.'

'And early yet, sir. The night coach is due in ten minutes and the yard at a stand, some gig come in like smoke, sir, and ran into one of our shays. You never seen such a rumpus. Language fit for heroes,' and he grinned, showing all his bad teeth, and darted away.

The Doctor descended through a fog of tobacco smoke, cooking smells and hot, hard-pressed humanity. In the yard the chaos had been cleared – almost. The damaged chaise was being trundled away by several men on foot and one of the ostlers was sweeping the entrance clear of onlookers by telling them in minute and bloody detail what they would resemble when pulled from under the wheels of the London mail. A lady in a hooded silk cape stood to one side, perhaps the late occupant of the chaise, and the Doctor had only just come to the conclusion by the set of her shoulders that she was smoulderingly angry when she turned round and he saw her face in the light of the torches – and it was Ann.

'My dear,' he said, hurrying forward, and she threw back her hood to reveal all her sprightly hair and a delightful, smiling face out of which all fury and frustration drained away in seconds. 'My dear, it was not you in the chaise?'

'It was. Can you not see I am covered in straw? I was catapulted on to my knees. They wanted to carry me in to revive me with sal volatile and tea but I refused to go until I could be sure of another chaise. They tell me there is no room vacant inside and I have no wish to be forgotten in a corner of the kitchens.'

He said: 'I am upstairs at a medical dinner, a few friends; too much to eat, too much to drink, too many tired old stories and poor thrice-told jokes. I shall not introduce you. They are no longer fit company for a lady.'

'I thought you looked the worse for wear. Your neckcloth is adrift.'

292

'I smell of wine and tobacco.'

'I do not mind it.'

A great strong fellow begged to be allowed to pass, there was no room in this here yard to chuck a kitten and the Mail due in five minutes, and he pressed through with a set of harness over his shoulder.

'Do you know if there is a chaise ordered for any of the medical gentlemen?'

'No, sir. Chairs, sir. The chaises are all bespoke by the political coves.'

'Come,' said the Doctor to Ann, 'there is a settle in the hallway. I shall go up and take my leave, make my excuses, and then we shall walk along a little and see if we can't find a coach elsewhere.'

'I have been with Tom all afternoon – ' as they pushed in, a crowd of rowdy youngsters in regimental full dress pushing out. 'He has signed the lease for Thorn. I was invited to Mrs Carey's for the evening and Mr Bridger kindly carried me here in his own chaise. He lectured me all the way on my folly, said I was a profligate Forsie and looked under his eyebrows in that way he has to see how I took it. It was arranged I should take a carriage home – an allowable extravagance, Tom said. The Careys could not keep me for the night, their house is full. But one of the horses trotted lame down St Giles, almost on his knees, and we were forced to turn in here to beg for another. Then this gig thunders in, knocks over two people and careers into us. The man was drunk, roaring drunk, calling down curses on Pitt, Addington, King George, and every tory who ever breathed. They bore him away singing. Do you think he did it for a dare?'

As they were thrown together by the settle – literally thrown together – he steadied her, looked into her face and said: 'I have bought Blackow Hall. I would like Tom to farm the land.'

She tucked in his neckcloth. 'I know. Clodie told me.

What an eccentrically generous man you are. But the land . . . There is a great deal of land.'

'Even with Thorn he will be well short of his thousand acres.'

She smiled bravely. 'Harry thought it so sensible to join Blackow and Thorn. And I . . . I had some bold dreams that came to nothing.'

'Wo ho,' shouted Menzies, tottering down the stairs. 'So here you are, you old rogue. Here you are with a woman . . . a woman . . . I beg your pardon. A lady. Alex, forgive me, I am not myself. I am away out for some air. We have drunk to your good health, your very good health, and to your generous donations, most generous, to the . . . to the Hospital. And I shall certainly toast the lady when I return.'

'May I introduce Lady Gerard. Lady Gerard, Dr Menzies.'

She had a small, expressive face, expressive of a courageous, difficult, embattled nature. Menzies stared into it a moment, swaying slightly. Who would have thought it: the cunning old dog slipping out after a woman. He thought: I saw them. He was holding her shoulders. Their faces were inches apart. She was speaking low. What was she saying, I wonder? Old dog. Never thought he cared so much for women. For men neither. A solitary, monkish sort.

'Lady . . . Gerard.' He bowed his head, grunted, and pushed away into the throng.

Out in the air again Ann said: 'You will not be surprised to know that Mr Neech has not proposed.'

The Doctor said nothing but walked resolutely on.

'He would not take me in my shift and without a penny,' she told his back as provocatively as she dared, running to keep up.

At the Cock he held the door for her. 'Alex, are you never going to speak to me again?'

'Not on the subject of George Neech. Do you think

Tom will be able to manage that land? Barsham is having the fifty acres by Lubbock's Hole, Mrs M'Cool has the use of the park and the Gorse is to be left untouched.'

'The Gorse. Tom and I have quarrelled over the Gorse.'

She was brave, generous, intelligent, he thought, at moments possessed of a shining loveliness. She would never love him as much as he loved her. As if aware of his thoughts her eyes opened wide. He had always admired those dark, beautiful eyes. He looked down, looked down at his own long slender hands clasped before him.

'Mrs Badcock – ' as the door opened – 'this lady must have your best room tonight, she cannot get home. She will take a dish of tea before she retires.'

'That is a lie,' said Ann, throwing off her cape and revealing a white dress with silver embroidery at neck and hem. 'Of course I could get home.'

'It is far too late to tramp about after a carriage. And I have something to ask you . . .'

'Tea, Doctor,' said Mary, carrying it in. 'Would the lady like to see the room?'

Ann shook her head. As the door closed again she said: 'How quiet this place is after the King's Head. I hope Tom is not worried. You should have seen his face when Mr Bridger brought out the lease and put the pen in his hand . . . Oh Alex, he is such a great sentimental fool: there were tears in his eyes,' and then, still smiling at the memory: 'I always knew it was the right thing to do.'

The Doctor did not appear to be listening. He had walked to the window, a small window and giving directly onto the street. There were two boys talking opposite, standing under a link. At the rattle of tea cups he turned, saw Ann's head bent over her task and said softly: 'I have a marriage licence in my pocket. My dear . . .'

A clatter and a small cry. 'I have knocked over the cream and broken the jug,' she wailed, jumping up.

'My dear, I know you do not love me but there is affection between us, close regard . . . Many marriages begin with less and thrive. I hoped . . . with Tom and Charlotte at Thorn and Blackow Cassandra's house . . . I hoped you might be willing to keep me company abroad, though you would only be the wife of a humble army surgeon. I very much fear my twenty thousand pounds is sadly diminished.'

She stood there, very pale, biting her lip. All she said, after a long while, was: 'It was bold of you to buy a licence.'

It was a whim, he might have said; he had asked Chapel about it when the lawyer put the deeds of Blackow Hall into his hands. He had never seriously thought of asking her again, knowing how she felt, but then again, he had not bowed and smiled and played the great benefactor these last days without being conscious of that dull continuous longing. 'There are still adventures to be had,' he said, 'Will you marry me?'

Her smile gave him his answer. But: 'I am not sure I shall be good for you,' she said as he put out his hands and cupped her face, 'Perhaps we'll come to quarrelling and regrets. But life is not the same without you,' as if she saw the way his heart contracted at her words, 'Last year . . . Last year I did miss you so.'

He leaned forward and kissed her mouth, perhaps the briefest, most impersonal kiss ever exchanged at such a moment. When he could speak he said: 'Would tomorrow morning be too sudden? Of course Tom and Miss Pennyquick . . .'

'Tomorrow morning will be perfect.'

A knock. Mrs Badcock entered. 'Doctor, I have put you in the little room down the passage. Oh,' seeing the spilled cream, 'I shall send Mary to mop it up.'

'Mrs Badcock, would it be an inconvenience to you to step across to St Stephen's in the morning and be our witness? Lady Gerard and I are to be married.'

A moment's hesitation, sheer astonishment. 'Lord! In the morning?' she cried, still staring. 'Oh, my goodness! Oh Doctor. I shall be glad to, at any hour. May I wish you joy. Madam too. Oh, all joy, sir, and a long life and a happy one.'

The first overcast morning, the first autumnal mist creeping up from the river; but by the time the small wedding party had stepped out from the church the sun was as strong as ever.

'Oh, Doctor, you have not kissed the bride,' admonished Mrs Badcock, exchanging glances with Mary who shared her anxieties about the Doctor's state of mind.

The bride looked very small and pale in the evening dress that was her wedding gown: no frills, no jewels, no bonnet even; and the Doctor's gold ring was just that and no more, a plain gold ring, obtained by knocking up the jeweller at six o'clock and paying double its value. She looked up and smiled, offering her cheek for his kiss.

Then away in the Cock's best trap, no rice, no ribbons. A long silence as they bowled away from Norwich, a long long silence as far as the foot of the Gorse when Ann said: 'There are swallows, scores of them. Perhaps yours are there.'

He slowed the pony. 'Can you bear to live in the gatehouse until we leave?'

'How absurd – we each own a house and cannot use it.'

The level green, the gorse clumps, the rabbits bounding away. At the crossroads he halted. 'I hope you do not regret this.'

She put her hand on his arm. 'No, dear Alex, I shall not regret it. It is you who . . . I only hope we remain friends.'

He swung right-handed for Thorn, taking the hill rather too fast as usual, Ann putting out her hand to the reins. Thorn smoked cheerfully amid its buildings: baking day.

My wedding day, she thought, stealing a look at the hard face, the long nose of her husband. This was a very different wedding day from her last, a very different homecoming from any she had ever had. For some reason, like Tom's lease, it had seemed the right thing to do.

The horse swerved and stopped.

'This is a fine time to come home,' said Miss Pennyquick, running out, 'Tom has taken off his splint, says he is going to do without. That Jim Wells has been down here twice asking if we had seen you, Doctor, and then if those bullocks have pushed the fence down once this morning they pushed it down three times, Hollin has been in and out every ten minutes.'

'Damned if I'll be pushed about in a chair,' came Tom's strong carrying voice from inside. 'I am going to walk. And let go my arm, I am not an invalid. Ann! Ann, there you are – and Alex.'

Old Spring padded out at his heels and it was as the Doctor handed Ann down and she reached to fondle the dog's ears that their senses bristled.

'Is anything wrong?' asked Tom.

'Lord, there was never some sort of accident?' cried Miss Pennyquick.

Ann looked up. 'The Doctor and I are married.'

Tom stared at them, a large handsome man with very blue eyes and the yellow Forsie hair, standing in the doorway of the house that was now his own. He looked from one to the other and back again, and disbelief and delight struggled in his face.

Delight won. 'How glad I am! Why, of course. Why did I never think of it? You should have done it long ago. Oh Ann,' stepping forward to swing her up and cover her with kisses, 'how very very glad I am!'

And: 'How he laughs,' said Hollin in the yard to the disgraced bullocks. 'They must hear him at Upgate. *Now* what, I wonder?'